Murder Made Her Wicked

ALSO AVAILABLE BY ELIZABETH HOBBS

THE MARIGOLD MANNERS MYSTERIES

Misery Hates Company

Murder Made Her Wicked

A Marigold Manners Mystery

Elizabeth Hobbs

NEW YORK

Books should be disposed of and recycled according to local requirements.
All paper materials used are FSC compliant.

Published in the United States by Crooked Lane Books, an imprint of
The Quick Brown Fox & Company LLC.

Crooked Lane Books and its logo are trademarks of The Quick Brown Fox
& Company LLC.

Library of Congress Catalog-in-Publication data available upon request.

ISBN (hardcover): 979-8-89242-323-6
ISBN (paperback): 979-8-89242-483-7
ISBN (ebook): 979-8-89242-324-3

Cover design by Marisa Ware

Printed in the United States.

www.crookedlanebooks.com

Crooked Lane Books
34 West 27th St., 10th Floor
New York, NY 10001

First Edition: November 2025

The authorized representative in the EU for product safety and compliance
is eucomply OÜPärnu mnt 139b-14, 11317 Tallinn, Estonia,
hello@eucompliancepartner.com, +33757690241

10 9 8 7 6 5 4 3 2 1

This story is a love letter (albeit murdery) to two of the most influential women in my life: my mother, Carol Craven Robinson, and my godmother, Marie Loupret Karanfilian, both members of Wellesley College class of 1954. Their dedication to lives of learning and adventure, constantly expanding their horizons and interests, and in so doing giving back to their communities, has given me a brilliant example for how to conduct my life. Non Ministrari sed Ministrare.

With deep love and affection, and enormous thanks.

Prologue

"It does not do to trust people too much."
Charlotte Perkins Gilman

What was it about hats that always seemed to catch Marigold Manners's eye?

This hat was outlandish—judged by Marigold's decidedly less flamboyant taste—an oversized, sodden, blue velvet tam-o'-shanter with an elaborate spray of pheasant feathers bristling out of a shining brooch.

Had she seen it before? No matter, someone had likely paid a very pretty penny for the chapeau and brooch and would want it back, even if it were dripping from its dousing in the lake. Let that be a lesson to young ladies to secure their fashionable headpieces with sturdy hatpins, especially while broaching the decidedly brisk fall winds coursing along the shore of Lake Waban.

Marigold shaded her eyes to look back up the hill, judging the distance to the gothic pile of College Hall, where she would need to return the hat if it were to be reunited with whichever young collegian had been so careless as to lose it. Or perhaps she would just take the hat with her, so as not to be late for her appointment at the boathouse.

But as she stepped off the path, careful of her footing in the soft, marshy ground along the edge of the dock, her gaze went beyond the hat, to the trailing skein of dark hair tangled in the reeds, rippling with the motion of the waves. And to the unmistakable shape of a hand, pale and shimmering white like the belly of a fish, below the surface of the clear, cold water.

Recognition screamed through her in the same instant panic propelled her forward, sloshing deeper, reaching frantically into the icy water, hoping against hope that this time she would not be too late.

CHAPTER 1

"I think I shall write books, and get rich and famous, that would suit me, so that is my favorite dream."

Louisa May Alcott

Boston, Massachusetts
October 1894

Marigold Manners paused in the chilly twilight along Back Bay's Park Drive and gazed at the row of townhouses glowing in the gaslight.

They were the sort of elegant, substantial houses that made one think nothing bad or tiresome or troubling could ever happen within. That if you lived there, you could not be hungry or worried or plagued by any of the ills of people who lived elsewhere, in meaner, less well-kept houses. They were the sort of houses that inspired equal amounts of jealousy and devotion. The kind one wished one had grown up in.

But the fact that Marigold *had* grown up in just such a house had taught her there was no true buffer against illness or misfortune. That grand houses could conceal ugly truths just as easily—if not more easily—than the meanest hovel.

That evening, with the sharp edges of the autumn wind scratching at the corners of her eyes, Marigold felt she would always be on the outside looking in. Always looking into the darkness hidden by the light. Always suspecting, if not expecting, the worse.

Murder, she supposed, had made her see wickedness in every corner.

Murder, and finding out she really wasn't who she thought she was.

"Marigold?" A cultured voice called from the dark before a portal was pushed wide in welcome. "There you are, darling!" Isabella Dana, friend, confidante, and all-around bonne vivante, ushered Marigold into her townhouse's opulent cocooning warmth. "I was beginning to grow concerned. It's gone quite dark."

"I am here, never fear." Marigold dashed away the self-indulgent tears and pushed aside the lingering chill of her malaise. She was a rational creature ruled by logic, not girlish emotions.

She pasted on a smile before she went in to be cocooned, carefully wiping her walking boots upon the polished iron scraper. One didn't track leaf dirt into such a house. Not if one wished to be invited back. And Marigold most fervently wished to be invited back.

She had nowhere else to go.

No. That was her strange melancholy restlessness, the hazy, dissatisfying feeling of having no true purpose of her own. In former years, the arrival of fall had always made Marigold glad. The start of fall school term, with its promising new beginnings had cheered her.

But without any money, there was no return to school.

No purpose.

Isabella, on the other hand, was fulsome with both money and purpose. "Come into the drawing room. There's a fire laid to chase off the chill." She hooked her arm through Marigold's. "I've poured sherry."

"Thank you," Marigold unpinned her hat and accepted her friend's hospitality for the gracious gift it was. It really was a marvelous thing to have rich friends.

But there on the tray that held the sherry decanter and two glasses was also a freshly pressed set of handkerchiefs. And a waxy beige envelope.

The lingering misapprehension crept back along the line of Marigold's shoulders like a stray cat. "What is that?"

"Come sit." Isabella led Marigold to the soft velvet sofa. "I wanted to be prepared. A telegram has come for you."

Marigold felt the unwelcome kick of dread in her midsection but would not give in to its tawdry clutch. "A wire doesn't always mean bad news."

"Good news arrives with fresh flowers," Isabella countered. "Bad news shows up uninvited and unaccompanied, wearing beige like a mother-in-law. Hence the sherry. It's from New York," she warned. "The telegram, not the sherry."

From New York, Marigold might expect the telegram to be from her half-sister, Daisy Manners Endicott, or Daisy's husband of a few months, Tad Endicott, who had recently relocated from Boston to Manhattan to start his publishing career. Or perhaps from her twin brother, Seviah—how strange it was to even *think* those words—who had been appearing on the vaudeville circuit in the city. Or perhaps from her dear friend Lucy Dove, her half-brother Wilburt's half-sister, who had recently traveled to the metropolis in search of a publisher for her remarkable book teaching cookery.

All of whom were now far too dear to Marigold to bear being the subject of bad news.

She took a quick, fortifying sip of the rich, golden wine before she calmly took the folded missive from the tray. She refused to let her hands shake.

She ripped open the envelope.

"Your sister?" Isabella was clearly thinking along the same lines as she.

"No," Marigold answered, before she was nearly overcome with surprise. "Oh, gracious!" She covered her mouth to keep from gaping like a goldfish.

"I knew it!" Isabella instantly wrapped an arm around Marigold, lest she succumb to an unseemly swoon. "What has happened?"

"Nothing," Marigold managed over her smile—and her absolute astonishment. "Everything. It's—" She swallowed around the unexpected lump in her throat. "It is the very last thing I might have expected. You may congratulate me, my dear friend, for it seems I finally have a profession! Mr. Matthew White—one of the editors Tad Endicott suggested to me—has bought my story of the Great Misery Island murders, to be serialized in *The Argosy* literary magazine!"

"Oh, Marigold, darling!" Isabella put a hand to her stylishly rounded bosom in relief. "What excellent news." She clasped Marigold's hand in delight. "It's not exactly *Scribner's*, but it's just as I told you it would be."

"Naturally," Marigold agreed, for indeed, Isabella had predicted her success. In fact, without Isabella's prompting and support, Marigold would never have thought to write the story of the Great Misery Island murders. "I have learned my lesson never to go against you! Mr. White writes that he is entirely receptive to my mystery story and not in the least surprised or hesitant to employ a female writer."

"Naturally. Just as I told you!" Isabella said staunchly.

Marigold laughed at her friend's easy shift from foreboding to fortune-telling. "And the best part is that once the magazine has run the full story, I am free to sell it to a novel publisher. But Mr. White will pay me well for the privilege of first printing." Marigold waved the wire like a parade banner in absolute delight.

"Well done, darling, and so well deserved," Isabella offered with her usual grace. "Especially after all you've been through."

"Been through" was not exactly the right euphemism for Marigold's involvement in the murders on Great Misery Island but was certainly the right expression for the crisis of confidence she had experienced after finding out the secret of her less than legitimate parentage, and her surprisingly complicated coterie of full and half siblings—as well as unrelated half siblings of her new half siblings.

It had all been, frankly, more than a bit much. Even for her.

"Champagne then, instead of sherry, to celebrate!" Isabella decided.

"Oh, yes! Let's," Marigold agreed. She was too happy to care if she got tipsy before dinner. She accepted her coupe with pleasure. "Here's to paying the bills!"

"Yes!" Isabella agreed. "Financial independence is the best sort of independence."

"Agreed," Marigold laughed. "But I'm ambitious enough to want all sorts of independence to go along with it. A matched set of independencies," she joked. "Style, substance, and spondulicks, as they say."

"A matched set." Isabella raised her glass.

"You know what this means?"

"No, but I'm sure you're going to tell me—as long as you don't start going on about repaying me for your room and board or clothes," Isabella began. "I won't hear of such nonsense."

As the couturier and owner of the House of Dana, Isabella had always been generous in making clothes for Marigold. "I've told you, time and time again," she went on, "young ladies daily visit my atelier vying to look as stylish and elegant as the inimitable Miss Marigold Manners and spending delightful gobs of money to do so. I should be much the poorer if you stopped wearing my clothes."

Marigold had learned to accept such convoluted logic with gratitude. "You have been very kind to me Isabella—overly so."

"That is what friends are for, darling. What kind of friend would I be if I couldn't see you through this terribly trying time you've had?"

"Everyone should be lucky enough to have such a friend." Not only had Isabella convinced Marigold to put pen to paper and write the story of the murders of Great Misery Island but had also given her the time and solitude needed to write it. "I have decided the best way to repay you is to resume the life I was meant to lead."

"You're going to marry Cab?"

A sharp pang of misapprehension landed in Marigold's midsection. Jonathan Cabot Cox had been Marigold's sometime—or at least onetime—beau. She had turned down his proposal of marriage, not because she didn't love him, but because she loved the life she had planned—and worked toward and wanted with an ache approaching feverish—more.

"Much as I admire and respect Cab, I will not be marrying," she answered firmly. "I meant that I am going to go back to college to finish my degree and my thesis of an English-language translation of the Greek myths. And graduate with honors and then finally—finally!—spend next summer on the island of Kefalonia, where I will complete my archaeological fieldwork on the Classical Period site at Leivathos. All just as I had planned."

Just as she had planned before her parents had died, leaving her near penniless. Before she had gone to live with relatives on Great Mystery Island. Before she had discovered the murders.

"I don't see why you couldn't get married and still do all that," Isabella groused. "You could do your archaeology on your honeymoon. I'm sure Cab wouldn't object to a summer in Greece."

"Isabella," Marigold chided. "Do you really think Cab is the sort of fellow to idle away his time doing nothing while I was busy with my avocation? Or that his law firm will simply let such a man take leave for five months so soon after letting him involve himself with Great Misery?"

"For a honeymoon, surely," Isabella answered. "It would hardly be unprecedented. My own wedding trip took six months."

"Your dear late husband had already secured his fortune and could do as he liked in those days."

"As I'm sure could Cab," Isabella pressed. "If only you—"

"—asked him to?" Marigold finished for her. "But I won't. Because if I did, then I couldn't go back to school to earn my degree—nor use that degree to gain a professorship if I were married."

"I don't see why not." Isabella was not giving up her point gracefully.

"Because it is against the rules, my dear." Marigold had explained to Isabella time and time again that all the major universities required their female professors to remain unmarried.

Of course, Wellesley was more progressive than most colleges—her favorite professor of Greek, Julia Irvine, had joined the faculty after her marriage, and even been promoted to the presidency of the college. But not every other university was as forward-thinking where women were concerned as Wellesley. And Professor Irvine had been a widow, like Isabella—the rules were different for them.

Marigold had to live in the world as it was, not as she wished it to be. "When they change their rules, then so will I. So, there you have it." She glanced at the clock. "I've got just enough time to get to the wire office to send my acceptance to Mr. White at *The Argosy* and send notice to the registrar of Wellesley College that I'll be returning for the first semester."

"You're that serious?" Isabella asked. "Hasn't the fall term already started? The Radcliffe girls were knocking down my doors, begging for fitting appointments more than a month ago, at the beginning of September. Surely, you're too late to start back now?"

"I'll wire my Classics professor to advise me," Marigold suggested. "But I'll send a bank draft to the bursar regardless—they'll welcome payment of my outstanding fees at any rate, even if I'm too late to register for the fall semester." She headed for the stairs to change into suitable attire for settling one's bills—something entirely respectable, like broadcloth or well-brushed wool. "Professor Irvine will surely advocate for me—she was exceptionally sympathetic when I had to leave last year. And she's president of the college now—she'll have more sway than before. She knows I'm capable, both of making up any work I've missed and getting ahead for the future. Oh, Isabella, don't you see what this means?"

Isabella pulled a face. "That you're leaving me."

"No, my dear friend." Marigold softened her tone of voice. "I'm not leaving you. Rather I'm rejoining *myself.* Despite everything—or perhaps because of it—I've found my way back to the life I was meant to live all along."

"I suppose so," Isabella finally agreed. "Just as you should. Though we've had such a marvelous time, I hate to see it end. I shall miss you. I shall even miss the sound of that horrible typewriting machine!"

Marigold had used the last of the annuity she had been left upon the death of her parents to purchase her reliable Dougherty Visible typewriting machine, upon which she had produced her manuscript for *The Argosy.* "I shall be happy to relieve you of its din by taking it with me to college, where I will astound my professors and fellow students alike with my professional acumen. See if I don't!"

"I'm sure you shall, darling girl," Isabella answered fondly. "For I've learned that you always do whatever it is you set out to do. No one should ever, ever bet against you."

CHAPTER 2

"Go confidently in the direction of your dreams."
Henry David Thoreau

One very full week of planning and packing later, Marigold disembarked from the train at the picturesque stone station in the center of Wellesley's town with her stack of trunks and her trusty bicycle, and was happy to find, this time, she had not been left to fend for herself.

"Miss Manners!" The cheerful driver of the college's horse-drawn omnibus, nicknamed the Barge, doffed his hat. "Good to have ye back amongst us, miss," Thomas Griffin said in his lilting Irish brogue.

"Mr. Griffin." Marigold reached for the Irishman's hand. "How very good of you to come to meet me so late in the term."

"Wouldn't have missed ye, miss. President Irvine set down a note herself, personal like, making sure I'd be here to meet yer train."

Marigold tried not to beam with unseemly pride at such an honor. "That is very good of you both, and much appreciated."

"Come right along." He led her toward the familiar omnibus and handed her up. "And we'll have ye back where ye belong in no time."

Yes, her heart sang in agreement. Her beloved college was the only place she had ever completely belonged. She was inordinately ready to return to the life she loved.

And no time it was, before Mr. Griffin had trotted the Barge across the town, down the road to East Lodge, and through the tall stone gates guarding the bucolic campus of her college.

Four and a half years ago, Marigold's first ride along the same scenic, rambling lane had passed in a blur of youthful excitement. Now she savored each glimpse of a familiar landmark, each notable vista. The rich fall colors wove a warm, welcoming tapestry around her, filling her with comfort and ease. And something more.

Gratitude.

And purpose. Perhaps because she had lost the privilege of her education after the death of her parents last spring, she appreciated it so much more now. Behind her were the doubts and worries of the spring and summer. Before her was her future, glistening and bright.

This was what she was meant to do.

And there it was at last, College Hall, the vast high-spired, tomb-like building that had loomed so large in her imagination over the past year. Sitting high on a hill overlooking Lake Waban, College Hall resembled nothing so much as a European abbey or Gothic monastery, far more than a typical, red-bricked American school. In fact, its floor plan was even in the shape of a papal cross—a 480-foot-long main axis intersected by three shorter wings, their spires capped with crosses—a nod to the college's quasi-religious beginning as a female seminary devoted to Christian thought and education. And though Marigold wasn't particularly religious, she did worship at the altar of education and knowledge.

"Here we are, Miss Manners," the driver said with a smile, as the Barge pulled up under the carriage porch. "Welcome home."

Silly, sentimental tears threatened at the corners of her eyes. "Thank you, Mr. Griffin."

While the porters and the custodian, Mr. Duckett, bustled out to unload her trunks—filled with fashionable clothing Isabella had insisted Marigold take—"Now, I'll have the whole of Wellesley College beating a path to my door along with the Radcliffe girls."—Marigold sallied forth through the entrance and into the soaring sanctuary of Center Hall.

"Miss Manners, I presume?" A bespectacled, middle-aged dormouse of a woman with a mildly irritated air immediately appeared at the door of the reception parlor.

"Indeed, I am Marigold Manners." She held out her hand to shake.

"Right on time," the woman said with some small satisfaction as she consulted the upside-down watch pinned to her immaculate, highly starched blouse. "Miss Burke," the woman introduced herself crisply, gesturing down the long, echoing east corridor. "This way, if you please. President Irvine has been awaiting your arrival."

"How gratifying," Marigold murmured as she fell into step behind the woman, who scurried toward the east end of the building, where the president had a suite of rooms.

Miss Burke rapped sharply on the door before she poked her head in. "Miss Manners has arrived, ma'am."

"Oh, thank you. Do send her in."

By the time Marigold had been ushered through the doorway, Julia Irvine, the president of the college, had taken her pince-nez glasses from her face, risen from her desk and crossed the room with her arms stretched forth in welcome. "Marigold!"

"Professor Irvine—or forgive me, I should say President Irvine." Marigold clasped her hands joyfully. "Please accept my heartfelt congratulations. What a pleasure it is to return to Wellesley and be reunited with all my friends."

"The pleasure is all ours," the woman replied with a smile. "And yes, a great many changes have occurred since you left us. But now that my former favorite student has returned to the Department of Classics, my hopes for you to succeed me as professor of Greek have been revived."

Marigold didn't know when she had been so flattered. Certainly, she had known Professor Irvine had valued her as a diligent student of both ancient languages and history, but to find herself spoken of as a potential favorite for the position of professor was immensely gratifying to her private ambitions. "I only hope I can live up to such generous praise. I will admit to being a little worried with nearly five weeks of classes already passed."

Julia Irvine waved away Marigold's concerns. "You will naturally have to work hard to catch up, but I have confidence in you, Marigold. I've spoken to your professors, and we've devised a revamped plan of study for the remaining classes required for your degree.

If you'd like to take a look?" She returned to her desk and drew out a manila folder, which she passed to Marigold.

"Certainly, I will agree to any course of study you should allow me." Her gaze scanned the listings of Honors Thesis, Advanced Latin and Greek Translation, and Senior Seminar of History of the Hellenes, as well as an unexpected course. "Independent Laboratory Study?"

"Trust you to pick that out straightaway. You see, I had been pursuing my own particular avenues of research before being called to the presidency, and I thought perhaps you could be persuaded to take up where I had to leave off." She picked up a thicker folder to hand to Marigold. "I had been working with Professor Judith Cleaver in the Chemistry faculty on some chemical solutions and processes for the treatment and long-term stability of archaeological artifacts, namely coins. We have been particularly keen on working out a superior method of electrolytic reduction, following on work by Olhausen and Rathgen at the Königliches Museum in Berlin and Rosenberg at the National Museum in Copenhagen. We are determined that our own country's scholarship should not lag so far behind the Europeans, and naturally want our own institution and scholars at the forefront."

"Naturally," Marigold agreed, looking at the folder with a wonderful admixture of enthusiasm and doubt—she had never been a particularly adept student of the sciences, despite her desire to excel. But as her sweet mother used to say—even if sweet Esmé had not given birth to Marigold, she had still raised Marigold well—"We can't all expect to be superior at everything, darling. Just try your best."

"Excellent." Julia Irvine took her assent for enthusiasm. "Professor Cleaver will be delighted to have such a mind as yours under her tutelage. I'm giving you the advantage of my notebooks on the subject to bring you up to speed, as it were."

"Thank you, ma'am." Marigold accepted the bound notebooks with something approaching reverence.

"You are most welcome. I hope you will be pleased to learn that, as president, I've focused on using my institutional powers to elevate our academic standing with our brother and sister universities, and in doing so, Wellesley has at last been invited to join the American School for Classical Studies in Athens."

This was astonishing news. Marigold felt as if her ambitions had been given room to take wing. "How excellent."

"Indeed. And as a member institution, I have requested and received a number of ancient coins from ongoing excavations—twenty-eight coins, to be exact—in need of restoration for our experiments. You'll be working with those artifacts, and with Professor Cleaver, one on one. But it will look very well on your own applications for fellowship with that same American School for Classical Studies in Athens, to which I am prepared to recommend you, if you can manage to regain your former academic footing."

The doubt flooded back. But with it came an equal share of determination. "I shall devote myself to nothing else, Professor—I beg your pardon, President Irvine."

Julia Irvine stretched out her hand to take Marigold's once more. "I have every confidence that you will do so. Because I have one more, hopefully welcome, piece of advice. If you can get up to proverbial speed and excel in these last few courses required for your undergraduate degree, we are prepared to accept you as a master's degree student in the spring semester. We'd like the privilege of keeping you at Wellesley as long as we may."

Ambition seemed a mild word for the soaring feeling of possibility within her. And after so much harder luck last spring, Marigold was more than astonished at such soft, good fortune. "I should like nothing better."

"Excellent. Now, I won't keep you any longer. I'm sure you're anxious to settle back in. Through Miss Burke's excellent offices, we've secured you one of the larger corner rooms on the third floor, in the west transept, where you'll be close to the Art Museum and the artifacts under study."

"Thank you." Marigold knew at this point in the semester, she was lucky to get anything bigger than a broom closet. "I am most sincerely obliged."

"I should hope so," President Irvine laughed. "And I will expect you to discharge your debt of gratitude by excelling at your studies."

It was a strange feeling for Marigold to have less confidence in herself than those around her, but she had always risen to whatever challenges had come. And she was desperately determined to rise to this one. "Thank you."

"Miss Burke will have your keys, and the porters should have delivered your trunks to your room by now." The president extended her hand. "Welcome back, Marigold."

"Thank you, ma'am." Marigold shook her hand warmly. "It is so very good to be back."

She collected her keys from the brisk Miss Burke, waving off any further assistance. "I know my way."

Marigold set off at a leisurely pace, taking her time, savoring the sense of familiarity and excited ease at being back in these hallowed halls. College Hall was the exact antidote to the malaise she had felt just a week ago in Boston—a place where nothing bad could happen. Wellesley had been designed to nurture young women, mind, body, and soul. The huge building seemed to be full of life—conversation and laughter mixed with footfalls on the floors and the clatter of steps on the stairways echoed up the open stairwells to the rafters soaring above. One could not help but be inspired to excellence in such a place.

She took the central stairway upward to the second floor, when she heard her name. "Miss Manners?" a voice called as she passed an open dormitory room. "Is that you?"

"It is." Marigold paused while the student, dressed in a shirtwaist and long wooly cardigan belted over her skirt, came to the door with a hat in her hand, as if she had been in the process of trying on the velvet tam when she had noticed Marigold's passing in the mirror. "You may not remember me—"

"Miss Newton, isn't it? First year Greek translation, two years ago, was it? Of course, I remember." The college was a little like a cloister—a closed community of dedicated souls where, after a short while, everyone was known to everyone else. While Marigold assumed she would have a great many new faces and names to learn, there were plenty of girls who remained well remembered.

Tall, athletic, auburn-haired Aggie Newton had seemed more suited to the sweep of the golf course than the classroom. She had scrambled her way through Introduction to Greek, persevering through grit and determination to realize her own ambition to become an archaeologist. Fortunately, the young woman had shown great aptitude in other areas of study, namely history, and that indefinable quality Marigold thought of as puzzle-solving.

Marigold extended her hand. "It is good to see you."

"And to see you as well," the young woman stammered with pleasure. "We were quite disappointed when you left last year."

"As was I, Miss Newton." It was a lovely thing to be remembered.

"Aggie, please. It's Agnetta, but everyone calls me Aggie."

"And I am Marigold." She held out her hand again. "For I am no longer your teaching assistant."

"More's the pity!" Aggie exclaimed as she shook Marigold's hand. "The girl who took your place has nothing of your generosity—" she stopped herself with a hand over her mouth. "Oh, I oughtn't have said that."

Marigold was forced to choose between what she knew was right—not engaging in the vulgar habit of gossip—and what she knew was expedient—engaging in gossip to gauge the atmosphere of the place.

She settled for something both nonvulgar and informative. "And who is the new teaching assistant for Greek?"

"Miss Appleton. Sarah Appleton."

"Naturally." Marigold should have anticipated that her former rival from both boarding school and the Department of Classics would have swiftly stepped in to fill Marigold's vacated shoes. Miss Sarah Sedgwick Appleton—of the Lenox Appletons—was a very distant relation of Marigold's through the Sedgwick line. But any trace of familial feeling for the girl had long been lost to her disagreeably superior personality—she had always been the sort of person who peppered her conversation with half-whispered phrases like "entre nous" and "not our kind" to elevate herself at others' expense.

"I oughtn't say—" Aggie hesitated but clearly wanted to unburden herself. "But she's just so—you know the type, the sort of girl who seems so . . . lofty and elegant and effortless. As if she never gets anything so mortifying and ignominious as pills on her sweaters."

Aggie held up the arm of her rather well-worn sweater. "Or lose their buttons. Or hats. I lost this one just yesterday—Mable Benkins retrieved it from the library for me."

"I am a great appreciator of hats," Marigold conceded. Isabella had taught her that a hat was essential to balance an outfit. "And that is a very stylish hat, well worth retrieving."

"Thank you." Aggie's smile was a charming mix of gratitude and relief. "It was meant to give me a bit of splash on the golf course. I spent a whole eight dollars for it at Jordan Marsh—which was a vast deal of my summer earning at the Concord Public Library, where I worked."

"Worth every penny." Marigold also understood that the value of clothing went beyond its cost. She was more grateful than ever for Isabella's generosity in the matter of wardrobe.

"But things will change now that you're back with us, I hope," Aggie suggested quietly.

"Naturally," Marigold agreed, while also intuiting that she needed to tread carefully. "I hope you'll find a friend in me, no matter who is officially the teaching assistant in the Department of Classics."

"Oh, thank you." Aggie said with open relief. "Plato has been giving me pure conniptions. So much more complicated than the Greek New Testament translations we worked through first year. And you know how much trouble those gave me!"

"You know," Marigold advised, "B's and C's get degrees too—not everyone needs to be a linguistic scholar. You have innumerable other talents that are just as important to an archaeologist as translation."

"Oh, thank you, again." Aggie's natural cheerfulness rose to the fore. "To heck with being a stickler! I just need to pass the danged course!"

"Just so." Marigold agreed with a smile.

What a joy it was to be so wholly consumed by collegiate concerns, so removed from the more visceral cares of the rest of the world. How nice it would be to confine her focus solely to academic concerns. If she could.

Because she had changed. She felt older, wiser. Tested.

For all its wickedness, murder had somehow made her more worldly.

And, if she was honest, far more weary.

Chapter 3

"Keep away from people who try to belittle your ambitions. Small people always do that, but the really great make you feel that you, too, can become great."

Mark Twain

Marigold was more than pleased to have been given the corner bedroom President Irvine had promised, along with a larger sitting room with a wonderful view over the lawns to the lake, and immediately set about organizing it into the cozy study of her academically minded waking dreams—tidying and getting organized always calmed her mind and eased her soul.

She opened her windows to the fresh country air before she set to work. Her trunks of clothing she unpacked first—she respected both Isabella's genius and her seamstress's hard work too much to ever take them for granted or mistreat such stylish clothing. Second, she set up her ingeniously engineered steamer trunk that unfolded into a three-tiered chest of drawers, so she would have all the extra storage she might need for her archaeological field gear, as well as her bicycling tools and accoutrements. Her bicycle itself she was sure had been uncrated by the efficient Mr. Duckett and now stood in the well-filled bicycle rack outside the building, awaiting her much anticipated first ride around the campus.

The ringing clarity of the Japanese bell hanging at the second floor of College Hall's atrium, signifying the supper hour had thankfully arrived was a welcome interruption.

After freshening up and checking her appearance in the modern and hygienic washroom adjacent to her rooms to ensure she was unsmudged by dirt and dust—one might alter one's standards to fit the occasion, but never let them down—she made her way downstairs to the dining hall. There, the students gathered in informal groups at tables designated by interest and field of study.

Marigold passed by the German table and the French table, where students were conversing in the foreign languages, looking for the familiar faces of the Classics table.

Only to find the familiar figure at the head of the table looking at her with something less than welcome. "Well, look what the tide's brought in." Sarah Appleton's smile didn't quite reach her eyes. "Decided to grace us with your presence after all, Marigold? Did you finally come into enough money to scratch together your tuition?"

"How kind," Marigold returned with her own crocodile smile—all bright teeth and cynical eyes. She had long ago learned from Jane Austen's example that one's courage should rise with any attempt to intimidate. "So like you to take an interest, Sarah. And yes, I did come into money, though I'm quite sure no one wants to hear the vulgar details. You're looking marvelously athletic, Aggie—I heard you made a hole-in-one on the golf course this afternoon. And Fannie, my dear girl—your sonnet in the last issue of the poetry magazine was sublime. You are to be congratulated." And so Marigold went, on down the familiar row of faces, moving at a measured but steady pace away from Sarah Appleton, who was left alone with no company but her own spleen.

Aggie pulled out a chair for Marigold at the far end of the table, where a lively group of students who were more interested in the study of archaeology than in the classical languages were gathered.

"How was Kefalonia?" Fannie asked guilelessly before being shushed by another, better-informed student. "What?"

"It's all right," Marigold said with a calm smile. "I don't mind. I am sorry to report that I was not able to join the field season at Leivathos on Kefalonia this past summer as planned, due to the unfortunate family circumstances our Miss Appleton so kindly alluded to. But as she also alluded"—Marigold sent what she hoped was an ironic nod up the table at Sarah Appleton—"my fortunes have reversed themselves, so I am hoping that I will be able to take up my forfeited position next summer—along with a number of you, who, I hope, will also be applying to the field school?"

What ensued was just what Marigold had hoped and longed for—a lively discussion on scholarship, research, and opportunity, now made broader by Wellesley's joining into the American School for Classical Studies in Athens.

"What do you think, Marigold—had you rather apply to the school in Athens, to better be able to work on your translations of the Greek myths, or will you take your chances with a field season on the island?"

"I'm not sure," she answered truthfully. While she had made some small progress on her intended Honors thesis translations of the Greek myths, her true goal had always been to become a working field archaeologist. "The thought of a summer in Athens certainly has its charms. And now that we American scholars have our own excavating concession in Greece, I shall have to look for deficiencies in my plan of study, so I shall be ready to apply."

"Are you sure you can afford all the extra credit hours that will require?" was Sarah's seemingly innocent query from the far end of the table—her clear blue eyes all but danced with a sparkling mixture of malice and privilege.

"Not sure at all," Marigold laughed. "But where would be the fun, or adventure, in that if life were always so predictably, stultifyingly set? I rather like rolling the dice and taking my chances." She spread her smile around her end of the table like butter over bread. "That's why I'm an archaeologist—we're naturally more adventurous than . . . others."

It was as if Marigold had issued a clarion call to adventure, so enthusiastically was her pronouncement met. But it served its purpose—to keep Sarah from spreading either her well-bred, well-camouflaged venom or her influence. Her day in the sun might continue—there was no way Marigold might take away her assistantship at this point in the school year—but Sarah's time as the leader of the table had all but come to an end.

And that was all the triumph Marigold would allow herself. She would not gloat or let herself be consumed by the passing pleasure of pettiness—she had far too much work to do.

Which she began as soon as she got back to her sitting room, settling into preparation for the following day's classes as well as the backlog of reading and translations she needed to complete to be up to date for the semester. It was a powerful load of work, as her old friend—or nemesis, depending upon how one looked at it—from Great Misery Island, Cleon, would have said.

But she, with her determination and her ambition, was just the person to do it.

And so, she burned the metaphorical midnight oil quite literally—using one of Seviah's old shuttered lanterns that she had brought with her from Great Misery Island as a preservation against the "ten PM rule" that all lights had to be doused as soon as the Japanese bell rang out the appointed hour. The tightly focused lamp gave her just enough light to read her text of Antiphon's oration, the "Anonymous Prosecution for Murder," along with his first oration, "Against the Step-Mother for Poisoning"—which, given Marigold's own recent experiences on Great Misery, made for absolutely riveting reading.

But while Marigold was keenly caught up in suspecting the poison used would prove to be the botanical *Atropa bella-donna*, or nightshade, the lamp's circle of light extended just far enough for her to catch sight of something being slipped under the crack of her door. The object proved to be a withered, dead rat, presumably plucked from one of the porters's many traps.

Marigold's first fleeting thought was that its appearance was nothing more than a collegiate prank. But due to her recent experiences on Great Misery Island, Marigold, like the Jane Austen heroine she had recalled at dinner, had a stubbornness about her that could never bear to be frightened at the will of others.

She was up and across the floor, wrenching open the door before the desiccated specimen had slid to a stop against the rug. "Good evening, Sarah."

Sarah Appleton reared up from where she had knelt to deliver her stealthy gift, handkerchief in which she had transported her rat still in hand, her mouth gaping open in a comic admixture of shock that she had been caught and horror that she would therefore be punished.

Neither reaction would serve Marigold. Humor was a more useful tool. "How thoughtful of you to welcome me with a gift."

Sarah was not wise enough to take Marigold's offering—her shock slid easily into disdain. "It *is* a gift. One to tell you you're as welcome here as that rat."

"Naturally," Marigold agreed as pleasantly as she was able, given the circumstance. "I can see how you might feel that way. But honestly, you needn't."

"Someone has to tell—"

"What's going on?" The ever-vigilant faculty member resident on the hall—recognized as such by her matronly personage as much as her air of inviolable authority—came striding down the corridor. In her wake, curious kerchiefed and braided heads popped out of the doors to witness the event.

"Good evening, Professor," Marigold answered, stepping into the corridor to block the woman's view of the rat's corpse, lest her apparent schoolgirl rivalry with Sarah Appleton blossom into something more volatile. "I had forgotten an important Greek lesson and Miss Appleton was kind enough to deliver the notes to me."

"Was she? Lights are out," the professor reminded them. "Which, as Miss Appleton *knows*, means no passage of the corridors or stairs. Perhaps *you* have forgotten the rules, Miss Manners, but I will brook no nonsense on my hall. Do I make myself clear?"

"Yes, Professor," said Marigold, while Sarah Appleton murmured a meek, "Yes, ma'am."

The compliance mollified the woman. "I will let this incident pass this once, as it is your first night, but let there be no repeat offenses. Have I made myself clear?"

"Yes, Professor."

The woman walked away, and if Marigold had expected Sarah to follow, she was surprised to find all signs of obedient meekness had vanished from the girl's long, patrician face. "You don't belong here," she all but hissed. "I know all the *vulgar*"—Sarah emphasized the word to echo Marigold's use of the adjective at dinner—"details of your tawdry, scandalous parentage. You're a . . . bastardess!" Her pleasure at her own cleverness painted smudges of color on her high cheekbones. "That you even dare to continue to call yourself a Manners—your audacity astonishes the family."

Marigold refused to let her own astonishment, or her sudden hot embarrassment at the bold-faced airing of her somewhat-soiled-despite-repeated-washings laundry, show. She might doubt her new-found sense of self all she wanted, but it was beyond the pale for this prig of a girl to do so.

"My audacity? At being born? But not my father's audacity at fathering illegitimate children? Which, by the way, is none of your business—nor mine—if my father did commit the so-called sin of sowing his wild oats before his marriage to dear blameless Esmé." Marigold would not allow any slander against her near-sainted mother—although mother wasn't exactly the right appellation for sweet Esmé. Not that it particularly fit Sophronia, either—though that lady had at least attempted to enjoin a correspondence with Marigold. Her letters, full of eerie, queer goings-on and recipes for healthful tonics, arrived with delightful regularity. But they were not the point—Marigold's self-worth was. "How intellectual and forward-thinking of you."

"You don't belong here," Sarah repeated one last time, sweeping her nightgown aside, as if any proximity to Marigold would sully its snowy white frills, before she paraded herself away.

Marigold forbade herself from retorting—she was too choked with the acidic admixture of pride and shame to say anything more. While she had learned that the easiest way to rid oneself of an enemy was to turn them into an ally, she had neither a plan nor any real inclination to turn Sarah Appleton to her benefit. Instead, she simply wrapped the rat in one of her least favorite handkerchiefs and disposed of it in her wastepaper bin.

"How childish. And ab-so-lutely vile" was the quiet comment from the stalwart girl directly across the hall. "Not to mention atrociously rude."

"Yes, I'm terribly sorry." Marigold misunderstood her on purpose, for as much as she agreed with her, Marigold herself was the one who had woken everybody up. "I shouldn't have created such a commotion. My apologies."

"You've nothing to apologize for," the girl responded staunchly. "Such a podsnapper that Appleton is, all nose up in the air, as if sharing oxygen with the rest of us were a con-dee-scension." Her vaguely southern accent added a charming flavor to her outrage.

"You don't say," Marigold encouraged.

"I do say. And leaving the dead *Rattus norvegicus*," the girl observed, eyeing the rotting rodent over her spectacles. "Well, I'm all for a fun prank, but that's just all too skilamalink for me."

Marigold was charmed by the young woman's easy usage of old-fashioned slang that Marigold had only ever heard from her grandmother's maids. "It's a bit too skilamalink for me too," she agreed. "But is that really a Norway rat? You must be a biologist or zoologist?"

"Chemist, although I've done many hours of biology and zoology, so I like plain old 'scientist' well enough," the girl corrected with a smile and a hand extended. "Ethyl's the name. Ethyl, spelt like the chemical, with a 'y.' Rautencranz, Ethyl Christine."

"Manners, Marigold Dianthus." She enjoined the handshake. "A pleasure to meet you."

"Likewise. Although I've known *of* you, of course. 'The Inimitable Miss Manners,' they called you. Thought you'd be an awful old stinker like Appleton and her herd of erudite effetes, looking down their noses at the tradesman-like sciences—their words, not mine."

"Nor mine," Marigold assured her. "I'm taking an independent study in chemistry, with the aim of conserving artifacts from archaeological sites."

"Aha! That's you then." Ethyl beamed her approval. "You'll be the last empty bench in the Student Laboratory and Apparatus Room, up in the attics, where we seniors have our experiments. Which means you'll be working with Professor Cleaver too. You'll be in good, if mighty stern, hands," Ethyl confirmed with a laugh, nodding up the hall to indicate that the faculty member who had come to investigate had been none other than Professor Judith Cleaver herself. "Danged clever woman, excellent instructor."

"I am glad to hear your good opinion. But I'm slated to work in the Art Museum, on museum artifact conservation. I don't think I've ever had reason to visit this Apparatus Room—it sounds positively arcane."

"Lights out!" Professor Cleaver reappeared out of the hallway's gloom. "Miss Manners, Miss Rautencranz. Any further hobnobbing at this time of night will not do. Back to bed, please."

"Yes, Professor Cleaver," Ethyl answered immediately and retreated to her door.

"And Miss Manners? I have noted your shuttered lantern." Professor Cleaver inclined her head toward Marigold's sitting room. "I am aware of the fact that you have, at the moment, a greater portion of study because of your late start this semester. But know that I will have my eye on you, to make sure your flouting of the rules becomes neither a habit nor a bad example to the other undergraduates. I'll see you in my chemical lecture room on the fourth floor bright and early tomorrow morning."

"Yes, ma'am."

"Hadn't thought of that," Ethyl whispered, venturing out only after the professor had retreated. "Nearly five weeks of classes behind. You have my sympathies."

"Thank you," Marigold acknowledged ruefully. "President Irvine said she had confidence in me to get the work done, but tonight I begin to have my doubts."

"Don't we all?" Ethyl laughed silently. "Lordy, don't we all."

Chapter 4

> *"Life is never fair . . . And perhaps it is a good thing for most of us that it is not."*
>
> Oscar Wilde

The sheer amount of work required to get up to academic scratch blew down upon Marigold like the fall winds off the lake, bending the treetops, testing her best intentions to meet the difficulty with discipline and diligent effort.

True to her word, Professor Cleaver had begun Marigold's tutelage in the science of archaeological conservation by outlining an ambitious plan for Marigold to set up her own experiments in the Student Laboratory and Apparatus Room on the fifth floor. "I know President Irvine envisioned you working within our museum, but I'm convinced that giving you a dedicated bench in the Student Laboratory, where your experiment will not be subject to the daily comings and goings of curious and often clumsy undergraduates—only those serious science students with ongoing experiments are granted keys to the room—will be better. It is far better ventilated, which will be a concern for your work."

The Student Laboratory and Apparatus Room was located on the very top floor of College Hall, where the mansard roof created echoing, high-ceilinged rooms punctuated by tall, drafty dormer windows. Other students had clearly marked out territories for their own experiments—Ethyl Rautencranz's chemistry experiment on the bench next to Marigold's consisted of an elaborate series of connected vials and flasks, while one whole corner of the room was partitioned off with heavy, dark curtains to shield it from the prying eyes of the curious.

But Marigold had more than enough to worry about without poking her nose into other people's business, so she set to work, hauling her equipment up the long flights of stairs—the Columbia dry cell battery she requisitioned from the chemical laboratory storeroom, along with the necessary wiring and clips, not to mention the gallons of chemical solutions and deionized water. Normally, she never shied from such demanding physical labor, but after more than an hour of heavy lifting, even Marigold's usual positivity was on the wane.

Especially when Ethyl took one look at her and laughed. "I was going to ask if you might be available to try to row for a seat in the senior class barge. But you look as if one more thing might plumb drag you under."

"One foot on a banana peel and the other in the grave," Marigold quipped, quoting her friend from Great Misery, Bessie Dove, while at the same time taking a surreptitious glance at her reflection in the window to gauge the extent of her shabitude. She tucked a stray hair behind her ear. "Haven't the seats on the boat already been decided by now?" Most oars won their seats when they were freshwomen and continued with their boats through their senior year.

"Bow oar came down with appendicitis," Ethyl supplied in her factual but charmingly accented way. "Thought you'd do on short notice—only senior girl with both experience and ready-made calluses on her hands."

"Yes, well," Marigold managed, even as she curled her palms into fists behind her skirts. Her time on Great Misery had clearly given her a number of new attributes besides suspicion. "How observant of you."

But Ethyl meant no harm. "Scientific process," she explained with an easy, confidential smile. "Teaches you to be observant."

"Naturally," Marigold agreed with welcome relief—she really was back amongst her own kind of thinking people, Sarah Appleton notwithstanding. "But to your first question—yes, I should very much like to row for the seniors." Regular physical exercise would do her a world of good. Mens sana in corpore sano, as the ancients would have it. "When might I try out?"

"Frankly, the seat is yours for the asking, though we might have to shift positions to make best use of you. Anybody who knows anything about rowing at Wellesley knows you can row."

Marigold was chuffed. "Thank you." That she was even better prepared than they could know—though she had been absent from college, her form had only gotten stronger with all the rowing back and forth to Great Misery Island—would no doubt prove another source of pride. "Then I will ask instead, when is your next practice?"

"Round about three-thirty, directly after the last class has ended and as soon as everyone can get changed into rowing attire and get down to the lake, so we can get a good hour in before the light starts to fade."

"Three-thirty at the boathouse it is." All work and no play would make Jill a dull girl just as surely as all play and no work would make Jill but a toy.

Marigold wanted to be no one's toy, so she applied herself strictly to memorizing the chemical solutions and pH levels cited in President Irvine's notebook, until the time came to change into a suitable rowing costume, which was the same sort of sensible, athletic wear she favored for bicycling riding—a well-knit athletic sweater over a stout tweed split skirt, which, like bloomers, were worn so often on campus that their propriety was never questioned. And while she was lacing up her supple leather boots, she decided she would give herself the pleasure of cycling down to the boathouse instead of walking. There was nothing like a little wheelwork to clear out the cobwebs from one's brain—and having her bicycle would bring her back to her work sooner than a walk.

She strode downstairs through the soaring center of College Hall with a renewed sense of purpose. And nearly walked into none other than tall, elegant Sarah Appleton.

"Sarah." Marigold spoke purposefully, in a quiet, even tone, mindful of her intent to make an ally of the girl. "Good afternoon.

You're looking well, despite our rendezvous in the night. I fear too many chemical formulations have left me in need of some exercise. Perhaps you'd like to join me?" Sarah had always been a keen sportswoman, though they had only occasionally competed against each other, being in different class years.

Sarah drew herself up but did not respond. Instead, she shifted her Greek grammar to her left hand so she could again sweep her skirts away with her right, lest the illegitimacy Marigold harbored leap across the floor and scratch its way up her skirts like a contagion. Once she had finished the gesture, she declared loudly to whoever might be within hearing, "Some people don't know when they are out of their depth."

Marigold raised her chin, even as she smiled. Sarah might have taken over Marigold's academic place as the top student, but clearly, it had not made her any more secure in her ability. Or perhaps it made her too sure—so sure she no longer felt the necessity to be fair, even-tempered, or polite. It gave her leave to be an ambitious shrew. Despite Marigold's antipathy for the word and its gendered stereotype, she could think of no other that fit the beautiful but callous Miss Appleton so well.

At least, no other word that was polite.

"Some people have been tested in the currents, Sarah, and know how to swim, no matter how hard the tide might try to turn against them."

Her riposte given, Marigold took her own dramatic step around Miss Appleton's skirts and made for the door.

It was only when she reached the drive that Marigold forced herself to take a deep breath and banish her unkind thoughts. She would be better. She would rise above such pettiness. The day was too fine to wallow in woefully unnecessary academic rivalry. There was room enough in such a progressive institution for any number of scholars to pursue their personal dreams. She would simply concentrate on pursuing hers.

Marigold took a turn around the circular drive before cycling down the lane that led to Lake Waban. It was a bluebird day, with high, clear skies under a warm autumn sun. She pedaled across the grass edging the water, past the small crescent of beach where the majority of the college's small pleasure boats were drawn up on the sand, and around the curve of the lake until she came within sight of the boathouse fitted snugly against the shore.

The entrance to the boathouse was marked by a tall rotunda that gave way to more traditional floating docks. Built in Marigold's junior year with funds the students themselves had raised, the memories contained within—of the joy of discovering rowing, of gaining prowess and building camaraderie—could not fail to made her soul glad and her heart light.

She had missed this sense of routine and ease, this elegant purpose. Here, within the verdant grounds she had dreamt about last spring and summer, all was peaceful and calm. All was right.

Marigold pushed her machine into the dock, past the meandering ducks and the waving stands of catkin reeds, taking her time, enjoying the afternoon, when some flash of misplaced color caught her eye.

She stopped and looked again, thinking she had seen the dark iridescent feathers of a mallard drake when she realized that dark blue hue was the plush velvet of a hat oscillating back and forth with the quiet movement of the waves.

A plush velvet hat with an elaborately feathered pin. Like Aggie's.

Her alarm was slow to rise. If Aggie had again lost her hat to the wind and waves she would undoubtedly want it back, for the pin alone—an incised silver base decorated with a brush of deer hair and adorned with three long pheasant feathers—looked properly expensive.

Marigold had already decided to retrieve it for her, even though the hat would be hard to reach—it wavered just below the corner of the boathouse, buoyed up by a raft of lake algae. And the algae looked odd, rippling in the shadow of the building, not fresh green like the specimens they had fished out of the lake to study under microscopes in freshman biology—Ethyl Rautencranz would no doubt remember the precise taxonomic name for the water plant.

But a longer look showed the algae that clung to the corner post of the boathouse was not colorless, even in the shadow. Because the oscillating plume was not algae but hair.

A woman's hair.

Long, dark auburn hair that wafted below the surface of the water, where Marigold could now make out the unmistakable shape of a long puffed sleeve and a bare white wrist.

Some echo of recognition—the memory of another girl, drowned under the waves of Salem sound—scoured through her like acid.

"Aggie!"

Marigold had already dropped her bicycle and was jumping, splashing into the shallows, sinking up to her waist as she plunged forward. Her wool skirts quickly became saturated, weighing her down as she struggled against the binding of the fabric wrapping around her legs. "Aggie!"

She plunged her arms under the water to reach for the girl, trying in vain to keep her head above water to see through the shadows. Finally, she caught up the fabric of the sleeve.

Somewhere at the edge of her hearing, Marigold heard footfalls. "Help me!" she called frantically. "Help me, please!" But her voice sounded weak and feeble against the lap of the water and the rush of the wind—and her own fearful panic. She strained to raise her head and her voice enough to shout. "Help!"

She caught hold of the girl's clothing with two hands and heaved back as hard as she might, trying to bring the poor thing to the surface, desperate to try and help. Desperate to be in time.

Against the soft crush of the fabric in her hands, the girl was cold, heavy, and stiff. "Aggie!" Marigold slipped deeper into the water, her feet sinking into the shifting sand on the bottom as she grappled her arms under the poor girl's shoulders. "Help me!"

"What—" came an aborted call from a railing overhead. "What are you doing?"

"Help me!" Marigold's cry took on a sharp edge. "Help me get her out!"

Footsteps rolled and echoed over the wooden dock. "What are you doing to her?"

"I'm not—" Marigold tried to get her breath, but the chill of the water and the cold of the sodden clothing under her hands, left her gasping. "I'm trying— Please help me get her out!"

"Hurry!" someone called from a different direction. "Into the boat!"

It took moments of Marigold struggling in vain to make any sort of progress before the unseen voices came back.

"Oh, my God!" someone cried from the water a few feet away, where the bow of a rowing barge had just nosed out of the boathouse bay.

"Mind your oars," demanded another, somehow more familiar voice, before the rest of the boat appeared, and she too gasped. "Lordy! Is she dead?"

"I don't know," Marigold gritted out, even as the logical part of her brain told her the opposite—that there was no hope. "I can't find out if you don't help me!" She levered her feet as best she could against the piling and pulled one more time—and heard the dampened sound of the slow rending of fabric. And all of a sudden, she was overbalanced and had toppled backward under the water as the girl's skirts at last floated free.

It was only a moment before she came up gasping and scrambling to find her footing, to see a line of girls in a boat staring down at her. And at what could only now be called the body in her hands, which was threatening to sink anew.

"Catch hold. You, Ruth," came the order from the boat. "And bow oar, reverse, to put us back in."

The aforementioned Ruth dutifully clasped Marigold's hand as she clung to the side, towing Marigold and the lifeless girl to the dock inside the bay, where reluctant hands finally reached down to help her out of the water.

Marigold heaved herself onto the edge of the dock to catch her breath, still clasping a puffed velvet sleeve, lest the poor stiff girl sink under again. But it was clear from the way the girls on the dock had shuffled back that she would get little if no help from them.

Because the young woman was clearly dead. Even in the dim, mottled light of the boat bay, her skin was eerily pale—faint blue veins spiderwebbed over chalky white, and her expressionless, flat eyes stared unblinkingly into the dark rafters. In the water, the young woman's auburn hair had streamed out like a fan, but against the sodden wool of Marigold's lap, it was a tangled into a lifeless mat.

And she was a young woman, of an age with the Wellesley undergraduates who now surrounded her. But she was not Aggie Newton.

"Thank God." Marigold muttered her relief before she gathered her strength and heaved against the wet weight again, pulling the poor girl's shoulders clear enough to drag her stiffened corpse onto the planks. "Please, if someone would get her feet?"

"Lordy, I'll do it." That take-charge, braver soul knelt down to take hold of the beautifully made, low-heeled half-boots—Marigold noted with an eye for fashion, though the boots were terribly scuffed—levering the lower half of the young woman's torso out of the water.

"Is she dead?" someone behind Marigold asked.

"Lordy, she looks it, doesn't she, with the rigor mortis and all." The familiar, take-charge voice belonged to Ethyl, who, thankfully, seemed less overwhelmed than the others. "You'll know better than us."

The poor girl did indeed look dead. "I'm afraid . . ." Fear and frustration made a hideous muddle in Marigold's middle. The sheer, awful helplessness rose like a tide within her.

But there was nothing she could do. Nothing she had learned that might help. Even in this modern day and age, in this progressive place of learning, full of the most brilliant minds and inventions, there was nothing she knew how to do to revive the poor soul.

"I'm afraid so," she finally finished, forcing herself to think logically. "But we had still best send for Doctor Barker. To make sure."

"Ruth, you go," Ethyl, who was still kneeling at the dead girl's feet, directed. "You're the fastest."

"Oh, yes!" Ruth was clearly glad of something to do other than stare at a dead woman. "I'll fetch her."

"And Mr. Griffin, the driver, if he's there. Or Mr. Duckett, if you would," Marigold added. The handyman would be a practical addition. "With some transport. And President Irvine ought to be notified, don't you think?"

"Lordy, yes," Ethyl seemed to be the only other one capable of clear thought. "Good thinking. Let me help you up. You're soaked."

Marigold gratefully took the hand stretched over the dead girl. "Thank you. Not exactly what I envisioned when you invited me down here today."

"Lordy, no. Golly, but this isn't much of a welcome."

"No." Marigold could only agree.

"Welcome?" A too-familiar voice behind them rose in something approaching the high tones of horror. The other girls stepped back to give the now sportily attired speaker room. "I saw you in the water, choking her. I saw you," Sarah Appleton accused. "If she's dead, you're the one who killed her."

Chapter 5

"You have done what you could; some blunders and absurdities no doubt crept in; forget them as soon as you can. Tomorrow is a new day."

Ralph Waldo Emerson

Marigold rallied her rational brain to challenge her accuser.

"I beg your pardon, but you most emphatically did not." The uncomfortable feeling of being prejudged for the sins of her parentage soured her belly. She might not be able to fight such ingrained bias, but she would defend herself the best way she knew how—with logic.

"I called out the moment I saw her body under the corner of the boathouse," she continued. "I called for help to retrieve her. And frankly, judging from the state of her, she has been dead for quite some time." Unlike the others, Marigold had an unwelcome advantage, in that this was neither her first drowned girl nor her first dead body.

"So you say," Sarah retorted hotly. "I know what I saw."

"So the doctor will say when she arrives, surely," Ethyl said staunchly. "So will anyone who has taken even introductory anatomy and physiology, where we learned that rigor mortis sets in several hours after death. *After*," she emphasized.

"I still think it's very suspicious," Sarah insisted.

"So do I," Marigold countered. "How long have any of you been here? How did any of you not see her here? She was desperately tangled on the corner piling, the poor little thing." Marigold took another long look at the girl's still face, cementing once and for all that this dead girl was not Aggie—she was smaller and her hair was darker.

But the important thing was this poor young woman was not someone Marigold recognized. "Do any of you know her?"

"No," Sarah said quickly—almost too quickly.

Which made Marigold entirely suspicious—the easiest way to get out of blame was to deflect it onto others. And the people who would have had both access to the boathouse and knowledge of its secret corners were the rowers. One of them might have easily done this poor girl in by—even accidentally—smacking her across the back of her head with an oar.

Perhaps seeing wickedness in every corner would prove useful after all.

Some girls took longer to look than others to answer—Ethyl took the longest time to make a closer examination before she, too, shook her head. "Never seen her before."

Marigold was nonplussed. "No one? But she must be a fellow student." Who else would be at a college boathouse?

"Perhaps a freshwoman?" Ethyl suggested. "We're all seniors—we're the senior class crew, just like I was telling you—and I for one haven't met all the new underclasswomen since term started."

"A very logical supposition. Thank you, Ethyl." Now that the pulsating panic that had propelled her into the water was draining away, the gravity of the situation descended upon Marigold like a physical weight, leaving her exhausted. And wet. And too cold to think of what else she ought to say.

So they all stood there in doleful, dripping silence as the chill began to set into Marigold's bones. And probably her brain—all she could think was how could none of them, the strong, athletic, intelligent girls around her, not have seen or heard the girl before it was too late?

How had they all paraded past a dead body in their boathouse?

Thankfully, speedy Ruth was soon back from her dash up the hill. "Dr. Barker is coming straightaway," she panted. "And I sent word for Mr. Griffin to bring the Barge or Mr. Duckett's cart, or something. Do you think that's right?"

"Absolutely," Ethyl said before she looked to Marigold. "Wouldn't you say so?"

"Yes." The caretaker's cart was perhaps not the most dignified substitute for a hearse, but it was the most expedient.

Marigold set aside her suspicions to focus her attention and observation on the unknown dead girl. At first glance, her clothing was stylish and very well made, if a bit dressier than the usual sort of things the students wore. Her jacket was of thick velvet, and her skirts were excellent broadcloth, well-tailored in an uncomplicated but elegant style Marigold would not have been ashamed to wear.

Whoever she was, she had taste. And money.

Isabella would likely know where one purchased such clothes.

"Did she drown?" one of the Greek chorus of rowers finally asked into the uncomfortable silence.

Ethyl answered. "As Marigold here said, Dr. Barker will know." She stood and Marigold saw that for all her take-charge personality, Ethyl was a diminutive girl—and therefore very likely the coxswain of her class boat, used to giving direction. "Let's all move back a pace, so that when the doctor gets here we're not standing about like a dang picket fence." She turned again to Marigold. "Should we perhaps move her"—she indicated the dead girl—"away from the edge so the doctor might examine her more easily?"

"Yes," Marigold agreed. "But let us first cement all our impressions of how we found her so we might give as factual accounts as possible to the authorities."

"You think the authorities will need to be called?" Ethyl seemed astonished at the idea. "You mean the authorities from beyond the college?"

"A young woman is dead—" Marigold's experience had taught her that at some point the authorities, in the form of the coroner at the very least, were bound to be involved in some way. Malice had found its way within their cloistered confines, and it would not find its own way out.

"So you say," came the sharp complaint from Sarah Appleton.

Allies rather than enemies, Marigold reminded herself in an effort to keep her own response from being equally sharp. "The facts, established by Dr. Barker, will establish the truth. I hope you will defer your allegation to her opinion."

"Lordy, yes, absolutely," Ethyl said with a pointed look to the taller girl. "All of us will certainly be guided by the facts, which are about to be established—here is Dr. Barker."

The young women dutifully shuffled back, giving way to the college's longtime physician, Dr. Emilie Barker, who immediately went to her knees in front of the dead girl. "What happened?" she asked as she began her examination—taking the girl's wrist first, before bending to put her ear to the girl's sodden chest.

"Marigold Manners found her, doctor." Ethyl spoke up. "And heroically brought her out of the lake."

Dr. Barker briefly glanced about. "Where?"

"I saw her just under the corner of the boathouse, doctor." Marigold responded. "Her skirts had become tangled with the post. Her skirt ripped—there—when I pulled her out."

"She was fully submerged when you found her?"

"Yes, ma'am. I think so." Marigold tried to clear her mind's eye of everything but the memory of what she had seen. "Just below the surface."

"I see." The doctor sat back for a moment, before she gently closed the girl's eyes. And then leaned hard against the girl's chest.

A sluggish surge of water gurgled from the girl's mouth and nose.

"Drowned, I must assume," was the doctor's opinion. "And in her Sunday best, it seems. God rest her soul. No idea how long she's been in the water, as the cold may have arrested the natural processes of decom—" She broke off, with a glance at the students arrayed around her, clearly not wanting to upset them with harsh clinical details. "But I'll have to take her up to the Hospital Wing to examine her more particularly—just as a precaution."

"Ruth called for Mr. Griffin or Mr. Duckett's cart at Marigold's suggestion, ma'am," Ethyl informed her. "Which I think shows some great presence of mind."

"Yes." Dr. Barker cast a long glance at Marigold. "Thank you both. You'll need to get out of those wet things as soon as possible, Miss Manners."

"Thank you, Dr. Barker, but I would prefer to stay." Marigold wasn't sure what compelled her, because she was frankly more than a little cold and wet. But she had lost at least one other drowned girl to the waves of Salem Sound—she was not about to let this one go. "Do you recognize her, doctor?"

"No." Dr. Barker frowned. "I do not. Any of you?"

"No, ma'am," Ethyl answered. "None of us recognize her."

"Then an underclasswoman who has not yet had the need to visit my premises, I presume," the doctor posited. "But I should think a bed check—or a modified sort of room check—will suffice to identify her."

There were other ways as well—ways Marigold would certainly pursue if checking of all the dormitory rooms within College Hall did not turn up a name.

Like asking Aggie if she had loaned anyone her hat.

And the dead girl's clothes—a look at the labels inside would probably prove instructive.

But looking at the girl's labels was certainly off limits at the moment. Especially when Dr. Barker carefully arranged the girl's arms into a gesture of repose before she began to organize the assembled young women.

"Now, if someone—or perhaps a few someones would be best—would care to have a look round the boathouse to see if there is some blanket or covering with which we might shield the body from curious stares? Or from horrifying the entire college campus. Thank you." While the rowers dispersed as instructed, Dr. Barker turned her attention back to Marigold. "I'll advise you again to go up and change as soon as possible, Marigold. By the way, it is good to see you back."

"Thank you, doctor," Marigold returned. "But I'm sure either Mr. Griffin or Mr. Duckett will be here presently, and we'll all progress up to College Hall. I'll change then."

"Yes, all right." The doctor's attention returned to the girl lying between them. "Your observations, Marigold?"

"Yes, ma'am." She truly was amongst her own kind—women who took other women's opinions and thoughts seriously. "Other than the fact that she seems quite dead, she has these curious pink dots all over her face, but particularly around her eyes, there."

"Petechiae," the doctor explained. "Mm. Yes." She reached to turn down the collar of the sodden velvet jacket and hissed in her breath.

But whatever explanation she had been about to make was interrupted by the return of the rest of the senior crew.

"We found a blanket, Dr. Barker." Ethyl was back, holding forth her prize. "Two of them actually—one to carry and one to cover her," she added solemnly.

"Very good thinking." The doctor's smile was kind if not warm. "And here are Mr. Griffin and Mr. Duckett to assist us," she observed as the men clambered down the wooden staircase to the dock level. "Thank you for coming so quickly, gentlemen."

What a solemn procession they made, bearing their makeshift blanket stretcher up to the rotunda, then trudging silently behind the cart as it wound its way back up the hill to College Hall. Whatever indignation or determination had made Marigold want to stay with the girl until she had at least been identified began to leach away with each cold, squishing step.

But when the wagon turned for the covered porch at the front of the building, Marigold felt her purpose return.

"Ma'am?" She called to Dr. Barker, who was seated in the well of the wagon with the draped body. "Do you think perhaps the west entrance—nearest to the stairwell leading up to your Hospital Wing—would be better? It would certainly be far more discreet?"

She could only imagine what might happen were they to bring the body in the main entrance—frankly, some onlookers had already begun to take notice, their mouths gaping open in astonishment, and not a little horror.

"Yes, certainly," the doctor agreed, directing Mr. Duckett to steer the cart toward the far side of the building.

Her part effectively done, Marigold briefly debated leaving the small cortege to go directly into the sheltering warmth of the Hall, but something about the way the other girls seemed to naturally close ranks—Ethyl looped her arm through Marigold's in unspoken support—kept her going with their discreet party.

But there was no keeping the situation a secret—especially not in such a tight-knit community of academically minded young women, who were trained and encouraged to be intellectually curious. Their peace—the peace of this beautiful sanctuary of female learning—was about to be shattered. Malice and wickedness had found their devious ways in.

At the far west end of the building, President Irvine awaited them like a vigilant sentry against such evils. "Thank you all for your assistance, girls," she said to the assemblage. "I hope I don't need to mention that discretion is very much required of all of you. Please, let us not set tongues to wagging with rumors and suppositions before we have been able to ascertain the facts."

"Yes, ma'am" was the answering murmur, though Marigold had little hope of the direction being fully followed—human nature could not be suppressed. The girls would need to talk about such an experience amongst themselves at the very least, and roommates and best friends not present at the boathouse were bound to be included in the discussions.

She herself had a number of thoughts and suppositions careering about her brain.

"Thank you, that is all. Again," President Irvine raised her voice as the girls turned to go. "Discretion is our watchword. Thank you. You are dismissed with my thanks."

Marigold would have gone with the rest, but President Irvine's voice stopped her. "Not you, Marigold. I suspect we'll have need of you."

Dr. Barker looked askance but kept her peace, so Marigold obligingly waited while the two older women conferred.

"I'd planned to take the deceased up to my Hospital Wing," the doctor was saying, "where I can conduct a more detailed examination. It seems the most appropriate place while you send for the authorities."

"Agreed. And I'd like to suggest Marigold—whom I have in the past found to be especially accurate in her observations—assist you for discretion's sake, as I understand she was the one who found her. If that is all right, Marigold?"

What else could she say, though she was still dripping, chilled, and uncomfortable? "Naturally, ma'am."

"Perhaps if she can take down notes for me while I dictate, I think we'll have a very comprehensive report done relatively quickly, for she did have some very astute observations in the heat of the moment," Dr. Barker conceded.

"As I expected." President Irvine agreed before she turned to Marigold. "If you could assist Dr. Barker while Mr. Duckett and the porters take the body upstairs, I would be much obliged."

"Naturally, ma'am," Marigold agreed immediately. "But wouldn't one of my classmates studying medicine be a better choice? Ethyl, for example—" She looked for her hallmate with her pertinent knowledge of rigor mortis, but Ethyl had dutifully disappeared with the others.

"The fewer people involved, the better," the president answered. "And I have faith in your powers of observation."

Marigold was in it now, whether she liked it or not. Death had followed her home.

Or had it? Maybe it was here all along and she had just been unlucky enough to chance upon it. But Marigold didn't believe in coincidences.

On Great Misery, it had been her arrival on the island that had set the murderous chain of events into motion. That could hardly have happened here—no one, aside from the president, had known she was coming. And she didn't know this poor dead young woman in the least.

But someone else had to. Even in a large community like the college, with over seven hundred young women living together, the victim could hardly be unknown. It had to be one of them.

But naming the victim was only half of the problem—they also had to find the person who had pushed this girl under the dock. And if there were over seven hundred young women who might be the potential victim—there were also over seven hundred potential suspects.

Looked at with less partial, more objective eyes than hers, the cloistered community of the college that Marigold found so close and comforting might be seen as—to use the clinical word of the Viennese physicians—claustrophobic and oppressive. A hothouse where disparagement might bloom into insult, and small slights might fester for years.

While that psychology might work if it were an older academic who had been strangled, it was not unheard of for a student to form their own academic rivalry that could spill over into something more sinister—witness Sarah Appleton's disgusting prank with the rat and her continued unwillingness to put down the gauntlet of competition.

Yes, malice had followed her home to college.

And Marigold would have to expel it.

Chapter 6

"My experience is that as soon as people are old enough to know better, they don't know anything at all."
Oscar Wilde

Once the poor dead girl's discreetly draped body had been laid out upon the Hospital Wing's sterile white enameled table, Marigold felt the fear and horror she had thus far been able to keep at bay well up inside her. "Are you going to perform an autopsy?"

Though Marigold had been privy to the information Doc Oliphant had shared after performing the autopsy in the Great Misery Island murder, she had not been present for the grizzly undertakings. It was one thing to know about and understand the importance of a postmortem examination; it was quite another thing to be confronted with taking part in one.

"Nothing so clinical," Dr. Barker assured her. "I'm not entirely qualified to do a complete postmortem, nor are my facilities set up for one. But I should like to make a record of my own preliminary observations, especially as symptoms and indications that are present at the moment may fade or change as the natural progression of death takes over."

But Dr. Barker must have sensed Marigold's trepidation. "Why don't you sit over here?" she suggested, indicating a smaller table to one side. "Let me find you some paper . . . Oh, and a blanket—you must be frozen. We ought to send up to your room for dry clothes. I can't have you getting sick on top of everything—" She removed to the wardroom, returning with a thick wool blanket. "Wrap this around you."

"Thank you." Marigold accepted the blanket, but she had rather be slightly uncomfortable in her damp clothes than have anyone going through her precisely organized drawers. "I'm warm enough now that we're indoors." She took up the pen and paper and seated herself so the examination table wasn't in the direct line of her vision. Not that she felt entirely squeamish, but it would not hurt to take some sensible precautions.

"All right then." The doctor took a deep breath and stilled, standing quietly in front of the draped body. "Let us begin. Tell me again, from the beginning, how you came to find her. When did you see her first?"

Marigold focused her mind's eye on the scene. "I saw the hat first. I thought it was Aggie Newton's. She had one—a hat—similar to this girl's. From Jordon Marsh, she said."

"Write that down," the doctor instructed.

"Yes, ma'am." As she did so, Marigold felt more of her poise and confidence return. "I did realize she had been in the water for some time—long enough for her skirts to become quite badly entangled under the corner of the boathouse."

"Yes?" The doctor encouraged. "And for her skin to exhibit vascular marbling and livor mortis—that is, darkening or discoloration. What else?"

"She had, or has, only one glove—black suede—as if she had lost its mate or . . ." Marigold trailed off, reluctant to make a supposition at such an early date. "Well, clearly, her other glove was lost, either in the process of her slipping or falling into the water, or before."

"Mm," the doctor made a vague sound of something approaching agreement. "Also write that down."

"Yes, ma'am," Marigold said again, concentrating on making sure her handwriting was both neat and precise.

"You took a good look at her once you'd got her out of the water, I gather?"

"I tried," Marigold confessed. "I noticed the top two buttons on her jacket were missing. Or are missing," she corrected herself.

"Though the jacket"—a plush, dark velvet with fashionably wide sleeves—"might still have a maker's label. It seems fairly new."

"Does it? What makes you say that?"

Marigold screwed her eyes shut so her mind's eye could picture the body of the girl arrayed before her on the dock. "The fabric was soft, even sopping wet. The pile was long and shiny, even in the light in the boathouse, not worn."

"Yes," the doctor agreed. "I can see the threads from the buttons here. They're short and frayed, as if—"

"As if someone had tugged at the lapel and torn them off—perhaps in a struggle? Oh, and there was a sort of scuffed gash on her boot that looked new, or at least unrepaired—otherwise her boots were quite well polished."

"Very observant. Yes." There was a moment of quiet. "There is a label sewn in at the back collar, but I'm going to need your help. I'm going to attempt to move her head. If you could read the maker?"

Marigold obliged with alacrity, grateful to have something so mundane to concentrate upon. "Wa—" she had to reach in to tug the tag straight. "Watteau. Oh, Madame Watteau, at Number Six Beacon Street. I know that shop." It was just down a block or so from Isabella's far more established—and expensive—atelier, the House of Dana. Which brought another thought. "Are there other labels on the rest of her clothes?"

"You check the hat," Dr. Barker instructed, gesturing to the sodden tam on the clean draped side table.

While Marigold had been taking her careful notes, the doctor must have freed the hat from the tangle of the girl's wet hair. "Jordan Marsh," Marigold read. "Just as I thought—or as Aggie said." It must have been a very popular hat for two girls in such close proximity to have purchased it. "I'll have to ask her if she knows of another girl on campus who might have owned it."

And the pin, which had first caught her eye, was fastened to the spray of feathers and was incised with some writing. "S.d.B.L.," Marigold read. "Does that mean anything to you?"

"No, I'm afraid not."

"I suppose I can look that up," Marigold offered, already trying out combinations in her head—South Dedham something Library . . .

"Good ide—" Dr. Barker rattled a nearby swivel lamp into place to get a clearer look at something. "Blast. Just as I feared."

Marigold immediately looked up from her examination of the pin. "What is it?"

The doctor had unbuttoned the high neck of the plaid-patterned blouse and held it away from the neck. "Marks of a particular sort. But notes, please, if you will resume. Take this down exactly."

The doctor only waited for Marigold to rush back into place before she began a terse narration. "Despite extensive livor mortis, there is distinct bruising all around the front of the neck, dark, well-articulated. Consistent with manual strangulation. Indeed, judging from the blossom of blood risen beneath the skin at the center of her throat, either her larynx or her hyoid bone was likely fractured by the pressure from—" Dr. Barker took a moment to take a deep breath before she resumed. "—bruises consistent with handprints, in a pattern showing individual fingers, can be observed. And judging from the color of the bruises as well as the rest of the skin, they were inflicted just before the subject's death."

A hideous chill settled deep into Marigold's bones—she couldn't help the shiver that crawled across her skin. "You're saying she was strangled, not drowned?"

"She was," Dr. Barker confirmed quietly. "By somebody with very strong hands. The marks are quite unmistakable."

Silence yawned between them, filled with growing horror.

Rowers generally had very strong hands.

Had one of the Greek chorus of the senior class oarswomen behind Marigold not an hour ago done this? Sarah Appleton and her too-quick denial came swiftly to mind.

But Marigold was getting ahead of herself. Rational thought precluded letting her personal animosity for her rival color her thinking.

"Those other marks?" Marigold sought refuge in logic. "The little red dots on her face and especially in her eyes?" she ventured over her suddenly tight throat. "What did you call them?"

"Petechiae," the doctor said again. "Formed when capillaries burst under strain and leak blood into the surface of the skin. Consistent with strangulation. The chill of the water may have acted to arrest the fading of the red marks and darker bruises."

"She didn't drown." Somehow it was a small relief to think that this poor girl might not have suffered like the others in Salem Sound, thrashing and fighting as the cold water closed over them.

"Perhaps." Dr. Barker frowned so hard she had to adjust her spectacles on her nose. "It would have depended upon the degree of strangulation—whether it was enough to only make her pass out before she was thrown—" The doctor's voice broke with emotion. "—or pushed into the lake. I'll have to measure these marks more precisely." She cleared her throat to collect herself. "But let us continue the visual examination. Her hands also show some bruising around the wrist. Less lurid or deep than the marks to the neck, but still visible. Consistent with being restrained. Her nails, which are neat and well kept—buffed regularly, I should think—show no obvious abrasions or detritus collected by scratching." The doctor took up a magnifying glass and carefully surveyed the girl's pale white fingertips, before she moved on. "But the water may have washed that away. And the cold temperature of the water will have also arrested the bloating that typically progresses along with the rigor of death."

While Marigold forced herself to focus on unemotionally recording the doctor's words, Dr. Barker moved her lens on. "Looking again at the clothing—what was it you noticed about her skirts?"

"The large rip at the hem—that was where her skirts had become tangled with the piling under the boathouse." Marigold tried to remember her exact words upon the dock. "Her skirt ripped—there—when I pulled her out." And then she remembered something else. "But when I was pulling her up onto the dock, I thought the button at the waist—or the material surrounding said button—seemed to have given way as if it were—"

"—torn at great force." The doctor had moved her glass to the aforementioned spot. "Yes, I agree. That possibility that it was ripped from being tangled with the post seems unlikely to me, as that rip is here, on the other side of her hems. Well, that gives us a definite suspicion of foul play, I should think. Of a malefactor or malefactors, at this point unknown, having at the poor girl. Whom I still do not in the least recognize—I think I should remember such Titian hair. Always wanted auburn hair as a girl. Still do if I'm honest. But that is neither here nor there."

Dr. Barker paused to listen to the sound of a key being turned in the lock. "I latched that so we wouldn't be disturbed."

"Emilie?"

"Julia? We're in here," Dr. Barker called to President Irvine, who led in a pair of rather unprepossessing men in worn wool jackets and faded plus fours, who looked as if they had come in to fix the plumbing.

"The watchmen from the town are here. Mr. Driscoll and Mr. Worthington." President Irvine introduced them in turn. "Dr. Emilie Barker, our resident physician, and one of our more accomplished undergraduates, Miss Marigold Manners, who has been assisting the doctor in the difficult duty of examining the body."

Marigold watched the watchmen's faces change when they realized that the table before them contained a dead young woman. They swallowed and belatedly doffed their hats.

"Drowned in the lake, was she?" the taller of the two posited.

Dr. Barker looked pained but prepared, as if she had anticipated just such an assertion. "That is to be determined by an autopsy conducted by the coroner's office. But it is my professional opinion as a medical doctor that the young woman did not drown—or if she did drown, it was due to injuries she received from person or persons unknown before her body was put into the lake."

"I was told she drowned." The tall fellow, Driscoll, looked to President Irvine, who had obviously tried her best to brief the men before she brought them in.

"As I said in the note I sent to the town hall requesting your presence," the president explained in a patient tone, "the young woman was *found* in the lake—by our Miss Manners here, to whom we are most obliged. That is why I requested she remain here to make herself available to any questions you might have."

The men looked at Marigold as if she were a strange species of insect they had never encountered. "You'll want to get out of those wet things," Driscoll finally commented in his nasal New England drawl, "afore you catch yourself pee-newmonia."

Dr. Barker spoke before Marigold was required to answer. "Pneumonia is caused by the bacterium Streptococcus pneumonia. Merely getting wet will not cause Miss Manners to contract the disease. I have—"

"My cousin caught it after falling in the creek over to Newton Falls," the shorter of the two fellows averred. "Water in his lungs gave him the pee-newmonia. Right near died of it."

"Thank you for your advice, Mr. Worthington." Marigold interrupted this recitation of woe. "Which I will take as soon as I am able. But in the meantime, we have a young woman who has already died—of injuries which Dr. Barker has catalogued."

"All righty then." Driscoll nodded his agreement, but then neither said nor did anything else to the point.

President Irvine shared a look with Dr. Barker, which Marigold would only characterize as a moment of silent, put-upon female communication, before the doctor took her turn to try and explain. "The evidence before us suggests that the young woman has been strangled, as you can see from the bruising around her neck." Dr. Barker moved to the table and pared back the poor thing's clothing to show the lurid purple marks. "She was either killed before she was put into the water, or she fell into the water in unconsciousness as a result of the strangulation."

The watchmen stared at her—in stupidity or incomprehension, Marigold could not tell.

"She was strangled." Dr. Barker spoke again, quietly but plainly. "She was killed."

Driscoll gaped at her. "You mean like . . . murdered?"

Dr. Barker nodded. "I mean quite exactly murdered."

After another very long, very painful silence, the man Driscoll finally said. "I don't know what you expect us to be able to do about that."

The three women exchanged speaking glances, and once again, Marigold was reminded what it was to be with women who were not only her equals but also superior in intellect, understanding, and experience.

President Irvine calmly took up the directorial reins. "We should like you to investigate the cause and circumstances of her death."

Worthington gaped. "Us?"

"Look, lady, ma'am," Driscoll stammered. "We're just the watchmen, meant to keep the peace. Keep people from moving their dairy herds into other people's fields. And keep old man Crutcher from letting his dogs get loose to get into Martin's chicken coops."

"Or keep Dewey Smalls from making a nuisance of himself around town when he gets too far into the drink," added Worthington.

"That sort of thing." Driscoll spread his hands in his earnestness. "We've no idea about . . . Well, the sort of thing you're talking about."

President Irvine clasped her hands together in a gesture Marigold knew to be one of mounting frustration. "Then, gentlemen," she asked precisely, "to whom in authority must we appeal? If the town of Wellesley does not have someone prepared to thoroughly investigate this murder, then who does?"

Driscoll shrugged uncomfortably. "Dunno. Maybe the county. Maybe the district fellows in Boston?"

Marigold interjected what she hoped was a logical train of thought. "If *you* are not prepared to investigate the young woman's murder, perhaps you might be able, at the very least, to help to identify her?"

"What does that mean?" Driscoll stepped forward briefly before he stepped back. "Do you mean that you don't know who she is?"

"Yes," Marigold answered. "None of the people thus far involved in recovering her from the water recognize her or know who she is."

Mr. Driscoll reached for the lowest hanging fruit. "One of your students, ain't she? Bound to be."

"Very possible," President Irvine conceded. "But that has yet to be determined. Our campus is not strictly fenced off, or forbidden to the townspeople or visitors, as much as we try to regulate the flow—"

"Well, that's for you to do, surely," Driscoll grew more positive. "Not us."

"Yes," President Irvine was as patient and polite as her position demanded, but Marigold could hear the sharpening edge in her voice. "We will certainly take account of all our students as soon as may be. But while we are doing that, we should like to know who amongst the authorities of Wellesley town or Norfolk County—or even the Commonwealth of Massachusetts—will be investigating her murder?"

"I can't like that you keep saying that—murder," Worthington muttered.

"I can't like witnessing it." Marigold's own patience in the face of their lack of urgency, or even some sense of responsibility, was wearing decidedly thin. "If the evidence before our eyes is of murder, then murder we must say. Using some other word won't make her any less strangled."

President Irvine tried to reimpose calm. "What Miss Manners means, gentlemen, is that someone—someone who might be abroad on our campus, or in the town, at this very moment—killed this young woman, for reasons we cannot yet comprehend. But until we find that person and find out why this was done, we—all of us at Wellesley College and in the town of Wellesley beyond—are in danger."

Driscoll looked nonplussed. "How do you figure that?"

"If you ask me," Worthington opined, "young girl, likely seeing some man like that—bound to come to a bad end."

"Yup." Driscoll nodded. "It's bound to be that she got herself in a bad way."

Marigold's sense of outrage rose like a wave within her. "First of all, we have no way of knowing anything about the circumstances of her death, other than the fact that she was strangled. She might have simply been in the wrong place at the wrong time—perhaps she saw something or witnessed some crime that had nothing to do with her. And secondly—" Her voice rose to match her outrage. "If you mean to suggest that this young woman might have been impregnated by someone whom she was seeing romantically, then that would not be an excuse to let her be strangled but would instead be strong evidence of a motive to murder!"

"Indeed," Dr. Barker chimed in. "Young—and even older—women are particularly vulnerable to violence when disclosing their pregnancies to their romantic partners. So you see why a coroner's examination is necessary as an aid to a thorough investigation into this young woman's death?"

"By jeezum," Driscoll said, as if he could not see anything so obvious. "Tell you what—we'll send over to Dedham to the county for your coroner, if you'll get to figuring out if the girl's your student." He hitched up his pants in a gesture of finality. "Then we can worry about romantical partners and murder or not."

President Irvine looked her question to Dr. Barker, who nodded. "That seems a sensible path to initiate an investigation." She nodded to the men. "We're agreed."

"All righty." Driscoll jammed his hat back on his head. "Likely 'bout the only thing we're going to agree upon. Because it won't be murder."

Marigold could no longer hide her disdain. Or her outrage. "Mark my words, gentlemen. Her death will be thoroughly investigated." Her chin went up in what she was self-observant enough to recognize as a gesture of defiance. "See if it isn't."

Chapter 7

"Let us not underrate the value of a fact; it will one day flower in a truth."

Henry David Thoreau

"Gentlemen, let me show you out." President Irvine led the men to the door. As they preceded her, she turned back to Marigold and Dr. Barker. "We'll call a chapel service presently, both to quell rumors and to take a strict counting of all the students and find out who is missing. You'd best go change clothes," she instructed Marigold. "But, Marigold?" She leveled her gaze over her knitted brow. "Not a word of this."

"Yes, ma'am," Marigold immediately acquiesced, because she had never gone against Julia Irvine's authority or questioned her judgment. "But why? Surely silence is dangerous? As you said, whoever strangled her"—she gestured to the poor soul still clothed in her Sunday best—"might still be out there, waiting in the dark to strangle another!"

Dr. Barker answered. "In my opinion and experience, until we know more, especially her identity," she said, "a careful prudence is best. My observations are naught but suppositions until she is properly examined by the coroner's office. They are not yet confirmed facts. And as such, are not to be bantered around the college. Please."

"Yes, Doctor," Marigold was chagrined. "I understand."

"Thank you. Do get some dry, clean clothes on at your first opportunity." The doctor shook her hand and rubbed a consoling hand up Marigold's arm. "Thank you very much, both for your quick thinking and assistance and also for your courage. Not many young women would have been able to do what you did today."

Marigold was equally surprised by such praise and such censure of her fellow collegians. "I'm sure any of the girls at the boathouse would have done the same."

"Perhaps," Dr. Barker conceded. "But I happen to think your kind of moral and physical courage is a rare thing indeed. So, thank you." The doctor's smile was bittersweet. "You had best go and get yourself into dry clothes before the bell rings for chapel."

"Yes, ma'am." Marigold went but hardly knew how. It seemed impossible to walk out of the Hospital Wing after what she had just heard and witnessed.

One of them—one of any of the girls who lived and studied and learned in rooms up and down this cavernous building—had been strangled to death in the boathouse by someone who had then pushed her lifeless body into the waters of Lake Waban for Marigold to find.

She shivered anew as she trudged up the stairwell that connected most directly to her own dormitory room two flights above.

Ethyl Rautencranz met Marigold at her door. "Well, this is a fine old kettle of fish. You look just about done in," she said, taking in Marigold's blanket-wrapped appearance. "What did you say this morning? One foot on the grave and the other on a banana peel?"

"Indeed."

"What did you learn down there?" Ethyl tossed her head in the general direction of the Hospital Wing.

"Nothing—not even her name." Marigold strengthened her necessary fib with a smattering of the truth. "Let me get out of these wet things."

Marigold stepped through her parlor and into her bedchamber where she quickly shucked her clammy clothes, leaving them, for expediency's sake, in a chilly puddle on the floor. "Is anyone missing from our hallway?" she asked through the open door as she chafed herself dry with a Turkish towel and pulled a fresh shirtwaist and skirt on—gray tweed, suitable to the solemnity of the moment, with a long deep-charcoal knit sweater for warmth as well as stylishness.

One might adapt one's standards but never let them down.

"No one that I know of," Ethyl answered from the doorway, with a quick look over her shoulder. "At least no one I wouldn't miss. Oh, Lordy—speak of the devil and up she pops. Here *she* comes again—looking like miles of bumpy road."

Marigold straightened her dry stockings and tied on her shoes—she would have to make sure to stuff her cycling boots with paper so they didn't warp while drying—preparing herself for another conversation with Professor Cleaver, before she was met instead with Sarah Appleton's preening disapproval.

"All this to-do is your doing, Marigold." She took her time with Marigold's name, elongating the first syllable in sarcastic emphasis. "How predictable."

Although from her vantage point with one knee on the floor of her bedchamber Marigold could not see all the way into the hallway, she could hear footsteps gathering in the corridor—a ready-made audience, just as Sarah had no doubt hoped. Her distant kinswoman's smile was a particularly upper-class mixture of superiority, pleasure, and malice.

"Naturally," Marigold answered as if she were entirely unperturbed. "But one doesn't like to make too much of oneself. It's a deplorable habit." As was letting someone as shallow as Sarah Appleton so easily knock her off her metaphorical balance. Marigold allowed herself a moment to try and restore something of her usual equanimity. "Especially in the face of such a tragedy. I feel certain President Irvine, in her steadfast wisdom, will shed light on the situation presently."

Almost as if she had wished it into action, the Japanese bell pealed through the building.

"A call to chapel—how eminently practical," Marigold said brightly before she headed toward the sanctuary at the far end of the building. "Shall we?"

Even as she charged ahead, Marigold chided herself for not taking the opportunity of letting Sarah go first so she might observe her—and perhaps see if those long, strong patrician hands of hers seemed scratched or abraded, as if they had been in some secret set-to at the boathouse.

But it was too late to turn back, and her progress with her own growing group of supportive rowers in tow, who seemed to have materialized out of thin air—likely thanks to Ethyl—had been noted. Marigold might no longer be the Classics scholar, but she still had some worth to her fellow students. And so she took the helm, steering her crew to where the president awaited them, standing on the dais of the chapel auditorium, with the faculty seated in an array behind her.

In the time that had passed since Marigold had pulled the poor girl out of the water, the chill autumn afternoon had waned into cold evening. The chapel was lit, but somehow the flickering amber gaslight only seemed to add to the eerily tense atmosphere.

"Come in, quietly now, please," President Irvine directed, "and sit with your dormitory halls, if you would."

There was some shuffling as girls removed themselves from their seats to comply, but in another minute or two the assembly was satisfactorily seated. Marigold and Ethyl seated themselves at the far end of their row, while noting that the house mothers and faculty members who were residents on halls were taking a not-so-surreptitious count of their charges.

"Good evening, ladies," Julia Irvine quietly commanded their attention. "I will come straight to the point. Rumors have no doubt been circulating amongst the student body"—even as she said the word, Marigold could see that President Irvine instantly regretted her choice—"of the *body* of a young woman, perhaps one of our own, being found by another of our own and her fellow rowers, down at the college boathouse. And I will tell you plainly that it is true."

A hubbub of distress arose from the gathering.

President Irvine held up her hands to quiet them. "I hope you will take comfort in the knowledge that your fellow students conducted themselves most honorably and bravely, immediately retrieving this unfortunate young woman, and subsequently calling for not only Dr. Barker but also myself. I will further inform you," she raised her voice to speak over the rising reaction from the assembly, "that the local authorities have also been alerted, to whom we shall look for assistance in identifying this unfortunate young woman."

"But who is it?" a girl asked over-loudly.

"Who's missing?" asked another.

President Irvine immediately quelled the simmering uproar. "In answer to the first question"—Julia Irvine was nothing if not logically self-disciplined and organized in her response—"I'm afraid we have not yet been able to ascertain her identity. And so, I would ask each of you to take this moment to look around for your friends, and classmates and colleagues, and if any one of them is missing, please report it to your nearest faculty member, or house mother, or my office, as soon as possible."

The babble rose to a near fever pitch as young women asked unthinkable questions. Marigold watched—tense with a new sort of anticipation—as everyone around her turned to and fro, frantically seeking out friends and acquaintances. Names were ticked off fingers in relief, girls stood, looking for classmates who were seated with other halls, while others gratefully clasped hands. The noise of the assembly rose and fell as panic waxed and waned.

But no one put forth a name.

Presently, after the assembly seemed finally to settle back into some semblance of order, the president spoke again. "No one? Are we quite sure?" She made eye contact with the staff and resident faculty, and one after another they all shook their heads.

President Irvine let out a tense breath. "Then we will take this moment to say a grateful prayer of thanksgiving. And we will also take this moment to pray for the repose of this poor unfortunate soul who found her death amongst us."

Along the rows, nearly all eyes were now returned to the front. Julia Irvine was by her own religious inclination a Quaker, but the chapel services she conducted for the college were marked by a simplicity and distinctive elegance that made her a favorite of the student body. Despite her slight build, she was still a commanding figure behind the chapel podium as she read them into service. "Let us bow our heads and pray."

The sobered assembly of students obediently did so.

Marigold did not. Of course, she ducked her head a little—a very little—so as not to seem profane, but she used the moment to make a quiet exit from the room and make her way up the chapel stairs to the fourth floor, where she came out onto the chapel gallery. From such a lofty perch, she could better observe the rows of her fellow students, taking notice if anyone was still turning her head this way or that. Assessing if anyone still seemed particularly distressed. Scouring faces for some furtive sign of knowledge. Or guilt.

She was disappointed to find Sarah Appleton's head was dutifully and beautifully bowed, as if she knew piety was a good look for her. Many other girls were tearful or quite understandably scared. Marigold knew better than most what had already transpired on their campus, and she would honestly have to account herself one of the scared. Or at least, one of the extraordinarily cautious. And extremely curious.

Although almost every head was bowed, the few that were not gazed respectfully at the dais. Marigold could mark no one out as being out of order—no one she could single out as too distressed or too calm.

As President Irvine's precisely plainspoken appeal continued without incident or interruption, Marigold began to think she must be wrong—that perhaps the girl might not be from the college at all, when her eye was caught by a flutter of handkerchief in the second row of the faculty.

Marigold immediately recognized tiny Professor Imogen Currier, who taught Moral Philosophy and Rhetoric—a required class for all juniors, no matter their preferred area of study—and who, in the row of thoughtful, concerned faculty members, was quietly dabbing her eyes with visibly trembling hands.

A quick study of the generally more stoic faces of the faculty told Marigold that Professor Currier was not alone in displaying her feelings—several faculty members looked upset. But none were as clearly distraught as Professor Currier. She looked pale and almost pinched, though she was normally a gregarious, outgoing sort of instructor with a warm, open disposition.

But not today. Today she was white-faced and tearful, all but obscuring her face behind a large white handkerchief that fluttered like a flag of surrender in her hand.

As if, amongst all those assembled, she alone had something to hide.

Chapter 8

"Nothing is a waste of time if you use the experience wisely."
Auguste Rodin

As soon as the short service in the chapel concluded, and the students dismissed to their dormitory rooms with the injunction to please not wander the grounds alone, Professor Currier left College Hall after a hurried stop in her first-floor classroom to collect her pocketbook and hat.

"Marigold? Are you leaving?" It was Aggie, coming along the corridor behind her.

"Yes, I—" How did one say that one was tailing a suspect, when one didn't even know exactly what one suspected them of? Or if one had any authority to suspect them in the first place? But those were questions for a less fraught hour. "I'm sorry, but I have to go."

"But President Irvine just said not to go out alone," Aggie objected. "It's nearly full dark."

"I need to . . ." Marigold grasped for a plausible excuse. "I need to speak to Professor Currier. It's urgent. But I do want to talk to you later, when I get back." From wherever it was Professor Currier was going in such a very great hurry.

"Oh, well, in that case, I suppose I'll see you at dinner? They can't cancel that, can they?"

"Naturally." Marigold did not wait to explain her haste—she had only enough time to realize her bicycle was likely still along the shore next to the boathouse where she had abandoned it before Professor Currier's short, agitated stride took her out of sight, down the path toward the town.

Marigold hied after the woman, trying all the while to remember what she knew of the professor from taking her class two years ago. She was a single lady—as all of their female professors were—and one of the few longtime faculty members who had survived President Irvine's purge of underqualified instructors in an effort to raise the academic standard of the college. Professor Currier's undergraduate degree was from Wellesley itself, where she had graduated in the first class of seniors in 1878, before she took her master's degrees in English and Rhetoric from Cornell.

She had returned to Wellesley to teach and had been on the faculty for something like fifteen years, which put her age somewhere close to forty. She was physically quite small—Marigold wondered if she was any more than five feet tall—but she was known as a jolly and engaging teacher, even gregarious, very often taking meals with the members of the Forensic and Debate Society in the dining hall, though she lived off campus.

Which was where Marigold assumed the woman was going now. She followed her as discreetly as possible down the carriage way, from each patch of gaslight to the next, stopping outside the flickering pools of lamplight once or twice, so as not to overtake the older woman. But Professor Currier seemed not to notice—she was entirely absorbed with her own mission, passing by the college lodge gate, and what was presumably her own well-lit boardinghouse on Washington Street, where the voice of a woman hailed her from the shadowy porch.

"Evening, Imogen. You're home early."

The professor merely waved her off, hurrying onward up Washington Street to a tall, gaslit colonial-style clapboard house on the corner of Blossom Street, nearer the center of the town, where she knocked and was immediately admitted.

Marigold idled as inconspicuously as possible behind a large white-oak tree, its leaves already turned reddish-yellow with the fall, before she engaged the passing iceman, whose horse was plodding homeward at an autumnal pace. "I beg your pardon," she called, "but whose house is this?"

The iceman was one of a particular breed of distrustful New Englander, squinting up one side of his face, as if he could better assess her character and trustworthiness with such an expression. "Why'd you wantah know?"

She combatted his native skepticism with a sort of over-bright, college-girl enthusiasm as she kept pace with his ice wagon. "Well, you see, I'm studying the vernacular architecture of the town for a class, and I thought this a rather fine example of clapboard federal farmhouse." She turned as if surveying the house. "Don't you think it fine?"

"I 'spose." The iceman eyed the house for a bare moment before he turned his narrow gaze back to Marigold. "You'll be from up the college then."

"Naturally." Marigold rewarded him with an encouraging smile. "I suppose they must be a very old, distinguished Wellesley family, to have such an old, distinguished house?"

"Thayers live there" was the iceman's response.

"Ah!" Marigold made a sound of interest. "And what do they do, to have such a fine house?"

The iceman scratched his bristling whiskers. "What do you call them philosophical kinds of religious think-ahs they're talking about nowadays?" he asked in his rustic New England accent.

Marigold stretched her mind into current philosophical events to find an answer. "Universalists?"

"Ayuh," he agreed with a sage nod. "Them, but more than them."

"Transcendentalists?" she ventured, thinking of the philosophies and writings of Emerson and Longfellow and their ilk.

"Ayuh. That's it." The iceman was no less grim in his satisfaction. "Don't matter what they're calling it, it always amounts to the same thing. Them that has, keeps. Always have, always will, one after another. Way of the world." And with that, the fellow harrumphed his mare onward and away.

But for all her sympathy with the fellow, Marigold knew that there were many different ways in the world, and that "them that had" were as vulnerable to losing it all as anyone else—more so if they were foolish. And Professor Currier's headlong rush appeared entirely foolish, not to mention culpatory—she was acting very guilty, if you asked Marigold.

But Marigold could only ask herself. And wonder if the girl she pulled out of the lake had been foolish. Some—the watchmen, certainly—would say she was obviously so, to get herself killed.

She could only ask herself if the girl had come from this fine, well-kept clapboard house with the two smoking chimneys to keep her warm and dry. Or was she just a girl like Marigold, doing her best in the world, despite not having such a solid familial foundation as the big white house might imply?

What would someone think if they had pulled Marigold from the lake—or from Salem Sound, where she was meant to have been pushed overboard and left to drown last spring? Would that person think she had been foolish?

They would certainly think she was well-dressed by the House of Dana.

That brought Marigold's mind back to the girl's clothing, which might be brought to bear in learning her identity. Under Isabella's keen gaze, an eight-dollar hat from Jordan Marsh, and a jacket from Madame Watteau would only be the beginning of the revelations the dead girl's attire might offer.

Marigold consulted her watch pinned to her shirtwaist and decided she could no longer afford to linger if she wanted to make it back for dinner. She would have to abandon Professor Currier, but she had just enough time to leg it up to the commercial district, where the wire office stood ready to send her telegram off to Isabella, before the dinner bell would ring.

She rehearsed several different messages in her head before settling on the most direct. "Need assistance, stop," she dictated to the telegrapher. "Information regarding fashionable clothing, stop. Potential murder, stop." she added in an ill-advised attempt to intrigue Isabella.

Ill-advised, because the clerk immediately eyed her from under his green cellophane visor. "Is it true then, what they're saying happened at the college—there's a girl dead?"

Marigold felt all the self-blame of so quickly and thoughtlessly contravening President Irvine's plea for discretion. "It's only a rumor," she hedged.

She quickly counted out the required coins and headed back toward campus before the full fall of night made the walk dangerous. But Professor Currier's boardinghouse lay along the way, at the corner of Weston and Washington Streets. And if the rumor she had so carelessly started regarding murder got out, she would need something—some progress or evidence against Professor Currier—to counteract her indiscretion.

The boardinghouse was a large, squat four-story edifice with rooms under dormers at the top, with a gaslit porch and balcony across the front. A wooden placard hanging from the second-floor balcony declared it "Noanett." Beneath that sign was another notice, posted on the screen door of the porch, nearest the carriage drive side of the house, advertising for a cook.

Marigold stepped into the carriage drive to get a closer look, when she was greeted by the same voice that had earlier hailed Professor Currier from the screened porch above. "There something you want?"

Marigold turned her eyes upward to find a stolid, middle-aged woman in rather dated clothing, with a tight knot of gray hair pulling her face as taut as a fireplace poker, staring down at her.

"Don't have any rooms open, if that's what you're asking."

"No, ma'am," Marigold replied with alacrity. "I was looking for my professor from the college—Professor Currier."

The woman's gaze narrowed. "Not home yet. Very regular in her habits, the professor. You girls, on the other hand . . ." The woman's put-upon sigh gave her opinion of flighty college girls. "Every hour of the day and night. Haven't got the sense to come in out of the rain." She folded her arms across her ample chest. "Best get back there, if you ask me."

Marigold had not asked her, and so did not mind staying put—and trying a new avenue of approach. "I see you've a notice up for a cook?"

"You cook? College girl like you?" Her scoff was huffed with laughter.

Marigold did not take her scorn personally—she was confident in her own abilities. "No, ma'am. But I have a dear friend who is an accomplished and experienced professional cook—she has even published a well-received book on cookery."

Even as she said the words, Marigold's mind was turning over with ideas and possibilities. Her friend Lucy Dove had recently returned to her own mother's boardinghouse in Pride's Crossing after her short stay in New York, seeing to the release of her book. Having Lucy's keen observations at this boardinghouse might be of great use.

"Has she now?" The landlady looked skeptical. "Good, healthful, elevated cooking, suitable for discriminating tastes?"

Marigold's idea might face a different sort of discrimination, but there was nothing in not trying. "Indeed, ma'am. Miss Lucy Dove is a Black woman who has considerable experience working for distinguished families on the North Shore." Although the Hatchets might not have exactly been distinguished, they were most certainly from the North Shore of Boston. "And Miss Dove's book of cookery has just been published by one such of those families—by Mr. Thaddeus Endicott, formerly of Pride's Crossing." Marigold's emphasis on the fashionable, old-money enclave was in the hopes that it might impress. "But now Mr. Endicott is with the Collier and Son Publishing Company of New York, and is my friend's editor. I would be happy to furnish you with a copy of her book—regardless—so you can vouchsafe the recipes." Marigold had a copy in her trunks at College Hall, purchased out of solidarity for her friend, not with any actual ambition toward cookery.

And the book might give her an entrée into the boardinghouse, even if she could not convince Lucy that her presence there was necessary. Not that she had really convinced herself—all of Marigold's speculations about Professor Currier and the unnamed and unclaimed dead girl might turn out to be nothing more than empty suspicions.

Perhaps her involvement with the Great Misery murders had made her see shadows where there really were none.

And yet, some indefinable force, some instinct told her that Professor Currier, along with Sarah Appleton, knew something—and whatever that information might turn out to be, an entrée into the boardinghouse could only help. "I'll bring that cookbook by for you, Mrs.—?"

"Barnacle. Mrs. May Barnacle."

"Marigold Manners, Mrs. Barnacle. Pleased to meet you."

The woman shifted her hands to her hips. "If you can get me a good cook, I will be pleased to meet you too."

"Then I will endeavor to do so, ma'am. I will wire her straightaway. And now, I will take your other advice and get back to campus. Thank you."

"You're welcome. Now, what about you?" The woman was presumably addressing someone else.

Marigold pivoted to see a tall, very handsome man in a long double-breasted Chesterfield coat doffing his hat in the circle of gaslight. "Are you the proprietress?"

"I'm the landlady, if that's what you're meaning," Mrs. Barnacle answered. "But I don't mind telling you, I don't rent to men. Ladies only. Keeps the peace."

"Now, that's a shame," the fellow answered with an easy, undeterred smile. "This seems a fine looking, well-kept house."

"It is," Mrs. Barnacle retorted. "You won't find better in Wellesley. But it's not for men."

"That will be my loss," the man lamented. "Might you direct me to a house that does let to gentlemen?"

"I might," Mrs. Barnacle alleged. "Say, you look kinda familiar." She narrowed her eyes at him again. "Haven't I seen you around here before?"

"I should think not," he laughed. "I have only just arrived in town, on the 3:45 train from Boston. James Wilkerson, ma'am. I'm here to cover the story."

"What story?" demanded May Barnacle. "You mean like a story in the newspaper?"

"I do, ma'am." He included both Mrs. Barnacle and Marigold in the beneficence of his unforced smile. "I do indeed. The story of the death at the college."

Clearly, despite all injunctions to discretion, the bad news had traveled, to use a particularly New England expression, faster than stink.

There was something in this man's voice, some lilt or cadence, that gave hint to an accent not of New England, though different indeed from Ethyl Rautencranz's rural drawl. But regardless of handsomeness or interesting cadences, the last thing Marigold needed was a nosy journalist asking her questions she did not want to give the answers to or insinuating himself into her own investigation. She had already violated the president's directive once for the day, and that was more than enough.

And so, she merely ducked her head at Mrs. Barnacle as a goodbye, but by the time she had walked briskly back to East Lodge, where the town gave way to the wooded campus of the college, night had fully settled into inky darkness. And the wind, which had chilled her earlier, now bit and nipped at any exposed skin. Her nose would be red and her fingers white by the time she made it home.

She slowed at the lodge gate, because although a good strong gaslight shone from the lodge building itself, and the gas lampposts were lit, leading the way down the winding road through the woods, between the patches of light, it was eerily, frighteningly dark.

And there might be a murderer loose somewhere out there.

Marigold hesitated, stuck between her own sense of self-sufficiency and her burgeoning fear. It had only been a few hours since she had sat on the dock and held a dead girl's head in her lap, and the horror of it all, the violence and waste and injustice, seemed to come over her all at once.

And then a movement—or was it the sound of a twig snapping underfoot—caught her fractured attention.

She started, but even as she chastised herself for being a jumpy, illogical fool, she stared back the way she had come. Had that man followed her down Washington Street?

She searched the shadows, but nothing came but the silent sweep of the autumn leaves falling from the trees. Still, the feeling of being watched—and hadn't she felt it a hundred times on Great Misery?—persisted.

But she had been right on Great Misery, hadn't she?

Which instantly helped her make up her mind—she would listen to her instincts.

She immediately rang the lodge's bell. And waited an anxious few moments until the porter answered the door.

"Miss Manners! Glad to see you back. You're out late." Mr. Breyer and his wife were fixtures of the college, though they rarely left their post at the lodge. "Thought there was an injunction against you girls going out tonight?"

"I am indeed out late, on business in the town that could not be delayed," Marigold explained. "But as I have no wish to contravene President Irvine's wishes that no one go about the campus unescorted, I hoped you might escort me back to College Hall." A glance over her shoulder betrayed her unease.

The porter stepped out of the lodge, peering hard through the thickening dark. "Is someone following you? Some tramp?"

"I-I can't be certain. But I just couldn't shake the feeling of . . ." Her concern felt even more ridiculous when she tried to explain. "I'm sure I'm just being silly."

It wasn't as if the polite young man with the charming accent had been dark and shadowy, or hiding beneath the brim of his stylishly dark homburg hat. He had been everything polite and aboveboard when speaking to the landlady. He had not made any advances toward her or even tried to speak to her directly. He was hardly the type for a murderer. And even if the fellow had inadvertently followed her, he might simply be looking for another boardinghouse that catered to men. Yet, there she was, shaking in her shoes like the verist peabrain.

But the porter did not object. "I reckon we're all a bit on edge this evening, Miss Manners. You let me tell my missus, and we'll be on our way."

"Thank you, Mr. Breyer. I am most sincerely obliged." She waited patiently in the thin glow of the gaslight, though she could not shake her unsettled feelings, despite telling herself that she was safe now.

Cab Cox would know better than to follow a woman—even inadvertently.

But why should she think of Cab Cox? Just because she was uncomfortable and a little bit spooked didn't mean she needed the protection of a man. *Mrs.* Breyer in a carriage would do as well as her husband. But who would protect Mrs. Breyer on the way back? And for that matter, who would protect Mr. Breyer? A strangler might take umbrage at a man as well as a woman.

Marigold's dilemma was solved when the couple came out together. "Quicker to hitch the carriage with the two of us." Mr. Breyer explained.

"Safer too" was Mrs. Breyer's softer but no less potent report.

Clearly, they were *all* on edge that evening. And Marigold, for one, did not object to finding safety in numbers.

"Well, then, Miss Manners." The porter returned her to her own original intent. "Let's get you home, shall we?"

Yes, the college was certainly home, even with the dark turbulence of the dead girl. Despite everything, the soaring gothic walls of College Hall were the best home she had ever had, and the only real home she was ever likely to know.

Chapter 9

"She had a womanly instinct that clothes possess an influence more powerful over many than the worth of character or the magic of manners."

Louisa May Alcott

"Miss Manners? Miss Manners!" Miss Burke scurried out of the reception room and all but accosted Marigold as she tried to pass through the soaring Center hall on her way to her advanced Latin translation class the next morning. "If you *please*!"

Lucretius's *De Rerum Natura* would have to wait.

Despite being weary from burning the midnight oil in preparing her translation—classes had resumed in an effort at "normality"—Marigold found just enough patience to address the president's assistant politely. One had one's standards. "Yes, Miss Burke? How might I be of assistance?"

"You have a *visitor*." The woman lofted her eyebrows as she said it, in some sort of emphasis which Marigold could not readily interpret. "If you will attend them in the reception room, *please*?" Miss Burke added with what seemed to Marigold some unnecessary asperity. As if Marigold had kept them waiting on purpose instead of being wholly uninformed about their presence, whoever they were.

"If I must," Marigold muttered under her breath. For some inane reason, her brain could supply only one suggestion for the identity of a visitor who might send Miss Burke into such a tizzy. But Cab Cox could have no reason for coming to call on her at the college on a Wednesday morning.

"You must," Burke snapped under her own breath. "Or be accounted extraordinarily rude."

Marigold's eyebrows rose of their own accord at the rebuke. "And we can't have that."

"No, we cannot," the sharp little woman sniffed. "We have standards of polite conduct at Wellesley College, Miss Manners. Perhaps you have forgotten that while you were away."

The rebuff, though certainly unearned from Marigold's point of view, stung. "So noted, Miss Burke. But I hope you will forgive me for being more concerned about being rude to Professor Lord, since she will be expecting me for my advanced Latin translation class, and I do not wish to be tardy or, worse, counted absent." She had spent far too many hours last night working diligently through the translation of Lucretius's masterwork to miss the class now.

"That can't be helped." Miss Burke drew herself up like an aggrieved squirrel, tiny, tense, and agitated. "If you *will* have callers, you need to attend to them. Promptly."

"Yes, ma'am, with all due haste." Marigold set herself to soothe—anything else would continue to be counterproductive.

It was the last person Marigold might have expected and the first person she should have anticipated—Isabella in all her fur-trimmed glory, holding court in the reception area as if it were her drawing room on Park Drive. "Ah, there you are Marigold, darling."

"Isabella!"

"You're looking well." Her ever-elegant friend ran a benign eye over Marigold's ensemble of a green and gray striped athletic sweater over a long linen split skirt of subdued gray wool. "Not exactly mourning attire, but very sporty."

Marigold kissed her cheek with both delight and consternation. "One does one's best. As do you look very well, naturally." Isabella's tweed suit of amber wool was in the height of fall fashion, dripping with an autumnally hued foxtail stole. "But what on earth are you doing here?"

"Taking an excellent cup of tea from your redoubtable Miss Burke. Thank you, my dear Miss Burke, but could you be so kind as to fetch a fresh cup?" She smiled warmly at the woman, who scurried out immediately to do her bidding.

Trust Isabella to tame the squirrel with soothing attention. Marigold made a mental note to learn from her example.

"Now," Isabella turned her attention fully to Marigold. "You didn't think I was going to send a tame wire after you oh-so-casually mentioned *murder*, did you? Not after I left you alone far too long last spring. I've decided murder is like tea—best when hot and shared. Now—" Isabella patted the upholstered settee. "I've ordered a fresh cup—that wee benighted mole of a woman must have brewed it from her own brow hair, so strong and dark is it! But it will sharpen our minds while we ponder your dilemma."

"Not now, I'm afraid" was Marigold's apologetic answer. "Tempting as tea with you might be, I'm late for a very important class. Lucretius," she added, as if that explained everything—because to a Classics scholar, it did. "Can we meet after? Where are you staying?"

"If we must." Isabella gave in with good grace. "The Wellesley Inn. Most of what I have to say can wait. Come to me for dinner. I'll send my driver."

"I'll cycle. Six o'clock?"

"Marigold!" Isabella's tone was chiding. "Have you mistaken me for a country bumpkin, or worse, a savage? Eight o'clock, not a moment sooner—civilized Boston hours. Though you should certainly come earlier for cocktails—seven-ish. But I will send my carriage—I heard the little mole say that there's to be a curfew imposed. If that's true, I suppose I'll have to come myself to sign you out, like a maiden auntie."

"Agreed. Thank you, Isabella." Marigold stooped to kiss her cheek. "Must dash."

"Yes, I don't want to keep you a moment longer than necessary, Marigold darling, but there is something I think you ought to know."

The quietly serious look on Isabella's face gave Marigold pause. "Whatever can it be?"

Isabella drew a copy of one of the Boston tabloids from her carpetbag. "I'm afraid you've made the front page." She handed Marigold the newspaper bearing a photogravure of "Miss Marigold Manners, late of Great Misery Island, and Dr. Emilie Barker, female physician, resident at Wellesley College, tending to the dead body of the unfortunate suicide."

"Damnation." Of both Dr. Barker and her, it was an excellent likeness. Of the poor unfortunate girl, thankfully, little besides a heap of sodden clothing could be seen.

"Yes, damnation indeed," Isabella agreed. "So I thought when I saw it. One doesn't like to appear in print other than at birth, marriage, and death." Isabella, despite being a rather modern widow, still held on to some of her early society teachings.

Marigold, as a New Woman, eschewed such things.

"Well, this is someone's death," she said with some heat. "How horribly irresponsible to label the poor girl a suicide when no such thing has been established—except for frankly the opposite."

"Your wire said murder," Isabella reminded her.

"Potential murder," Marigold corrected in a quieter tone, remembering both President Irvine and Dr. Barker's requests. "I'm not supposed to say."

"Marigold," Isabella's tone was once again chiding. "I know you—I read every draft of your story about Great Misery Island. You wouldn't have said murder unless you had reason to suspect murder. Now, tell me why."

"I should very much like to," Marigold agreed in a whisper. "But I haven't got time to go into all the particulars now." And certainly not in the public reception area where the little mole held sway—and might at that very moment be listening at the keyhole. And although she trusted Isabella's discretion on the matter, she had made a promise. "Suffice it to say Dr. Barker and I have a number of reasons to suspect."

"Then you intend to investigate? And solve the murder just like you did last time?"

"Perhaps." Marigold likely needed permission from President Irvine, if no one else. But then again, the college president had already asked Marigold to assist Dr. Barker in her inquiries—and the so-called authorities had been no use. Perhaps that was all the permission she needed. "I suppose I do."

"Excellent." Isabella relaxed. "You come to dinner, and we'll begin to get to the bottom of this."

"Thank you," Marigold said with some relief. It really was an excellent thing to have generous—and conveniently rich—friends. "You really are an absolute darling. Would you mind terribly, on your way through town, sending a wire for me?"

"Not at all, darling." Isabella was all gracious accommodation. "Dare I ask who it might be to?"

Marigold could tell from Isabella's nearly coquettish smile that she was thinking of Cab Cox, but Marigold was not about to admit that she too had been thinking of Cab not a few minutes ago. "I am sorry to disappoint you, Isabella. But it is to Lucy Dove, who I think may also help us get to the bottom of this unfortunate event. Oh, and if you would also be so good as to deliver this copy of Lucy's cookbook—"

"Ah, yes, I know it well. *The Domestic Cook's Book: Containing a Careful Selection of Useful Recipes for the Kitchen*," Isabella recited. "Very superior. My cook found it eminently useful."

"Naturally." Marigold wondered how many of Lucy's recipes she had been served by Isabella's French chef without knowing. "I'm glad to find you think so! If you would be so kind as to deliver it to Mrs. Barnacle at Noanett House on Washington Street on your way to sending Lucy this wire? And perhaps put in a good word for Lucy while you're there?"

"Anything to assist a friend—and any friend of yours is a friend of mine."

"You are an absolute darling to think so. I must introduce you to some of my new friends here at college." Isabella would no doubt love creating an elegant golfing ensemble for tall, trim Aggie Newton. "But first—" Marigold paused to write out a very short plea begging Lucy's assistance, which she passed to Isabella, who read it immediately.

"Seems an eminently sensible precaution" was her verdict.

"Excellent." Marigold kissed her cheek once more. "Must dash, darling. Mind to expand, opinions to inform, ancient civilizations to explore!"

"Off you go!" Isabella waved her away. "Leave it all with me."

★ ★ ★

An hour and a half later, Lucretius was still ringing through Marigold's mind—*summon to judgments true, Unbusied ears and singleness of mind, Withdrawn from cares*—when the Japanese bell called her to luncheon.

The Classics Society table was as full as ever, especially the "Diggers" end, where the archaeologically minded gathered. Of suspicious Sarah Appleton and her superior linguists, there was no sign.

Another mark of distrustful behavior, if you asked Marigold.

But she would take advantage of their absence. "Aggie. Ladies. Good afternoon, all."

"Oh, hello, Marigold. How goes it? I missed you at dinner last night," Aggie said cheerfully before she seemed to recall herself. "Isn't it awful?"

Marigold strove for the discretion the president had asked for. "I assume you are referring to the death on campus. Yes, it is awful, poor girl."

Aggie reached for Marigold's hand. "I hear you're the one who pulled her out. Ethyl Rautencranz said so. She said it was very brave of you."

How gratifyingly loyal of Ethyl to say Marigold had looked brave rather than desperate.

But one never wanted to make too much of oneself. "I hope I only did what any one of us would have—what was right."

"Well, you did," Aggie affirmed. "She said that you were as cool as a summer cucumber. I would have been shaking in my shoes."

"I was shaking too, Aggie. I certainly was cold—the water was absolutely chilling this time of year. It was quite a shock."

"As I imagine it was seeing her all dead like that." Aggie's face was as wide and wondering as a goldfish. "Did you really touch her?"

"No more than was necessary to pull her out of the water." No need to add to the rumors piling up the place.

Aggie shook her head in admiration. "You really are the bravest person I know. I don't even want to leave my room, what with President Irvine saying that it's not safe to move about the campus alone. And we might as well stay home, safe in our rooms, with so many extras canceled or postponed. The golf course is closed, as is your boathouse."

"Clubs can only meet within College Hall," another girl complained.

"And anything open to the public, like the music concert on Friday night and the Forensics and Debate Society's upcoming special lecture on Saturday have been canceled too," added another.

"I'm sure the concerts and lectures are only postponed," Marigold assured them. At least she hoped so—the Forensics and Debate Society's lecture had been slated to address universal suffrage, a topic dear to Marigold, as well as many other Wellesley girls. "We will solve the question of the unfortunate young woman's identity and our academic lives can return to their natural rhythm."

But even as she said the soothing words, Marigold knew they could not possibly be true. That girl had been strangled, and strangled by someone who might still be about campus at that very moment. The thought sent an unwelcome shiver of alarm up her arms.

But Aggie seemed relieved. "You really are a wonder, Marigold."

"Thank you." Marigold decided protest was only prolonging this line of questioning, when she had questions of her own. "I wondered if later this afternoon I might take another look at that extraordinary hat you showed me the other day?"

"Certainly!" Aggie was all eagerness, until she caught something of Marigold's seriousness. "But . . . why?"

"I hate to bring up ill tidings, but the reason I waded into the water at the boathouse to help the girl was that I thought she was you."

"Me?" Aggie gaped at her. "But what would I be doing at the boathouse—I don't row. Oh! You mean you thought I was the girl who you pulled from the lake—" She covered her mouth with her hand. "The dead girl?"

"Yes," Marigold answered as gently as possible. "You see, she had a hat just like yours. I must say, I was extraordinarily relieved to find it wasn't you."

Aggie's eyes grew as wide and glassy as tea saucers. "But she killed herself, didn't she? Isn't that what the papers are saying?"

"Tabloids," Marigold said the word with all the disdain she felt. "Out to sell papers with lurid content that has very little to do with the actual facts."

"Those weren't the facts?"

"I should think not. Or rather, that is my opinion," Marigold hedged, again attempting to recall her promises to both Dr. Barker and President Irvine.

"Then why don't the better newspapers print the real facts?"

"Perhaps." Marigold tried to be as circumspect as possible—there were impressionable young women around, and none more impressionable than the young woman before her—while still cleaving to the truth. "Perhaps there are extenuating circumstances that forbid the college from making all the facts well known."

"Why?"

"Because they have not yet identified the poor soul." Marigold tried to be logical. "And they don't want someone to find out about the death of their daughter or sister or friend from the front page of a lurid Boston tabloid."

"Oh, yes, I suppose that would be awful."

"We must trust President Irvine and Dr. Barker to know what's best." But the truth was, these girls—these vulnerable but thinking young women—deserved to know that they were likely still in danger. Marigold didn't think she was ever going to forget the way Dr. Barker had said the word "strangulation." "I have my reasons to think President Irvine's cautions quite necessary. It is her duty to keep us all safe."

"Does that mean you think we're not safe?" Aggie barely whispered the thought. "Did something happen when you went out alone last night? You never said—"

"Not at all. But note that I asked the lodge porter to accompany me across the campus, rather than walk home alone." Marigold addressed the rest of the table as well. "And until this unfortunate incident has been completely resolved, I would urge you all to do the same. Now, if the speaker on universal suffrage is postponed, perhaps we should have our own lively debate amongst ourselves."

"Who are you going to find to argue against universal suffrage?" Aggie asked with a laugh.

"Perhaps those who are well-versed in biblical studies, as well as Classics, who feel their Christianity requires them to take a different view."

They turned to find Sarah Appleton had made her return to the table.

"Well said, Sarah," Marigold said with all the equanimity she could muster. And in truth, she felt strongly that such differences of opinion ought to be expressed—how else were they to educate their minds and form their thinking? "In such cases, I would advise those who do not believe in voting to exercise their conscience by simply *not* voting, while those who do want their voices to be heard within government should have the right to exercise their prerogative."

"A very balanced, civilized solution," Aggie opined before Sarah might say anything more cutting. "Thank you, Marigold."

Marigold merely smiled—one never wanted to make too much of oneself—and turned her attention to her excellent roast-chicken soup.

Luncheon progressed with a thoughtful discussion of what changes they would vote for once they got the vote. "For it's only a matter of time," asserted one girl. "We'll wear them down eventually, like water on stones—drip, drip, drip."

"I'm tired of us being the drips. I'm ready for the rest of womankind to join us in a torrent," another girl declared.

"I had hoped that the speaker on suffrage, Olivia Thayer, might address this in her lecture," Aggie added, "but I understand she's young and idealistic, and might not be as concerned with practical actions as we are."

The name immediately sent an alarm bell ringing in Marigold's head. "Thayer?" she echoed, while her brain clamored that there was no such thing as coincidence and her mind's eye pictured Professor Currier scurrying into the Thayer house on Blossom Street. "Is she local?"

"Yes, I think, but you should ask Professor Currier, or someone in the Forensics and Debate Society—they're sponsoring her."

"Yes, I think I shall." She would definitely be speaking to Professor Currier at her first opportunity. Because Imogen Currier clearly knew something—and something about Olivia Thayer—the rest of them did not.

And Marigold meant to find out exactly what that something was.

Chapter 10

"Money is the root of all evil, and yet it is such a useful root that we cannot get on without it any more than we can without potatoes."

Louisa May Alcott

As soon as luncheon was finished, Marigold returned to her prior intent. "Aggie," she spoke to her young friend before she might depart. "Would you mind showing me your hat?"

"My fancy tam? Certainly."

They walked to Aggie's room, where she dutifully fetched the flamboyant blue chapeau.

It looked much the same as the one Marigold had fished out of Lake Waban—the velvet was plush and new, the feathers sewn in an artfully arranged cluster around a gleaming pin. But this one was a bright gold, while the other had been a somewhat dimmer silver.

"Is this pin your own?"

"Oh, yes, it is my prize pin from when I won the golf championship at Nashawtuc Farm where I'm from in Concord. It's ever so much nicer than the one from the store—it's gold, you know—so I took off the tin one that came with it, because I thought this one made the hat more my own. I mean, it's not exactly a one-of-a-kind hat—there's at least one other around."

Marigold was instantly alert. "Who else has the same hat?"

"I don't know, but I know someone must." Aggie twirled the hat admiringly. "I was wearing it one day out on the golf course—I wanted to practice my putting at the nearest green, you know—" She turned to point out the window toward the college golf course situated just to the west of the building. "Anyway, this fellow spoke to me roughly. 'What was I doing?' sort of thing, and he grabbed my elbow, all proprietary, quite the masher, which I didn't care for in the least."

"Just as you ought." Marigold had strict feelings about elbow-grabbing, rough-talking young mashers.

"I thought it must be one of the groundskeepers telling me off because the green was too wet—it had rained the day before—but it was just some man looking for his sweetheart or something, because once he realized it was me and not his girl, he begged my pardon, saying he mistook me because she had the same hat, and shied right off. And a good thing, because I was hot enough to give him what for with my putter for grabbing my arm—except that it was my good Robert Forgan putter, from Scotland that my dad bought for me, and it was too expensive to crack on some wiseacre's back."

Marigold was all admiration for Aggie's plan of self-defense as well as her descriptive vocabulary. But her instant curiosity prompted her to ask, "And what did this wiseacre look like?"

"Oh, you know, some fellow—they're all alike, if you ask me. Coat and hat, proprietary air, thinks the world is their oyster and nobody else's. Well, not here, it isn't."

"No," Marigold agreed, equally proprietary about the sanctity of their college as a woman's place. "You didn't get a good look at him?"

"Not really. He went straight away, with his back turned, and I got back to my putting." She sighed. "I thought it was the perfect hat for golfing. But now I don't know."

"It is very fine, Aggie." Marigold weighed satisfying her curiosity against President Irvine's request for discretion—but doubtless, such indiscretions were happening all across College Hall. "I think there was a different pin on the hat I found at the boathouse yesterday."

"Do you think the dead girl had her own pin on her hat too? Is that important?"

"Yes, maybe." Marigold wasn't exactly sure—a personal or prize pin like Aggie's might help identify where the dead young woman came from. Or it might mean nothing. "Do you have the original pin?"

"Maybe." Aggie went to her wardrobe and began to dig through a small jewelry case. "I thought it was just a blank piece of tin or pewter in the shape of a shield—you know, a sort of generic suggestion of Scots heraldry."

Then the pin on the dead girl's hat had also been individual and personal. She tried to recall the inscription exactly. "Do you have any idea what S.d.B.L. might be?"

Aggie frowned. "No idea. And I'm sorry, but I can't seem to find the original pin."

"That's all right," Marigold said. "Though I can't help but feel as if I am missing something terribly obvious." Starting with the poor girl's identity. "Have you heard anything about any classmates absent from class? Is no one missing a roommate or hall mate? Surely someone has some information, however small?"

"Not that I've heard," Aggie offered. "Not a peep."

Which was odd. In such a closed, close-knit community of women, people tended to know everyone else's business. It was a rare person who could keep a secret in such an intimate society.

But someone seemed to be keeping the greatest secret of them all.

"Well, there she is, the college's latest cover girl." It was Sarah Appleton, standing just outside Aggie's doorway with her coterie of apple polishers. "So desperate for notoriety that you couldn't spare a thought for the rest of us or the reputation of the college."

"I assume you refer to the tabloid photogravure of Dr. Barker and me?" Marigold asked in as conversational a tone as she might manage. "How interesting that you should bring it up, Sarah." The easiest way to deflect blame from oneself was to purposefully heap it upon others. "I only had a glance at it this morning—tabloids aren't my preferred reading—but as neither Dr. Barker nor I had any knowledge of our likeness being taken, we can hardly be made responsible for the reputation of the college."

"We should have expected as much from *someone like you*" was Sarah's snide retort.

Marigold had already learned better than to bite at that particular bait, but sweet Aggie was not so forbearing. "What do you mean by that?" she demanded hotly.

"I mean that I know all the *vulgar*"—Sarah emphasized the word to echo Marigold's own use of the adjective at dinner the first night—"details of Miss Marigold Manners's tawdry, scandalous parentage. Her audacity astonishes."

"Does it?" Marigold worked a little—a very little—to keep her crocodile smile in check, but she stood and used every inch of her slight height to crowd the taller girl from the doorway. "My audacity is nothing compared to my manners, which find this conversation *vulgar* in the extreme." Then she lowered her voice so that only Sarah could hear. "But if you insist on discussing family matters publicly, I'm sure I can speak with some assurance of your father's well-known affinity for a certain Mrs. Lake's house on Endicott Street in the North End." Marigold was never more thankful for having spent the summer with Isabella, listening to her encyclopedic knowledge of both society and gossip. "I'm sure he goes there," she continued in her quietest, kindest, most ironic tone, "to an area well known for its brothels, for the intellectual conversation and not any *tawdry* or *scandalous* purposes. I'm sure his audacity is at the forefront of your thinking."

"Why—" Sarah's face drew white with outrage. "That is none of your business!"

"Correct," Marigold agreed matter-of-factly. Her only business was getting to the bottom of the dead girl's identity, not trading veiled barbs with Sarah—unless Sarah continued to act in this highly suspicious manner. "Do you by any chance have a copy of this vulgar tabloid at the ready?"

Sarah gestured to one of the girls behind her, who quickly brought the newspaper in question out from behind her skirts.

"Naturally, you do. Thank you." Marigold took it from the girl's hands and smiled upon them all, gracious in her small triumph.

"That will be all." And she shut the door in their collective faces so she might take a good long look at the image before her.

At least the photogravure had captured her from a good angle.

Aggie was thinking along the same lines. "It is a nice shot."

"Of a dead girl, Aggie. Vanity must certainly take a backward-facing seat to more important issues. Like her identity." Marigold strove to take a more logical approach. "From the angle, this photographer must have been right here on campus—I wonder that no one noticed them about the place with the equipment they must have had to take such a photograph." She took a close look at the attribution at the bottom of the image. "Mr. E. Anthony."

"Oh!" Aggie exclaimed. "That is likely not a mister at all!" She snatched the paper from Marigold's hands. "Yes! I am sure that is bound to be Eliza Anthony—she's a sophomore, so you might not know her."

"She is a photographer?"

"And how! Always about the place with something she calls a patented detective camera, snapping away when one least expects it. She's got all the equipment—her father is the Anthony of the New York Anthony Camera Company. She's put it about that her father's company has several patents for cameras, and I think that Eliza has them all, to try them out."

"And sell the images to the tabloids for photogravures?"

"This is the first time I've heard of her doing so, but clearly, she must have done."

"And where is this Miss Eliza Anthony's room?"

"She's commandeered a good portion of the Student Laboratory and Apparatus Room, up in the attic story, where she has set up her 'darkroom.'"

"I think I know just the spot. Well, then." Marigold rose. "I think it's time for me to give our Miss Anthony a visit."

Eliza Anthony had clearly curtained off her portion of the Student Laboratory and Apparatus Room to control the amount of available light. But in her righteous fury, Marigold cared not for whatever delicate or unstable process Miss Anthony was engaged in. She threw back the heavy blackout curtains. "I hope you made a tidy profit for your illicit piece of voyeurism?"

Miss Anthony jumped back, dropping whatever it was she had been doing. Shiny liquid splashed down the front of her heavy waxed muslin smock. "I didn't hear you."

"Nor I you." Marigold employed her smile to good effect—Miss Anthony took a further step back. "From the angle of your photograph, you must have concealed yourself in the woods just up the slope from the boathouse, where you snapped away without announcing your presence. Did you hear the commotion and then come, or did you chance upon it by accident?"

"I . . . Well, I . . ."

"A detective camera, was it?" Marigold moved toward the shelf where several cameras were housed. "No matter which one—I'm tempted to break them all."

"You won't dare!" The young woman moved to protect her precious equipment. "That's against the rules!"

"I would dare," Marigold said quite simply. "I'm Marigold Manners. We haven't met, but you should know I have a reputation for doing exactly what I say I will." And at that moment, she was angry enough not to care about the rules.

Miss Anthony took up a defensive posture between Marigold and the cameras. "These are not your property, and the student code of ethics expressly forbids one student from stealing or destroying the personal property of another."

"What does the student code of ethics have to say about spying on your fellow students with said personal property—to wit, a camera? I should think it an egregious violation of their expectation of privacy." Marigold might not be studying the law, but she still had read enough to have a thorough understanding of the correct vocabulary.

Miss Anthony stilled, and then tried a different tack. "You have to understand—" she began.

"I do not," Marigold contradicted. "You violated my privacy and Dr. Barker's, whilst she was in the midst of her professional duties. But more importantly you violated the privacy of this as yet unidentified young girl. Did you not think of her?"

Eliza Anthony put up her chin, in a gesture Marigold recognized well from her own mirror. "I can't afford to."

Marigold was taken aback, by both the evident sincerity and the deep bitterness in her fellow student's voice. "I fail to see how."

"I am a photographer," Eliza Anthony declared. "And I'm proud of it. But I need to be paid to be a professional photographer. You can't imagine how hard it is as a woman—a young woman—to be taken seriously as a professional in this field."

Marigold's antipathy softened slightly. This was a complaint she had not only heard before but often made herself. "I can imagine, Miss Anthony. We all can, or I doubt we would be here." It was one of the great dilemmas of their age, the changing place of women within American society and indeed the world. At the college, women's education and women's suffrage were felt to be urgent and nearly sacred goals. It was, to a great extent, the work of all their lives.

"I want to be a paid professional photographer, like the men, so I need to take advantage where and when I can. I must use the resources at my disposal, or I will not be given other opportunities. Frankly, I will never be *given* anything. I will have to work twice as hard to achieve half the results."

Marigold was almost taken in. Almost. "You were *given* these cameras." She picked up one piece of apparatus and turned it over to see the manufacturer's stamp. "The Anthony Camera Company of New York?" Marigold looked her up and down. "I feel certain you weren't charged full price."

"Do not be so certain." Eliza Anthony gave Marigold as good as she got. "Everything comes with some price, especially from family."

As this was a lesson Marigold had lately learned the hard way on Great Misery Island, her indignation deflated a little. But not entirely. "If we accept your need to be taken seriously as a professional photographer, why on earth did you sell the print to the *Boston Evening Journal*, the worst of the yellow-dog sort of tabloids? Why not one of the more reputable newspapers that would have printed the facts instead of this lurid sensationalism?"

Eliza Anthony was not to be cowed. "The more reputable papers won't even see a young woman like me." Up went that pointed chin. "The tabloids are not so *nice* in their standards. And they pay better."

Marigold rearranged her indignation. "And I assume it costs a lot to maintain this setup?"

"It does," Eliza confirmed. "The college only supplies a very little materiel for the fine arts classes on artistic photography, and the chemicals for development do not come cheaply." Perhaps she could see that Marigold was softening, because she took a deep breath herself and assayed a smile. "That's what I was meant to be doing that day." She gestured to the tabloid. "Taking artistic landscape photographs for composition class. But landscape and buildings are boring—I like capturing people. I like portraits even better. Look."

She turned to range in her cabinets and in another moment thrust several striking portraits of young collegians into Marigold's hands.

If Marigold had expected stereotypical posed photographic portraits, with the subjects sitting stiffly in their best clothes, she was rather surprised to find Anthony's sitters both relaxed and individual, adorned with both smiles and the implements of their prowess—rackets and oars and field hockey sticks and bicycles. And books. Lots and lots of books.

Young woman in the first flush of confidence and competency.

Marigold tried to resist being charmed.

But Miss Anthony saw her opening. "I've made something of a studio here, behind these curtains." She swept back another set of dark draperies to reveal a studio area full of soft, colorful pillows and fabric that reminded Marigold so strongly of her brother's Scheherazade's cave in the barn on Great Misery that she was momentarily taken aback.

"How lovely." But very likely flammable—especially with all those volatile chemicals.

"I could take your portrait."

Marigold could see the excitement—or was that avarice—that pinked Miss Anthony's fair face. "And sell to the tabloids an even more recognizable likeness of the woman who found the body?"

Eliza Anthony didn't bat an eyelash. "You could be famous."

"I have no desire to be anything of the sort," Marigold lied. Because she had always aspired to be famous—as an archaeologist, with famous excavations of important digs and famous papers published in important journals, not in a seedy tabloid. She wanted to be famous for her accomplishments, not for the fact that she had chanced upon a body. Or two.

Or three, actually.

Or did that make it four now?

"I'd split the profit with you." Anthony tried a different approach. "The way I figure it, they'll print what they like anyway, without so much as a by-your-leave, so you might as well get what you can out of them when they do."

"How exceptionally mercenary of you," Marigold accused.

"How eminently practical," the young woman countered. "The world is the way the world is—my photographs are the only means I have of making my way in that world. I'm going to use them to my best advantage every chance I have."

"And what if your best advantage is to someone else's detriment? What then?"

Eliza Anthony crossed her arms over her chest, the very portrait of defiance. "I suppose I'll cross that bridge when I come to it."

"My dear Miss Anthony," Marigold sighed. "You already have."

CHAPTER 11

"The truth is the only safe ground to stand upon."
Elizabeth Cady Stanton

Eliza left the Student Laboratory and Apparatus Room, but Marigold decided to spend the time before she would need to change for dinner with Isabella working on her own experiments in electrolytic reduction, securing the terminal wires and clips to the battery, while also learning more about the other inhabitants of the laboratory—namely Ethyl, whose bench was marked by a handmade skull and crossbones and "Do Not Touch" placard.

"Why the theatrical sign?"

Ethyl eyed Marigold askance. "Because my experiments are extremely dangerous."

"Really?" Even as she said it, Marigold realized she still thought of the college as a place of safety and comfort, where nothing dangerous could ever happen, despite the recent tragedy in the boathouse demonstrating exactly the opposite. "The Jolly Roger is not just for show?"

"Not by a long shot," Ethyl assured her somberly. "I am not the kind of person who tries to scare the bejeebers out of somebody just for fun or notoriety. This stuff is poison."

"Really?" Perhaps Ethyl would have some insights into Antiphon's first oration. "Wellesley College is letting you make poison for your honors thesis work?" Marigold asked while wondering idly where her own mother Sophronia's knowledge of plant poisons had been learned.

"You bet!" Ethyl was amused at Marigold's skepticism. "No, really it's just the opposite—I'm trying to isolate a specific active compound in one organic poison to create an antidote for another."

Marigold was fascinated. "Do tell."

Ethyl warmed to her subject. "You see, that active compound, physostigmine, is a parasympathomimetic alkaloid, specifically, a reversible cholinesterase inhibitor, which is an antidote for nightshade poisoning. It occurs naturally in the calabar bean and the fruit of the manchineel tree, which is common where I come from. If I can successfully isolate physostigmine from manchineel, that will certainly earn me honors, but more importantly, it ought to get me into medical school."

Marigold was all admiration for Ethyl's ambition.

"I don't want to be a medical doctor, like a sawbones," Ethyl continued. "I really want to work in disease eradication. Like identifying the pathogen in this last Russian Flu epidemic, which is still ravaging parts of the globe."

Her words hit Marigold with a pang. "I am well aware of its ravages—both of my parents succumbed to it last winter. And I am also aware of the ravages of poisoning. I helped solve a case of digitalis poisoning last spring."

Ethyl straightened. "Domestic poison, homemade?"

"Indeed." Marigold might have had reservations about admitting her involvement in the murders on Great Misery to such a new friend, but *The Argosy*'s publication of her story would soon render the point moot.

"Happen we do have that in common," Ethyl said quietly. "Poison took my father."

Marigold was astonished into silence. "Is that why you're conducting your research?" she finally asked.

Ethyl shrugged. "Seemed a good place to start."

"What a strange world." Marigold moved closer to the maze-like miscellany of tubes and vials.

"Don't touch that—or breathe it in," Ethyl warned. "That's why I'm careful to keep the vent hood running and the window wide open, to vent the distillate outside. It's all extraordinarily toxic—poisonous—at this stage."

"And what is this stage?" Marigold asked.

"Preliminary—I'm distilling the raw sap of the manchineel tree, which grows wild where I come from along the coast and mangrove swamps in North Florida. Beach apples or little apples of death are what the fruits are called, and rightly so—they're powerful poisonous, every bit of the tree. Even the bark."

Ethyl took a long moment before she seemed to come to a decision. "Made an applesauce she fed to my pa to kill him before she disappeared, my ma did," she said so quietly Marigold had to lean closer to hear. "Out back, over an open fire, like she was making soap. I'll never forget the look in her eye. The things you remember. Not that he was the pleasantest of fellows, my pa, but no one deserves to die that way."

"No." Marigold was all agreement. Because her own memory filled with the image of old Alva Hatchet dying from the poison she had made and taken herself.

"Anyway, my interest in botany took a turn for the chemical after that. And then I got to high school and read Dr. Thomas Fraser's work on physostigmine as an antidote for poisons and then his treatise on isolating the chemical physostigmine in calabar beans. I got to thinking about manchineel trees. And there you have it."

It seemed strange to be discussing domestic poisons, homemade, at Wellesley, which was a world away from the events on Great Misery Island last spring. But malice seemed to have a way of finding its way where it was least wanted. Or expected.

"But please—" Ethyl held out her hands in open appeal. "If you wouldn't mind keeping that rather unsavory information to yourself. Not that I'm ashamed, but—" She shrugged again. "Professor Cleaver knows everything, of course, but we think it best not to let everyone—or anyone—else know what I'm doing up here. Someone might get the wrong impression. You're the only one I've told."

"Thank you for telling me Ethyl." Marigold took her hand in a gesture of solidarity. "You may be assured that I will honor your confidence. I understand all too well the potential savagery of our fellow students' innuendo."

"Sarah Appleton?"

"Indeed." A lovely sort of fellow-feeling—or perhaps just a peaceable sort of sisterhood—filled Marigold and momentarily banished sour Sarah from her thoughts. But it couldn't be for long—Marigold knew she would have to reckon with her suspicions about Sarah shortly.

The Japanese bell broke their moment of accord and sent them on to their next classes, but when Marigold went rapidly down the west stairwell, who should be coming slowly up but President Irvine, along with Dr. Barker, and a couple of somberly dressed men—the "authorities" made real and put into white suits.

"Marigold," President Irvine greeted her. "If you have a moment to wait here, while Dr. Barker and I see to these gentlemen from the county?"

"Naturally, ma'am," Marigold answered, before her conscience reminded her of her class schedule. "If you wouldn't mind writing me a pass for Professor Chapin's History of the Hellenes?" Not even a murder was going to get her excused from classwork.

"Yes, of course. One forgets that young women are trying to get an education here in the midst of all this . . ." Julia Irvine let whatever vocabulary choice she might have made fade away as she turned back to the men that Marigold assumed were from the coroner's office—they had a much more professional, serious nature about them than the watchmen from the town.

"This is one of our students, Miss Marigold Manners. She was the one who found the deceased down at our campus boathouse," she told the gentlemen. "She also assisted Dr. Barker in her preliminary assessment of the body. I've asked her to remain here," she indicated the oak bench, "so she can answer any questions you might have of her."

The more corpulent one of the gentlemen raised his brows, though his face was a studied blank. "Don't expect we'll need anything but the doctor's report, if that."

Dr. Barker barely twitched at the implied insult to her professionalism. "I should hope so. I'm sure you're well aware that many of the observed marks and discolorations that were made when the body was newly found will have faded or disappeared in the interim. I made my report to fill in the gaps in your knowledge as it has taken the better part of a day for you to retrieve the body."

The younger of the two men had the grace to look chagrined, while the older of the two looked cross at having been told how to do his job by someone clearly better educated than he.

"Shall we?" was all President Irvine said, as she gestured Dr. Barker forward with the keys. "I'll be back presently, Marigold."

Marigold found herself pacing back and forth along the corridor, nodding absently to anyone who passed, too absorbed in her own thoughts to make small talk. She wanted to get the logical sequence of her suppositions in order before she presented them to President Irvine. She was about to accuse a valued, treasured, respected member of the faculty of being—what? *Knowledgeable* seemed the only sensible word.

Presently, President Irvine returned. "Marigold." She held out her hand to shake in her forthright, unsentimental way. "If you'd be so kind as to accompany me to my office, where we might speak privately?"

"Did they perchance make any identification yet?" Marigold asked.

"No, but they have agreed to take possession of the body, as we have neither the facilities nor frankly any legal right, since she has not been identified as one of our students." President Irvine looked even more aggravated than usual. "Come, let us proceed as if we are in close conference—which we are—so we might make our way to my office unmolested by some new care or worry before we can address the first ones."

"I assume you've been made aware of the tabloid article and photogravure?" Marigold asked quietly as they made their rapid way down the long hallway toward the president's office at the opposite end of the building.

"Indeed." Julia Irvine's sigh was more than frustration. "No less than three faculty members have come to me, clutching their pearls and pinstripes, bemoaning the dragging of the college's name through the mud and demanding to know what I plan to do about it."

"I am sorry, ma'am."

"I informed them there was little I could do about the photo, under the First Amendment to the Constitution." Julia Irvine adjusted her spectacles but did not alter her steely gaze. "And since neither I nor the college are in any way empowered to act on behalf of this unfortunate young woman who has had the misfortune to die amongst us—"

"Are we positive that she is not a member of the college?"

"As sure as we can be that she is not one of the young women residents this semester." President Irvine risked a sigh of relief. "There is no one unaccounted for in College Hall. We have also naturally made inquiries about the very few of our students who live at home in the town, but thus far, all our students have thankfully been accounted for."

"I am glad to hear that. But I do have . . ." Marigold lowered her voice, though the corridor they passed along was relatively empty. "I have a . . ." She hesitated, working for that discretion the president had requested. ". . . a suggestion of a name."

President Irvine came to a standstill and turned the lamps of her keen gaze on Marigold. "And?"

"Miss Olivia Thayer, the young woman who was scheduled to give the lecture on universal suffrage this Saturday evening. Do you know her?"

"Yes, of course. Well, I know *of* her" She turned to gesture toward a bulletin board hung at the confluence of corridors. "The notices are put up in half a dozen other places about the college." She turned back. "How do you come by this name when no one else has put it forth?"

"During the chapel session, I noticed Professor Currier was overcome with some emotion, and immediately after the service concluded, she left the campus for a house on Washington Street—the Thayers' house. And when I found that the intended speaker for this

Saturday's lecture was a young woman named Olivia Thayer, I thought that bore further investigation."

Julia Irvine's brows rose in question. "Marigold." President Irvine's tone was only a little chiding, but it was entirely serious. "I hope to heaven you've been discreet."

Marigold swallowed the guilt that threatened to rise in her throat. "Yes, ma'am, although asking questions is never entirely discreet."

"Well, then." Julia Irvine took a deep breath. "Let us see if we might sever this Gordian knot with one blow."

Marigold let President Irvine lead the way to the large amphitheater-like Rhetoric classroom, with its three rows of risers where debates and speeches were practiced. Professor Currier's desk sat off to one side, away from the dais, so her students might take center stage.

As they approached the open doors, President Irvine said, "If you'll wait outside? Imogen is more likely to be more candid with a colleague than with a student present."

"Naturally." Marigold tucked herself behind the oaken door, giving herself permission to flout her own prohibitions against eavesdropping—President Irvine would just tell her everything anyway.

"Imogen?" President Irvine called as she went in.

Marigold heard the sound of a chair scraping back, "Julia. President Irvine."

"Julia will do amongst colleagues, Imogen. Please sit back down. You look as if a stiff wind would blow you over. Are you unwell? Can I get you anything for your relief?"

"Thank you, but no. I have my medicine. It's just been . . ." Professor Currier could be heard sitting heavily before she sighed. ". . . a rather trying few days."

"Yes." President Irvine took her cue. "I noticed you appeared rather overcome during the chapel service yesterday."

"Yes, I was . . . greatly distressed. I . . ." For a professor who taught rhetoric, Imogen Currier was having an extraordinarily hard time coming up with the requisite words.

"Yes," Julia Irvine put in for her. "A tragic situation." She could be heard drawing up a chair. "So tragic, you absented yourself from teaching your classes today?" Julia Irvine's tone was kind but still somehow steely. "Is there something you know that you ought to share with me, Imogen?"

"No, no." Professor Currier was quick with her denial. "I mean . . ." She seemed to take a deep breath. "The truth is, I did think that perhaps, I might know who . . ." She heaved out another sigh.

Marigold edged closer to the cracked door, willing her heartbeat to stop filling her ears.

"But it turns out not."

"Then that is good, surely?" President Irvine's calm tone reflected none of Marigold's overwhelming disappointment or agitation. "Yet—please forgive my curiosity, but you are still clearly upset about something."

"Too true." Another heavy sigh accompanied the admission. "I had hoped to keep the news quiet as long as possible, but it will all come out in a day or two anyway. I was concerned for a young woman from the town, the daughter of some dear, dear people, and a senior at the wonderful new Wellesley High School, whom I had been mentoring in the hopes that she would come to us at the college. She showed such great promise as an orator—Miss Olivia Thayer."

Marigold was instantly riveted. She edged closer so she might see into the classroom through the crack in the door.

"She was to speak on universal suffrage at the Forensics and Debate Society lecture on Saturday," Professor Currier explained.

"Yes," President Irvine encouraged. "The students have been talking about their disappointment in the postponement of the lecture."

"Well, I'm afraid it will have to be canceled now."

Julia Irvine's face was carefully, stoically blank. "May I ask why?"

"Because she's gone."

Marigold's curiosity careered into confusion.

And inside the room, President Irvine's patient stoicism cracked. "What do you mean—gone?" Her voice was horrified.

Marigold swiveled her gaze to Professor Currier—who frankly looked diminished, even more than last afternoon.

The professor heaved out another sigh. "Let me explain. I had been worried—dreadfully worried—because she did not come to an appointment we had, regarding the lecture, that she might be this . . . girl."

"The girl found dead in the lake?"

"Yes. But she wasn't that girl, thankfully." There was only the tiniest relief in the professor's voice. "But the reason Olivia missed the appointment, you see, was because she had run off—eloped with a most unsuitable young man." Imogen Currier's emotions got the best of her as she swore, "A damn ne'er-do-well!"

Marigold was both completely surprised and completely disappointed all at once. Although her own experience of ne'er-do-wells was limited to her reading of *Pride and Prejudice* and therefore hypothetical rather than experiential, Marigold felt that such reading as a college-bound suffragist like Olivia Thayer must have undertaken should have been a ward against such an occurrence.

The president's response also seemed to come straight from Austen. "What has been done to recover her?"

"Nothing could be done," Professor Currier averred. "He made sure of that. They sailed that very day, before his telegram to her parents could be delivered. By the time her parents arrived at the White Star Line's dock in Boston to stop her, the ship had long sailed. And though they immediately appealed to the port authorities, there was nothing the port police could do to help them at that point—the ship was already outside territorial waters."

"Oh, Imogen, that is terribly disappointing."

"Just so. I just hate to think of her with such a . . . *rotter*," Professor Currier said, as if this were the strongest approbation she could utter. "But I don't know when I've ever been so crushed as when I feared that this poor anonymous girl found in the lake might be Olivia, when my darling Olivia was already gone with that abominable boy."

CHAPTER 12

"It takes two flints to make a fire."

Louisa May Alcott

"I am sorry, Imogen. It is a trial, to be sure," Julia Irvine agreed. "And a very great blow to the movement of woman's suffrage, but at the very least you have the comfort of knowing that however lost, she is at least not dead like this poor unfortunate soul who remains unidentified."

"Indeed, Julia." The professor took her consolation like bitter medicine. "I will, of course, call the Forensics and Debate Society together this afternoon and inform them of the news. And have them take the notices down."

"Yes. That seems a sensible first step." Julia Irvine nodded her agreement. "Thank you for telling me."

"Of course. Well, then. What must be done was best done soonest." Imogen Currier rose and briefly clasped President Irvine's hand in thanks.

Marigold stood as well, but her attention was momentarily riveted by the sight of a diploma or award of some kind on the wall behind Professor Currier's desk—from the Société des Belles Lettres.

S.d.B.L. The letters on the pin recovered with the hat.

Marigold hurried after President Irvine, too convinced by what she had just seen and heard to wait for privacy or discretion. "I just don't like it, ma'am. If I've said it once, I've thought it a hundred times—there are no coincidences. I think we ought to have Professor Currier take a look at the body just to make absolutely sure before they take it away."

President Irvine frowned. "Do you really think that's necessary? I feel she ought to be spared any further distress—she looked so ill."

Marigold worked to contain her impatience. "Yes, of course, as much as possible, but the letters on the girl's hat—"

"I understand your frustration, Marigold," the president said. "And your particular passion for justice. I commend you for it. But Professor Currier's health is of greater concern to me at the moment."

"But I have another—"

"No buts." Julia Irvine shook her head. "Not in public. Come with me, where we might talk more privately and freely. Because I can see you really are not going to take no for your answer." The president led the way into her office, where she sat behind her desk and knit her fingers together across her lap before she spoke again. "Now. I understand from Dr. Barker that you were privy to certain disturbing information resulting from her preliminary examination of this unfortunate soul?"

"If you mean the signs that the girl was strangled? Yes." Marigold gave way to her frustration—and disgust. "They didn't put that in their tabloid, did they?" she said, looking at the copy on the desk. "All this revolting 'threw herself into the lake' business—why must they always say things like that, when it isn't in the least bit true?"

"Because fiction sells papers, Marigold. You of all people should understand that. But believe me, if the newspapers get hold of the chance of a mad strangler running wild about the college, they will splash that across their front pages without a second thought or a second's remorse. And if that happens, every parent from here to Maine and back down to Washington, D.C., will come steaming up the train tracks in an unthinking panic, hellbent on taking their daughters away from such a threat." She took a sip of the clearly cold tea in her cup before she set it back with distaste. "So, we must tread a very fine line indeed."

A line which Marigold could not see for the wide path of evidence before her. "But—"

"I know you see things others don't, Marigold. And you think of things before you are asked. You are already investigating, aren't you? Your observations of Professor Currier's response to the announcement and your finding the girl's name are proof enough of that."

"There is more," Marigold confided. "The pin on the girl's hat—the one we pulled from the water—was engraved with the letters S.d.B.L. And just now in Professor Currier's office, I saw a certificate or a citation from the Société des Belles Lettres on her wall. That *cannot* be a mere coincidence."

"The Society of Belles Lettres is one of the oldest literary societies in the country and a well-known student organization—we have a chapter at the college," the president said. "Professor Currier is the faculty sponsor."

"Another reason the girl in the lake must be someone Professor Currier knows," Marigold insisted. "Even if it is not Olivia Thayer—for her to have such a pin shows she is clearly *someone* educated and . . . one of us!"

"I see your point." President Irvine's response was characteristically measured. "I will speak to Professor Currier again, but at the moment, I should like to take her word that it is not Olivia Thayer. And what reason could she have for lying, especially about something that will be another hard blow to the reputation of the college—in a different way—when it is known that Olivia Thayer has abandoned her principles to run off with this young man?" She took a weary but fortifying breath. "Men are not the enemy, my own dear Mr. Irvine used to tell me frequently. But they do seem to make it difficult for the rest of us."

"Indeed," Marigold agreed.

"But our involvement with this unfortunate business is near its end—the coroner's office have to make their official findings independent of Dr. Barker's report. Only if they come to the same conclusion about the cause of death will the case be passed on to a higher authority, whoever that will be—neither the coroner's men nor the town watchmen were sure." She shook her head. "They don't even have a telephone exchange! They were completely flummoxed when I offered our telephone so they might communicate with the police in

Boston to see if any young women who might answer to the description of our unfortunate soul might have gone missing from there."

Marigold's frustration found a new avenue of approach. "There are people in Boston to whom *I* might communicate that question." And if Marigold was also alarmed by the alacrity with which a certain man's face had leapt into her mind's eye at the thought of Boston, she kept it to herself.

"You were always my keenest student, Marigold." President Irvine's compliment was offset by her tone of warning. "Your intellectual curiosity is an asset I have come to rely upon, now more than ever. As I said, you see things others don't—it is what will make you a dynamic force as an archaeologist."

Marigold was humbled by her mentor's faith in her. "Thank you, ma'am."

"But I fear your attention to this affair will be a hinderance to your studies. You have taken on an exceptionally full academic burden this semester—at my encouragement—and your studies need to come first. Do I make myself clear?"

Marigold felt all the weight of the woman's gaze—and her expectations. There was no one on this earth she was less prepared to let down that this formidable woman she admired so. Julia Irvine was said to be prickly by many who were intimidated by her straightforward personality. Marigold, for her part, had always rejoiced in Professor Irvine's forthright, clear, and lucid instruction.

And she did so now. "I'm sure I can manage some small inquiries on the college's behalf without interfering with my studies. You can rely upon my discretion, ma'am, just as surely as you can rely upon my curiosity."

"Marigold, I will be frank, for we have not the luxury of being evasive." The president stood and adjusted her spectacles upon her nose in a rare gesture of frustration. "This death could not have come at a worse time. Suffice it to say that the changes we have made to the curriculum and the resulting necessary changes amongst the faculty have placed a necessary but undue strain on the budget. We need this cleared up—and by that, I mean investigated in a thorough and unbiased, professional manner and the truth found by the requisite authorities. I expressly mean that you should not do anything to sacrifice your academic standing—and the future that awaits you as a scholar, by imposing yourself into this tragedy. Am I being clear?"

"Yes, ma'am." As much as Marigold disliked being told off—and stymied—she knew the president was right. Still, her suspicions of Professor Currier were not going to go away. "I hope I may offer my testimony as well as Dr. Barker's to see that justice is served."

"Yes, that will do." Julia Irvine was unflinching in her gaze. "Only the truth will serve the college in the end."

"You have my word."

"Thank you." President Irvine nodded and sat, already returning her attention to the tasks upon her desk. "Then I will trust you to it."

Marigold had her marching orders.

It remained to be seen if anyone else might try to set the tune.

After her dressing down from the president, Marigold wanted the exercise of her bicycle. She always seemed to think better when she was cycling, and she needed some time to reconcile the opposing evidence and opposing choices before her. Despite her promise, she knew she would never be able to concentrate upon her studies with her mind at loose ends about the murder.

It was still light enough that she did not feel in any danger at going alone, and she would take a satchel with an appropriate evening dress and accoutrements—sportswomen's attire would never do when Isabella had made sure to outfit her with dinner gowns—but for the moment, action was the thing.

She packed and pedaled toward East Lodge via the longer, lesser-used path closer to the water so she could pass by the boathouse and take stock of what she knew as fact and what she only supposed might be true.

Thus far, the only thing she knew beyond a shadow of a doubt—no matter what the coroner's office might "independently find"—was that a girl had been strangled. An unknown girl, who was not a Wellesley student but somehow found herself on the campus. She had been assaulted by another unknown person strong enough to strangle someone, and cold-blooded enough to toss her body into Lake Waban.

It did not make a pretty picture.

Marigold slowed as the path skirted by the tall rotunda at the entrance to the boathouse. Days ago it had seemed lofty and inspiring, but today it was full of slippery, sinister shadows that kept her from lingering. Indeed, the starkness of the fall afternoon seemed to cast a pall over the boathouse, which had before been such a source of ease and joy—and would be again, she was determined, once this terrible murder was solved, and the murderer brought to justice.

She pedaled on toward the Music Hall on the south side of the path, passing by the fork that led away from the shore, up toward Stone Hall. Just past that fork, Marigold paused along the edge of the changing wood, trying to find ease in the rich riot of fall color, when a spark of refracted light caught her eye.

Marigold muttered an irreverent prayer that forbade the object from being another hat.

And was calmed, and then swiftly alarmed to see a dark glove—the empty fingers outstretched on the damp ground. A right-hand glove in black suede. Identical to the left-hand black suede glove the strangled girl had still been wearing.

Could she have been strangled with this glove?

No. It was impossible, surely—the glove was too small, and Dr. Barker had quite specifically noticed the handprints on the girl's neck.

But they had also noted signs of a struggle—the bruising at her wrists and the ripped buttons on the jacket and skirt waist. Had that struggle happened here?

Mindful of her foot placement, Marigold carefully moved her bicycle off to the side of the path and picked up the glove before she began to methodically survey the ground for anything resembling a black button. Or rather, she looked steadfastly for the brown dirt of the path, because she knew her clever, curious brain would do the rest of the job for her and find the thing that did not belong—as long as she didn't look for it.

And there it was on her third pass—the small, shining, glass beaded button that must have first caught her eye. As small as a pea, easy to miss amongst the pebbles and berries and fallen leaves, and yet unmistakable. Ripped from the rounded neckline of the girl's jacket.

This was the place, then, where the murder had begun, even if it had ended in the boathouse.

Marigold looked back to see if she could make out the roof of the boathouse's rotunda, before she looked ahead in the other direction to where the path curved back toward the main road and the East Lodge, gauging the distance between the two—she was far closer to the lodge than the boathouse.

But the boathouse was where the body of the girl who had lost—or been forced to lose—this glove was found. It seemed too great a distance for someone as diminutive and frail as Professor Currier to manage—even on her own, not to mention hauling the body of a young woman. But who knew, perhaps the professor's frailty was all for show?

In contrast, any number of strong athletic Wellesley women, whose curriculum was famed for favoring physical exercise, would likely have been able to manage the distance. Sarah Appleton's patrician physique came strongly to mind. And there was her distant cousin's evident antipathy for universal suffrage to be considered as well.

Yet, for all her own antipathy for Sarah, Marigold could not picture the young scholar doing something so obvious or vulgar as giving way to the brute force required to strangle someone. Sarah was all for passive aggression, not active violence.

But practical consideration before the hypothetical—Marigold turned in the direction of the East Lodge. If the girl had fought her assailant here, on the very public pathway, perhaps someone—especially the lodge keepers, protective Mr. and Mrs. Breyer—might have had some sight of such a person. Or had heard something—surely the girl would have called out in her fright?

Or perhaps not, if she was with someone she knew. And trusted.

Marigold almost thought of calling out herself—of trying the distance—but as she looked, just over the knoll, four young collegians came into sight. And in the other direction, larger groups of girls—clearly mindful of the direction not to wander outside alone—walked across the lawns closer to College Hall.

The path was far too well used to have allowed an altercation, in which the buttons were torn off a girl's coat, to go unnoticed—unless it had happened later, at night, when the cover of dark would have cloaked their passage. And when even a seemingly frail person could have taken their time—or slowly coerced their protégée to go the rest of the distance.

But the reminder of the coming night had Marigold stowing the artifacts of the murder safely in her pocket and setting off for the entrance lodge. And after she had spoken to the Breyers, she would see Isabella, who with any luck, would be able to help shed light on a new avenue of inquiry with the clothes. Well-dressed young women, with eight-dollar hats from Jordan Marsh and velvet jackets with expensive glass bead buttons, didn't just disappear without anyone—someone—noticing.

She came to the joining of the path with the carriage road and was about to turn to head toward East Lodge when a deep voice called her name. "Miss Manners?"

Marigold instantly recognized the tall, handsome journalist from the boardinghouse, who jogged to her side, lest she pedal off without speaking to him. "It is Miss Manners, isn't it?"

There was no way of politely evading the introduction—and no real reason to do so. She was safely within sight of the lodge. "Sir?"

"James Wilkerson." He doffed his hat and introduced himself with an equitable offer of a handshake. "I didn't get a chance to introduce myself the other evening. You left before I could get in a word edgewise."

"Mr. Wilkerson." Marigold shook his proffered hand—a handshake was very often a good measure of a man. Too hard and one knew he was aggressive. Too soft and he might be wishy-washy—or might not respect women enough to give them an actual handshake. Too limp—well, that one spoke for itself.

His handshake was exactly firm enough and exactly quick enough to inspire some small confidence. "It is Miss Marigold Manners, isn't it? I thought I recognized you from the paper."

"It is." Marigold dismounted her bicycle keeping the machine safely between them—a precaution she had learned on Great Misery. "What might I do for you, Mr. Wilkerson?"

His smile was a bonfire of pleasure—bright, even teeth gleamed in the afternoon sun. "Pleased to meet you, Miss Manners. I understand you're the one who pulled her out—the jumper."

All confidence in the fellow fled. "The jumper?" Marigold heard herself repeat with barely disguised contempt.

"The suicide." He was indifferent to her outrage. "I'm a journalist, Miss Manners, sent down from Boston to cover this incident. You were the one that pulled her out, weren't you?"

Marigold was compelled to set the record straight. "There is no evidence to suggest that the poor creature jumped, Mr. Wilkerson. Indeed, Lake Waban hardly holds a bluff that counts as height enough from which to jump."

"Now, that's the kind of information that might come in handy." His smile, she supposed, was meant to be her reward for being so clever. "So, you didn't see her throw herself in?"

"Again." Marigold firmed her voice. "There is no evidence to suggest that the unfortunate young woman did herself in. As a journalist, you should know better than to jump to unfounded conclusions. What newspaper did you say you wrote for?"

"Come on, Miss Manners," the fellow cajoled with easy confidence. "What else could it be but a suicide? Place like this?"

"A place like this?" She did not care if her voice was frosted with a rime of outrage. "A temple to the education of women? A place of learning and erudition?"

"You must know what people say about this place, don't you?" His smile became so kind it was almost patronizing. "All these women closeted up together—it's unnatural."

"But not unnatural for young men to be closeted up together at Harvard, or Brown, or Yale? No? What is your excuse for any bad thing that happens in those places?"

"All right now." His chagrin was almost gracious. "I take your point, Miss Manners—which is why I'd like to interview you. If you don't mind my saying, you're quite a gal. Our readers are curious about what happened, and you, Miss Marigold Manners, seem to have all the answers."

Chapter 13

"Let me be dress'd fine as I will, / Flies, worms, and flowers exceed me still."

Isaac Watts

"Not all of them," Marigold was honest enough to admit. "I do not even know the name of the young woman who died."

Mr. Wilkerson's eyebrows rose in disbelief. "Still no leads as to her identity, huh? Now, that would be a shame to have to bury a pretty young woman in an unmarked, paupers grave."

"Gracious, but that's a melodramatic take. This is the 1890s, sir, not the Middle Ages. I have confidence that she will soon be given her rightful name."

"But surely she's just a Wellesley student."

His casual dismissal of the place that gave her life meaning and shape was insulting. "There is no such thing as *just* a Wellesley student, sir."

"Call me James, please."

"I don't think so, Mr. Wilkerson. Which paper did you say you wrote for?"

He looked a bit sheepish, as if he really did not want to answer, before he finally admitted, "The only paper really interested in the story is the *Boston Evening Journal*."

"Naturally," was her tart response. The very tabloid that had splashed the photogravure across its front page, jumped to unfounded conclusions and told the story of finding the poor girl's body in the most lurid way possible. "Your work is a prime example of Mr. Pulitzer's style of yellow journalism that has taken over the newspapers."

He seemed to enjoy matching wits with her—his smile was amused. "Mr. Pulitzer says the American people want something terse, forcible, picturesque, and striking. Something that will arrest the public's attention, enlist their sympathy, arouse their indignation, stimulate their imagination, convince their reason, and awaken their conscience."

"Memorized that from the masthead, have you?"

"You've got me there, Miss Manners. May I call you Marigold?"

"No, I don't think so," she responded pertly. As engaging as he was, she knew nothing of him, nothing of his background. Nothing of his credentials.

But she was having fun. It was something of a pleasure to engage in such lively, spirited debate. But her debate had a purpose. "I'll tell you what, Mr. Wilkerson—I will do an interview with your *Boston Evening Journal* on one condition."

"Now what could that be?"

"That you, and thereby the *Journal*, truly investigate the death of this girl. No throwaway assumptions about her cause of death being a suicide without any shred of evidence."

"And you think evidence of whatever it was that might have happened actually exists?" he countered.

"Isn't that what an investigative journalist is supposed to find out?"

"I could find out if you let me interview you." His smiling charm was on full display. "Find out everything you seem to know."

Marigold saw her own opening. "I will tell you what I suppose, if you meet my condition."

"Well, that's not rightly my decision to make," he hedged. "I'm just a lowly scribe, not the almighty editor."

"I should think a thorough investigation into a potential murder would suit the *Journal* far better than a lovelorn drowning."

He looked alarmed. "Now, who said anything about murder? If she wasn't a suicide, she drowned, surely? You found her in the water, didn't you?"

Marigold felt all the assurance of knowing she was in the right. "My condition, Mr. Wilkerson."

He eyed her for the barest moment before he tipped his hat back off his forehead and smiled warmly. "You sure are a peculiar thinking woman."

Marigold felt her spine stiffen and soften all at the same moment. This was not a new insult, this charge of peculiarity, but it had never been delivered in such a charming manner. It was almost disarming. Almost. "I am not peculiar, Mr. Wilkerson. I am educated, trained in the use of logic and reason and facts. There is nothing peculiar about that. This place abounds in such women."

"Maybe so," he conceded, even as he lowered his chin to look up at her from under his brows. "But most of them aren't as pretty as you."

Marigold refused to be taken in by such an obvious piece of flattery. "And how is that of any significance? Many women are prettier. Many are smarter." She gave him what she hoped was a leveling gaze. "Many are much more patient with importuning men."

His laugh was surprisingly good-natured. "Well, aren't you just a peach. I guess there's just something about you." He offered his smile to her as if it were a gift. "Something fine."

She did not disagree. But neither would she agree. "That is good of you to say. But to what end do you say it?"

He laughed. "You take a compliment all peculiarly too."

"Am I meant to be coy and pretending?" Marigold challenged. "I have a mirror, Mr. Wilkerson, as well as a very keen sense of who I am." And while she knew she was no great beauty, Marigold knew without a doubt that she had something more—she had panache.

And she wasn't afraid to use it. For any ends she deemed necessary.

And murder was one of them.

But clearly the journalist felt the same. "And who are you, Miss Marigold Manners?" James Wilkerson pressed his question as assertively as he did his smile. "Our readers surely want to know. I want to write your account of finding the drowned body—it might make you famous."

Marigold nearly laughed at the repetition of the offer. And immediately chided herself—she ought to have thought her own offer through before she made it.

As she had told Eliza Anthony, she was only interested in being famous on her own terms, which frankly included keeping her account for herself. If there might be a story in how the unfortunate young woman was murdered, Marigold would want to pen her own account for *The Argosy*. And hopefully make some money—spondulicks were still very much in demand.

But she had already given her word. "Do we have a deal?"

He stuck out his hand for a delightfully firm, decidedly equitable handshake—no limp wrist for Mr. Wilkerson. "Meet me tomorrow evening, at . . ."

"Marigold?" It was Isabella at the window of her elegant private carriage, which Marigold had been too involved to hear drive up.

"Isabella!" Marigold took a deep calming breath to fight the rise of any blush in her cheeks. She hated to admit to Isabella any connection with the opposite sex—she invariably got *ideas*. "How lovely. I was just on my way to you when—"

"Yes. I can see that." Isabella made no subterfuge of her frank assessment of Mr. Wilkerson's admittedly fine person.

"James Wilkerson, ma'am." The journalist swept his hat from his head and made a respectable sort of little bow. "How do you do?"

"Mr. Wilkerson" was all Isabella would deign to say before she turned her gaze decidedly to Marigold. "I was worried for your curfew, so I rang up the Hall and told them to expect me to collect you."

"How thoughtful, Isabella. Thank you. Clearly, I left before your message could be relayed."

"Yes, I can see—you're dressed more for sport than for a dinner engagement."

"Yes, but never think I have not come prepared." Marigold indicated her satchel, but also saw her opportunity for a neat end to her encounter with Mr. Wilkerson. "Perhaps you could take me up?"

"But of course," Isabella said brightly. "I shall conduct you there directly." With a wave, she directed her groom up on the box with her driver to assist Marigold by storing her bicycle in the boot.

Marigold surrendered her bicycle but turned back to Wilkerson—one might alter one's manners but never forget them entirely. "If you will excuse me, Mr. Wilkerson, I have, as you can see, a prior appointment."

"I won't try to keep you," he said graciously. "But you think about my offer for that interview."

"Only if you will honor my offer, sir. You can leave word for me at the lodge at the gate." Which he should not have been able to pass without the specific invitation to enter. "They'll get any message up to the college. Or telephone, if you're modern."

James Wilkerson settled his hat back upon his head. "I'll do that, Miss Marigold Manners. You can bet that I will."

Marigold accepted the groom's assistance into the carriage and settled in for the interrogation she knew was coming.

"Who was *that*?"

Marigold did not demure. "A journalist looking for an angle on reportage of the as yet unidentified girl."

"Still?" Isabella cradled her furs closer to her body in a gesture of ill ease. "Poor thing."

"Indeed. But I have hope that you might be able to assist me. I have some of her actual clothing—only a glove and a button, which I just found, but I'm sure you can trick some information out of them, however muddy they might be."

"Hmm." Isabella turned over the items carefully so as not to soil her own gloves.

"Also." Marigold felt the information well up out of her, like floodwaters behind a dam. "The label inside her jacket—black velvet, very much à la mode with stiffened gigot sleeves and a rounded, edged collar dotted with these glass bead buttons, which I judged had been recently purchased—read Madame Watteau of Beacon Street."

"Oh, yes, I know her. Her shop is just down the block from my atelier," Isabella acknowledged with a smile that hinted at the corners. "*Madame* Watteau is really plain Essie Waters, from the far side of Dorchester. Not that there's anything wrong with changing one's name to suit the current mode." Isabella was as egalitarian in her praise as she was with her condemnation. "She's a very competent, clever seamstress and frock maker, even if she does lack some originality. But she uses good quality fabric, I'll give her that. Has a good eye and an elegant touch. Silk velvet with these buttons, you said?"

"I didn't say, but very likely." Marigold recalled the feel of the jacket in her hands. "The fabric felt remarkably soft and plush, which is why I thought the jacket was new, despite having been immersed in the lake."

"And what was she wearing with it—the whole of her ensemble?"

"A well-tailored skirt of a plaid wool. Mostly blue. I'd judge it was also good fabric well made, even though it ripped while getting her out." Marigold controlled the shiver that stole under her skin at the memory of that moment. "The velvet jacket was worn over a plaid-patterned blouse, gathered at the neckline, under a high, lace collar that came almost up to her chin."

"Forest green, black, aubergine, and royal blue?"

"Yes!" Marigold ought not be surprised at Isabella's acuity, but this kind of clairvoyance was a little unnerving. "How did you know? The blue of the plaid almost exactly matched the velvet of the hat—a tam which I am sure came from—"

"Jordan Marsh." Isabella nodded. "Stylish for someone of good but not unlimited means. Not custom—Watteau has a version of the same ensemble in her window now, as we speak—or at least she did yesterday, when I departed the city."

"You check your competitor's windows every day?"

"Not a competitor really—my clients are more interested in exclusive designs. Watteau sells ready-made ensembles. Very good at their price, but not . . . exactly the equal of the House of Dana."

"Naturally," Marigold said. "Forgive me for my lapse of understanding."

"You are always forgiven," Isabella answered. "We're almost to my inn. So." She began to sum up. "Your girl is well-heeled enough to buy her clothes at Madame Watteau on Beacon Street but not—"

"—rich enough to venture up Beacon Street to the House of Dana?"

"Indeed," Isabella affirmed.

"What does that tell us?" Marigold posited. "Is she a local girl? Does a girl who is not from the area come to Wellesley College, but take the train into the city and venture up to Beacon Street to shop for a wardrobe?" To Marigold's mind, anyone who would be so concerned about her appearance would already know where to shop. "Or would she be someone local who knew Watteau's would have high-quality ready-made clothing that was better than what might be available on Wellesley's commercial street?"

"Why don't I just ask her who bought that ensemble?"

"Ask Madame Watteau?"

"Essie." Isabella smiled in her assured, serene way. "I'll invite her to dinner. Explain it all—about your dead girl and how you need to know. She's a good egg, our Essie Waters. She'll tell me, even without the good champagne."

"You're a wonder, Isabella." Marigold reached out to touch her friend's hand—briefly. One never wanted to make too much of oneself or one's sentiments. "Give her the good champagne anyway."

"Of course I will, darling. I always do."

CHAPTER 14

"Principles have no real force except when one is well-fed."
Mark Twain

The next day was more of a return—or perhaps for Marigold, an establishment—of blessed routine. She put aside her investigation and did nothing but act as a college girl and future archaeologist. First, she tended to the chloride content of her experiment in artifact conservation before attending her classes. After that, she retreated to the intellectual fortress of the library, where she spent several hours preparing an essay for History of the Hellenes as well as getting into the nitty-gritty of Lucretius's Epicurean philosophy.

It was difficult and exhausting and sublime all at the same time. The work made her, dare she say it, happy. Or at least as happy as she might be with an unidentified girl and an unsolved murder tumbling in the back of her mind.

From that worry, there was no respite.

But toward that end, she was presently stymied. No one seemed to be missing a girl.

"Oh, Miss Manners?" Miss Burke was only marginally annoyed at her this afternoon, waving from the doorway of the reception room as she passed. "Telegram for you."

Marigold wondered idly if she ought to be tipping Miss Burke the way she might a hotel bellhop who might bring her a wire, but her funds were too closely budgeted to permit such a thing. She settled for effusive politeness. "Thank you, Miss Burke. Oh, it is from my friend, who is my half-brother's half-sister," she added with a delighted smile just to confuse the poor little woman, "who is now become a famous cookbook author. Her book is being published in New York."

"Is it now?" Miss Burke looked suitably impressed enough to allay Marigold's feelings.

She tore open the waxy envelope with alacrity. "Oh, she's coming on the train this afternoon." She consulted the watch pinned to her sweater. "I've just enough time to change into my cycling boots, pin on my hat, and meet her train. Thank you, Miss Burke. You have no idea how happy you've made me."

"My pleasure." The little woman beamed with her own subdued happiness.

But not nearly as much happiness as Marigold. After a long day of single-minded academic endeavor, there was nothing, simply nothing, half as liberating and invigorating as a brisk bicycle ride. Marigold felt her mood lighten and her mind clear through the simple pleasure of physical exertion.

What she needed was a fresh approach—a fresh perspective. She must be concentrating on the wrong thing or have taken the wrong approach. And yet it nagged at the back of her mind that no one seemed to be missing such a well-cared-for young woman. It boggled her imagination.

And worried her—if she were to go missing, would no one look for her?

Her newfound family were sprawled across the region—Wilburt had sold Great Misery back to the Endicotts to be developed for a hotel and was happy making a new life for himself and their mother, Sophronia, on a tidy farm on the Rhode Island coast, far away from the North Shore of Massachusetts and the notoriety of the murders. Daisy and her husband, Tad Endicott, had relocated to a brownstone in New York, where Tad was establishing his publishing career. Seviah was traveling the world over, filling theater seats as a matinee idol for the Keith Vaudeville Reviews. And Lucy—

Marigold's smile returned. Lucy was here, come to help Marigold—who reached the depot just as the train was steaming into the station.

Lucy was one of the first people off the train, exiting from a car at the far end of the platform with her valises in hand. She was just as tall and forthright and beautiful as Marigold remembered, with her dark skin gleaming in the morning sun, but she carried herself with a newly acquired elegance along with her usual quiet assurance and understated panache.

Marigold ran down the platform and immediately embraced her friend, which seemed to fluster Lucy as her arms were filled with bags. "Well, hello to you too, Miss College Manners."

But the last time they had parted, Lucy had been the one to hug her, so Marigold wanted to return the affection. "Hello to you too, Miss Published Author. I can't thank you enough for coming. You're looking marvelous. I love your hat. Very chic." The dark felt chapeau complemented Lucy's very continental ensemble of a plaid suit embellished with passementerie.

"It's French, from Paris, France," Lucy enthused.

"Naturally. Very sophisticated." Marigold felt comparatively dowdy in her plain, dark straw boater.

"Got it in New York City as a special present to myself when Collier bought my book. My momma says I wasted good money, but I told her I need to look like I'm a successful authoress and chef. And besides, it's just pretty."

Marigold knew the feeling. "I think you made a wise investment in your image. A hat is like the punctuation mark of one's look—no ensemble is complete without it. You look every inch the accomplished authoress and discerning chef. Which is why I fear I may be wasting your time, sending you on a fool's errand here. But I do thank you profoundly for coming."

"It's all right. I like how we've managed to look out for each other, in our way," Lucy said as Marigold linked arms with her. "You helping me with the introduction to Mr. Endicott, and him taking me on at Collier. And his wife, your sister, Mrs. Endicott, why, she had me to dinner at their place, sweet as you please—right through the front door. And she invited their cook to come out and take tea and coffee with us after dinner and discuss recipes, and she was just as comfortable and nice as you please. And I know it was down to your influence. Kindness like that needs to be repaid any way it can be."

Marigold felt her heart swell with fellow-feeling—both for Lucy and for her half-sister, Daisy. "All I asked was for Tad Endicott to give you a fair shot—which your work had already earned you and which, clearly, he did. But Daisy's kindness was all her own."

Maybe Daisy felt she had some repayment of past support, albeit secretive, from Lucy to make up for. Whatever the reason, all that really mattered was, as Lucy so aptly said, that their strange, assorted family kept managing to look out for one another.

"So, what's gone on?" Lucy asked. "I understand that you need me to try out for a cook, but I figure you've got some deeper play going on here."

"Well . . ." Marigold wanted to stall her until they were safely out of the station where no one from the town might hear her theories. "I'm really not sure—" She took her time retrieving her bicycle.

"Don't try to bluff me, Marigold. I remember how you were about all those drowned girls up in Pride's Crossing—like a dog who can smell a fox in the henhouse. I know you must be digging into something."

"I am trying—discreetly," she admitted as they passed down the sidewalk. "Because there is another girl dead here—you may have seen it in the Boston tabloids?"

"I don't read those rags."

"Good for you," Marigold shared Lucy's disdain for the kind of irresponsible stretching of the truth that the tabloid engaged in on a daily basis. "Because true to form, they got the facts wrong." Marigold felt secure in telling Lucy the truth without compromising her promise to President Irvine. "While the *Boston Evening Journal* published that she was a suicide, she was in actuality strangled before she was put in the water so she would appear drowned."

Lucy's expression was shocked but, sadly, not surprised. "Who is she?"

"That is one of the particular difficulties—we don't even know her name. Yet. But someone *must* know her."

"And you think that someone is at this boardinghouse?"

"Yes." It was a wonderful thing to find herself with such an intuitive person. "Something is potentially amiss with one of the boarders, Professor Imogen Currier. She is a professor of rhetoric at my college, very well respected by the faculty and equally admired by her students—I liked her very much when I took her class two years ago. But I do feel there is something she is trying to hide." There was too much out of character in her recent behavior to make her seem entirely innocent.

"And you want me working on the inside of this boardinghouse so I can find out what it is she's hiding?" Lucy shook her head. "I'm no snoop."

"I am not asking you to snoop. I'm just asking you to keep your ears open. People tend to be more unguarded in domestic situations than they might be in professional ones," she said, thinking of President Irvine's observation regarding Professor Currier. "She might talk to her landlady or the woman who makes her beautiful breakfast differently than she might talk to say, the president of the college. She might mention her protégée who allegedly eloped with some rotter, or her dear friends the Thayers and their friends in Transcendentalist circles in passing. Just keep your eyes and ears open—within your professional context."

"And this is that important?"

"It is. A girl has been murdered—strangled to death. And no one seems to care or want to do anything about it." Marigold heaved out a sigh of frustration. "Well, I care. A great damn deal."

"Oh, I can see that, Miss College Manners." Lucy patted Margold's arm. "No getting away from that. You always do. I'll bet you got everything figured out, just like you did last time, don't you?"

"No." Marigold felt another sigh push its way out of her lungs. "To be honest, I have very little figured out. And to be even more honest, I don't know if the landlady will hire you. She's a mite bit crotchety. May Barnacle is her name."

"Oh, Mrs. Barnacle'll hire me—if I want her to." Lucy smiled and hefted one of her valises, which clinked and clattered meaningfully. "You hear that? That's all my special sauces and flavors I got ready to make her—what did you call it?—'proper and elevated cooking'? That's what she wants, that's what I'm going to give her."

Lucy closed her eyes and nodded in a gesture of confidence. "She'll hire me."

Marigold felt her worries give way before Lucy's assurance. "Then let us get you there straight away."

Marigold led the way, walking her bike down the well-tended sidewalk at Lucy's side until they reached the house, where they were greeted before they might even ring the bell.

"S'pose you must be that cook she was talking about."

Lucy took charge of the situation directly. "Yes, ma'am. Mrs. Barnacle, I presume? How do you do? I am Lucy Dove, and I am prepared to give you a demonstration of my cooking."

That put Mrs. Barnacle a bit on the back foot. "Well, I don't rightly know, I s'pose."

"But first, I should like to see the kitchen, if I may, ma'am, to make sure it is everything that I will need it to be to make the most proper and elevated kind of cooking that you require. If you would lead the way?"

The woman could be heard clomping her way down the second-floor balcony's stair before she came through the screen door. "Kitchen's round the back. Easier than finding your way through the house." She stopped a moment to take in Lucy's stature. "You look a tall strong woman. I like that in a cook."

Mrs. Barnacle nodded to herself, as if she had made up her mind. "Can't cook a decent meal myself. No taste for it. But we can't all be geniuses. I'll show you my private entrance, where you can come and go to shopping and whatnot." She waggled a finger at Lucy. "Now, I'll want you to use Henry's butcher shop up off the square. I keep an account there," she told Lucy in a confidential sort of voice. "So I know he won't cheat you if you tell him you're buying for my house."

If Lucy took any offense at being walked around to the back instead of being shown in the front door, she kept it to herself, although Marigold saw the slight lift of her chin. But she was smiling as Mrs. Barnacle held the door for her and showed her into the private entranceway with some pride.

"This way is just for my particular friends. These are my own rooms. Kitchen and housekeeper's closet—well, that's me, you see—just through here. I get a woman in a few days, but most of the house, I look after myself. Makes a difference, that personal touch."

Lucy blessed May Barnacle with a beaming smile. "I could not agree more, ma'am."

Marigold followed mostly from curiosity and was pleased for Lucy's sake to see that the kitchen, with its gleaming, up-to-date Hub Grand Range—spelled out on the shining front grille—was as immaculate as her mother's.

"Now, that's a stove," Lucy said admiringly as she surreptitiously ran a gloved finger along the top of the oak cabinets.

"Seven medals at the World's Fair in Chicago," May Barnacle said with evident pride.

Lucy took a full turn to take in the whole of the kitchen before she nodded in satisfaction. "Now, let me cook you something your boarders are going to love, Mrs. Barnacle. You can get along now, Marigold—I know you've got a powerful lot of scholarly work to attend to. I'm sure Mrs. Barnacle and I will come to a right agreement, but we thank you for your assistance with the introduction." She patted Marigold's shoulder as she gently shoved her toward the door. "I'll keep in touch."

"Naturally." Marigold squeezed her hand in pleasure and thanks before she saw herself out the kitchen door.

"Now, you know my momma keeps a boardinghouse for Black folk up on the North Shore, Mrs. Barnacle, but she will be pea green with envy when I tell her about this range. Well, let's get this beauty up to heat. . . ."

* * *

Marigold cycled back toward the campus without any of the strange feeling of being watched she had experienced the last time she had come this way. Granted, it wasn't yet gone dark—perhaps the afternoon sunshine had its own salubrious effect upon her mood. Or perhaps it was the satisfaction of having taken action in installing Lucy at the boardinghouse. The sight of her, pinning on her apron to begin cooking in that extraordinary hat—

Which gave her another idea—now that she had someone monitoring her prime suspect, she needed to look out for some others.

Sarah Appleton with her strong arms and convenient antipathy and easy assignment of blame returned to mind. And although Marigold could not picture Sarah as the physically violent type, she did seem the type who would be a member of the Société des Belles Lettres.

"Miss Manners!" The journalist James Wilkerson came jogging up the sidewalk of Washington Street, his camel hair overcoat flaring out behind him, cutting him a dashing figure. "I was hoping I'd run into you. Have you thought any more about my offer?"

Marigold did not miss a beat. "Have you thought about mine?" Isabella had promised to buy the full run of the Boston papers for her daily, but no further articles regarding the death seem to have been published.

Wilkerson gifted her with his smile. "As a matter of fact, I have. And I've decided to join your cause."

"Excellent." Marigold would have rubbed her hands together in anticipation if she were not holding her handlebars. "What do you know so far?"

"I am more interested in what you know so far." His smile was meant to flatter. "You're clearly the one in the know."

Marigold was experienced enough of the world to be leery. "What makes you think that?"

He smiled and flicked his gaze over his shoulder toward the boardinghouse. "You put a woman of your own on the inside. Very clever. Might I ask why you're so almighty interested in that boardinghouse?"

Marigold was instantly uneasy. She had no want to expose Lucy to any aspect of tabloid journalism, especially when she was just on the cusp of success in her new career as a cookbook writer. Her hat deserved to be on the cover of *McCall's Magazine* or the *Ladies' Home Journal*, not a second-rate yellow-dog tabloid.

"I am not almighty interested in that boardinghouse. I had a friend in need of a job as a cook, so I told her about it. That's what I was doing there, two days ago, when I first took notice of you there asking after rooms—inquiring about the position."

"So, you took notice of me that day?" His smile grew more relaxed, appeased, she thought, by this version of himself as unforgettable.

"Certainly." Marigold decided to try her own hand at flattery to see where it got her. "I was pleased that my friend might be working at a ladies-only boardinghouse, as it seemed safer, but your presence told me that the neighborhood must be eminently salubrious to have such a handsome, well-spoken gentleman wanting to live there."

His smile deepened, scoring soft little lines at the corners of his eyes. "What else did you think?"

"About you? I was surprised to find you a journalist, I must say, for I thought you were a gentleman—in the old-fashioned sense of the word." Marigold said what she thought was useful, not what she actually believed. "You don't look the sort of a man who has to make his rough and ready way in the world. You look much more . . ." She searched for the right word to flatter without being too obvious. ". . . cultured than that."

"Well, I thank you." His smile was as broad as his accent. "I'd like to think I'm a cultured sort of gentleman."

"Do I detect a hint of a refined accent in your speech?"

"Do you? Well, aren't you clever. I hail originally from Virginia. I was raised to think a great deal of gentlemanly behavior and conduct." He took the liberty of taking her arm to steer her away from the lodge gate and back up the sidewalk toward a tearoom. "For instance, you seem all parched and worn out from this bicycling, and I would be remiss as a gentleman if I didn't offer you some refreshment."

Marigold spared a thought for her studies—she would likely miss her class on the History of the Hellenes—but decided that a fish on the line was well worth landing. And she wanted to see where Mr. Wilkerson's apparent vanity might take them.

He was, in the common parlance, a very good-looking man—her fellow Classics scholars would have dubbed him an Adonis. She, however, felt a comparison to the more vain Narcissus was more appropriate—as they walked into the tearoom, he could not help but check and momentarily admire his appearance in the mirror hung in the hallway. And when they were shown to a table, he sat himself facing a very pretty mirror hung on the wall behind her head.

Wilkerson, it seemed, could not resist the temptation to look at himself and, occasionally, to preen. More than once, he raked his hand through his hair, lowered his chin and looked up at her through his luminous brown eyes, all the while watching himself perform as if he were in a melodrama.

She would have to tell her brother Seviah about the move—it might go down a treat in his stage performances.

While Wilkerson was clearly not what she might call her ideal man—that position remained securely taken by another—what remained was to find if *this* man might be useful.

She batted her own lashes at him. "Tell me more about how you made your way from Virginia up to Boston to work for a tabloid?"

"Well, that's a long tale," he began, sitting back a little as if settling in to regale her with his favorite subject—himself. He hooked one arm over the back of the chair and rubbed his thumb over his signet ring in a small gesture that Marigold attributed to familial pride.

"Marigold?" A different voice had her turning.

Directly behind Mr. Wilkerson, her one-time beau and all-time favorite Jonathan Cabot Cox seemed to have materialized, as if she had called him forth from her unspoken desires. As if the universe, in its infinite wisdom, wanted to be sure Marigold would stop making unconscious comparisons and confine herself, once and for all, to the real thing.

Chapter 15

"I felt it shelter to speak to you."
Emily Dickinson

"Cab!" Marigold was up and out of her seat, moving instinctively to embrace him like a long-lost friend before she knew what she had done. "What a surprise!"

"I hope not an unwelcome one?" He smiled at her before nodding politely to Wilkerson. Behind Cab, naturally, was Isabella, looking entirely inscrutable.

"Of course not." Marigold tempered her excitement. "I'm just surprised. Isabella didn't tell me you were coming." A glance at her friend showed not a trace of remorse on Isabella's face—she looked as smug as a cat in cream.

"Oh, didn't I?" Isabella said airily. "I had a business proposition I wanted to talk through with my lawyer, so naturally, he came to me."

"Naturally." Marigold recalled herself to her manners. "Mr. Wilkerson, may I introduce you to two very dear friends of mine? Mrs. Isabella Dana, I believe you've already met, when she came to pick me up in her carriage. And Mr. Jonathan Cabot Cox, of the law firm Armory, Dana, and Cox."

Wilkerson's manners saw him rising politely, but he made the typically male social blunder of speaking to Cab before he acknowledged Isabella. "A fellow would have to be from far away from Boston not to know the name Cox, not to mention Cabot. How do you do, Mr. Cox?"

Cab, being the gentleman he was, nodded briefly in acknowledgement before he too introduced Isabella. "Mrs. Dana—Mr. Wilkerson."

"How do you do," Isabella said with some ice. Her second impression of Wilkerson was going the way of her first—not favorable.

But Wilkerson still knew how to charm. "Pleasure's all mine, ma'am. Any friend of my friend Miss Manners's is a friend of mine."

It was a bold thing to say to people who were already her dear friends. "Not so fast, Mr. Wilkerson. For we are not friends but professional acquaintances."

"Then not friends, *yet*," he laughed. "But I have my hopes up. I'd ask you to join us—" Wilkerson turned his charm on the others. "—but I'm afraid my time with Marigold is limited and we do have important things to discuss."

"Indeed," Marigold seconded before Isabella could get that martial look in her eye. "It is lovely to see you, Cab. To see you both. But I made this appointment with Mr. Wilkerson in order to give an interview in the hopes that the exposure will help identify the unfortunate young woman who was found in the lake."

"Marigold here's got some wild theories," Wilkerson added.

Before Marigold could even object to such a thing, Isabella came immediately to her defense. "Miss Manners *here*," Isabella began with some disdain, "has rather considerable experience with such things. I don't believe I've caught your byline in any of the major papers, Mr. . . . ?"

"Wilkerson, James," he smiled, stepping closer in a manner that some might take as being cozy and confidential, but also looming a bit, as if his height might somehow intimidate Isabella into being more pleasant.

It did not. "Good to know" was all she said, but she lofted an eyebrow in a manner that told Marigold that Isabella was about to have Mr. Wilkerson thoroughly investigated.

"And we won't keep you," said Cab graciously. "Always a pleasure, Marigold."

"Cab." She hoped her smile said what she felt she could not.

"I'll be in touch, darling. I'll be heading to Boston tonight." Isabella made it sound like a warning, before she and Cab withdrew—though only to a table across the room, where Isabella kept a not-very-surreptitious eye on Marigold.

"That your fella?" Wilkerson asked when they were all seated again.

Marigold had her pat response at the ready. "Mr. Cox is a very old, very dear friend whom I esteem greatly."

"You know him from those Misery Island murders?"

"Ah. So you know about my connection to the Great Misery Island murders?" Although her story for *The Argosy* had not yet been published, the murders had been widely and luridly reported in Boston's tabloid press, so it would make sense if a journalist for one of those same tabloids remembered her name.

Wilkerson's smile was just a little smug. "I like to know who I'm talking to. I asked around." He knit his hands together on the table, touching his signet ring again in that small gesture of pride.

She felt her polite smile slipping into crocodile-infested waters. "And where is around? The offices of the *Boston Evening Journal*?"

He was unabashed, setting his elbows on the table to lean in toward her in a confidential manner. "Journalistic privilege," he said with a wink. "Never give up your sources. But you weren't hard to find. And Cox too. His name was prominent—solved the case, didn't he? But Cox is a Boston name that people know."

"Is it?" Marigold set herself to annoy Mr. Wilkerson. "Rather it was Mr. Cox who helped *me* in the matter. Mr. Cox acted as my attorney, as well as representing several other parties interested and involved in the events that took place on Great Misery last spring."

"Well, one thing's for sure, it sure made for a ripping tale."

Marigold agreed sweetly. "Then let us get on with telling *this* tale, so that someone somewhere will recognize this poor dead young woman and help us put a name to her."

"Say the word." Wilkerson took out his notebook.

"Words, actually," Marigold demurred as she drew her typewritten sheets out of her pocketbook. "I've already done your work for you. All you have to do is submit it."

He read her title out loud. "'An Appeal to the Populace'?"

Marigold had pecked it out on her doughty typewriting machine last night—in a vain attempt to assuage her guilt that she had not yet used the machine for any of her classwork. "You're the one who said the American people want something that will arrest their attention, enlist their sympathy, and awaken their conscience. Someone out there knows something, and you're going to help me awaken their conscience."

He sat back and regarded her for a long moment before he seemed to make up his mind. Finally, he smiled, giving her the benefit of the full butterboat of his smile. "Well, I guess it might be worth a try."

"I promise you," Marigold swore. "It will be."

The moment Mr. Wilkerson donned his stylish hat and took his leave, Marigold went in search of a very different sort of man.

The comparative differences between Cab Cox and James Wilkerson could not have been more pronounced. Cab would have moved his seat rather than gaze at his reflection in such a manner. And if there had been no reasonable way to move his seat, he simply would have had the self-discipline not to stare at his own reflection like Narcissus enthralled.

The very important fact of the matter was that there was really only one man in Boston whose discretion and know-how she could safely rely upon—and that person was Cab.

She found him with his head bent toward Isabella in earnest conversation. "I hope you will forgive my intrusion."

"Not at all," Isabella responded immediately, scooting her chair over to make room, as if she had wished for just such a result. "Do come sit with us."

Cab, who had immediately risen from his chair—and also, she noted, swept up the notes he had been making, stowing them into his suit coat pocket—added, "Please do," as he held a chair for her.

"Thank you." Marigold seated herself, even as she said, "I can only stay a short while—I've already missed one afternoon class. I had asked for Isabella's assistance with some matters regarding a murder at the college—"

"Yes," Cab nodded his immediate understanding. "Isabella has filled me in on all the particulars."

"Has she?" Was that what Cab had been taking notes on? "What do you think?"

"About who might have killed such a girl? Well, according to my reading about murders in Massachusetts in the *Journal of the American Statistical Association* published last September—" Cab's steely intellectualism came to the fore. "—rural areas, like Wellesley, have the least resistance to the homicidal tendency."

"The homicidal tendency?" Marigold had not imagined that there was such a thing. "But this is not a rural area—this is Wellesley College, bastion of enlightenment and learning."

"And in opposition to the statistics, in such a community of academic women, one might expect some rivalries to turn sour in one way or another—poisonings or a push down the stairs. But strangulation—" He shook his head so that his hair fell across his forehead in that near-perfect way. "That's a man's method."

"Don't count the women out," Marigold felt compelled to say. "Wellesley women are well known for their stout, athletic constitutions. And in any academic community there are contentions and rivalries—was it any different at Harvard?"

"No, I suppose not."

"Why should it be different just because we are women? Old Alva Hatchett was as homicidal a person as I should never hope to meet again."

"True," Cab acknowledged. "But the statistics regarding the rate of murders within the state definitely point to a preponderance of perpetrators being men of low character and sensual impulses."

"Cab, what a font of interesting and useful information you are." Judging from Isabella's very satisfied expression, Marigold did not doubt that the murder was not the only thing she had filled in. "I'm having dinner with Essie Waters tomorrow," Isabella supplied, "to sort out what information we can from her clothes."

"Thank you. I so appreciate your help," Marigold assured her. "Both of you." Despite her present annoyance with her dear friend, Marigold was mindful of the fact that she could not be everywhere, nor know everything or everyone at once. She had to rely upon others to help her investigate—especially since she was not supposed to be investigating at all. "I have another point on which I would like to ask your help, Cab."

"Name it."

And there was that divine rush of fellow-feeling she always seemed to get in Cab's presence. "Thank you. In your experience as a lawyer within the criminal justice system, to what authority might the college appeal to take up an investigation into the cause and circumstances of this young woman's death? I've done so only because the town's watchmen are unprepared to do anything."

"Only?" Cab's smile was both teasing and knowing.

"I am trying to do so discreetly," she admitted quietly. "Very discreetly."

Cab cast an eye toward where she had just been sitting with Wilkerson, but thankfully made no comment on her discretion, instead turning to more serious matters. "Has the county coroner's office been contacted?"

"Indeed. They came yesterday, but as far as I know, no official identification has been made."

"But your doctor was sure of her findings?" he asked.

The image of the dark purple bruises across the poor girl's neck were seared into Marigold's brain. "Quite sure."

"Then once the coroner's office has corroborated that finding, the case should be moved to the Special District Police, who have both the authority and the experience to investigate murders—unlike your local watch." He firmed his jaw—although Marigold doubted that such a clean-cut jaw could get any firmer. "If you like, I could put in a *discreet* word—they are under the authority of Mr. Augustus Endicott."

"A relative?" Like most of Boston society, who tended to intermarry, Cab was related to the influential Endicott family through one of his parents.

"Distantly, but I have enough of a connection to him through the law to ask that one of his officers be assigned to this case as soon as possible."

While Marigold hated to rely on something so variously available as influence, she would take the gift for the benefit of the college. "Thank you, Cab."

"Happy to help where I can."

"Naturally." The lovely sense of fellow-feeling dissolved into reassurance. "I also wondered if it would be possible for you to make *discreet* inquiries at the major ocean liner docks or offices? Despite some recent information, I can't shake the feeling that a local girl who is said to have eloped on a transatlantic liner—Isabella told you my suspicions about Miss Olivia Thayer?—is somehow tied into this unfortunate affair. It's just too coincidental."

"I understand." Cab was nodding in that wonderfully thoughtful way that made a person feel as if they were being taken seriously and not pandered to. "What line was cited in the telegram?"

"White Star, I think." Marigold gave the name of the most prominent of the Boston Route lines. "And I also wondered if there was some way to tell if the purported elopement did actually happen—would there be some record of a marriage? I'm assuming a civil marriage and not a religious one?"

"I don't know of any religions that will marry a couple without notice," Cab offered. "But justices of the peace and city and county clerks could certainly do."

"You see," Marigold felt emboldened to carry on thinking out loud, "before the report of this elopement, I would have considered Olivia Thayer an ambitious, academically minded young woman, judging from her speechmaking. So I have some doubts as to whether she would agree to eloping to Europe in the first place—with or without a legal marriage."

"Would you do so?" Cab asked quietly.

Marigold was momentarily taken aback. Because if she were honest with herself, given the right circumstances—the right man—she certainly would not need, nor want, the surety of a marriage to embark upon any trip. She eschewed the very idea of marriage. Even with *this* man—though she would certainly embark upon a transatlantic voyage with him at any time he might agree to do so.

But only with this man.

She lifted her chin to give him a level gaze. "You know I would, Cab. But I am several years older"—and hopefully wiser—"than Olivia Thayer. And we are not speaking of me."

"Not everyone shares your antipathy for marriage, Marigold—even amongst your peers," Isabella pointed out.

"Naturally," she agreed. "But the question is if Miss Olivia Thayer, a well-educated, academically minded seventeen-year-old from Wellesley, whose family were prominent in religious, Transcendentalist circles, and who was making a name for herself speaking on universal suffrage—nothing conventional about her so far," Marigold commented. "Would this girl insist upon a conventional marriage or not? And assuming for argument's sake that she did, would there be, somewhere within the town or county or city of Boston, some record of said marriage?"

Cab did not exactly answer the question but said instead, "I will endeavor to find out."

"Thank you, Cab. I am very much obliged." Marigold's admiration mixed with gratitude. "The date of sailing was said to have been Sunday, October seventh."

"And the name of this young man she eloped with?"

"I don't know. A local boy, I assume." She would have to look into that—Professor Currier had only identified him as a ne'er-do-well and a rotter.

"That will make it more difficult, but I will see what I can do." Cab duly wrote all the information down on the back on one of those folded papers he extracted from his pocket. Which was none of her business.

"I so appreciate your assistance," she added, just in case she had not made her own fellow-feeling clear. "And even if I weren't seeking assistance, it is always such a pleasure to see you." She stopped herself from laying her hand over his—just.

"You are most welcome," Cab responded graciously without any physical demonstrativeness of his own. "I hope you know I feel the same."

Marigold would not allow herself to glance at Isabella, who was all but radiating her I-told-you-so aura. "Naturally," Marigold said easily. "It is something of a pleasure to find oneself taken seriously."

"You can always be sure of that with me, Marigold," Cab responded. "Always."

Marigold felt something of a dart to her heart when Cab used that word—always. She had to remind herself that speaking in such a fashion was part and parcel of who Cab was as a man—hadn't she just been ruminating on his self-discipline and steely disposition? No doubt he spoke that way to Isabella too, not just to her.

Although, if she were honest, in her heart of hearts, she certainly hoped he didn't.

Chapter 16

"The only difference between the saint and the sinner is that every saint has a past, and every sinner has a future."

Oscar Wilde

"Miss Manners?" came the summons the next morning while Marigold paused by the mail slots, attempting to read a letter from Sophronia. "Miss Manners, I should like to speak to you, please."

Marigold left off her contemplation of Sophronia's turkey rhubarb tonic recipe—Ethyl would have to be consulted on the possible toxicity of the ingredients—to find Miss Burke with her hands on her hips and a frown on her face.

She immediately set herself to soothe. "Yes, ma'am. What would you like to speak to me about?"

"There was an . . . urchin!" Miss Burke pronounced the words with the same effrontery one might display over the discovery of a cockroach. "Here, in my reception room with his dirty fingers and smudged face."

Marigold wondered how this complaint might have anything to do with her, but still, confusion was no reason to abandon one's manners. "I am so very sorry that he upset you, Miss Burke."

"As well you should be, Miss Manners, because he came for you!"

"Me, ma'am?" Marigold feigned astonishment. "I don't believe I am acquainted with any local urchins."

"He left a note. A sticky, smudgy, filthy note." Miss Burke held out the article in question on a white handkerchief, presumably to keep herself from any contact with said sticky, smudgy filth.

Marigold took possession of the scrap of paper, which still bore the faint traces of rhubarb jam. "Thank you, ma'am. I do apologize."

"If you will keep having people come here, Miss Manners, I don't know what I'm going to do."

"Naturally, ma'am." Marigold tried to give appropriate gravity to the situation. "I'll see what I can do to curtail the flow of urchins."

"Thank you," Miss Burke said with some small relief.

Marigold decided discretion was definitely the better part of valor and moved well away from Miss Burke's reception room to read her note, which proved to be from Lucy, asking for Marigold to stop by the boardinghouse at her earliest convenience.

While she had planned to spend the time between her classes checking on her experiments—she was hoping that at least one of the fifth-century coins from the American School of Classical Studies at Athens's preliminary survey of Ancient Corinth were ready to come out of solution. But maybe she could convince . . . "Ethyl?" she called as she ran up to the Student Laboratory, "Are you here?"

Ethyl poked her head out of her ventilation hood. "How now, brown cow? What's got you all up in a pother? Got another of your mother's tonic receipts for me to translate?"

"Something else—I need to cycle into the town for a short bit. Do you think you could check on my second electrolytic tank for me? I'll be back later, but I don't want—"

"Lordy, Marigold! You know Professor Cleaver is due up here any minute to make her biweekly evaluation. You'd best take the pH of your solution and check the battery connections, at the very least. Normally, you know I don't mind helping, but I've got to have this distillate ready for her to test for purity. Just make sure your monitoring data is up to date, and she'll likely be satisfied. But I'll tell you what I will do—I'll be sure to take up all of her time with my questions, so she won't have but a half second to spare for yours."

"You are a darling."

Ethyl smiled in her easygoing way. "You go ahead and tell that to everyone you know. You know, you're lucky old Professor Cleaver likes me so much, she's too taken up with praising my experiment to do anything more than steal a quick glance at yours. And you're danged lucky I'm so good at my work and attentive to my experiment that I can cover for yours."

"I am damnably lucky!" Marigold agreed. "Always have been."

She finessed her way through the work Ethyl recommended and whisked herself out of the laboratory before any sign of Professor Cleaver, smiling all the way to the bicycle rack and most of the way to the boardinghouse on Washington Street, where Lucy awaited her on the carriage drive.

"Only got a moment or two," Lucy said as soon as Marigold was within earshot. "Mrs. Barnacle's due to come back any minute now. I sent her out to the butcher herself—to prepare them that I'm going to be shopping on her account—and so I could have a little snoop around."

Marigold had to laugh. "I thought you said you wouldn't snoop."

"Well, I ended up poking my nose in a few of the rooms—collecting breakfast trays that I had sent up to the boarders. Reminded me of taking trays to old Mrs. Hatchet," Lucy added in an aside.

Marigold felt as if a chill had settled onto her shoulders at the very mention of the old woman's name. "Let us pray that none of your boarders are as homicidal as old Mrs. Hatchet."

"Amen to that," Lucy rejoined. "But I wanted to tell you that I saw something you might want to know in the Professor Currier's room."

"Yes?" Marigold's curiosity prickled along her spin like an errant electrical charge.

"She has a photograph, up in a nice frame and all. A photograph of her and a girl. And that girl is looking at her pretty special like, if you know what I mean."

Marigold did not know exactly what she meant. "Do you mean amorously?"

It would not be unheard of for an educator to have a fancy for one of their students—especially one termed a protégée—nor for a student to develop an infatuation for a teacher. Nor for two teachers to form an attachment. The region had even given a name to the phenomena of two women seeming to prefer each other's company to that of men: a Boston Marriage, which was a snide euphemism for the cohabitation of two women in a quasi-marriage of convenience.

Never mind that women had been forming romantic friendships and life partnerships since the dawn of time—and certainly during the Archaic Greek period Marigold was currently studying, in which Sapphic poetry from the island of Lesbos featured prominently—and most certainly long before there had been a Boston, Massachusetts, for lesbians to cohabit in!

But that didn't make a woman's preference for the company of women any more socially acceptable.

Perhaps this was what the professor had to hide? But . . . "A girl? How old a girl?"

"Okay, maybe I misspoke," Lucy considered. "A young woman would be a better description."

Marigold's feelings were only a little relieved. "Let me see it."

"Well, that's the thing—it's gone!" Lucy exclaimed. "I'd got a good eyeful and was thinking I ought to tell you about it, when not a half an hour later, that Professor Currier came down asking everyone—staff and boarders alike, if they had seen it, because she couldn't find it anywhere. Which is odd, because she only has the two rooms. It's not like you could get lost up there."

"Where is Professor Currier now?"

"She's still up there, in a taking, turning over every pillow and scrap of linen because she 'can't lose it now!' And 'If I didn't know better, I would think that horrid bully Valentine had done this.' That's what she was saying, all anxious and fluttering. So, I helped her, thinking I might learn something. All she would say was that the photo had sentimental value, as it was of somebody who was no longer here. I asked her if that meant had the girl passed and she didn't say anything, just searched all the harder, pulling up cushions and looking behind curtains like a madwoman."

"Did she seem more concerned that people might have seen the photo or more concerned that it was gone?"

"That it was gone," Lucy said emphatically, before she broke off, her gaze focusing over Marigold's shoulder. "Morning, Mrs. Barnacle. You remember my friend, Miss Manners, who gave you my cookbook? Now, what have you got for me today? Oh, that looks to be a nice lamb shoulder. I'll be right in, ma'am, to decide upon the menu for your guests after I see my friend Miss Manners on her way. She came by to see how I was getting on, and I was just telling her this is the best equipped kitchen that I have ever had the pleasure of cooking in."

Marigold took her cue. "I won't keep you any longer from that lamb, Lucy." And when the landlady had taken herself out of earshot, she added, "Is there anything else you can remember about the photo? About the girl, what she's wearing?"

"Plain white dress."

"Or where the photograph was taken—" Another thought occurred. "Never mind. I think I know where the photograph might have been taken. Thank you for letting me know, Lucy. I am very much obliged."

"All right then. I'm glad I let you know."

Marigold returned to campus all afire with the idea that she might be able to find the photographer, if not the photograph. If Professor Currier was trying to publicly conceal something that might shed light on the girl's identity, Marigold was hopeful she could circumvent her.

Eliza Anthony was exactly where Marigold had hoped she would be—deep into her darkroom processing.

"Did you take a portrait of Professor Currier recently?"

This time, Eliza Anthony was far less alarmed by Marigold's interruption—she didn't even pause in tonging her photograph out of its solution bath. "Don't you ever knock?"

Marigold was startled out of her outage but not her determination. Yet Eliza Anthony had a point. One might adapt one's standards but never let them down.

"I am sorry. Forgive me." She stepped back and rapped upon the nearest cupboard. "Miss Anthony, might I have a word?"

Eliza drew back one of the curtains to let in the light. "It depends upon which word you want."

"The word I want is photograph, and the subject is Professor Currier."

Eliza frowned. "I don't have the concession to take faculty—only seniors, or other graduate degree recipients, who get their portrait made for the *Legenda*."

Marigold changed her tack—one didn't need to make an adversary of everyone. As her Grandmother Manners used to say, one might catch more flies with honey than vinegar. "I am a senior—again—but I never got my portrait for the *Legenda*," as the annual college yearbook was called, "made last year. How does one get that done?"

Eliza Anthony crossed her arms over her chest. "You didn't come up here breathing fire to get your portrait taken."

"No, but I had forgotten about the senior portraits. And you were all invitation to take my picture the day before yesterday."

"That was before I knew you."

Something about Eliza's prickly intellect earned Marigold's respect. And sharpened her determination. "I did not know you were the one commissioned to take the seniors' portraits."

"Commissioned is not exactly the right term—while I am allowed to take portraits, I am not being paid by the *Legenda* board."

"So, you're doing it out of the goodness of your heart?" Such an arrangement seemed entirely too altruistic for the mercenary Miss Anthony.

"And you're surprised to find I have any goodness in my heart, aren't you, Miss Manners?" Eliza's slight smile was wry.

"A little," Marigold admitted with her own wry smile. "But I am happy to be proven wrong."

"Don't get your hopes up too high—I'll make my money in the end. You have to purchase a ticket, which I will sell to you for a reduced rate, as compared to last year's senior class photographer, Mr. Charles Hearn of Boston, who charged more, and to whom everyone had to travel for their portrait."

Again, Marigold had seen the almost bitterly determined smile on Eliza's face before—in her own mirror. "So, the discount is part of your goodness?"

"Partially—and the convenience to my fellow students. But fortunately, I am able to make that discounted rate back by selling the portraits—printed and matted and framed, all at a considerable markup—to the loving parents and families of our graduates, who will want some small commemoration of where their money has gone for the past four years."

Another thought occurred. "Did you sell a portrait to Professor Currier?

"No." Eliza looked genuinely puzzled. "Not that I remember. Who was it of?"

"I don't know," Marigold admitted. "I was hoping you would tell me."

"Because you're such a nice, polite, altruistic person?" Eliza Anthony's smile was just on the polite side of snide. "Sarah Appleton warned me about you."

"Naturally." Marigold let her own smile slide into scorn. "Such a public-spirited soul, my cousin Sarah. So concerned with the well-being of others. So above reproach."

Eliza Anthony surprised Marigold by laughing. "Rivalry from the cradle? I didn't know you were cousins."

"Distant ones. I'm sure she doesn't let that particular information out, since I'm such an embarrassment to the family—here spending my own hard-earned funds for my education instead of being entitled to generations of prim, faultless puritan wealth."

That gave Eliza pause. "Are you really paying for your own education here?"

"I am." Marigold found she was quite proud of the fact. "I have begun to make my way through the world by writing stories that are to be published in *The Argosy* magazine. So, I do understand your plight to be taken seriously as a professional, Miss Anthony."

"What do you know," the young woman mused, turning back to her pans of solutions, as if perhaps she were beginning to change her mind about Marigold.

Which gave Marigold leave to have a good look at the labels on the drawer pulls. While the drawers above had the descriptors Landscapes and Buildings alongside others with sizes of paper and equipment—stereopticons and lanterns—the bottom cupboards were labeled with the names of various chemicals. Sodium sulfide, hydroquinone, and borax figured prominently.

"Do you make your prints yourself?" she queried.

The photographer's answer dripped with sarcasm. "No one else here, Miss Manners."

"Call me Marigold, please. May I call you Eliza?"

"Call me anything you like," Eliza countered, "if you commission your portrait. You'd be an easy ticket—you're very photogenic."

"Thank you." Marigold took some time to look over the other accoutrements of the studio. "What about other portraits—ones that aren't these senior class pictures?"

The girl shrugged in an offhand manner that Marigold was sure was meant to convey her indifference. "Occasionally. I've taken a few portraits of townspeople."

Something in Eliza's tone was . . . slippery. "Is that allowed—having townspeople here in the student laboratory?" Professor Cleaver had said that access was restricted.

"Not really." This time, the shrug was more defiant. "As I said, I'm trying to make my own way as a professional."

"How exceptionally mercenary of you."

"How eminently practical," the young woman countered. "And don't try to tell me you're anything different. Because I've read stories in *The Argosy*, and I know what they're like, so I simply won't believe you."

Marigold could really have nothing to say to that—nothing that wasn't entirely hypocritical. But she could not let the girl's cynicism stand. "The trick, dear Eliza, is to mix the mercenary and the practical so that no one else gets taken advantage of. Or hurt."

But even as she said the words she knew she herself had done just that—the image of Cab Cox, stunned and hurt by her rejection of his proposal last spring, filled her mind's eye.

But he had got over that, surely—he was still her friend. He still said *always.*

But what about others, who weren't so understanding or so forgiving? What were young women like her—or like Eliza—to do in a world that rarely forgave them for the sin of being ambitious? That called their hopes and dreams selfish?

And how were they to make their supposedly selfish way when that way was often purposefully barred to them? Barred by men who were unlike Cab and who demanded their fealty or their obedience instead of their genius?

The answer, she feared, was that they had to continually steel themselves against the pressures to make themselves always likable.

And Miss Anthony, like herself, had already fashioned herself with that steel.

CHAPTER 17

"There is nothing more deceptive than an obvious fact."
Arthur Conan Doyle

"Miss Manners!"

Marigold had learned to recognize the sharp summons from Miss Burke in the reception area. "Yes, ma'am?" She immediately left off collecting her correspondence from the mail slots at the end of Center Hall—her latest letter from Sophronia would have to wait. "How may I be of assistance?" She crossed her fingers against there being any urchins involved.

"You have another wire." Miss Burke led the way back to her desk where the waxy beige envelope lay in some state in the center of Miss Burke's blotter. "From Mrs. Dana."

"Oh, thank you, Miss Burke. I am much obliged. I hope it will be some news that will help solve this terrible dilemma of the young woman we found."

"Oh, I hope so too," the tiny woman confided. "Such a burden on President Irvine, this has been."

Marigold understood in that instant that loyalty was the key to Miss Burke's heart. "I hope I am doing everything I can to relieve her, Miss Burke." She tore the telegram open so she might begin to do so as soon as possible.

"News from Mme. W.," it read. "Vivid recollection of girl. Miss Olivia Thayer of Wellesley. Bought for speaking tour."

The confirmation of her suspicions sat like cold fish stew in Marigold's belly, allowing her absolutely no satisfaction in being right.

"Miss Manners?" Miss Burke's normally concerned expression deepened. "Are you quite all right?"

"No," she heard herself say. "I am not at all right." Nothing was right.

Miss Olivia Thayer, who had purchased her ensemble from Madame Watteau in Beacon Street specifically for a speaking tour sponsored by a professor she was suspected to have a crush upon, and who had then been thought to reverse course to elope with her rotter the day before the murder, was the girl Marigold had pulled from the lake.

It seemed both inevitable and impossible.

And when one eliminated the impossible, whatever remained, however improbable, had to be the truth. Even if the evidence contradicted itself.

Marigold felt as if she needed to take an hour or two to tidy her room and organize her clothes to sort out the problem. But she didn't have the time—direct action was necessary. "Might I please use your telephone, Miss Burke? It's very important."

"Well." Miss Burke clasped her hands tidily at her waist as if she were preparing herself to refuse.

"Please. It is of vital importance in identifying the young woman who died." Marigold did not mince her words. "I have a very alarming report via this wire"—Marigold held forth the telegram as if it were evidence—"that needs must be confirmed as soon as possible. You will be doing me, and therefore President Irvine, an immeasurable favor if you would so kind as to let me use your telephone exchange. Immediately," Marigold pressed.

Whether it was the appeal to President Irvine or not, her plea worked. "If you'll come this way." Miss Burke led Marigold into a small annex behind the reception room, where the wooden box housing the telephonic machinery was mounted on the wall. "I'll ring up the exchange for you, shall I?"

"Please."

Marigold watched with fascination as the woman began to grind the handle to rotate the cylinder she then spoke into. "Exchange?

Wellesley College, Miss Burke. Will you connect me with—" She raised her eyebrows to Marigold in question.

"House of Dana, Beacon Street, Boston," Marigold supplied. "Mrs. Isabella Dana."

"Beacon Street, Boston, House of Dana," an eerie voice crackled back.

"All right now," Miss Burke instructed. "You stand here and hold the receiver up to your ear and speak into this small horn."

"Thank you." Marigold took up the required position, stooping a little—for the machinery had evidently been installed to Miss Burke's diminutive height—and listened as the tinny, electric sounds crackled and snapped down the line.

"House of Dana? I have Wellesley College on the line."

"Oh, one moment."

More static and noise before a faraway voice come on. "House of Dana. Isabella Dana. Marigold, darling, is that you?"

"Yes, Isabella, it's Marigold."

A squawk was her seeming answer.

"You'll have to speak up," Miss Burke instructed. "Enunciate clearly. As if you were giving a speech. And put your ear closer, here."

Marigold did as instructed. "Isabella? Marigold here. I got your wire."

"Yes, darling! There you are! I feel positively sleuthish to get you the name so easily."

"But it's impossible," Marigold insisted. "Olivia Thayer was supposed to have sailed from Boston the day before the body was found. Professor Currier had it from Olivia Thayer's father himself."

"Can't be," Isabella rasped back. "Essie was sure."

"How sure?"

"She remembered the girl perfectly—how she and her mother bought the whole ensemble straight off the mannequin in the bay window. Said it would go perfectly with her hat—from Jordan Marsh. Lovely young girl from Wellesley, beginning to make a name for herself as a passionate speaker for women's suffrage. The mother was beaming with pride."

"When?" Marigold called. "When did she buy it?"

"Let me see." The line subsided into crackles as Isabella presumably looked at something. "She showed me her order book, Essie did," she came back on the line to explain. "I saw the girl's name myself. Thayer—copied it all down for you exactly. Two weeks ago, on Friday, the twenty-eighth of September."

That was the date that Marigold herself had gotten her telegram from *The Argosy* that had reversed her fortunes and sent her back to Wellesley.

"Marigold? Marigold, are you there?

Marigold didn't know what to say. It all seemed so impossible and conflicting.

"Marigold?"

"I am here." She pulled her muddled mind back into some semblance of order. "Thank you. You've done yeoman's labor."

"Hardly, darling," Isabella laughed. "Unless yeomen drink champagne at luncheon."

"Yes, no," Marigold answered nonsensically. "Thank you all the same. I'm going to ring off now. Thank you."

Whatever response Isabella might have given was lost to the crackle of the line as Marigold replaced the earpiece on its hook. "Thank you, Miss Burke."

"You are most welcome." Miss Burke's usual persnicketiness was absent. "And it does seem quite a dilemma," she added in a quiet show of sympathy.

"Truer words were never spoken, Miss Burke." Marigold felt deflated, as if all the air had run out of her lungs along with all the logic from her brain. "What I am going to do about this dilemma, I do not know."

"Did you never meet or see her here?" Miss Burke asked.

It took Marigold a long moment to understand. "Olivia Thayer, do you mean?"

"Yes." The lines that normally bracketed Miss Burke's pursed-up mouth seemed to soften—she was quietly pleased to help. "But I suppose you came late this year. She came here often at the beginning of the semester, as I recall. A very polite, well-mannered girl. Beautifully spoken, as you might imagine. But never a hint of the firebrand when she was here in my reception rooms, waiting to be given permission to visit Professor Currier. She was bringing her along, you see, the professor. Teaching her, though she wasn't a student here yet."

"She came here," Marigold gestured to the reception room. "Often? Often enough that you might recognize her?"

"Yes, certainly," Miss Burke affirmed.

"I am sorry to ask this of you, but do you think you could identify her body?"

"Oh, no," Miss Burke said with evident horror. "No, I couldn't possibly. I couldn't possibly leave the reception room unattended."

"We'll leave a note on the door. I'm sure no one would mind." Marigold would remove all obstacles—the sooner the young woman could be positively identified, the better.

"No, no." The little woman waved her hands in front of Marigold as if she could shoo her away. "That would mean going out—" Miss Burke's eyes darkened with imagined terrors.

"It is not very far at all, Miss Burke," Marigold cajoled, trying to gauge the distance to the county seat in Dedham. "And not for very long. Just long enough for you to take a look at—" Marigold stopped herself at the look of panicked horror on the woman's face.

"I couldn't possibly," the poor woman stammered. "I mean. No, I don't think I could. No."

"I am sorry to ask, Miss Burke," Marigold attempted to soothe, not quite understanding what seemed to her like a disproportionate response to a reasonable request. "But you would be doing a great service to the college."

"I don't see how." The woman's panic seemed to expand within her—she began to speak more and more rapidly. "That girl wasn't even a student yet, I know she was meant to be, and had already passed the entrance examination because Professor Currier had prepared her, but . . . but . . ." She seemed to run out of excuses. "I just couldn't possibly."

Marigold tried another tack. "What if . . ." She searched her brain for something that would satisfy them both while easing the woman's seemingly irrational anxiety.

"Oh, no, please!" Miss Burke's eyes seemed to roll back in her head, as if she were going to succumb to a sudden swoon. "I don't think I could."

Marigold fought against being unkind. "Someone must, Miss Burke. And you are the someone best positioned to do so." She appealed to the woman's sense of loyalty. "Think of your service to the college. Think of all the other girls here—of President Irvine and Professor Currier—who are counting upon you to be a Wellesley Woman. To be of service. Non Ministrari sed Ministrare." Marigold quoted the college's Latin motto. "Not to be ministered unto, but to minister."

But her appeals were in vain. Miss Burke shut her eyes as if she was also shutting her ears. "I cannot." Her voice grew so thin Marigold had to lean down to hear her. "Please don't be so cruel as to ask me again. I cannot."

Marigold stepped back. And chastised herself—no one had ever called her cruel. Determined, yes. Dogged even, in her pursuit of justice. But never cruel.

She immediately apologized. "Please forgive me. I am sorry to distress you so, ma'am. I will not do so again." Barring an unforeseen infestation of urchins, of course.

But what was she to do with the information she had received? Where was she to look for confirmation? And how was she to do so discreetly?

She had to be logical. And far more thoughtful.

"Do you think it would be possible for me to speak with President Irvine about this, Miss Burke?" she asked in a quieter, more considerate tone. "I do think I ought to inform her of the information in the telephone call."

"Oh, yes." Miss Burke drew a steadier breath. "Yes, certainly. Let me conduct you to her."

"Thank you for your kind assistance, Miss Burke. And I apologize again." One might alter one's standards to help solve a murder, but never let them down.

Marigold was forced to pace in the corridor as Miss Burke gained access to the president's inner sanctum.

"Khairete," her classmate in History of the Hellenes, Fannie Arbuthnot, hailed her as she came down the hall with Mabel Benkins. "How now, Marigold. We missed you in class yesterday."

"Kalimera, Fannie. Mabel." Marigold greeted her fellow classicists in Greek and tried hard not to feel too guilty about the missed class—sometimes other things, like murder, took precedence. "Mabel, you're in the Forensic and Debate Society, aren't you? Did you, or either of you, know Olivia Thayer, the proposed speaker for the Saturday lecture, personally?"

"I think I saw her once, hanging about at the back of Professor Currier's class," Mabel answered. "And I did ask for a photograph of her from Professor Currier to include on the flyers, but it hardly matters now, does it, with the lecture being canceled."

"Did the professor give you a photograph? Could you recognize her from that, do you think?"

"I suppose, maybe. Wait!" Mabel put her hand over her mouth. "Word is you've been trying to identify the drowned girl. You don't mean—"

"She wasn't drowned." Marigold was done with untruths. Her sense of right rebelled at the thought that all their discretion and careful respect for young women's sensibilities and sparing older women distress had actually been a hinderance to identifying and solving this young woman's murder.

If she had only held her tongue and had let Dr. Barker take the poor girl's body in through Center Hall, in the middle of the afternoon, in the middle of the college, where everyone could see, the chances that some one of the many people who had seen or met her before—Professor Currier, Miss Burke, or any number of other students—would have recognized her right then and there.

"Miss Manners?" President Irvine stood in the doorway. "You needed to see me?"

"Yes, ma'am." Marigold ducked her head and followed Julia Irvine into her office. As soon as the door was closed behind them, she said what she had come to say. "I fear it really is Olivia Thayer after all."

President Irvine froze halfway to her chair. "But Professor Currier—"

"Was told by Thayer's parents—who were informed by telegram, which I now believe must have been a deliberate lie."

"Why do you think that?"

"The labels on the girl's clothing were from a Madame Watteau on Beacon Street—and Madame Watteau herself has confirmed that the clothing in question was purchased by Olivia Thayer and her mother, specifically for her speaking tour."

"Are you positive? Might it just be a coincidence? Professor Currier seemed sure—"

"I don't believe in coincidence. I am as positive as I can be without having someone who knew Olivia Thayer personally identify her body. And that is what I recommend. As soon as possible."

President Irvine, normally so stoic, blanched a little. "Ah, I begin to see now why you asked Miss Burke." She drew a considering breath. "I also hate to ask Imogen, given her health, but I fear it were far better to ask her than the Thayers," she mused. "Cruel either way."

"Crueler than having them think their daughter abandoned all her principles and ran away with a rotter?"

"Yes," the president said simply. "Far crueler. At least with the rotter they might hope that she would be happy. And alive." She sat abruptly, as if the weight of all her responsibilities had, of a sudden, become too heavy. "Let me send for Professor Currier at the bell. What must be done, however unpleasant, ought to be done soonest."

Chapter 18

> *"This appetite of the mind for particulars of great crimes and criminals has been stigmatized as vulgar. It is only vulgar in so far as it is universal, the common attribute of every age, people and clime."*
>
> The *Daily Telegraph*, 1881

Professor Currier was sent for, but as it was a good fifteen minutes until the class period was slated to end, President Irvine invited Marigold to take a seat to wait. "For we have other things I should like to discuss with you—namely your missing classes."

"I am sorry, ma'am," Marigold began. "But when the information came to me—from others, as I promised you, professionals in Boston—I felt I had to act." For a moment she wondered if she might appeal to the president's sense of history. Wellesley originally organized itself as a strictly nondenominational female seminary, to raise up a generation of genuine but practical Christian young women, for whom doing good was always seen as equal to merely being good.

"You have also gravely upset Miss Burke," the president rebuked her. "She was greatly distressed."

"I am sorry," Marigold apologized again. "I realize I was rather too single-minded in my quest to find someone to identify the body, and she seemed eminently suitable."

"Please don't be too hard on her. She has her own reasons to refuse, Marigold. Which I will ask you, as a favor to me, to accept without going into private matters and histories that are not yours to know, nor mine to tell. Suffice it to say, we are not all so steely as you."

If before Marigold had felt herself rebuked, now she felt as if she had been slapped.

As if she were steely by nature. As if she had not *chosen* to steel herself to make her way in the world. To be both diligent and determined. And as if that choice had not cost her.

Marigold raised her chin and firmed her resolve. "You, of all people, ma'am, should know that every piece of steel has to be tempered and purchased, for a price." She blinked furiously to keep herself from an unseemly display of frustrated emotion—it would only delay their doleful mission. "Today, Professor Currier will have to pay the price that Miss Burke would not."

Julia Irvine raised her gaze to look directly into Marigold's eyes. "In case you did not understand, Marigold, I appreciate your steel, greatly, for I understand the very grave cost. To you and Professor Currier both. But pray do not make the mistake of thinking that no one else has ever tried to carry such a burden. Some people, through no fault of their own, the burden breaks."

Only Julia Irvine could make Marigold so ashamed while complimenting her.

"Yes, ma'am." Her voice sounded as vanquished as she felt. "So noted. And my apologies."

"Thank you. If I am hard on you, Marigold, it is only because I know you and want to help you find your better self. The better self I seek for myself daily. You have both a rare ability and a rare opportunity, if you will return your focus to your academic studies instead of—"

Miss Burke stuck her head in the door. "Professor Currier, ma'am."

"Imogen. Do come in."

"Julia," Professor Currier greeted her colleague. "You wanted to see me? I've only got a moment between classes."

"Yes. I'm afraid this is not going to be a pleasurable conversation, Imogen. Please have a seat." Julia Irvine gestured to the other chair in front of her desk before she turned to Marigold. "Let me reintroduce you to Marigold Manners."

"Yes, I remember Marigold well." Professor Currier put out her hand to shake, even if she was clearly confused about both Marigold's presence and the potentially unpleasant news. "What has happened?"

"I'm afraid Marigold has discovered some unsettling information with regard to the identity of the young woman found in the lake," President Irvine explained.

Professor Currier put her hand to her chest as if she might ward off whatever bad fortune was about to come her way. "Yes?"

Marigold sat in the other chair opposite the professor and tried to be as gentle as possible. "The young woman's clothing bore several labels indicating where it had come from—which store. In Boston," she added incrementally, parsing the unhappy information out in small doses. "Beacon Street. Madame Watteau's."

Professor Currier gasped. "But . . . it's a popular shop," she stammered.

"Yes, ma'am. But Madame Watteau herself confirmed that she sold the exact ensemble that the deceased was wearing—black velvet jacket with stiffened gigot sleeves and a rounded, edged collar, over a plaid-patterned blouse of forest green, aubergine, and royal blue, worn with a skirt of the same plaid wool—to Miss Olivia Thayer and her mother."

"No." Professor Currier closed her eyes as if in pain. "No, it wasn't her mother. It was me." She swallowed before she could speak again. "Her mother, however accomplished in her own right, is . . . unworldly, and dressed Olivia in simple girls' dresses, all bows and cambric. Olivia wanted something . . . more mature. Something suitable for an aspiring Wellesley girl and a passionate, educated young orator making a name for herself in the world." She opened her eyes that were now filled with tears. "I took her to Madame Watteau."

"I am so sorry," Marigold said. "But I would also like to ask if Olivia was a member of the Société des Belles Lettres?"

"Ah." Professor Currier's tears coursed down her cheeks. "The pin—on her hat. She was so proud."

Julia Irvine came around her desk to put a consoling hand on her colleague's shoulder and offered a fresh handkerchief. "I wish we had better news."

"Is it settled then? You're quite sure?" Professor Currier asked.

"Unfortunately, it has not been made official," Marigold clarified. "Some one of her family would likely need to make the formal identification of her body."

"Oh, no." Professor Currier put her hand to her heart again. "Have they been informed?"

"No, Imogen, not yet. We wanted to speak to you and make sure, before we made our findings available to both the authorities and to the Thayer family."

"She's dead, then." Professor Currier blotted at her fresh tears. "It must—don't you think—it must have been Valentine?" This was the name the professor had inadvertently given to Lucy. "That bully Valentine."

"And who is Valentine, ma'am?"

"Her suitor, for lack of a better word. Wilkie Valentine. But he wasn't really her suitor, was he, if he could do this?"

Marigold agreed in principle, if not yet in fact. She could certainly cast her own suspicions toward the young man, while still reminding herself that the surest way for anyone to deflect blame from oneself was to offer up another suspect.

Professor Currier remained a person of interest in Marigold's eyes. "Did you have occasion to meet this young man, Wilkie Valentine?" She must have done so, to think he might be behind the disappearance of the photograph from her room.

"Yes. Unfortunately." Professor Currier wrinkled her nose in an expression of dislike. "He was persistent in his wooing of Olivia despite her avowed disinterest."

"Can you describe him? His physical appearance, his style of clothing or his habits?" She would need to give such information to Cab at her earliest opportunity—although, if the dead girl did prove to be Olivia Thayer, then the search of the ocean liner records was nothing but a wild-goose chase.

"He was, to me, a moderate-looking young man," the professor said, "the sort who gets along just fine without any great appearance of intelligence. I suppose he had good looks, but what he had, in overabundance, was charm. A vast deal of it, which he spread like manure, fertilizing and polluting equally, if you ask me. I found him ghastly."

"When did you meet?" Marigold asked.

"Oh, well, I suppose . . . when he took serious interest in Olivia, and she came to me for advice on how to dissuade him. Her mother, you see, despite being progressive in most of her views, still believed in romantic love—being very much in love with her own dear husband, Reverend Thayer. She was willing to give Valentine the benefit of the doubt—at first."

"But you weren't?"

"No!" Professor Currier said vehemently. She closed her eyes again, as if even the thought of Wilkie Valentine was too much for her. "It didn't take much to see he was up to no good."

"Might we trouble you for the introduction to the Thayers?" President Irvine asked.

"Yes, of course." Professor Currier shook her head as if she were trying to organize her thoughts. "They—especially her father—were supportive of her career, or rather, the fact that she wanted to have a career. Olivia, that is. Once her father found out that Valentine had been surreptitiously courting Olivia, he did everything in his power to try and keep her head from being turned by the boy."

"How so?" Marigold asked.

"Asking me to do more things with her—take her shopping, have her come to the college after her classes at Wellesley High School were over. But I suppose that was when Valentine made his appearances, walking with her to campus. We did too little, too late, I suppose." The professor drew in an unsteady breath, as if she might resuccumb to tears.

President Irvine must have heard it too. "What can I do for your relief, Imogen? I know it's been quite a shock."

The professor's laugh was close to a sob. "Not nearly as much of a shock as I had thinking Olivia had gone with that absolute rotter."

She pronounced the last word with some venom, before she drew in a steadier breath. "My only comfort now is in knowing I was not wrong about her after all."

"Yes," President Irvine agreed consolingly. "That will be some small consolation to the cause. But I'm afraid there will be little consolation for the Thayers, who will have to be told, so they may identify and claim her body for burial."

"And if it's not her?" Professor Currier asked, hoping against hope.

"Then it's not." Julia Irvine was sanguine.

"Then they will have been put through another ordeal. No." Imogen Currier seemed to sit up a little straighter, as if she were firming her convictions. "I'll go. I'll make sure. And then, if it is she—if Olivia really is dead—well, I should be the one to tell them."

"Are you quite sure, Imogen?" Julia Irvine asked. "It's all the way over in Dedham."

"I am sure I can arrange private transportation for us." Marigold hoped that Isabella might be persuaded to return with her town carriage for their use. "This is not the sort of thing one ought to do alone." She offered to accompany Professor Currier not only out of kindness—the fact that she would also be able to keep a close eye upon the professor's demeanor was an added bonus.

Because Marigold's instincts told her the professor was still hiding something important.

For the first time in the conversation, Professor Currier turned to look—really look—at Marigold. "Forgive me if I'm wrong, but that advice seemed to be given in a tone of experience, which is not what I might have expected from one so young as you, Miss Manners. You young women these days seem to have ice water in your veins."

At that moment, Marigold felt she had the opposite of ice water within her veins—every bit of her seemed hot with suspicion. It gave her no pleasure to know she had been right about the identity of the dead girl, and less pleasure to know she would be watching Professor Currier like a hawk when she identified the young woman.

Murder had indeed made Marigold see wickedness in everyone she met.

"It is unfortunately true that I do have experience in identifying a deceased person, Professor. And so, I know the toll it might take upon a soul. You should have some support."

Professor Currier seemed a little taken aback. "That is very kind of you. Thank you," she said with obvious relief. "I would appreciate that."

"And I will ask Dr. Barker to accompany you as well, Imogen," added Julia Irvine. "It is only right that you have a colleague with you as a sign of the college's support."

"Thank you, Julia."

"You are very welcome, though I am deeply sorry for the occasion."

⋆ ⋆ ⋆

If the wait to tell Professor Currier about Olivia Thayer had been melancholy, the drive the next morning, from Wellesley to Dedham, the county seat, was funereal. Isabella had been gracious in the loan of her carriage, but even while they sat in relative comfort—the professor and Isabella sat on the plushly upholstered forward-facing seat, while Marigold and Dr. Barker were on the backward facing bench—the drive was undertaken in churchly quietude.

But that was no reason why the time spent in transit couldn't also be informative.

Marigold began with what she thought were less intrusive—but no less important—questions. "How long had Olivia Thayer been your protégée, professor?"

"Oh, she came to my formal attention at the college little over a year ago. A former classmate of mine now teaches English composition and rhetoric at the new Wellesley High School—she told me that she had a student who showed exceptional promise as an orator. And I agreed. I could see that Olivia was a very bright young thing," the professor mused. "Quick and curious and clever in a way that never triumphed in other's mistakes or mischances. Such a waste of talent and time and ambition. She could have been . . . something. Something more." She shut her eyes and drew in a deep breath to restore some portion of her equanimity. "Something truly influential. But now . . ."

"Yes." They all sighed collectively. Yet Marigold still probed. "And when did she meet this Valentine?"

Imogen Currier's mouth cinched up in a look of extreme distaste. "Shortly after he came, I suppose."

"Came?" Marigold wanted to make sure she understood every particular. "From where?"

Professor Currier frowned and pursed her lips again, as if she found the subject—or perhaps the man—beneath her consideration. "I'm not exactly sure." She turned to look out the window, before she closed her eyes again. "Richmond or Baltimore, I thought. I think I heard Olivia say he came from down south somewhere."

A vague sense of alarm spread under Marigold's skin—she endeavored to find its source. "How did she meet him, exactly?"

"Oh, I don't know." Again that desolate sigh that had her turning her head to gaze dolefully—or was it evasively?—out the window. "She didn't really say."

Marigold decided to be direct. "What *did* she say?"

"That she had met a rather charming gentleman by chance, and that they had talked and she thought him very intelligent and thoughtful at first—which was all a ruse, I'm sure. If he was thoughtful, it was like a fox. He did it all quite purposefully, I'm sure, to lure her away from her calling—from speaking." Her voice grew more vehement. "In fact, I am sure he chose her—chose to speak to her, chose to woo her—because he wanted to strike a blow against suffragism."

"What gave you that impression?" Dr. Barker asked.

Professor Currier looked at Emilie Barker as if it were obvious. "Well, he's killed her, hasn't he, to prevent her from speaking."

This was an angle Marigold had not considered. "I suppose the more conventional thought would be that he might have killed her because he was crossed in love."

"He wasn't in *love*," the professor scoffed. "How could he be—they had only just met? What could a man like him, or a child like her, know of real love, of the sacrifices and burdens that come with the elation and joy? How could he say he loved her when he didn't even *know* her?"

"I don't know," was Marigold's honest answer. "But the important question seems to be if you think Olivia was even a little bit in love with him?"

"No." Imogen Currier shook her head vehemently. "She was certainly pleased to find an attractive man who seemed to listen to her and flatter her abilities—at first, as I said. She began to see through his charm from the moment he began to pressure her. But she was not in love with him. And she did *not* mean to marry him, of that I am now sure. Or I will be if . . . if it really is her."

"But three days ago, you did believe she had eloped?"

"Because that was what *he* said. What *he* told her father! But she told me differently," Professor Currier insisted. "She told me she did not want to marry him. She told me she was going to refuse him. I had encouraged her to do so."

"Then why did you think she had changed her mind?"

"But she hadn't changed her mind, had she? And that's why she's dead." The professor was close to tears. "I should have helped her. I should have gone with her." She took the handkerchief Isabella solicitously supplied. "And I never should have been persuaded that Valentine convinced her otherwise. I should never have believed it when her father told me she had eloped with the man. I should have insisted then that she had no intention of marrying him." She began to sob even as she spoke. "And I think she told him that, Valentine, that she had no intention of marrying him. And that is why she is dead." Her voice broke into a sob.

Dr. Barker reached out a consoling hand but looked at Marigold, as if to warn her not to distress the poor woman any further.

But not distressing people, not upsetting the status quo, had got them exactly where they were. And the professor's vehement protestations after the fact seemed a little too convenient. "That would make it a crime of passion—of Valentine being thwarted in love—whereas before, you said you thought he killed her to stop her from speaking?"

Imogen Currier raised her red-rimmed eyes to Marigold's. "If he knew Olivia at all, even a little, he would know that the only way to stop her from speaking her mind would be to kill her."

Chapter 19

"They were inconveniently reasonable, these women."
Charlotte Perkins Gilman

Marigold felt an awful chill, as if she were back in the lake. The words were frightening to hear but ought not be surprising. After all, she had seen with her own eyes the violence done to Olivia Thayer.

And other women.

Still, the clammy discomfort crawling across her skin was personal. The threat to any woman of education or opinion was overt—men so often stopped women from speaking with violence.

But there was something else tickling at the back of Marigold's brain. "You said this Valentine character began to pressure Olivia—pressure her to do what?"

"Go with him, be with him, to the exclusion of all else." Professor Currier spoke with some heat. "Perhaps he was also pressuring her to be physically intimate with him." She closed her eyes again in that gesture of distaste. "She did not say that exactly, only that he had begun to make her uncomfortable and dissatisfied with his demands."

"Did you let her know that you disapproved of Mr. Valentine?" Isabella asked more pointedly.

"I told her I distrusted him," Professor Currier answered. "But I wanted her to make up her own mind. In this day and age, it is one of the few choices left to young women—who they will love. Or not love. I wanted her to choose for her own self, with no pressure from me. I chose that word purposefully, pressure, so she might have a reasonable, intelligent comparison with Wilkie's approach."

The use of the familiar first name caught Marigold's ear. "Wilkie? Did you know him well enough to use his first name?"

"No, not really." The professor turned her head away again, gazing out the window before she shut her eyes, as if she were trying to blot the man from her memory. "That was how Olivia referred to him."

"Had the Thayers met Mr. Valentine?" Isabella kept asking astute questions. "What was their reaction to this young man they didn't know suddenly wooing their daughter?"

"They were cautious, I suppose," Professor Currier said. "I really don't know how much she told them. But I don't think they ever met him in person. I think that Valentine simply importuned her, especially when Olivia was on foot, going between the high school and our Wellesley College campus. I can imagine him loitering about, almost lying in wait for her to come by."

Marigold made a mental note to ask the protective lodge keepers, Mr. and Mrs. Breyer, if they had seen this Valentine fellow "lying in wait" for the young aspiring collegian. Or at least warn them—even if it were too late to protect Olivia Thayer, it was not too late to protect the hundreds of other young women who shared Olivia Thayer's educational values and ambitions.

And innate vulnerabilities.

But the carriage was being reined to a stop outside an official-looking municipal building in the center of Dedham. Thankfully, there was little traffic to impede them, as it was Saturday and the court was not in session. As it was, Professor Currier was clearly very anxious about the ordeal to come, gripping her handkerchief tightly in her gloved hand.

Was it guilt, or simple fear?

Compassion urged her to assume it was the latter, until proven otherwise. "Why don't I go in first, to ascertain the correct place to enter," Marigold volunteered as the groom opened the door and let down the steps. "And once I know that, we'll all go together. We'll be with you the whole time, ma'am. You needn't fear you'll be alone. I've already seen her, that day at the lake. And Dr. Barker as well."

"Yes, of course." Professor Currier sniffed her gratitude into her handkerchief. "How terrible for you two."

"It was terrible," Marigold admitted. "Mostly because I felt so frustrated that there was nothing I could do to save her."

"Was she—did she look . . . terrible?"

"No, ma'am," Marigold lied quickly, before Dr. Barker might interpose with facts. "She looked very serene. Quite beyond pain or suffering." She glanced at the groom waiting patiently. "I'll be back as soon as possible."

Marigold ascended the long, sloping front steps to the Norfolk County Courthouse, and immediately found herself under the notice of two uniformed bailiffs who loitered in the foyer with no other seeming employment than to amuse themselves with unaccompanied young women.

"All alone, miss?" one miscreant asked, with what Marigold was sure he thought was solicitous charm.

But Marigold was in no mood for either charm or loiterers. "I seek the coroner's office."

"The dead body office?" was his joking rejoinder. "Why not stay here where we are all alive and well?"

Despite several easy ripostes that came readily to her lips, Marigold was, for the sake of expediency, tempted to say nothing, serving only to let her coldest, most reptilian hint of a smile speak for her. But the events that had brought her to this moment—the missteps and frustrations that brought them to this place—prompted her to speak. "It remains damnable how easily the sight of an independent woman brings out the littleness in so many men."

She ought to have left it at that, but something about the trials of the day—the trial of what was to come, the sheer unnecessary, futile unfairness of it all—goaded her on. "Is it impossible for a man to simply let a woman go about her business without his confounded interference? Are you not capable of any form of self-restraint? Must you always, always, always make yourself, if not a mere nuisance, then a threat?" She advanced upon them with each word. "Are you incapable of simply shutting up?"

She did not wait for their response but turned on her heel and noisily—so she might not hear their no-doubt ribald response—stomped away to seek out the lone female clerk lodged in the corner behind a wide oaken desk. "I seek the coroner's office in order to identify a body, if you please."

The woman's gaze flicked between Marigold and what had happened behind her. "I am sorry," she said before she supplied the information. "You'll want to go back out and go downstairs, basement level. Entrance round on the Ames Street side. Dr. Prescott should be on duty today. He'll help you."

"Thank you." Marigold strode back to the entrance, wishing she had the foresight to bring her steel-shanked umbrella as a precaution against importuning men—today she felt wicked enough to do someone a deliberate violence.

But petty vengeance was not why they had come—justice was.

The coroner's office was entered from an unmarked side door on the west side of the building, next to a carriage drive and stable gate where hearses presumably came and went.

Marigold retraced her steps and directed Isabella's coachman to drive around to the appropriate entrance before she assisted the other women from the carriage.

Dr. Barker paused at the threshold. "I do want to prepare you that the place might seem sterile and cold and uncomforting," she told Professor Currier, "but Olivia feels none of that now. It is only our feelings that pain us, not hers."

"Yes, yes, I will remember that." Professor Currier gripped the doctor's hand. "Thank you for that small mercy."

"I'll wait for you here," Isabella said quickly, "And stay out of the way. And have things ready for your return." She gestured to the hamper stored under her feet.

"Thank you," Marigold said as she handed Professor Currier to the pavement.

"One always prays for courage," the woman said quietly. "But one never likes it when God presents one with the opportunity to show one has it."

Were those the words of a murderer? Or a grieving lover?

"No," Marigold decided. "One never likes it." She clasped the professor's hand and tucked it under her own, hoping against hope her compassion was not misplaced. "But we are all glad to have it all the same."

Inside, a darkened vestibule gave way to a long, creaking pine hallway that ended at a desk. "Dr. Emilie Barker, Professor Imogen Currier, and Miss Marigold Manners to identify the body of the young woman who was found in Lake Waban this past week."

"Ah, yes, the lady doctor?" The round-faced clerk in the short white smock smiled with casual, everyday impudence. "Brought more of yourselves, so I see."

Marigold instantly recognized the corpulent fellow from their meeting outside the Hospital Wing when he had come to collect the body. "So you see."

"Marigold," Dr. Barker cautioned quietly.

Marigold curbed her ire against insolent, insignificant men—for her colleague's benefit, not the clerk's.

"Well, sign here, and initial here." The clerk was efficient, if nothing else. "Both of you. All of you? Well, then, sign here and here too."

"We were told to ask for Dr. Prescott," Marigold said.

"Were you?"

"Yes." It remained damnable how easily the sight of more than one independent woman brought out more than littleness in so many men. The clerk's good opinion hardly mattered, but on such a day, with such a task before them, the casual cruelty of his assumed superiority—and indifference—ate at Marigold like acid.

Clearly Dr. Barker was thinking along the same lines. "Marigold," she murmured again in warning. "As long as the coroner himself has followed the facts and physical evidence that presented itself, justice will be served."

"I can only hope so," Marigold huffed.

"We do not need to simply hope," Dr. Barker told her calmly. "We will *insist* upon the truth. *I* will insist."

"Naturally." Marigold felt herself relax out of her belligerent posture. "Thank you for that reminder."

The official register signed, they were ushered to the end of the hallway and told to wait until the coroner would be ready to see them. Marigold looked about for some place of repose, but no benches or seats—other than the one the commodiously sized clerk had occupied—were available.

Poor Professor Currier valiantly tried to hide her distress, but clearly the ordeal was already taking its toll. And so rather than let the woman collapse to the floor, Marigold decided upon logical expediency. She followed the clerk through the swinging doors to find him, and now a second attendant she recognized as the younger of the two men who came to the college, engaged in a pleasurable smoke before they stirred themselves to the business at hand.

"Excuse me, please, but—"

"You're supposed to wait," the older clerk protested.

"You were supposed to inform the coroner that we were here," Marigold countered.

"You've got some nerve," he sniped.

"I have," she answered with her crocodile smile. She was quite done with putting up with mediocre men. "We are ready to proceed," Marigold informed them, moving purposely to the table where the subject of their visit lay, easily recognizable by her Titian hair peeking out from underneath the enveloping white sheet.

The clerk immediately disappeared through another set of swinging doors and returned with a serious-looking young doctor—identified as such by his long white coat over his pressed shirtfront and tie.

"I am sorry to have kept you ladies waiting." He adjusted his spectacles. "My apologies. We don't usually get women on their own here."

"Do you not?" Dr. Barker seemed to have absorbed some of Marigold's mood. "Because here we are."

The young doctor, who was perhaps not used to sarcasm, and so did not recognize it, continued earnestly. "I expect most women would find it distressful in the extreme to identify—"

"Nonsense. *I* expect," Dr. Barker continued with only slightly less patience, "you will not have yet recognized that my name and signature were the ones at the bottom of the preliminary report made at the scene of death. Dr. Emilie Barker, how do you do. I am the resident physician at Wellesley College, responsible for the health and welfare of over seven hundred young women under my care. I performed the preliminary examination of the body on the day this young woman was discovered in Lake Waban." She put out her hand as an equal—if not superior. "And you are?"

"Dr. Wallace Prescott. I am very pleased to meet you, ma'am." He shook her hand with alacrity. "I should have realized. Your reputation precedes you, Dr. Barker."

"Thank you, Dr. Prescott. May I introduce you to Professor Imogen Currier and Miss Marigold Manners." She indicated them in turn. "And now that introductions are complete, let us get on with the identification, if you please." She paused, as she had in the carriage, to address her colleague. "Dr. Prescott is going to turn back the cover over her in a moment, Imogen, but I want you to remember what Marigold said earlier—she is beyond care and beyond pain."

"Yes." Professor Currier nodded her understanding. "Thank you."

Dr. Barker signaled to young Dr. Prescott, who very methodically drew back the cover to reveal the face that had hung like a painting in the walls of Marigold's memory.

"This is the girl I pulled out of Lake Waban," she said.

Professor Currier drew her handkerchief to cover her mouth.

"I am sorry this is distressing for you, ladies," the coroner began, before a pointed look from Dr. Barker caused him to switch his approach. "Do you recognize anything that might—"

"Yes. Yes, I recognize her." Professor Currier stiffened her spine and lowered her handkerchief. "She is Miss Olivia Thayer, daughter of the Reverend and Mrs. Thayer of Wellesley. They live—she lived in Wellesley. The town, not the college," Professor Currier clarified. "Blossom Street. She was seventeen years old."

"You are sure," the coroner asked as he carefully took that information down, "beyond any reasonable doubt?"

Professor Currier swallowed again before she spoke carefully. "I am."

The coroner pulled the sheet back up over the body. "Thank you for coming in."

If the coroner was done with them, Dr. Barker was not done with him. "Official cause of death, doctor?"

The coroner nodded but frowned, glancing at Professor Currier. "Perhaps, Dr. Barker, you and I might meet privately to discuss the findings of the autops—"

"No, please." Professor Currier rallied again. "I think it would behoove us all to hear the facts—the unvarnished truth, doctor."

Marigold could only agree with her—enough time and energy had been wasted on discretion. "Perhaps a chair?"

"Yes, certainly, please come into my office." Dr. Prescott led them to a small, functional room with a utilitarian desk, two straight-backed chairs and a solid wall of oaken filing cabinets. "Please make yourselves comfortable," he said even as his apologetic tone recognized the futility of the offer.

"I'll stand," Marigold volunteered, as the two older women took their uncomfortable places.

"Now, as to your question—" Dr. Prescott consulted his findings. "Although it was difficult to ascertain, due to prolonged exposure to the cold water, which we estimate to have been approximately twenty hours, the time of death has been established as seven PM on Sunday, October seventh."

The very day Marigold had arrived at College Hall. The evening she had been rejoicing that she had found her way back to her sanctuary of learning.

The college had proved no sanctuary for Olivia Thayer.

"Cause of death?" Dr. Barker asked succinctly.

The corner swallowed. "I was asked for discretion regarding . . ."

"Perhaps with the public, Dr. Prescott. And certainly, with the press. But I hope you will understand that whatever you choose to release to the press or the public, I have all the information from my preliminary report to take into account in my very real responsibility for the welfare of over seven hundred young persons under my care." Dr. Barker's patience was deep but not unlimited.

"Yes, ma'am."

"Doctor," she corrected without rancor. "And you understand that sharing your findings with the investigating authorities will be critical to the prosecution of whoever murdered this girl, do you not? And will also help prevent other girls, similar to this unfortunate one, from sharing a similar fate at the same hands?"

"Oh, I see. Yes, doctor. It was strangulation." Dr. Prescott swallowed around the word before he clarified. "Manual strangulation, that is, by hand, not a garrote or ligature."

"And was her hyoid bone fractured?" Dr. Barker pressed.

Dr. Prescott hesitated, frowning down at his paperwork before glancing at Professor Currier as if to ascertain her state of mind before he answered.

Dr. Barker helped him along. "I observed the livid bruising and scratches on the neck signifying strangulation, as well as petechiae in and around the eyes. But I could not confirm whether the young woman's hyoid bone was fractured, which is the typical result in a good three quarters of all strangulation cases. And consistent with a much larger, stronger individual performing the strangulation. So I hope that your postmortem examination has made a definitive finding?"

"Yes, ma'am."

"Doctor." Dr. Barker's voice would brook no further disrespect, even if it was clearly unintentional. "So was her hyoid bone crushed or was it not?"

The young doctor seemed to overcome—or discover—his scruples. "Yes, Dr. Barker, it was."

"And the size of the hand marks, doctor?"

"The extant bruises, as you so keenly observed, are consistent with a male perpetrator. That is," he began to clarify for Marigold and Professor Currier's benefit, "the size suggests the crime was done by a male of slightly over-average size. Or perhaps an extraordinarily large-sized, strong woman."

Which quite definitively was not Professor Currier—the tiny, nearly fragile professor seemed physically incapable of something requiring such strength. As it was, she could barely sit—she slumped back in her chair in obvious distress.

Marigold's mind ran back to tall, conveniently athletic Sarah Appleton, with her strong rower's hands and penchant for picking fights and holding grudges. Was she of "over-average size"?

"And the other bruises, on both wrists," Dr. Prescott went on, "suggest forced constraint, which, along with the evidence of tearing on the victim's clothing, suggests a physical struggle. But I did find something more—one distinguishing mark," Dr. Prescott added. "A darker contusion occurring on the left side of the victim's neck, observed as part of the fourth finger of the handprint. I would put this down to a large ring—I am thinking a man's signet ring—worn on the fourth finger."

And that put paid to elegant Sarah Appleton with her long, articulate, decidedly ring-less fingers. Not that Marigold had ever had any real evidence against the girl. Despite her own instruction not to let her personal antipathy for her distant cousin color her thinking, Marigold had done just that.

Clearly, it was time to stop thinking about the rivalries of women and place the blame squarely on men. Where it perhaps should have been along.

CHAPTER 20

"Fame is a vapor, popularity an accident, and riches take wings. Only one thing endures and that is character."

Horace Greeley

Marigold turned the full focus of her suspicions on the would-be suitor, Valentine.

If only Professor Currier and her friends the Thayers had believed what Olivia said about Valentine instead of what Valentine said about her.

"There." Dr. Barker was bringing their meeting to a conclusion. "We have our information. And you have yours. Thank you. We are much obliged. I should like a copy of the formal report for my files, if you please, Dr. Prescott." Emilie Barker was nothing if not polite, though her tone said she would have the report even if he didn't please.

"If I might ask one more question, doctor?" Marigold asked.

"Certainly," Dr. Prescott said.

Marigold phrased the question that had remained unanswered since their first interview with the town watchmen as delicately as she could. "Given the evidence that you have shared, combined with the circumstances in which we found Miss Thayer's body, I feel compelled to ask—was she by any chance with child?"

"No," he answered quietly but immediately, though his face colored hotly. "The subject was found virgo intacta."

"Thank God," Professor Currier whispered. "She was spared at least that indignity."

"Indeed, yes. Thank you, Dr. Prescott." Dr. Barker extended her hand a final time. "Good day."

They made their way back to the carriage with Professor Currier leaning heavily on Marigold's arm. While they had been inside, Isabella had not been idle—as soon as the three Wellesley women returned to the carriage, she was pressing glasses of sherry into their hands. "I thought we might need something warming and fortifying."

"Naturally. Thank you for your foresight, Isabella." Marigold accepted the drink gratefully.

"Oh, yes. Thank you." Despite her ordeal Professor Currier was still in full possession of her manners. "You have no idea how welcome this is." She took a sip and then promptly burst into tears.

Isabella reached for the professor's hand in a gesture of comfort, even while she sent a fond little smile Marigold's way, for Marigold had often said the very same words to her dear friend, who always seemed to know when comfort was needed. "I am happy to give what small comfort I can."

To do so, Isabella began to raise the window shade to give them greater privacy, but her instant expression of reproof as she glanced outside, made Marigold crane her neck to see a familiar figure—the journalist James Wilkerson striding past on the pavement, bound, she assumed, for the same place they had just been.

Marigold's first instinct was to hope that Dr. Prescott would remember his pledge of discretion when it came to the press. But her second was that the time for discretion and obfuscation were well and truly past. It would be good for Wilkerson, and by extension the *Boston Evening Journal* to learn the very real and very brutal facts of Olivia Thayer's death. Then they might at last print something truthful in their otherwise shoddy newspaper.

Marigold had been vigilant in canvassing the tabloids, but she had failed to find her plea to the public seeking the identity of the young women amongst them. It was something of a blow to Marigold's considerable pride that she had so clearly failed to sway Mr. Wilkerson in any way.

She must be slipping.

But despite her personal failings, some small progress, if she could call it that, had been made—Olivia Thayer had been identified, and her family and friends could mourn her, bury her in peace, and seek justice on her behalf.

She would not be one of the girls who were forgotten.

⋆ ⋆ ⋆

Marigold awoke the next morning with a strange feeling of flatness. If she had hoped that the identification of Olivia Thayer might lead to a sense of relief, she was mistaken. Instead, she felt a strange listlessness that wore on as she went through the motions of checking her experiments and preparing her homework for the week ahead. And that would never do.

She attempted to reorder her brain by tidying up her dormitory room, but as she was habitually neat, there was little work to satisfy. It had now been a full week since Olivia Thayer had been murdered, and Marigold had little to show for her efforts besides the identification of the poor girl.

And so she took to her bicycle. The physical exertion of pedaling never failed to lift her spirits and clarify her thoughts. If she had been able to identify Olivia Thayer, then she ought to be able to identify this Valentine fellow.

The last thing anyone had heard from the young man was the telegram he sent to the Thayer family, telling them that Olivia and he had eloped. In this modern world, surely there would be a record of what office the wire had been sent from? And perhaps the clerk at that office might remember something about the man?

But first, she needed to do what she ought to have done the moment she suspected the dead girl was Olivia Thayer—speak to her parents. Yet as she approached their house on Blossom Street, it was clear that a quiet chat was not in the offing—carriages of all sizes and shapes were parked under every available tree, and as she approached the front door, she saw a man taking down the knocker to drape the doorway in the black crepe of mourning.

"Excuse me, sir," she approached him. "I would like to speak to Mr. Thayer."

"Receiving condolence calls inside," the fellow gestured for her to simply proceed through the door and into the crowded house.

Marigold checked to make sure that her sporty charcoal-gray tweed ensemble and black straw boater hat was presentable—one might alter one's standards for a bicycle ride, but mourning required a different set of customs and protocols.

But she needn't have worried that she might stand out—she was only one amongst many paying condolence calls. Clearly, the Thayer family was both well respected and well liked in the neighborhood. Within a few minutes of entering, Marigold had learned that the iceman's information had been correct—gray-haired Reverend Mr. Thayer was a former Unitarian minister, who had taught at Harvard before retiring to his family's home in Wellesley. Likewise, his white-haired wife was a prominent Transcendentalist thinker and writer who had published extensively on theological and philosophical matters while raising their only child.

Other than the chill temperature—the fires were not lit—the house seemed to Marigold as if it were designed with nothing but her own happiness in mind. Every wall seemed to be filled with a bookshelf, every window housed a comfortable chair positioned to take best advantage of the light for reading. The place was a temple to the power of the written word and the value of a lifetime of education.

No wonder Olivia had excelled at a young age. And no wonder Professor Currier had felt herself amongst friends.

Marigold found herself joining an informal line of people waiting to speak to Olivia's parents, who were seated in wing-backed armchairs on either side of the cold parlor hearth. Imogen Currier was seated close by Mrs. Thayer, who very often held or touched the professor's hand for comfort. Both women appeared diminished and fragile—Mrs. Thayer's skin seemed nearly translucent, as if it had been worn away by her grief.

Olivia Thayer had been dead a week—old news to Marigold, but fresh grief to everyone gathered in the Thayers' household.

"My condolences, Reverend Thayer," she began when it was her turn to step forward and take the man's outstretched hand.

"Thank you, thank you. Alas." He patted her hand consolingly before he asked, "And who are you, my dear?"

"I was an admirer of your daughter's rhetorical excellence. My name is Marigold Manners, and I am a student at Wellesley College, where we had so been looking forward to hearing your daughter speak."

"Yes, yes, of course. Such an unimaginable loss to the cause as well as to us, her poor family. We are all the poorer." The man shook his head sadly before he seemed to come to a realization. "Miss Manners? At the college? My dear girl, don't tell me you are the one who found her? Who brought her out?"

Around them, the low murmur of conversation came to an abrupt halt.

"Was it you?"

Marigold hesitated—one never wanted to make too much of oneself. But in such a circumstance, she had nothing but the bare truth. "Yes, sir, I am afraid it was."

"My dear girl." The man rose and embraced her stiffly but with great emotion. "Come and sit with us." He moved so she might take the seat he had just vacated but held on to her hand almost tenaciously. "We are deeply indebted to you for all you have done. Our dear Professor Currier has spoken warmly of your physical and moral courage, and your compassion and determination in bringing our Olivia back to us, and for that we are most profoundly grateful."

Marigold hardly knew what to say to such effusive praise. For a moment she was nearly overwhelmed with feeling—this was the sort of approbation she would have given almost anything to hear from her own father. To be held in such esteem had been a guiding principle by which she had fashioned her life in order to give herself purpose and direction.

And to hear such words from a relative stranger—her heart ached anew for their loss.

And her conscience chided her for ever having suspected Professor Currier. "I am glad I could be of any help, sir," she managed. "Although I am deeply sorry for the occasion."

"Yes, of course," he nodded and patted her hand again. "You are very kind. And our dear friend the professor has also told us that you are just the sort of scholar our Olivia would have aspired to be. Just the sort of intellectually strong and morally secure person we would have wanted her to become."

"You are too kind," Marigold answered. "And though I never met Olivia in person, let me say on behalf of the entire student body of Wellesley College, how much we were looking forward to hearing her speak and being inspired by her extraordinary gift for oration. Clearly, she was well on the way to being the sort of person we *all* would admire."

"Bless you. Indeed. True, true." The gentleman shook his head as if this might ward off the tears that were brimming in his eyes. "Come, come, we must do something for her, mustn't we, Mother?" He addressed his wife. "Some token to show our thanks."

"Oh, yes," his wife agreed solemnly. "Perhaps one of Olivia's books? Dear Imogen has told us you are a scholar of the Greeks—I recall there is a particularly nice edition of Thucydides on Olivia's shelves that you might like."

Marigold had to work to control her own nascent emotions with the thought that she could not imagine her own sweet mother, Esmé, even knowing the name Thucydides, or any Greek philosopher or historian for that matter.

What a gift for Olivia Thayer to have been raised by such people. At one time in her young life, Marigold might have thought she would do anything to have such parents. Mr. Thayer, especially, was so perfectly the ideal father of her daydreams—educated and thoughtful.

But now she hoped she knew better. Even if Harry Manners had not been a scholar, he had given Marigold many gifts of character—not the least of which was the gift for taking a chance at the right time.

She glanced briefly at Professor Currier, who seemed to give her a sort of smile of encouragement, before she answered. "You are very kind, ma'am." She nodded respectfully to Mrs. Thayer. "But I will admit to wanting something different."

Mrs. Thayer raised her thin white eyebrows in silent question.

Marigold gave way to a small embellishment. "As Professor Currier is aware, I am making inquiries on behalf of President Irvine of the college, who feels that the Wellesley authorities"—such a woefully inadequate word, authorities, when they seemed to exert no authority whatsoever—"might need some assistance from those to whom Olivia's death matters most—her fellow suffragists."

This brought a different sort of regard from the Thayers, who looked at her with less grief and more interest. "Yes?"

"Do you still have the telegram you received from this Valentine fellow?"

It was as if a cloud had passed over his eyes, so profoundly did Mr. Thayer's entire countenance change. "That . . . black-hearted, vacuous, unctuous, insinuating viper!" He all but vibrated with his rage and grief. "I rue the day he darkened our door."

"And which day was that?" Marigold asked carefully. "How long had this Valentine known Olivia?"

Mrs. Thayer was the one who answered. "I believe my husband is speaking metaphorically, for the young man never did have the courtesy or the good manners to come to our door. No, he snuck around, making trouble and making himself a nuisance trying to turn poor Olivia's head behind our backs, away from the better influence of those who loved her best. We dismissed him, of course—never thinking that it would come to anything in the least. But he was dangerously persistent. We should have done more to drive him away, but Olivia said she wanted to deal with him herself. That it was the only morally correct thing to do."

Marigold agreed with their assessment of the unseen Mr. Valentine. "That seems entirely in keeping with his low character. So, you never worried he was going to succeed in turning Olivia's head?"

"No." Her mother's negation was plaintive. "She said she thought him a nuisance and his words and blandishments as empty as his understanding. Those were her words."

"He made her uncomfortable, she said," Professor Currier added vehemently. "She found it all so embarrassing, his attention."

"Which is why we were so shocked . . ." Mrs. Thayer turned away, burying her face in her handkerchief.

Marigold looked to Professor Currier, who had taken up Mrs. Thayer's hand, to also take up the tale. "So shocked . . . ?"

"So shocked that she would reverse course and go with him—elope to Europe the way the telegram said," Professor Currier finished, shaking her head. "We should have known Olivia never would have done such a thing—she wouldn't have ever thought it."

"But you accepted the contents of the telegram as fact?" Marigold probed. "Even as you pursued them to the docks?"

"We felt she had been coerced and only needed the support of her family to turn him away. But we were told the ship had already sailed. We were too late."

The three—Mr. Thayer, Mrs. Thayer and Professor Currier—exchanged what Marigold could only characterize as agonized looks. "And then, much to our shame—" Mr. Thayer began.

"And to our loss—" his wife added.

"—we thought of the scandal. Of the waste. Of ourselves," Mr. Thayer explained.

"But not of Olivia," Mrs. Thayer finished with an anguished sigh. "We should have thought of Olivia. And how such a thing was entirely out of character."

"Please don't think you might have prevented what happened," Marigold said, with feeling. "I am convinced that Olivia was already dead when that telegram was sent."

The news was not taken as the help Marigold had intended—her pronouncement was met with gasps from some, and fresh tears from the Thayers.

"I do apologize for my clumsiness," she managed. "All I meant was that you should not reproach yourselves. If it weren't a plausible lie, Valentine never would have gotten away with it. So, as to my first question—do you still have the telegram?"

"What good would it do to read it again?" asked Professor Currier.

"I don't know," Marigold said honestly, "other than the fact that I hope to glean some factual information from it—such as the office that he sent it from. With that knowledge, the clerk might be interviewed—they might remember some pertinent information that might help us locate Mr. Valentine."

"Surely he is across the sea on his ship—beyond the reach of the law?"

"Perhaps," Marigold allowed. "But as I understand it, that ship was to have sailed the night Olivia was murdered."

Mrs. Thayer flinched, as if in physical pain inflicted by the word *murder.*

"I am sorry," Marigold apologized again. "But there is no way to sanitize what was done to her—she was strangled. And Valentine had the strongest potential motive to kill her. But he could not be on a White Star liner out of Boston at the same time that he was in Wellesley, strangling Olivia and pushing her—" Another glance at Mrs. Thayer's pained, tearful expression moved Marigold to greater prudence in her speech. "He could not be in two places at once. It is impossible."

Mr. Thayer stared at her for what felt like a full minute before he walked away into another room, from whence he finally reappeared, holding the familiar waxy brown envelope of a telegram.

"Take it," he said to Marigold. "Take it and see if you can extract some justice from it. But I fear my sorrow will find no end, no matter what—no revenge will bring Olivia back."

"No," Marigold agreed. "But it will stop him from being able to do this to another young woman ever again. And if that is revenge, so be it."

Perhaps the first murders she had been involved with had made her personally conversant with how much wickedness was in the world. But this murder—this waste of an important life—made her feel so wicked, she was ready to exact that revenge herself.

Chapter 21

"There is nothing so powerful as truth—and often nothing so strange."

Daniel Webster

Marigold had what she had come for—the telegram, with its limited information to pass to Cab to decode. She had just reached her bicycle and was about to mount when a voice stopped her.

"Marigold! Miss Manners." It was Professor Currier, tying the tapes to her bonnet and cape as she came through the door. "I hoped I could catch you. Are you heading back to campus? I feel I want the noisy companionship of my students at dinner this evening. As much as I share my sister's grief, I feel as if I must—"

Marigold heard something she had not before. "Your sister?" she asked to be very clear, as sisterhood was a concept with a vast reach at Wellesley that had little to do with family trees.

"Yes, my older sister, Almira. Almira Currier Thayer. I thought everyone knew," she said at Marigold's rather too-obvious frown. "Almira, Imogen, and Lucinda, the Currier girls from Newton. Olivia is my niece, so it was no surprise to me when she excelled at rhetoric."

"You never said she was your niece," Marigold exclaimed. "When you were telling President Irvine about how you feared the dead girl might have been Olivia, you never said she was your niece."

"Didn't I?"

"No." Marigold was sure she would have remembered such an important piece of information—it would have saved her from a number of incorrect, unsavory conjectures. "You said she was the daughter of dear friends. You said she was your protégée, nothing more."

Color rose across the professor's pale cheeks. "I must apologize. But I suppose I made a habit of keeping the connection quiet for Olivia's sake, so her work might rest upon its own considerable merit. I didn't want people to think that the only reason I took Olivia on was because she was related to me." Professor Currier seemed to belatedly catch the accusation in Marigold's tone. "But I never lied about it intentionally, with an object to deceive. The people who mattered knew."

"The people trying to solve her murder didn't know."

"Well, it hardly matters now," the professor said.

But the exercise of having to explain herself seemed to wear out the professor's thin store of strength—she wavered a bit, unsteady on her feet.

Marigold instantly dropped her bicycle and took her arm. "Professor?"

"Yes, thank you. I fear I've overdrawn my strength." She drew in a steadying breath. "I had wanted to thank you for your kind words, in the house, but find I am weary body and soul. Would you mind terribly walking me home? It's just down Washington Street."

"Certainly, ma'am." She would come back for her bicycle later.

Professor Currier leaned heavily on Marigold's support as they made their slow way back down the street, pausing when the professor said, "Let me just catch my breath." She sat heavily on a stone wall. "That Wilkie Valentine has certainly caused a great deal of ungodly harm."

"Wilkie Valentine?" Something about the name sounded familiar—perhaps the similarity to the infamous actor John Wilkes Booth, whose name was, even after nearly thirty years, still synonymous with "traitor." Certainly, the feeling of betrayal—of goodness and right, and the cause of women's suffrage, and of Olivia herself—left a sour taste in Marigold's mouth.

Thankfully, the ever-vigilant Mrs. Barnacle was at the front door to usher them in. "Oh, Imogen," she fussed. "You've overdrawn yourself. Come rest in the parlor for a spell before you go up. I'll have Miss Dove bring you something bracing. Lucy!" she called. "Professor Currier is in need of a restorative."

"No, no," Imogen Currier insisted. "I just need my nerve pills. For my heart, really, not my nerves," she explained to Marigold, "though that's what the doctor calls them, the pills. I'll just rest a bit before I go up to take them."

Lucy had come at Mrs. Barnacle's call. "I've got just the thing for you, ma'am—a good bone broth of my own recipe. I'll have it to you in no time. You just rest easy."

"Yes, I think I will," Professor Currier said. "Just for a minute."

"Thank you, Lucy." Marigold added her own thanks that Lucy was "on the inside," as much to care for the poor woman as to give Marigold information—information that was no longer necessary.

There was nothing untoward about an aunt being worried for a beloved niece. There was nothing tawdry about her having a photo of a relation. There was nothing out of character in a college professor wanting that young woman to excel in her chosen field.

The professor's interest was, contrary to Marigold's first impression, entirely innocent.

It was no wonder the woman was, quite literally, sick with grief. Grief that Marigold had done little to allay, when she ought to have known better. She ought to have recognized that the strange admixture of great sadness, anger, guilt, and despair was as unpredictable as it was powerful.

Her own grief for her parents' deaths had been muted at first—they had been estranged due to her choice to become a New Woman and her devotion to her education. But it had compounded over time—each new revelation at Great Misery Island had made her feel their loss anew.

So it must be for Professor Currier, who had not only lost a beloved niece, and who had to suffer her sister's grief, but also had to weather the professional loss of a prized student and protégée. Not to mention the philosophical blow to universal suffrage, a cause particularly dear to her. It had been a series of hardships, indeed.

Marigold could only hope that the worst was over—the poor woman didn't look as if she could stand another blow.

★ ★ ★

"Miss Burke?" Marigold stopped at the reception room on her way back into College Hall. She had collected her bicycle along with her aplomb and decided decisive action was necessary. "Might I be able to use the telephone? I am more than willing to pay for its use, if need be. I have some information regarding the murder of Miss Thayer that I need to share with a colleague in Boston."

"Yes, of course. Do come in." Miss Burke immediately ushered Marigold back into her inner sanctum. "Normally, students are not allowed the privilege, except in emergencies, you understand. But Miss Thayer was a particular favorite."

"Thank you, ma'am. I greatly appreciate your help." Marigold was mindful of both the privilege and the responsibility. "I'll need to ring up the Boston exchange again, if you please."

"Do you remember how to do it?"

"I think so," Marigold answered. "I crank the cylinder here?"

"That's it," Miss Burke encouraged. "Go ahead."

Marigold stooped down and cranked the cylinder to ring into the exchange. "Boston, please."

"Boston exchange for Wellesley College," came the disembodied rejoinder. "One moment for Boston."

A series of static clips and plugs indicated the various connections the switchboard operator made. "Boston exchange. Your party?"

"Armory, Dana, and Cox law offices, State Street."

Another series of static and electrical noises preceded a posh clerk's pronouncement of "Wellesley College? Armory, Dana, and Cox. Your party, please?"

"Mr. Cox, please. Mr. Jonathon Cabot Cox," Marigold added in case there were multiple cousins or uncles in the family firm.

"And whom shall I say is calling?"

"Miss Marigold Manners."

"Oh! Miss Manners. One moment, ma'am."

Marigold didn't know whether to be excited or diminished in being recognized at Cab's place of business. But she did not have long to contemplate, because in no time at all Cab was on the line. "Marigold, is that you?"

"Yes!" She shouted her answer into the speaking horn. "I'm sorry to tell you that I have new information that may throw my former request into disarray."

"How's that?"

"The dead young woman has been identified as Olivia Thayer."

"So you were right—your instinct was correct," came Cab's reply.

"I wish I weren't." One never wanted to make too much of oneself—especially when one was shouting one's private thoughts into a machine attached to a wall. "But I've got the wire Wilkie Valentine—that's his name, Valentine—sent to the Thayers regarding their supposed elopement, and although it contains no new information in the text, it does tell us the elopement was fabricated out of whole cloth."

"How so?" Cab's muffled shout came back.

"The date, for one—it was sent on the Monday morning, and the autopsy results said that Olivia Thayer had been dead since about seven the night before. So the whole of the wire was a lie, designed to throw the Thayers off the truth and delay her identification."

Cab made a filthy noise that Marigold interpreted as a curse word.

"Indeed. But there are also some other miscellanea on the telegram that I hoped might be of use in deciphering more of the truth. Do you think you might be able to help me with that?"

"Absolutely," was Cab's immediate answer. "Fire away."

"It's a Western Union Telegraph. And there are three little boxes with coded information, I think—Number, Sent By, and Received By, which are SN, then JW, and a sort of a swoopy sign. At the very top box it says '15 Paid.'"

"The sender paid for fifteen words, which is standard."

"I see. Then on the left side it says, 'Received, 7:57 AM So. Natick' and opposite, on the right side, it is dated October eighth."

"Which means he sent it from South Natick—that's the SN, and the clerk will be the JW—at nearly eight o'clock in the morning, well after the RMS *Utopia* sailed from the Boston docks. So our checking of the passenger lists wasn't entirely an exercise in futility."

"Lies," Marigold confirmed. "All lies."

"What else does it say? Read me the exact text."

"To Mr. Thayer, Blossom Street, Wellesley."

"No first name?"

"No." She paused. "Is that significant?"

"Perhaps?" She could all but see him shrug and run his hand through his hair in that well remembered gesture of agitation. "But I would guess it means the sender of the telegram likely didn't know Mr. Thayer's name, as you're not charged for the recipient's name and address, only the contents of the message."

"Well, that would certainly comport with what I've learned about Wilkie Valentine—he had never actually met the Thayers."

"So, they have no description of him?"

"No one seems to." If she weren't standing in front of Miss Burke, shouting into a box, she might have cursed herself. "And all the time he was sending that blasted wire, Olivia was already dead."

Cab made a sound that might have been either consolation or compassion, but the distortion of the telephone was too much to decipher. "Read me the rest, if you would."

Marigold quoted the text. "'By time you read, will have sailed Sunday for Liverpool on RMS *Utopia* on honeymoon.' Those are the fifteen words. And at the bottom it reads 'Olivia Valentine,' as if she were married when she sent it."

"When she was already dead. Damnation." Cab gave vent to his feelings.

"But I should also hope that might make this wire more memorable for the clerk—JW at the South Natick wire office—Valentine's signing a woman's name to the wire. I'll try to go there after my classes tomorrow—"

"No. Please. You leave it be, Marigold. Now that the coroner has made their findings, a Special District Police detective will be assigned to the case. I've got some connections with their office—I'll go on over and hold their feet to the fire and give them all this information so *they* can go to Natick to question the clerk."

There was something—was it something paternalistic or almost patronizing in his tone? "Cab, Natick is only the next town over." She enunciated clearly to be sure of his understanding. "I can get there and back on my bicycle in no time."

"I know, but—"

"And you know I can look out for myself."

"Of course you can," he all but shouted back. "But you've worked too hard and sacrificed too much to get back to college to let an only marginally important conversation with a wire clerk interfere with your studies now. Isabella told me you're already in hot water with your Professor Irvine—"

Isabella was an awful snitch. "She's President Irvine now."

"Then she has even more influence over your future. Please, Marigold, let me do this for you."

His appeal was too logical to dismiss out of hand. "You're right, I suppose. Police assistance wouldn't go amiss—that is, if they prove themselves sufficient to the work and don't jump to unfounded conclusions."

"They are men trained in the specific requirements of criminal detective work, I assure you," Cab promised.

"I will take your assurance but hold you to it."

It was almost as if she could feel his smile coursing through the wires. "I look forward to being held. Always."

⋆ ⋆ ⋆

Always came sooner than Marigold expected—the very next afternoon.

"Miss Manners?" Miss Burke waved her over to the reception room as if she had chocolate to share. And in a way, she did. "You have a telegram from Mr. Cox."

"Oh, thank you."

"You are fortunate in your character—or should I say *we* are fortunate," Miss Burke clarified confidentially, "that you have been so persistent in working to solve this unfortunate matter."

"Thank you, ma'am." Marigold recognized this overture from the timid woman and returned it with praise of her own. "You are very kind to help me."

"You are most welcome. I realize our dear president has discouraged your involvement in this dreadful affair, but I know how this death has hung over her like a veritable sword of Damocles. You seem to be the only one holding up a shield to protect her—and protect us all."

Marigold didn't know when she had been so truly flattered. "I will continue to do so, Miss Burke, especially with your kind assistance."

"Thank you." Pleased roses appeared in the older woman's pinched cheeks. "One tries one's best."

"You do more than try, ma'am, you succeed. I am glad Olivia Thayer was a favorite. I am sorry I never met her."

"Lovely girl. Such a tragedy. Such a loss."

"Yes," Marigold agreed. "For both the college, and for women's suffrage, and of course for her family. I made a condolence call to their house on Blossom Street and found them quite lovely. Did they ever come here with Olivia?"

"No, not that I recall. It was generally Professor Currier who either met her or accompanied her."

"Was there ever anyone else? A gentleman, perhaps?" Marigold suddenly remembered Aggie's proprietary fellow looking for a girl in a blue velvet tam. "A young man who might have hinted that he was Miss Thayer's beau? Or were there any men that Mr. Duckett or Mr. Griffin or any of the staff noticed on the grounds, or out on the golf course when they ought not have been? Anyone in the last two weeks? Anyone the porters or the lodge keepers noticed?"

"Well, I don't know about the others, but I keep a strict eye on the comings and goings here. Unescorted males are never allowed to pass freely." Miss Burke nodded fiercely. "And Miss Thayer must have told her young man that, for he did walk her to the front of the building, the one time I did see him, but he did not attempt to come in."

Marigold felt that strange tingling awareness course through her, silently urging her to action. "Her young man—what was he like?"

"I only had a glimpse of him, you understand, but very respectful," Miss Burke opined. "Very gentlemanly. He tugged his hat politely and went back out the drive." Miss Burke pointed the way. "I'm sure Mr. Duckett or others on the custodial or grounds staff kept an eye on him when he was unescorted by Olivia."

"How often?"

"Well, I only saw him that once, but I'm sure Mr. Breyer at the East Lodge has a record—"

"Yes," Marigold agreed. "I shall ask him directly."

"You do that," Miss Burke approved. And then looked at Marigold expectantly. "Miss Manners? Your telegram?"

"Oh, yes!" Marigold recalled herself to the present. "Thank you!"

She tore open the missive. "No Valentine listed White Star Line. On hunch, found Mr. & Mrs. Valentine embarked Cunard Line to Liverpool on 11th."

Valentine was still in the area until last Thursday—four days ago!

Marigold tried to logically parse out the facts. Firstly, whoever had embarked as Mrs. Valentine was not Olivia Thayer. Secondly, if Valentine had indeed embarked on the eleventh, then there might still be time to file official charges and wire to Liverpool to have him arrested before he could disembark—the transatlantic voyage now typically took only five to six days on modern, up-to-date ocean liners.

Which meant they had one or two days, at most, to find some conclusive proof linking Valentine to Olivia's murder in order to have him taken into custody.

The clock was ticking down.

Chapter 22

"This is quite a three-pipe problem."
Arthur Conan Doyle

Which meant Marigold needed to get in touch with Cab immediately. "Miss Burke, may I again trouble you to use your phone to call Mr. Cox?"

"Oh, but I thought he was meant to be here presently? Mr. Breyer just called to admit him at the lodge gate."

"Excellent." Marigold felt herself breathe for the first time since Miss Burke had shared her surprising information. And then she checked her watch, consulted her class schedule, and decided she had just enough time to change her clothing into something a tad more flattering—not that anything Isabella had made for her could possibly be unflattering, but there was a time to raise one's standards to meet the occasion.

It never hurt to look one's best.

Isabella had included all sorts of evening wear that was still packed in tissue to preserve the delicate fabrics, but Marigold passed by the elaborate tea gowns in favor of a beautiful autumnal sateen skirt and double-breasted jacket ensemble that fit her like a glove. And instead of her usual white, well pressed shirtwaist, she chose a darker, paisley-patterned blouse with a black silk tie.

Yes, something out of her usual but still precisely tailored. And the wonderful wide puffed sleeves gave her consequence—not that she lacked any, but it never hurt to be prepared where Cab Cox was involved.

Marigold didn't have to wait long—she was about to descend to the reception room when Aggie came pelting up the stairs to bring her the news. "Marigold!"

"Where you coming from in such a pother?" Ethyl asked from her doorway as the girl all but skidded to a stop in the corridor. "You're as all aflutter as a moth in a mitten!"

"I came to tell Marigold that Miss Burke has sent for her, but that awful Sarah Appleton went and made herself at home in the reception area with Marigold's beau."

"Thank you, Aggie," Marigold could only smile, even as she said, "Mr. Cox is not my beau."

"He's not?" Ethyl lifted a brow in sly skepticism. "Then how did you know it would be Mr. Cox down in the reception room being romanced by old Sarah?"

"Because Mr. Cox, who is helping me with some particulars related to Olivia Thayer's death, wired that he would be arriving. That's how I know."

"Which explains the very elegant togs. Well played, Marigold." Ethyl waggled her eyebrows in teasing approval. "Now, off you go to give Appleton a run for her terribly old money. My only comfort is that she's got her nose so high in the air she'll surely drown herself in a rainstorm someday."

Marigold kept that cheering thought in her mind as she swept down into the reception room like a bright, brisk gale. "Sarah! How kind of you to entertain Mr. Cox. I do appreciate your being so welcoming." She beamed crocodilian warmth at the girl.

While Cab immediately stepped back from Sarah to turn to greet Marigold, Sarah sidled herself closer, sliding her hand through the crook of Cab's arm. "Why, Marigold, what an unexpected surprise. Whatever are you doing here?" Sarah was all wide-eyed astonishment.

"Keeping my appointment with Mr. Cox," Marigold answered simply, keeping in mind that she needn't make a greater enemy out of someone who was merely an academic rival.

But Sarah had her own version of reptilian chill and was not to be outmaneuvered. "Why, Cab and I are such dear old friends, aren't we, Cab?"

"Sure, I suppose we are," said Cab easily. "Families have known each other for ages. And as I was saying, Miss Manners and I are dear friends, as well." And to put paid to any more unseemly pettiness between herself and Sarah, Cab very wisely, and very smoothly, turned and shook Sarah's hand. "Awfully nice to see you, Miss Appleton, but I hope you will forgive us—Miss Manners and I have some urgent business to attend to."

Sarah was not about to take her dismissal with anything like good grace. "Don't tell me—you're here on behalf of a client to whom the Manners still owe money?" Sarah asked with a maliciously bright smile. "Is that why you brought a bailiff?"

Marigold noticed for the first time a fourth party present—a upright, mustachioed young man in a blue frock coat uniform, emblazoned with the badge of the District Police.

"Not at all," Cab answered flatly. "And I would never discuss confidential client matters, in any circumstance. But allow me to introduce Detective Pratt, who has come at President Irvine's request in the delicate matter of the murder on campus."

"Murder?" Sarah said the word with the same disinterested intonation one might reserve for tenement diseases—unfortunate, but nothing to do with her.

"How do you do, Detective." Marigold offered her hand. "I am Marigold Manners, and I am the one who found Olivia Thayer's body."

"Yes, so like Marigold to concern herself with such tawdry goings-on," Sarah put in.

"Yes," Cab said pleasantly. "How very like her to concern herself with justice—especially on behalf of the college. It is something I always admire in people, that kind of altruism and sense of right. Don't you?"

Which left the poor girl with nothing to say except, "Well, I suppose I'll leave you to it."

"Thank you, Sarah," Marigold responded with all the equanimity she might spare the young woman—for whom she still had unmet suspicions. "But before you go—are you at all familiar with the Société des Belles Lettres?"

"I am the president of the association this year."

"Naturally."

"Is that all?" Sarah asked.

"For now," was all the answer Marigold was prepared to give her.

Once Sarah had made her sweeping exit—did the girl know any other kind?—Marigold turned her attention back to Cab and the blue-coated officer. "My apologies for that display of schoolgirl pettiness, gentlemen, especially when we have more important matters to attend to. Now, where were we, Detective?"

"Officer George Pratt, Miss Manners." The policeman introduced himself. "Pleased to meet you. Mr. Cox has brought me abreast of all your findings to date, and I must say, I am glad to have your assistance—and experience, so Mr. Cox has also told me. This is only my second murder case."

Marigold had decided not to count anymore. But she was pleased that the young detective seemed to be the opposite of Officer Parker in Pride's Crossing, who had done everything he could to bar her participation in the Great Misery Island murders, and whose every utterance had been a condescension.

"I am more than happy to share my information, Detective. But what news have you come to tell me?"

Cab made an unhappy face. "As I hope I made clear in my wire, there was no listing for Valentine on White Star."

"The telegram was an obvious effort to confuse," Marigold concluded.

"And confound the chase," Detective Pratt agreed. "If the Thayers were in Boston, searching the White Star dock, they could not be in Wellesley, searching for their missing daughter."

"That's another thing," Cab said. "Before I had the information that the wire actually came from South Natick, I took a chance and visited the Western Union office directly across from the Cunard docks in East Boston."

"You went all the way to East Boston on a hunch?"

"Oh, you know me," he demurred, brushing his hair off his perfect brow in a familiar gesture of chagrin. "Much like you, I don't like to do anything by halves."

"Naturally." It was one of the things she admired about Cab—his brand of well-bred intelligence seemed to come with a large share of well-camouflaged, steely determination.

"The passenger rolls show he embarked on the eleventh—and that he did not do so alone. There was a Mrs. Valentine listed as sailing as well."

"So . . ." Marigold could hardly keep up with her thoughts. "Was he already married to someone else? Was his purported proposal to Olivia entirely spurious and he never meant to marry her in the first place? Why, he certainly was an out and out rotter!"

Her fury for poor Olivia Thayer grew exponentially. But at the same time, something in her bones had told her that Olivia Thayer was a like-minded young woman to herself—that however much she might have been attracted to this Valentine fellow, she never would have been taken in by such a double-dealing bounder.

"There's more," Cab warned.

"How much more iniquity can there be?"

"A vast deal more. After I ascertained that Valentine had bought two third-class tickets for passage on the Cunard liner *Ultonia*—"

"*Utopia*? *Ultonia*? How confusing!" Marigold complained. "But do you think he chose the ships on purpose to be confusing?"

"Sailing schedules are set months in advance," Pratt answered. "Probably just coincidence."

"There are no coincidences," Marigold averred.

"And on that theory," Cab said, "I went to talk with the stevedores at the Cunard dock, to see if anyone remembered anything about Mr. and Mrs. Valentine."

"Did they?"

"Considering I had no description of him, it was a difficult thing—"

Where was Eliza Anthony and her patented detective camera when Wilkie Valentine had been escorting Olivia Thayer to the doors outside the reception room?

"—but one of the dock hands did remember Mrs. Valentine, because she, while she was out of earshot of her husband, asked nervously if there might be some difficulty with her passport, as she hadn't had time, she said, to change it to Valentine after her recent marriage."

"Recent?" Marigold's outrage soared to new heights. "Valentine was romancing two young women at once? The bounder! I hope I never get my hands on him or I, I'll—"

Murder no longer made her just see wickedness in every shadow—it made her feel as hard and wicked as a murderer herself.

"You are not alone in your feelings, Marigold," Cab added, "I assure you. But the stevedore," Cab consulted a note he pulled from his pocket, "Mr. Ames, said that the ticket he copied—so he could make sure he had the right information to stow the couple's luggage—indicated that Mr. Valentine was from Richmond, Virginia, but that his accent was all wrong. Mr. Ames said he would have recognized a southern accent since he formerly hailed from that part of the world. He said Valentine's was pure South Boston."

"What . . ." Marigold was stumped. "What does that mean?"

"That is a question I asked myself and Detective Pratt. But to be thorough, I checked—or to be more honest, I had my law clerks check, but they're bright, curious young fellows, who know their way around a records office. And they could find no record of a Valentine marriage in any of the past four weeks in either Norfolk County or the city of Boston."

"So . . . was he already married the whole time he was wooing Olivia?"

"Perhaps." Cab shrugged. "Or perhaps this ostensible Mrs. Valentine is simply a modern woman who has no interest in the social convention of marriage. Or—"

Perhaps Cab was letting his own personal experience with Marigold color his thinking. "Or . . . what?"

"Or perhaps this couple who has no marriage license, no updated passports in the name Valentine, and no indication that they were from Richmond, Virginia—Mr. Ames said she sounded as if she were from Dorchester—are just another ruse to throw us off the chase."

"Damnation," was all Marigold could think to say in the face of so many lies. A strange unease crept back under her skin—probably just the idea that Valentine might have done *all* of those confusing things and *still* be on a ship somewhere escaping justice. "But if we don't treat his embarkation as a fact, then we have absolutely no hope of having him arrested on suspicion of murder once he disembarks in Liverpool."

"Indeed," the detective agreed. "It would certainly help our inquiries to have a better description of this Wilkie Valentine, to see if he matches the description of the man at the dock. We also need physical evidence connecting him to the murder."

"There are at least two people who might be able to give some description." If not Miss Burke, then they ought to be able to press Aggie, who had seen the man who had mistaken her for another. A wild thought occurred. "Do you think there is more than one man? That this Valentine had a twin brother or cousin who has taken his place?"

Cab shook his head even as he smiled. "Now that sounds like a made-up story in one of the tabloids. But speaking of tabloids, I'm sure you won't be surprised that I called in some favors from some rather shady characters I know in the press—"

"Is there any other kind of person in the press?" Marigold asked, thinking of the fast-talking, slow-acting Wilkerson, who had not yet managed to get any article published in his paper—not even the one she had written for him.

Cab chuckled. "Probably not. But I thought you ought to know that I got no purchase trying to track your Mr. James Wilkerson down—no one at the *Boston Evening Journal* will claim to know him."

Marigold was taken aback. "He is not *my* Mr. Wilkerson—especially if he proves not to be the *Boston Evening Journal*'s Wilkerson."

Cab relented a little in the face of her obvious objection. "I suppose it's not that surprising—the tabloids generally hire on only a few full-time writers and string the rest along on a speculative basis. Still, you'd think someone would have heard of him."

"Indeed." Someone was keeping him in camel hair coats and fashionable homburg hats. "But Mr. Wilkerson does not matter." Marigold tried to rein in her frustration and force herself to be rational and logical in sorting out the known facts. "Wilkie Valentine does. I do have some physical evidence—I found her glove and a button on the path halfway between the lodge gate and the boathouse, where they must have originally fought."

Officer Pratt gestured toward the door. "I should like to see exactly where that was. And the boathouse, as well. The scene of the crime."

"Naturally. Let us go there at once, before the light goes from the afternoon." Even as she said it, Marigold chastised herself for not revisiting the boathouse before—for letting her own feeble fears keep her from pursuing the truth. If she were honest—and she was trying to be both scrupulously honest and unfailingly logical—since the day she found Oliva Thayer's body, she had not yet had the courage to go back.

Now they would need more than courage—they would need luck. Because time was running out.

Chapter 23

"It is curious that physical courage should be so common in the world, and moral courage so rare."

Mark Twain

"We'll start with where you found the body, if you don't mind, Miss Manners," Detective Pratt said.

"Yes. It was just this side of the boathouse." She pointed down the lawns toward the building. "At the closest corner of the floating dock."

The detective paused at the crest of the hill to survey the scene. "You said you found the article of Miss Thayer's clothing where?"

Marigold pointed east along the well-trodden path toward the lodge gate. "At the crest of that next knoll, just past the Music Hall, there on the right."

"They came from that direction? Walking this way?" He narrowed his eyes to gauge the distance. "It's half a mile from there to the boathouse. He might have killed her anywhere along that path and carried her. The shore there is closer. Perhaps her body floated by chance to the boathouse?"

"I don't think so," Marigold countered. "It's marshy there so the shore is difficult to access. And there was something about the way her skirts were tangled under the pier that made me think she had been purposefully stuffed under there where she might potentially not be found."

"And I have learned not to go against your instincts, Marigold," Cab added. "You have a singular way of imagining what happened that ought to be given full rein."

Marigold was not entirely sure that this was a gift that ought to be complimented. "Thank you, I think. If it is an instinct, it is not exactly a comfortable one."

"Perhaps not, but it is useful."

They walked in silence the rest of the way down the path, taking exactly the same way she had come that fateful afternoon exactly one week ago. "I saw the hat first, from here." She pointed. "Just there."

"That looks to be about four feet deep," the detective assayed. "You went in there?"

"Off the side." She led the way to the floating dock. "Here."

Cab reached down to test the water. "Damnation, it's cold."

"It was then too," she assured him. Just the thought of the cold water sluicing down her back had her rubbing her arms for warmth.

Cab didn't miss much. He reached out a casual hand to touch her ever so briefly just on the inside of her elbow in that way he had. "Brave girl."

"I wish people would stop saying that," she said to stave off the feeling of disappointment that the touch had not been longer. Or more comprehensively personal. "I didn't feel brave," she went on. "I felt desperate. And awful. And it's been awful since, first not being able to identify her properly and now not being able to identify her killer or bring him—assuming it is *him*—to justice." She led the way onward. "You'll want a look at the boat bay where we brought her out," she continued. "This first stair leads down to the water level."

"Are there boats available we might use should the need arise?" Detective Pratt asked. "Although I'm not much of a waterman."

"My days on a crew shell are over," Cab answered, "But I think I can still row one of these skiffs anywhere you might want to go."

Even though the relatively crisp fall weather had Cab's forearms covered in sleeves, the memory of the way the sun had glistened off the tanned skin as he had taken the tiller on Salem Sound last spring on one of their many sails back and forth to Great Misery Island never failed to raise a frisson of delight within Marigold.

"What are we looking for?"

Cab's question brought Marigold back to the chilly present. "Something that would tie the strangulation to this place?" She looked to Detective Pratt for the answer. "Some piece of physical evidence—like the tonic bottle or the Bible," she said, referencing some of the clues she and Cab had found on Great Misery, "that might point us to the identity of our killer, or confirm that Wilkie Valentine is, in fact, the young man we seek?"

"Just so," the detective confirmed. "Lead on."

Marigold preceded the men down the bare wooden stairs leading down to the open bay, where the various rowing barges and skiffs were tied up, ready for use.

She had thought the gentlemen's company would banish the sinister shadows, but even with Cab at her side, it was eerie—echoing with sounds that ought to have been familiar but were now exaggerated and made frightening by her ridiculous fear. The short hairs at the top of her nape seemed to stand on uncomfortable end. "It was likely here, wasn't it?"

Cab paused and took a considered look. "Perhaps," he agreed.

"Just so," the detective said more unequivocally. "Here, their struggle would have been concealed, out of sight of College Hall and any passersby. So, if they first had some form of altercation on the path half a mile away, he might have begun to think of killing her there, but likely thought he was too exposed."

"Yes," Marigold agreed with his line of reasoning.

"Once they were out of sight," Cab mused, "he might have strangled her at any point from the rotunda on and then just brought her body down here to put into the water."

"Perhaps." Marigold felt that eerie, fearful anger roil through her, chilling her to the bone. "The way her skirt hems were tangled with the post in the far corner, I felt as if he might have purposefully stuffed her beneath the dock, so she would not be seen."

Cab walked around the U-shaped dock to where the skiff was tied up. "That seems plausible." He stared down at the dark water. "How about a lantern?"

"Yes," Marigold agreed quickly. "I know just where they're stored. I won't be a minute."

She was more than a minute going back upstairs to the storeroom, taking her time in an effort to dispel the strange uneasiness that had come over her, but in that time, Cab had stripped off his overcoat and houndstooth tweed jacket and tossed them into the skiff. And in another moment, he was rolling up his shirtsleeves to expose those well-remembered forearms.

All traces of internal tumult subsided at the sight. And the scent—when had the homey aroma of starch become so welcome and pleasing?

Marigold fumbled to light the lantern.

"Let me," Cab offered, retrieving a box of safety matches from his coat pocket. He struck the match and the smell of sulfur and heat mixed momentarily with the scent of starch and lake water.

Normally, Marigold would have been thrilled to find herself in a conveniently shadowed boathouse with Cab Cox. Normally, she would have been thinking of gripping those beautifully laundered and starched shirtsleeves and pulling him close to kiss. Of breaking through his usual puritan reserve.

But there was nothing normal about what they were doing.

And the thought of a kiss in the place where a young woman might have been strangled to death was unappealing in the extreme. And there was also an upright young detective, who was searching for evidence of that strangling, along with them.

Marigold forced her brain back to the task at hand, organizing her thoughts as if she were an archaeologist making sense of finds or patterns on an archaeological site. "So, Olivia had already lost her glove and had buttons missing from her jacket and the waist of her skirt from some physical altercation on the path." She pushed past her own discomfort to put herself in Olivia's place, so imagine the scene through Olivia's eyes.

"Judging from the way her skirt was ripped, he likely had her around the waist, from behind?" Marigold could see it in her mind's eye like a flickering nickelodeon reel. "He picked her up and was forcing her down the stairs, to here?" She could all but feel the steely band of the stronger man's arms pulling at her waist as she kicked and tried to stop his progress, scraping her half-boots against the rough plank walls.

No. At Olivia's torn waist. Olivia's scraped boots.

Cab moved beside her, nodded. "So, he brought her to the edge there, and—" He broke off.

"He strangled her," Marigold finished for him. "And then he carried her over there, where it was darkest, and purposefully pushed her into the water under the corner of the dock."

"By God," Detective Pratt muttered, staring at her with a deep, concerned frown etched between his brows.

"Yes," Cab assured him. "I've seen her do it before, but it still gives me the willies. Just keep going, Marigold. Don't let us delicate men slow you down. Keep going."

She ignored Cab's ironic tone and did just that, gauging the distance between where they stood at the edge of the dock, to the far pillar, where Olivia Thayer's skirts became tangled with the dock post. "Yes. I don't see how she could have become entangled in the corner post," Marigold walked around the large, U-shaped bay, "on the outside edge of the dock, behind this wall, without her murderer's direct action or interference."

"Simple motion of the water and waves?" Pratt posited. "Does this small lake get that stormy."

"There wasn't a storm that night." Marigold had a clear memory of her first night back at the college. "I had opened my dormitory room windows in College Hall just before I went down to dinner. The coroner, Dr. Prescott, had put Olivia's time of death at seven o'clock that Sunday evening a week ago, the exact time that the Japanese bell had rung the dinner hour, and sent hundreds of collegians heading toward the dining hall, at the far opposite end of the building away from the boathouse." She drew in a steadying breath. "If Olivia had called out for help, there would have been no one to hear her."

"Just so," the detective said quietly.

"I wonder if she was still conscious at all?" Marigold asked. "If she could swim or somehow try to get away?" Physical education, including swimming, was a required element of every Wellesley woman's plan of study, but Olivia wasn't an official member of the college yet. "But if she were still conscious and could swim, perhaps she might have tried to get away from him, under the dock. I'm fairly certain one could even stand under there—the water isn't above four feet deep."

"Let's have a look." Cab shone the lantern down into the dark but clear water.

The beam of light illuminated a rippling sandy bottom that gave way, closer in toward the shore to flatter, to a muddier, silty lakebed strewn with algae-covered rocks.

"Let us project the light back and across in a logical, thorough, archaeological grid pattern so we don't miss anything," Marigold directed, before she amended. "If you please. Slowly now."

"Aye, aye," Cab said without rancor and did as she bade, going down on one knee at the edge of the dock to sweep the bottom with the beam of light from the lantern, working from one side of the bay to the other. "Wait." He swung the lantern back. "Did you see that—"

"Gleam? Like a little flash of metal?"

Detective Pratt came to the edge opposite Marigold. "Just so," he confirmed. "Yes. There." He pointed.

She saw it—the flash of momentary brilliance catching her eye, much like the glass beaded button she had found on the path above.

Marigold knelt down upon the edge of the dock to get a closer look. "Hold the light steady now," she instructed, as she fixed her eyes on the shining little dot. "Do you see it?" She put her archaeologist's eye to work. "It doesn't look like metal . . ."

"No," the detective agreed. "More like a block or a stone."

"But there was a gleam—" She sat and began pull off her suit jacket and her shoes. She would have to make her apologies to Isabella for the ruin of the ensemble, but a potential clue against Wilkie Valentine was more important than any outfit.

"Marigold?" Cab's voice rose in alarm. "Don't—"

She had already slipped into the cold, cold water. And immediately gasped for breath.

"By God," Detective Pratt muttered again.

She sucked in a breath through her teeth. "Just, just hold the light steady," she instructed grimly, before she put her face into the water and opened her eyes. As soon as she spotted that singular gleam coming from the otherwise unreflective object, she immediately stroked down toward the pool of illuminated light, moving as economically as possible so she didn't stir up the silty soil to cloud the water and obscure the dark shape nestled into the sand on the bottom.

Marigold dug her hands into the silt and was surprised to find the thing, whatever it was, was smaller than it looked, soft and light, not heavy.

She pushed off the bottom and broke to the surface, gasping against the cold. "Here." She half swam her frigid way back to the edge of the dock to grapple the sandy little thing onto the planks, where Cab quickly knelt down to retrieve it.

"I've got it," he said. "Let me help you out—"

"No. Over there." She fought to speak without her teeth chattering. "Turn the light. Over there."

"Beneath the dock?"

"I saw something in the light over there."

"It's probably outside, in the sunlight. We'll take the skiff and I'll—" Cab reached down for her. "Just come out of there."

"Get in the skiff, then, and come around." Marigold knew if she got out now, she would never be able to convince herself to get back in.

Cab bit down a curse, but did as she asked, handing the artifact she had recovered to Detective Pratt before the two of them clambered into the skiff and pushed off.

Cab rowed close, so Marigold could cling to the side of the gunwale as he piloted them through the low open end of the bay and into the sun.

"Here," she judged.

They were just a little further out into the lake from where Marigold had found the body, which had been on the pier closest to the shore.

She put her face back into the water and fought for a moment against the driving shaft of cold though her skull. She refocused her eyes on the sandy bottom, waiting as long as she could for the dark ribbonlike shape she had seen to come back into view. The moment it did, she kicked down to the bottom, digging her hands into the gritty soil at the bottom, immediately obscuring whatever object she might hold clutched in her hand.

She broke the surface with a gasp, and immediately Cab was there, taking the thing from her clutch before he clasped her forearm and hauled her straight up out of the water and into his lap, puritan reserve be damned.

"I'll get you w-wet!" Marigold protested.

But Cab was already wrapping her up in his tweed jacket as well as his overcoat. "Of all the tomfool things to do in October—"

"Yes, yes. Don't f-fuss," she chattered, until she realized that her wet clothes might be plastered quite revealingly along her body. She gathered the edges of his coat around her as best she could with nearly numb fingers. "What was— is—" She tried to turn their attention to the evidence, but she was panting with the cold.

"It looks like a pocketbook." Cab kept his arms around her. "Black—"

"Suede," she finished for him. "Like her gloves. M-matching." She reached her hand out of the cocoon of clothing to touch the soft leather. It was not as new as the rest of Olivia's ensemble had been—the strap was worn in the middle, and the clasp was broken.

She pushed the purse frame open to find a waterlogged piece of thick paper, folded in half. But her fingers were too cold and unresponsive to do anything other than poke clumsily, ripping a piece off. "Damnation. What is that?"

"Looks like a . . . liner ticket, perhaps?" Cab observed. "That's a star—"

"May I?" the detective asked, and Marigold reluctantly handed him the waterlogged pocketbook.

"From the White Star Line?" Detective Pratt mused. "But your information was that Wilkie Valentine and his wife embarked on the Cunard Line?"

"It was," Cab confirmed.

"It makes no sense," Marigold complained over her aching jaw. "And it's too wet and fragile to look at here," she mused over her shivers. "Let's get it back up to College Hall where we can try to dry it a little so we can read it without ripping it any further."

"That is the best idea I've heard all day." Cab set her away only so he could row them directly to the beach, which would put them closer to the hall. And which would give her two or three more minutes of Cab's marvelous forearms flexing on the oars, distracting her from the chill.

But not too distracted—practical considerations came first. "We need to go back to the boathouse for my shoes and coat, if you please. I can't very well trudge back up to the hall in stocking feet in this weather. Or at least I would prefer not to." She was cold enough already.

"I could carry you," Cab offered, even as he swung the skiff around to return through the first bay of the boathouse. He rowed them in and neatly debarked to tie off the painter before he extended his hand to help Marigold out of the boat. "Your hands are like ice."

For once, she was grateful for the assistance. "I know it seems a stupid thing to have done," she began to explain, but when Cab pulled her into his arms again to warm her, practical considerations went the way of the dodo bird.

All she could see before her was Cab.

All she wanted to see was Cab.

"Marigold," he said in a voice that was full of warmth and regret all at the same time.

She waited for the return of his puritan reserve—for him to set her away.

But she hung on to him and willed him to kiss her anyway.

And for no reason that she could fathom, he finally did.

Chapter 24

"The respect that is only bought by gold is not worth much."

Frances Harper

There was something about being kissed by Cab that made her lose her mind and find it all at once. That made her happy and hungry and scandalous and safe simultaneously. That made her want the kiss to never end.

But those pesky practical considerations, like breathing and dripping water down one's legs and not freezing to death, and the presence of a professional police detective could not help but take precedence.

"Let's get you out of here," he said before he handed her her shoes.

"I've got the evidence," Detective Pratt had already headed for the stairs.

Marigold was glad of the policeman's discretion—not that she was embarrassed by their display of affection. It was both natural and right. But there was still a murder to be solved. "You have the other thing?" she asked him. "What was it?"

"Not sure," he said. "A box of some sort, maybe."

"Let's discuss this someplace warmer, shall we?" Cab suggested. "Come on." He put his hand around her waist to bundle her up the stairs and out onto the path the way they had come.

"Oh, no," she said again when he would have steered her toward the closest doors at the east end of the building. "This way, if you please. It will make far less of a scene if we go in the far door."

Discretion and prudence might not have been expedient in the cause of identifying Olivia Thayer, but Marigold would enlist them to her own cause—she did not want to try Miss Burke's patience and loyalty by dripping across College Hall.

"You need to get warm and dry as soon as possible," Cab was instructing.

"Which I can do best if we go in the west door," she insisted, "which is closest to my rooms. I'm not made of spun sugar, Cab—you of all people should know that. And besides," she added fuel to her fire. "If I have to sign you both in and out officially, it will take forever, and you'll be gawked at, not to mention ogled, and I'll have to explain why I'm wet, and we will be unnecessarily delayed in finding out just what's in the pocketbook."

"Have it your way."

She did not say that she always did—or at least frequently did have things her way. One ought not make too much of one's self. And at the moment, one's self was in desperate need of dry, warm clothes and a very stiff drink. And another deliciously warm kiss.

She must have shivered again, because Cab's hand came more snugly about her waist. "I do wish you'd let me carry you."

"Suit yourself," she said as they entered through the side door Detective Pratt held open. "It's four flights up. I'll advise you to pace yourself."

Cab settled for a very solicitous arm at her waist. "Just in case."

Detective Pratt doffed his blue uniform hat, tucked it beneath his arm and said in the same clear, calm voice Mr. Duckett and the porters employed, "Man on the hall."

As if he had extensive experience navigating female-only places. For such a young man, Officer Pratt had untapped depths.

"Thank you, Detective. Well done. You might as well come in," she said when they reached her floor. "It's the safest place for you both." She let the two gentlemen into her parlor.

Detective Pratt stood stiffly by the open door, while Cab took an expansive look around. "I don't think I've ever been in a young lady's dormitory room before. It feels quite scandalous."

"It is extremely scandalous." For the second time that afternoon, Marigold wished that she was not in the middle of a murder investigation, with clues in need of their attention. And that she really was as scandalous as she said and had no care or caution where Cab was concerned.

But even if she didn't, she knew Cab did—he had caution and respect enough for both of them. And that was why she admired him so.

Still, he had warmed her once with a kiss—what else might he be persuaded to attempt?

Marigold shivered so violently she nearly fell into the nearby chair.

"You're still soaking wet and chilled to the bone," Cab observed with some small degree of rancor. "You ought to get changed."

Practical considerations before the theoretical. And definitely before the romantical.

"Pour me a drink, will you?" Marigold waggled a finger at the left side of her steamer trunk bureau. "Sherry's hidden up there. Water glasses on the table. I'll be right back," she promised before she dashed across the hall. "Ethyl?"

Ethyl looked up from her study table. "Well, don't you look like you were dragged backwards through a briar patch. Or maybe a beaver dam. Been in the lake again?"

"Naturally. Come play chaperone with Mr. Cox."

"Oh, goody." Ethyl jumped up with alacrity. "I'd like to get a gander at what you fancy."

"Ethyl," Marigold announced as she came through the door. "Cab. Cab, Ethyl. Miss Rautencranz, Detective Pratt. Detective Pratt, Miss—"

"Ethyl will do," her hallmate finished cheerfully. "And drinks! How nice."

"Oh, thank you." Marigold took the proffered sherry gratefully. "Ethyl, chaperone our guests while I change into something less pneumonic."

"I don't think that's a real word, Marigold," Ethyl said.

"It is now." Marigold shut the door to her bedchamber and took a deep breath before she laboriously peeled each layer of wet clothing, from her saturated satin skirts down to her elasticized sporting corset, and chafed herself thoroughly dry with a Turkish towel.

She could hear Cab and Ethyl in easy conversation in the next room, and so took her time getting dressed, rearranging her hair and hanging out her wet clothing to dry—again, she respected Isabella and her seamstresses too much to treat such skillfully made clothing with anything but the utmost care.

". . . so you think the manchineel plant, or is it a tree?" Cab asked.

"Tree in my part of the world."

"And what part is that?" Detective Pratt asked.

"Florida, just outside St. Augustine."

"Long way to come for school," Cab observed.

"You don't know the half of it," Ethyl laughed. "Say, do you have a cigarette? Or better yet, a cigar?"

"Are you allowed to smoke in the dormitory?"

"Nope." Ethyl said. "But that hasn't stopped me yet."

"Ethyl, you will get us in deep trouble if we're caught smoking and drinking at the same time," Marigold said as she returned to the sitting room. "One or the other might pass, but not both."

"Spoilsport! Well, now you look like yourself," Ethyl commented. "Ah, well. It was fun while it lasted." She rose and made a valedictory sort of bow to Marigold's guests. "Pleased to meet you, Cab Cox. Detective."

"Don't go." Marigold waved her back. "We have a scientific conservation quandary to solve. Detective, do you have the pocketbook?"

Detective Pratt gestured to the wet suede artifact on Marigold's worktable.

"Thank you. Inside," Marigold opened the clasp as she spoke, "there is a sodden piece of paper—a ticket, we think—which is terribly fragile. Is there some solution that might help dry it so it doesn't rip?"

"Let me see." Ethyl adjusted her spectacles. "Maybe ethyl alcohol, but I'd reckon the most expedient thing would just be to manually dry the paper. Blot it with a towel on one side, then flip it over and add another, like a clean washrag or—"

"Handkerchief?" Cab produced an immaculate square of Irish linen.

"Perfect." Marigold took the proffered piece of fabric. "And I've got some Turkish hand towels in my trunk."

Together they swaddled the suede exterior in the towel and slid the linen handkerchief on top of the paper ticket.

"Maybe if we turn it over and prop it open." Marigold flipped the purse over, so the paper now rested on the handkerchief. "And we can pull it out?"

"I'll hold the clasp open, and you slide," advised Ethyl.

Marigold did so. "Let me get a tweezer—"

"Wait," Ethyl instructed. "I've got a set of surgical forceps. Be right back."

"Naturally." Marigold was all admiration for Ethyl's preparedness.

And so was Detective Pratt. "If you ladies aren't the most resourceful young women I've ever met, I'll eat my hat."

"It won't make much of a meal," Marigold tried for wit.

"No, it won't," he agreed. But for the first time that Marigold noticed, the young detective smiled. It wasn't one of Cab's ready smiles, full of charm and fellow-feeling, but it was companionable enough to make Marigold sure that the women were being treated as equals.

"Glad to see you're no worse for wear from your dip in the lake," Cab said quietly.

"Thank you for your concern, but you'll find I have the constitution of a moose."

"An otter, perhaps," Cab countered. "Far more elegance."

That compliment she let slide as Ethyl came back with the promised instruments in a small case. "We'll want these long-nose forceps, I think."

Marigold blotted the folded paper one more time before she slid the nose of the instrument between the layers and gingerly pried the paper apart.

The four of them crowded closer, craning their heads to see.

"White Star Line." Marigold read the printing across the top, and below that, "Second Class? Cheapskate—what kind of man tries to take a young lady of Olivia Thayer's caliber on a transatlantic honeymoon in second class?"

Her question was rhetorical—obviously Wilkie Valentine was a rotter—but Cab answered with another consideration. "The Cunard Line tickets for Mr. and Mrs. Valentine were *third* class—which I'm assuming was the best he could afford after already having purchased this one and, I'm also assuming, his own. But what day—which sailing—was this one for?"

Various parts of the ticket were printed or stamped, like the port of Boston and the name of the steamship, RMS *Utopia*, but the rest of the pertinent information was filled out faintly in ink. "Purchased . . . September sixth for . . . sailing October . . . eighth?" Marigold read. "So that was the original plan, made well in advance—over a month earlier? That they elope to Boston on the Sunday evening and sail the next day?"

The ink had run, making the passenger information difficult to read. But not impossible.

"Mr. W. Valentine . . . thirty-two years of age. Oh! He's much older than I had assumed."

And where had Marigold made that incorrect assumption—from Professor Currier's calling him a young man?

"Mrs. Olivia Valentine . . . well, I suppose that shows he was sincere about the idea of marriage," she commented as an aside. "And age . . . twenty two." Marigold drew back. "She was only seventeen!"

"Which shows that Valentine likely knew the age of consent for the Commonwealth of Massachusetts is eighteen years of age," Cab noted. "But you're right—it does show that the plan to elope was well thought out in advance—not just something he made up to cover the fact that he had already murdered her."

"A plan that she thwarted?" Marigold theorized. "Because here she was in Wellesley on Sunday, arguing, or at the very least struggling with him, on the path by the lake, with this ticket for that next day in her pocketbook—and no evidence that she had a suitcase with her to suggest a different intent."

"And the ticket was lost to the lake when he killed her," Pratt observed. "Forcing him into the necessity of buying more—third-class—tickets."

"He didn't just kill her," Marigold felt compelled to say. "He strangled her. With his own two hands." Marigold refused to use euphemisms. Violence had been wrought upon Olivia Thayer and violence ought to be described unflinchingly.

"Just so," Pratt agreed. "Perhaps as a direct result—" He reached into the pocket of his long blue uniform frock coat and brought out Marigold's first artifact, a small, sand-flecked velvet box held closed by a bright gold metal hasp.

"Y'all?" Ethyl immediately began to blot the sand off the box with her own wrinkled but clean handkerchief. "That looks to me like it's going to be a ring."

Detective Pratt carefully thumbed the hinge open. "Just so. It is a ring."

"Well." Marigold's head was full of conflicting thoughts as she gazed in astonishment at the beautiful, old-fashioned rose-cut diamond ring. "If I have nothing else in favor of a murderer, I can at least allow that he had taste. Or he inherited this from someone with taste."

"And some money," Cab added. "Enough to buy both of their steamer tickets and that ring, and the replacement liner tickets? All of which would have set him back a pretty penny."

A new thought occurred. "I never thought to ask the Thayers—or Professor Currier—if Olivia Thayer could be expected to come into any money on her majority?" The Thayer house on Blossom Street had looked prosperous, in a subdued, old Yankee sort of way, but gave no indication that there were untapped buckets of money available to underage girls. "Professor Currier said that Valentine was a ne'er-do-well with no apparent profession. But clearly, he must have had some ready cash—one can't buy trans-Atlantic liner tickets on credit."

"No," Cab agreed.

"But does this show that she likely had no intention of marrying him—that she was likely carrying the ring to give it back?"

"From where it was found," the detective answered, "I would venture that she either had it in her bag and it fell out when she went into the water—"

"Or she threw it in, to show him what she thought of his proposal." Marigold supplied a narrative that better suited her aggrieved feelings. "But no matter which it was, he wouldn't take no for an answer." Marigold could see it in her mind's eye, starting back on the path where there were signs of a struggle.

Olivia would have told him her answer and perhaps held out the ring box to him for the first time. Did he swat it away or push it back at her before he stalked off in the direction of the boathouse? Did he start formulating his plan to kill her there? Either way, Olivia held on to it, even as he dragged her by the wrists until she was in the boathouse. Perhaps she was still holding it tight when he broke her neck and pushed her into the water.

"What does it take to do something like that—to kill the person one has professed to love, just because they said no?" Marigold's question was rhetorical—she could fathom no answer that might suffice. "What kind of a person must they be?"

"I have no idea." Thankfully, Cab seemed as baffled as she. "And I frankly think the whole idea—that she would elope with him—is legally nearly impossible. The county and city clerks are generally sensitive to matters concerning the age of consent and ought to have refused to grant a license in the first place."

"Talk about your poison apples," was Ethyl's summation of the man.

"Indeed," Marigold agreed. "He is a damned strangler and murderer. And he's sailed off into the sunset and gotten away with it."

"Not yet." Detective Pratt began to collect the items on the table, carefully stowing them in his pockets. "We're on to him now. Mr. Cox, if you could accompany me to the courthouse, I think we may get our warrant as soon as may be."

"Of course." Cab was immediately at the policeman's disposal. "And once we have the warrant, I'll do what I can through official channels to see what can be done to arrest Wilkie Valentine before he debarks in Liverpool. This should be enough evidence to convince a grand jury. Oh, wait, Marigold, do you still have the telegram delivered to the Thayers? Thank you. Along with this, we should have more than enough to indict him. If so, he can be taken no matter where he might be. Unless he has a false passport—which I somehow doubt, or Mrs. Valentine, whoever she is, would not have voiced her concerns about her passport to the stevedore."

"Thank you, Cab." Marigold finally felt some small measure of relief.

"Don't thank me yet. Extradition is a complicated matter, but I will definitely give it my all." Cab stood. "Which means I must return to Boston with Detective Pratt as soon as possible to find out."

"There's a five-fifteen train at the Wellesley station." Marigold glanced at the clock. "Mr. Griffin should be able to take us in the Barge—that will be the quickest."

"Not *us*." Cab's tone would brook no argument. "You're staying here where you're warm. You need more than a sherry to recover from such a dousing. You may have the constitution of a moose, but you need a hot bath. And a good hot dinner." He turned to Ethyl. "You're in charge of her."

"Oh, sure," Ethyl laughed. "Marigold Manners is just the type to let other people take charge over her. I'll just force her to take that bath, sure. Sure."

Marigold could only laugh. And be thankful for such friends. "Thank you, Cab, for your vote of confidence in my constitution. I will at the very least walk and sign you out—or face the wrath of Miss Burke, who guards the door like a sentinel." She linked arms with Cab. "Come on, Ethyl—chaperone us all the way so we stay in Miss Burke's good graces."

"What's in it for me?" Ethyl asked.

"A bumper of sherry on our return. And a very nice claro cigar I've been saving for a bribe."

Ethyl took a very surprised-looking Detective Pratt's arm on the other side. "Chaperone at the ready."

Thus, they proceeded through the corridors and stairwells, unremarked by anyone—not even Miss Burke, who merely nodded at them with satisfaction when Marigold formally signed the two gentlemen out.

"Mr. Cox, Detective Pratt. It was a pleasure discussing the distillate of manchineel with you." Ethyl stuck out her hand. "Good luck in Boston, boys."

"Miss Ethyl." Detective Pratt shook first her hand, then Marigold's. "A pleasure to work with you, Miss Manners. Rest assured you can leave the matter safely with me."

"Thank you, Detective."

And with that, Ethyl and the detective left Marigold alone to make her own goodbyes to Cab. "Thank you for your assistance today. And your . . . support."

Cab tucked his chin, even as he smiled. "That's a strange way to talk about a kiss, Marigold."

"It is," she admitted. "But it does make it easier to ask for more . . . support."

Cab took a quick glance around the empty entry hall before he ducked his head and kissed her lingeringly, but entirely discreetly, on the corner of her lips.

It was not the kiss she wanted, but it would do. For now.

"Wire me with any news," she asked.

"I will." He squeezed her hand one last time. "And for God's sake—if not for your own—be careful." And with that he jammed his hat on his head, turned on his heel, and was gone.

"I will," she promised anyway. "Always."

Chapter 25

"It is astonishing what force, purity and wisdom it requires for a human being to keep clear of falsehoods."

Margaret Fuller

"Oh! Miss Manners!"

"Yes, Miss Burke?" Marigold immediately left contemplation of Antiphon's tetralogies to come to the little woman's aid. "How may I be of service, ma'am?" She made a quick scan for any urchins that might need banishment.

"Mrs. Dana has come to call for you, but she went straight up to your room, even though I told her it was against regulations. She didn't even wait for tea!"

"My apologies, Miss Burke." Marigold put a consoling hand to the tiny woman's shoulder. "I fear Mrs. Dana is a force of nature that none of us could contain. But not wanting tea—that is grave indeed. I will attend her immediately."

And indeed, Marigold all but ran up the three flights to the fourth floor to find Isabella already pouring herself a sherry. "Hello, darling." Marigold kissed her cheek. "Drinks for breakfast? What's the occasion?"

"You can't drink all day if you don't start in the morning. I've poured you one too," Isabella said, pointing to the stem of fortified wine next to a chair. "You're going to need it."

Marigold knew Isabella well enough to take her at her word. She took up the sherry and sat down in the chair. "Let's have it."

"I hate to be the continual bearer of bad news, but this time it's the infamous *Morning Standard*." Isabella passed over a tabloid newspaper. "They've pipped their rival *Boston Evening Journal* to the wire."

Marigold felt as if she knew what she would see before she looked. And indeed, splashed across the cover of the *Morning Standard* was a photograph in which Olivia Thayer might be said to be gazing adoringly at Imogen Currier. The one Lucy must have seen in Professor Currier's room. The one which Marigold now knew depicted a young, impressionable niece gazing adoringly at the doting aunt who was opening up the world to her talents.

But like the *Boston Evening Journal* before it, the *Morning Standard* had predictably gone for the lowest hanging fruit. The caption under the photogravure—which was curiously uncredited—read, 'The Boston Marriage Made in Wellesley?'

"Damnation." Marigold gave vent to her feelings with a curse.

"Indeed," Isabella agreed. "Crudely but accurately put."

Marigold's concern immediately turned to both the college and President Irvine, but also to Professor Imogene Currier herself. She could only imagine how deeply the barely veiled innuendo of the tabloid would hurt her and her sister. By her own admission, Professor Currier was deeply attached to Olivia Thayer—as any aunt might be to an only niece. And even without that familial tie, as any teacher might be to a prized pupil—as President Irvine was attached to Marigold, helping to shepherd her academic career.

But President Irvine was shielded by her marriage.

Neither Professor Currier, nor the college itself, had such protection.

Without even reading the whole of the article, Marigold knew what it would undoubtedly say. What did one expect from such a place, with all those women closeted up together? That it was unnatural for women to prefer each other's company. That women's minds were made by God to be weak, and that the college could only do them irrevocable harm. And that some prominent local clergyman or physician had long warned that for every woman's college, the citizenry was going to have to erect two insane asylums and three hospitals.

No matter that Julia J. Irvine's career as an exemplary scholar—as an undergraduate student, she had outright won prizes in Greek language and literature over men at competing academic institutions—and as a clear-headed leader and tough-minded Quaker moralist stood in direct and shining contradiction to such nonsense.

Still, it was printed. And people like Professor Currier—and all women in a similarly vulnerable position—were hurt.

"It always has to be salacious with them, doesn't it?"

Marigold's question was purely rhetorical, but Isabella answered anyway. "Facts don't sell papers, darling, stories do. I thought your Mr. Matthew White at *The Argosy* would have taught you that by now."

"Oh, I suppose it is a lesson that I learned a very long time ago, long before either Mr. White or *The Argosy* magazine, but it nevertheless never fails to disappoint. Listen to this drivel." Marigold read from the accompany article. "'A gentleman in the know, who wishes to remain anonymous, tells us that Wellesley College is a breeding ground for the 'Boston Marriage.' 'It is well known,' he says, 'to be a gathering ground for ladies of certain unnatural instincts.'" Marigold's personal feeling boiled over into outrage. "Of all the unmitigated slander."

"Naturally," Isabella observed dryly. "One would think it is positively libelous. But of course, the source is anonymous and they have used all the usual words—'tells us,' and 'it is said,' and such rot, which lets them lie as they like, while serving to protect them from prosecution."

"Naturally," Marigold fumed. "Poor Professor Currier. The deceased was her niece, so all this Boston Marriage nonsense is not only woefully mischief-making but woefully wrong. I wonder if I should go to her at her boardinghouse, to check on her? She seemed so frail the last time I saw her, I fear this might do her some great damage."

"Her boardinghouse? But Lucy Dove is there and will look after her, surely? She's eminently sensible and eminently capable." Isabella nodded confidently. "Lucy's got an exceptional head on her shoulders. You need have no worries."

Marigold had no idea that Isabella even knew Lucy well enough to make such an assessment of her character. It was a very true assessment, but nonetheless. "But Lucy may not understand the psychological implications," she fretted.

"Don't sell Lucy short, darling," Isabella countered. "I feel certain you can have complete faith in her."

"Well, short of rushing back over there, I suppose I must."

"You must. Now." Isabella put her chin up in the air in an attitude Marigold recognized as rather dangerous for whomever Isabella had in her sights. "The best way to combat such slanderous falsehoods is to meet them head-on while appearing not to care a whit, nor believe for any moment that they are true. You know." She struck a careless pose. "'Don't be ridiculous, darling!' That sort of thing. But you'll need a tame reporter to print your version of the story: 'Wellesley girls, as red-blooded as any American girl.' That sort of thing. Perhaps your Mr. Wilkerson can finally make himself useful." She cast what Marigold interpreted as a slightly jaundiced eye her way. "Or were you cultivating him for some other reason?"

"No, you have me exactly—I had hoped to make use of him," Marigold admitted. "But he has sadly not come up to scratch. I already tried to feed him an article, but it never ran in his paper." Marigold pulled a face. "I must be slipping."

"Or he was feigning his interest from the first. He's certainly feigning something," Isabella finished under her breath.

This had never occurred to Marigold. That the man had tried to flatter and flirt his way into her good graces, she had accepted as the natural product of her panache. That his interest had been false from the start— Well, surely she hadn't slipped that much!

"I might try to contact him, but . . ." For the first time, Marigold realized she had no notion of where to find him—Cab's efforts at the *Boston Evening Journal* had already proved fruitless.

"I'm sure he'll simply turn up like a bad penny." Isabella stood. "I don't trust him. I don't like him, and I certainly don't like his untoward attention to you."

"You don't like anyone who isn't Cab."

"Naturally," Isabella rejoined. "I have standards."

Marigold could only smile. "So you do. And, as it turns out, so do I."

"Now that is the first good news you've had for me in days!"

"We shall see," was all Marigold was prepared to say with regard to Cab. "But what ought to be done, if anything—"

"Marigold?" It was Ethyl, looking blustery from her usual morning walk. But today, instead of holding a particularly interesting leaf or rock, she was holding a copy of a tabloid newspaper.

Marigold sighed. "Please don't tell me the *Boston Evening Journal* is trying to rival the *Morning Standard*'s low version of yellow journalism?"

"Close but no cigar for the little lady. Or not so little lady," Ethyl corrected herself. "You have stature."

"Thank you." There was no reason to abandon one's manners, no matter the circumstance. "But what is it?"

"The *Morning Standard*." Ethyl tossed the folded paper into Marigold's lap. "And they have outdone themselves. It's a doozy. But I can see I'm bringing you old news."

"Indeed, but I thank you anyway." She really was blessed with wonderfully loyal friends. "May I introduce you to another of my dear friends? Mrs. Isabella Dana, meet Miss Ethyl Rautencranz, scientist and all-around good egg."

"Now you go on!" Ethyl beamed even as she held out her hand to shake. "A pleasure to meet you, Mrs. Dana."

"Likewise," Isabella said. "Call me Isabella—all my friends do. Marigold is a marvelous judge of character, so now we're to be friends as well."

"Well, I'm just luckier than a rabbit in a briar patch," Ethyl enthused.

"Ethyl is from the south." Marigold clarified.

"And I may have been born at night, but it wasn't last night." Ethyl pulled a face. "Did you read what they said all the way through? They're implying a Boston Marriage."

"Yes, I saw that."

"But did you read it all the way through to the end? To where they're implying that the professor killed that girl because she was thwarted in love? The professor, that is, not the girl. Down at the end." She pointed to the very last paragraphs.

"Damnation," Marigold swore. Not that she herself was blameless. Hadn't she originally thought Professor Currier might have done exactly what the paper implied—that she might be a thwarted older woman in love with an innocent younger girl.

But now Marigold was livid with the injustice of it all. Especially since the photograph seemed to offer visual proof of such a dynamic—the photo had captured nothing more than Olivia Thayer gazing admiringly up at Imogen Currier, who steadfastly faced the camera, seemingly unaware of the younger woman's adoring gaze.

"No need to ask who took this photograph." The proof was in the intimacy so thoughtfully captured, even if E. Anthony's name was absent from the bottom of the photo.

"She is a convincing sort of creature, isn't she, that Eliza?"

Marigold gaped at Ethyl. "Don't tell me you've sat for her?"

"I have." Ethyl confirmed without any evasion. "Sent the photograph to my grandmother, home in St. Augustine, as a present, where it was well received. Glad I did it, anyway. Can't speak for the others."

"How many others do you think, have posed for her?"

"A great many, since her charge for the sitting is a pittance—less than a cup of cocoa at one of the tearooms in town. You only pay for the printed photograph if you like it enough to buy it from her," Ethyl considered. "Not cheap, but not exorbitant. A fair value, as far as I can see."

"But this," Marigold insisted as her outrage overtook her. "This selling of photographs without the sitter's permission—for I cannot imagine that Professor Currier should have consented to such a thing—is highly unethical."

"Then I should imagine it is highly profitable."

Trust Ethyl to get right to the heart of the matter.

Marigold tried to calm herself into thinking as logically as her friend. "I imagine you are entirely correct." Hadn't Eliza Anthony herself said she needed the money? Which begged the question. "So just what else do you think she's been selling? And to whom?"

"Shall we go see?" Ethyl suggested.

"Yes." Marigold firmed her resolve. "Let us do just that."

Chapter 26

"Few things are harder to put up with than the annoyance of a good example."

Mark Twain

The darkroom portion of the Student Laboratory and Apparatus Room proved empty of Eliza Anthony's pernicious—at least according to Marigold's feelings—presence. Which gave them free rein to look around. Marigold began poking into cabinets and drawers.

"Just what are we looking for?" asked Ethyl.

"The picture from the tabloid."

Although Eliza Anthony had stated clearly that Professor Currier had not sat for her portrait, Marigold had the evidence before her own eyes. Had the young photographer simply lied outright? She wouldn't be the first liar involved in this murder, but Marigold hoped to perdition she was the last.

Ethyl had begun opening drawers from the other end of the long oak cabinet, so Marigold continued from her end. On the bottom shelf of the next cabinet was a large accordion-pleated leather file—with a promising small brass lock.

"Miss Anthony is trying to keep secrets." And Marigold was just the person to reveal them. She laid the file on the cabinet top and tried to force the lock—with no result.

"Wait," Ethyl hustled back to the far end of the counter. "I thought I saw—yes!" She held up a small string of brass keys.

"Sometimes," she said with a smile, "the oven cleans itself. We'll try them one at a time."

"Excellent plan," Marigold enthused, as if there was some other way of fitting keys into locks.

But Ethyl was as efficient as she was logical, and the third key obediently popped open the lock. "Q.E.D.," she enthused. "Thus, it is demonstrated."

Marigold, whose working knowledge of Latin had not needed the translation, was equally enthusiastic. "Now, let us see what our slippery Miss Anthony is hiding in here."

Each of the file tabs was hand-labeled. Marigold flicked through Portrait, Candid, Landscape, and most interesting, Occasional. "Let's start with the portraits." She pulled out the small stack of photographic prints and handed Ethyl half.

Marigold leafed through the sheets, not finding anything of particular value—or potential—that caught her eye. She moved on to "occasional," which seemed to be various artistic shots of furniture, including several of the corridors and rooms of College Hall and other buildings.

Nothing that might be interpreted as useful—nothing out of the ordinary.

She might have given up, but Ethyl took out the stack of landscapes, and Marigold's eye was immediately drawn to an artistic shot of the boathouse—almost from the same angle as the one Eliza Anthony had taken of Marigold and Dr. Barker with the body.

But this one, Marigold thought, must have been taken earlier in the semester—more leaves were upon the trees, as if they had not yet begun to fall. And in the foreground was a couple—at least it was a man and a woman—that drew Marigold's eye.

Ethyl took a sharp intake of breath.

"What?" Marigold peered harder at the grainy photograph. "What do you see?"

"Looks like Aggie Newton," Ethyl said finally. "I recognize that hat. Wears it every chance she gets."

"No!" Marigold immediately contradicted. The silhouette of the young woman—and she was a young woman, with her hair in a braid down her back—was smaller, more petite, and altogether neater than lanky, athletic Aggie. But the hat should have been seared upon Marigold's brain. "I think that is Olivia Thayer."

"The dead girl?" Ethyl crowded in closer, but immediately came to the salient point. "Then who is that man? I know they say 'cherchez la femme,' but I think we should cherchez le gent."

Ethyl's paraphrase of Alexandre Dumas was apt. In the murky graininess of the photograph, the tall, almost looming man was certainly the very sinister picture of a murderer.

"Cab and Detective Pratt are already looking for him—presumably on an ocean liner docking imminently at Liverpool. But it would help if they had a description of the man." Marigold peered hard at the photograph, trying to glean any other details that might help identify him. "Do you think there's a magnifying glass anywhere?"

"What are you doing here?" an outraged voice intruded.

Eliza Anthony stood in the archway at the top of the stair, dressed in a smart traveling ensemble of velvet trimmed broadcloth, and carrying what Marigold could only assume was her small, portable detective camera.

"Looking for evidence," Marigold refused to be cowed for prying. "As well as you. What can you tell me about this photograph?"

"When did you take it?" chimed in Ethyl.

"What do you remember of this couple?" Marigold kept up the rapid-fire questions. "Did you not recognize Olivia Thayer from your other photographs? Especially the one you sold to the *Morning Standard* of Professor Currier and the girl?" Marigold held out Ethyl's copy of the tabloid.

Eliza flicked a glance at it. "I didn't sell anything to the *Morning Standard*," she insisted sourly.

"And yet, here is a photo only you could have taken, with your acute eye for personality." Marigold thrust the tabloid paper at her as if it were a lance.

But Eliza Anthony remained stubbornly uninjured by Marigold's attempt at physical irony. Instead, she was pleased. "Do you really think so? I mean I've tried to cultivate a singular style, but—"

"It was evidence," Marigold scolded, shaking the paper at her. "Not a compliment."

Eliza Anthony rearranged herself into a defensive posture, crossing her arms over her chest. "I don't care."

"I do. Tell me about this photograph. Please," Marigold added. One might be forceful in one's approach, but rudeness was unnecessary and probably unhelpful with a girl like Eliza Anthony, who had little conscience to counteract what was obviously a great deal of ambition.

Not that Marigold was against ambition—she championed it, especially in other young women. The entirety of their college was a support for ambition.

But never at the expense of others. Never.

Eliza Anthony took the print, walked to the cabinet, and reintegrated it into the stack of landscape pictures. "It was of the boathouse—specifically the rotunda entranceway. I was trying to capture the soaring height of the columns, the way the shadows fell—"

"When was it taken—specifically? Date and time?"

Eliza turned the print over. "October fifth."

"Two days before she was killed." Marigold felt as if someone had walked over her grave—her skin felt tight and clammy under her shirtwaist. "Please, Eliza. Please try to remember everything you can about this moment."

Eliza looked at the photo more critically. "I was concerned about the aperture—about getting the right amount of light and keeping a high depth of field."

"What does that mean?" Marigold's frustration at the young woman's apparent lack of understanding at the gravity of the situation began to rise.

"I was trying to capture the architecture of the columns and the way the light slanted through the rotunda. It was for an independent study I've undertaken in Studio Art—even though the professor doesn't consider photography to be an art. She's a painter," Eliza explained. "Very superior in her attitude."

Marigold tried to get the information she needed out of Eliza's preoccupation. "So, the figures were not intended to be part of the composition?"

"No," Eliza looked askance, wrinkling her nose in distaste. "The focus was on the rotunda. I waited for them to move out of the way. But they didn't, though they moved back and forth—that's what makes their images fuzzy like that. They just wouldn't keep still. But I set the exposure anyway because I was going to lose the effect of the light. I might have even said something—I don't remember. But they still didn't move. They were engaged in some deep discussion or something."

"Were they arguing? Could you hear them?"

"Not really." Eliza shrugged. "The wind was from the west, blowing down the lake. You can see that from the trees in the background."

"And her hair, I suppose. Perhaps that's why her elbow is up like that—brushing her hair out of her eyes?" That lovely auburn hair that had floated on the surface like algae and had wrapped itself around Marigold's hands like a vine.

"Maybe." Eliza was noncommittal, clearly still not interested in the figures that marred her composition.

"And you didn't recognize her? Or think that this might be the same girl who was found beneath the boathouse? You clearly recognized her enough to find that portrait you took of her and Professor Currier?"

"Oh, I recognized the name, once it was out who it was—the Thayer girl, who was supposed to come talk? But I never took her portrait."

"Then how did a portrait that you claim not to have taken, and not to have sold to the tabloids, end up in a photogravure on the front page of the *Morning Standard* ?"

"I don't know. I didn't sell it to them."

"And yet, here it is, on the front page." Marigold fixed her with what she hoped was a no-nonsense, gimlet stare. "So perhaps the better question is—to whom *did* you sell it?" For certainly the mercenary photographer would never have given away such a prize for free.

Eliza looked acutely belligerent. "I didn't sell it at all. I haven't seen so much as a dime, not that it's any business of yours."

Marigold crossed her arms over her chest. "Care to prove it?"

"No," she said staunchly. "I would not. But I can see that you're set on being an everlasting pain in the backside if I don't, so . . ." Eliza snatched the tabloid from Marigold's hand and took a long moment to study it. "This was taken in the Boston studio of Mr. Charles Hearn, who used to have the concession for portraits, as I told you before." She thrust the newspaper back at Marigold. "His background is entirely different from my studio here."

Marigold could immediately see that she was right. "Damnation."

"Indeed," Eliza sniffed. "But now that you've found this other picture of Olivia Thayer in my files, I think I just may dig out the negative plate and see what can be done to sell it."

Marigold did not hide her disapprobation. "How exceptionally mercenary of you."

"How eminently practical," the young woman countered once again. "As was Hearn. For once."

Marigold worked to curb her frustration—it was getting her nowhere. Still. "Leave it to a man to put them in such a pose."

"Who said he did?" Eliza's mouth twisted into a little snicker of a smile. "Who's to say if Professor Currier or Miss Olivia Thayer didn't pose herself?"

"And what does that mean?" Marigold asked.

Eliza tossed up a shoulder in sophisticated unconcern. "None of my business if a young girl has a crush on a professor. If I may say so, it's not the first time anyone has had a crush on dear Professor Currier. Nor, I daresay, the last." She chuckled. "She has that effect."

Marigold wanted to say something cutting, but now that she thought back upon it, there had been at least two girls who had sighed and hung on Professor Currier's every word two years ago, during her junior year. And she herself had had something of a crush on her own favorite professor, Julia Irvine, when she had been an impressionable freshwoman.

Marigold chose her words carefully, working to untie the knot that was the murder and revisit her own feeling that Professor Currier was still hiding something. "And did you think the professor . . . reciprocated that infatuation?" Marigold had formed—and reformed—her own opinion regarding Professor Currier's relationship with her niece, but she was curious as to other people's.

Eliza Anthony shrugged. "Not particularly . . ." She trailed off, then shook her head. "Do you know what—no. She treated those girls in her rhetoric classes with an amused, even affectionate tolerance, not . . ."

"Amorous in any way?"

"No. Not amorous," Eliza confirmed. "Not that—" She broke off.

"Not that . . . ?" Marigold repeated.

Eliza tossed up her shoulder in indifference again. "Not that I didn't think she might be inclined that way, if you know what I mean."

"If you mean like a 'Boston Marriage' of convenience and companionship between consenting ladies—"

Eliza's smile turned back to amused. "Is that what we're calling it now—*companionship* and not attraction?" Her tone was arch and knowing. "But as you said, not my business." Eliza Anthony pulled that purposefully sophisticated pose. "I've got maiden aunties who lost their sweethearts and beaux in the last war. Never married and lived with each other in a brownstone in Clinton Hill, Brooklyn. People always said they had a 'Boston Marriage,' and it used to make them as angry as magpies."

"Yes, it is none of our business," Marigold agreed, "until one of the people involved is murdered."

"Murdered? You mean Olivia Thayer? The paper said she drowned—a suicide."

"And this one says Professor Currier was in love with her. The papers are wrong, Eliza. And now that you know that, don't you think you would want to know you had done everything you could to find the killer?"

"Me?" The girl looked more than astonished—she looked petrified at the very thought. "What do I know?"

"That picture you took of the couple in front of the boathouse likely shows Olivia Thayer with her killer."

Eliza stared at her. And then took her chance. "So don't you think it would be a good thing to show that killer to the public? To warn people so they might be on the lookout for just such a fellow?"

Marigold did not like the answer she had to give. "Yes. I suppose." Hadn't she come to the conclusion that quiet discretion had already done them a great disservice? "Go ahead. Publish and be damned."

"I'd rather publish and be paid," Eliza said, before some of her defiance seemed to fade. "Just like Mr. Hearn. For what it's worth, if he sold that photo to the *Morning Standard*, I'm sure he didn't do so knowing what the article said. He was a nice man. He wasn't that sort of fellow."

Who was? Someone out there? Or someone in here?

Her mind went to the photo missing from Professor Currier's rooms. Had that photo ever been recovered? Or was that missing photo the one that found its way to the front page of the *Morning Standard*?

Then who at Professor Currier's boardinghouse might have had the opportunity to steal the photo from their fellow lodger? Was May Barnacle either more mercenary or more wicked than she seemed? Was there another lodger—perhaps a fellow professor—that Marigold had overlooked? Or were there other parties involving themselves?

"When you approach the *Morning Standard* to sell your photo, ask them where they got this one."

"I may," was Eliza's defiant answer. "Not that it's any business of yours how I conduct my business."

Marigold's patience was near the bitter end. "But it is my business, Eliza, not only when a young woman has turned up murdered, but when you have key evidence you may or may not have deliberately concealed. Not to mention the fact that you are using college facilities to turn a personal profit."

"Unethical," Ethyl decreed.

"Unauthorized," Marigold added.

"Nosy Parker," Eliza grumbled.

"Naturally," Marigold countered. "Olivia Thayer is dead—strangled at the boathouse where you took a picture of her, Eliza—and here you are with all these photographs of the dead girl."

"And what about you?" Eliza shot back. "You're the one who thinks she knows everything. What makes you so sure this really is Olivia Thayer? The figures are entirely out of focus. It could have been anyone."

"Anyone with that hat? Anyone standing in front of the place where a girl wearing that hat was found murdered?"

"Why do you keep saying that?" Eliza grew petulant in her defense. "The paper says she threw herself into the lake because she was heartbroken."

"The paper has made that up out of whole cloth." Marigold didn't care that her tone was scathing. "And we, if we have any heart or brains at all, must ask ourselves the question you seem so fond of asking—who profits? As educated, logical, thinking creatures, it is incumbent upon us to do as the great Roman statesman and orator Marcus Tullius Cicero urged us to and ask, 'Cui bono?' To whose benefit?"

"Certainly not to Olivia Thayer's," said Ethyl.

"Nor to Professor Currier's. Nor to the college," Marigold continued.

Ethyl sighed. "To the benefit of the murderer."

"Naturally," Marigold agreed. "But the murderer is still unknown to us. So, logically, we must examine each person and the benefit they receive for their involvement in this unfortunate affair to find out who benefits the most?"

"Not I," Eliza Anthony averred. "I haven't made hardly any profit on these photographs you're so set about."

Marigold returned her gaze to the newest one—the one with the couple facing each other in front of the boathouse and rephrased her earlier question. "Do you remember anything more about this man in the photo—about what he did, or how he acted while he was in your frame? Any description?"

Eliza's expression grew only slightly less annoyed. "He was a man," was all she would admit. "Couldn't see much more than that. He was just tall and . . . in my way."

Marigold tried another tack. "What was he wearing?"

Eliza shrugged again. "What any man wears." She looked around absently, then gestured to the photographic print. "As you see—a coat and hat."

"Not every man wears a coat and hat," Marigold contradicted. "Mr. Duckett downstairs is in overalls or coveralls and a cap every day. Mr. Griffin drives the Barge in dark blue livery. Professor Hemmings in the Music Hall is in his black morning coat and dove-gray vest every day."

"Which needs laundering something fierce," Ethyl added with characteristic candor.

"I suppose I meant like a professional man." Eliza tried again, without much effect. "A gentleman."

"The color of the coat? The style of the hat?" Marigold pressed, trying to glean any advantage from the grainy black-and-white image. "Can you not recall some distinguishing mark or piece of apparel? Can you not call to mind some hint of color—eyes, hair, clothing? You, who strive to capture those same details in your photographs? Surely you remember something?"

"What, and you do notice such things?" Eliza's response was surprisingly defensive. "Can you describe every person you see on the street?"

Marigold shifted her mind's eye to picture the last person she had met on the street—her charming, if obvious, journalistic friend, although friend was too strong an association. Perhaps she might call him a journalist acquaintance, with his dapper camel hair coat and creased homburg hat with the spotted guinea and hackle feather tucked into the dark brown hatband. "Yes. That is what archaeologists do—describe things in detail. As someone who aspires to be a professional photographer, I am deeply surprised that you cannot."

Eliza shook her head in disagreement. "My eye is for the shot," she explained. "I tend to remember details only after I've photographed them—when I'm looking at the print, you see? The details show up in the printing. And that's how I remember them. Call it a professional hazard. Or handicap."

"Are all photographers like that?"

Eliza pursed her lips and shrugged. "I have no idea. I don't really know any other professional photographers. Which is why I'm trying to sell my photographs, like I told you, to establish myself."

Marigold steeled herself against this plea—for she'd been thoroughly bamboozled by the girl's appeal before. "Will you at least think about it, please? This man in your photograph is probably the man who killed her, and anything—absolutely anything—you can recall about this fellow would be of grave importance. Will you promise to tell me?"

Eliza's agreement was reluctant. "I suppose I could try."

"Thank you." As unsatisfactory as it was, it was the best Marigold could hope for.

But at least, unlike Eliza, she did not feel as if she were entirely on her own—she had friends helping her. President Irvine, Dr. Barker, Isabella, Lucy, Cab, Detective Pratt, Aggie, and Ethyl.

If nothing else, Marigold might take strength in their numbers.

Chapter 27

"Always do right. This will gratify some people, and astonish the rest."

Mark Twain

Marigold and Ethyl were trudging back downstairs when the sound of footfalls in the stairwell diverted their attention.

"Marigold!" A familiar strong voice called up the stairwell. "Come quick!"

Both Marigold and Ethyl immediately ran down the stairs in time to see Lucy cresting the fourth-floor landing.

"Something is wrong with the professor!"

"You see," Isabella, who came to Marigold's dormitory room doorway—and who had clearly spent the time since Ethyl and Marigold had gone upstairs in sampling more sherry—seized her moment. "I told you Lucy would have it in hand."

"Not even a little bit," Lucy rejoined as she immediately turned back the way she had come. "Come on! Something is seriously wrong."

The four of them went pelting down the stairs—well, Marigold and Lucy and Ethyl pelted. Isabella followed a brisk but decidedly less pell-mell pace.

"Where is she?" Marigold asked as they went down.

"I left her in her classroom—"

"This way!" Marigold caught Lucy's hand and tugged her down a short corridor to the porter's stairway, which brought them down to the first floor much more directly than the grand staircases might. "What's happened?"

"The professor took a fright. I was upstairs at the boardinghouse, in the corridor, collecting trays the way I do—"

They clambered down another turn of flights.

"And I heard her cry out and a crash," Lucy panted, "like something fell." She paused to catch her breath. "I ran up there and then she came to the door all white as a ghost, saying, 'This is his doing.'"

"Was it the tabloid?" Marigold resumed her descent.

"Maybe—there was a paper on the floor behind her, when she came out of her room."

"Damnation."

"There was a chair on the floor too—turned on its side. And she kept saying, 'This is his doing. He's here. I know he's here.'"

"Who?"

"No idea. I looked. Wasn't another soul in the place."

They spilled out into the wide first-floor corridors and turned for the Rhetoric classroom.

"She said she had to get out of there, the professor." Lucy took up the tale again. "Said she wasn't safe."

"Safe from what?" Marigold demanded as they ran the last few yards. "Or whom?"

"No idea. I told you, I looked. But she said she wanted to come here, where she would be safe, so I brought her. Figured you'd know what to do."

"Me?" While Marigold had always prided herself on being a take-charge, take-action sort of person, she took one look at the professor and knew without any doubt that she was well out of her depth.

Professor Currier stood unsteadily at her desk, pale and nearly shaking from some force within, gripping the edges of the heavy oaken table as if it were a lifeline in a storm. "I need my medicine. Will you—"

"Yes, of course," Marigold began. "Where—?"

The enfeebled woman could only point toward her desk drawers, so Marigold started at the closest one and began pulling out drawers, filled with ink bottles and steel pen nibs, until she came to the bottom drawer, which contained a small, medicinal-looking amber glass bottle labeled "Atropine Sulphur granules." "Is this—"

"Yes," Professor Currier gasped. "Please. Two."

Marigold measured out two of the granules, which the shaking woman pushed onto her tongue.

"No!" Ethyl shouted suddenly and went for the professor's face, gripping her jaw and forcing her mouth open to scrape out the granules with her fingers.

"What are you doing?" Marigold asked with growing horror. "Have you lost your mind?"

"Please," the professor begged. "I need—"

"No. I swear, they'll only do you harm," Ethyl explained. "I swear. I think you've already had too much."

"Took them at home," Currier panted. "But they didn't help. Made it worse."

"Yes," Ethyl agreed with her before she turned to Marigold. "I think she shows all the signs of atropine poisoning—dry mouth and dilated, nearly black pupils." She took up the professor's wrist. "Low, slow, reedy pulse and agitated, labored breathing."

"It's because of him," Currier cried in a weak panic. "I saw him! He was there."

"Agitation and confusion," Ethyl continued, pointing to the professor's stained shirtwaist. "Sweating and elevated body temperature. We need to get Dr. Barker."

"I'll go!" Marigold immediately responded, happy for something to do besides watch with dawning horror—Lucy wouldn't know where the Hospital Wing was.

And so she ran, racing into the corridor and up the nearest staircase, calling out, "Dr. Barker! Get Dr. Barker!"

By the time Marigold had made it to the second floor, Dr. Barker, dressed in a hygienic white smock and cap over her usual dark dress, was coming through the Hospital Wing doors. "What on earth is going on here?"

"Professor Currier has been poisoned—we think," Marigold added as an explanation for something that she could not really explain. "Ethyl thinks she's had too much atropine?"

"But she's so careful. I prescribed her dosage myself." Dr. Barker frowned before she shook her head and seemed to understand the urgency of the moment. "Where is she?"

"Her classroom." Marigold was turning to lead the way back down to the ground floor, while continuing to try to explain. "She came from her boardinghouse because she said she'd be safe here. And she tried to take the medicine—the atropine in her desk, but Ethyl stopped her and told me to get you."

Dr. Barker said nothing, but when they burst back into the classroom—which was now slowly filling with collegians who had been attracted by all the commotion—she found her voice. "Clear the way! Let me through!"

Marigold and Dr. Barker pushed their way through to the desk where Imogen Currier was seated, attended by Lucy, who had somehow found a cool cloth to press to the professor's brow, and Ethyl, who kept hold of the professor's wrist.

"I counted her pulse at twenty-eight the first time," Ethyl said immediately as Dr. Barker came beside her. "Times two is fifty-six beats per minute, which is—

"Not good," was the doctor's simple response.

"But it's weakening still," Ethyl explained. "Twenty-seven now."

"Imogen," Dr. Barker said sternly. "How much did you take?"

"The usual." The professor's voice was nothing more than a whisper. "One granule when I felt . . . when I felt so weak and anxious." She swallowed and tried to rally. "But it was all wrong. Different. I immediately felt—" She subsided back into her chair as if she were shrinking before their eyes.

"Are you sure?" Dr. Barker demanded. "You didn't accidentally—"

"No!" The professor's protest was feeble but sure. "Tampered," she muttered. "I saw him. I'm sure. He did it."

"Who?" Marigold pressed. But the woman closed her eyes tight and gave no answer.

"If her medicine, or the dose, were tampered with," Dr. Barker theorized, "you might be right about the poisoning."

Marigold felt that horrible feeling of helplessness wash over her, like the water closing over her head when she tried to reach Olivia Thayer. "What can we do to counteract it?"

Everyone in the room looked to the doctor for the answer, but it was Ethyl who supplied a response. "The physostigmine!" Ethyl gasped. "If it's atropine poisoning— I've successfully isolated the compound. Should I get it?"

She looked to Dr. Barker for the answer. And so did they all turn as one to await the doctor's decision.

"Professor Cleaver has confirmed that you have isolated an antidote?" the doctor asked.

"Yes. Twice."

"Then yes, please," Dr. Barker finally answered. "Go! Now!"

"Help me," Ethyl appealed to Marigold, catching her hand as she went for the door, so Marigold ran with her, hard on her heels—or as hard as she could muster after already having run up the flight to the Hospital Wing—up the full five flights to the attic level.

Thank goodness for Wellesley's commitment to physical education and fitness, which made them as strong in body as their academics made them in mind. Still, Marigold was out of breath from the exertion as she followed Ethyl into the Student Laboratory and Apparatus Room.

"Hold this—there. Tightly," Ethyl instructed as she began to pull apart the complicated structure of clear glass flasks and angled condensing pipes. She extricated a tube from a rubber gasket and freed the receiving flask at the end. "I just finished this yesterday morning," she explained as she pawed through a drawer looking for a rubber stopper to seal the flask. "Professor Cleaver and I tested it to make sure it was chemically pure, but—" She left the doubt unspoken as she headed for the door, carrying the flask in front of her as if it were the crown jewels.

"No, Wait!" She turned around. "Get a calibrated measuring pipette—third drawer!"

Marigold quickly rifled through the drawer until she found a thin stem of glassware with ruler-like marks all down the edge, like a clear thermometer, but larger and without the mercury. "This?"

"Yes! Carefully now!"

They went at a careful trot, carrying their respective treasures in front of them as they descended past young women who seemed to be acting as sentries. "They're coming," one bawled down the corridor to the next, who then relayed the message on, until Marigold felt like she had a centurion-like escort back into the classroom, where the doors were held wide and the students had formed a sort of gauntlet to let them through.

"Dose?" Dr. Barker demanded tersely.

"I—" Ethyl's nerve began to give way. "I don't exactly— Safest would be one drop at a time?"

"Yes," the doctor agreed. "Sound plan." She took the pipette Marigold offered her and measured out several drops. "Imogen, open your mouth."

Marigold felt as if the whole room was holding their collective breath. Lucy held one of the professor's hands while the doctor reclasped her other wrist, monitoring her pulse. Next to Marigold, Ethyl had her arms wrapped tightly about herself, as if she feared she might fall apart, her knuckles white with tension.

Marigold put her arm around her shoulder in comfort and support.

But no one said anything. Moments ticked by, turning into minutes.

And then Dr. Barker said, "Her pulse is stronger, less erratic."

It was as if they all drew breath at once, so audible was the room's sigh.

"Well done, Miss Rautencranz." Dr. Barker looked to Ethyl. "Well done, indeed."

Ethyl—so unflappable and easygoing—burst into tears and hid her face in Marigold's shoulder as her fellow collegians, murmured their praise and patted her on the back and shoulder.

"Oh, well done, Ethyl."

"How brilliant."

"It's decided—Senior Class Genius, Ethyl Christine Rautencranz," Marigold told her, as her fellow collegians said, "Hear, hear!" and "Absolutely!"

"Now then." Dr. Barker took charge. "Phyllis, Daphne, please go to the Hospital Wing and bring back a portable stretcher. Nurse will know where it is."

In the hubbub of action and recounting of the event, Marigold was able to give Ethyl's shoulder a squeeze. "I have never been more grateful for our shared experience with poisoners than I am at this moment. If Professor Cleaver doesn't pass you with honors for this moment alone, I'll eat my gown and mortarboard."

"No need, Marigold," counseled Dr. Barker. "I'll be sure to make that recommendation myself."

"Thank you, Dr. Barker." Ethyl was a puddle of gratitude.

"No, thank you. Thank you both." Dr. Emilie Barker looked from Marigold to Ethyl and back. "You're both a credit to your educations and your college. As is your friend here." She acknowledged Lucy. "Intellectual rigor combined with moral courage—the ideal Wellesley women."

Chapter 28

"Three may keep a secret, if two of them are dead."
Benjamin Franklin

The moment the following morning Dr. Barker declared Professor Currier sufficiently recovered to speak from her bed in the Hospital Wing, Marigold was at her bedside.

"She is still very weak," Dr. Barker explained quietly. "So I beg you not to tire her out. She's had a terrible shock, both physically and emotionally. I'll end the interview if I think you're adversely affecting her recovery."

"Yes, ma'am," Marigold answered. There was only one question she needed to know the answer to—she had barely been able to sleep for thinking about it. "Good morning, Professor."

"Marigold." Imogen Currier held out her hand in thanks. "Where is your fellow scientist, Miss Rautencranz? I find that I am very much in her debt."

"I'm sure she doesn't feel so, ma'am. She's just glad she could help."

"As am I. Please tell her so for me, if you would."

"Yes, Professor, I will." Marigold pulled a chair next to the bed. "All of your students are anxious for your recovery."

"Bless them," Imogen Currier breathed. "Such wonderfully loyal girls. And brilliant. Especially you and Miss Rautencranz."

"Thank you, Professor." Marigold accepted her share of the compliment. "I hope you understand my commitment to bringing your niece's murderer to justice."

"Understand it? I agree with it," the professor declared.

Marigold began with a rather round-about approach, easing her way into the professor's confidence. "In that vein, I'm trying to find out all the information I can about Wilkie Valentine—and we don't have much time. He left Boston on the Cunard liner *Ultonia* last Thursday, and there is only a day or so left—at best—before the ship docks in Liverpool and the authorities' ability to have him taken into custody will be gone."

"I see." The professor turned her face away, as she had before—in the carriage when they had traveled to Dedham to identify Olivia's body. And almost every time Wilkie Valentine's name had come up.

Marigold had once thought it was because Professor Currier was trying to conceal something she had done. And now she was not sure what it meant—only that it was important. "I sense you have a very great aversion to Mr. Valentine, Professor—with good reason, I agree."

"Horrible, terrible boy."

Marigold also noted that she had based her own impression of Wilkie Valentine as a very young man of a similar age to Olivia, on the professor's labeling him as such. "The ticket that we found for Wilkie Valentine amongst Olivia's possessions listed his age as thirty-two—hardly a boy."

"Really?" The professor pulled a face. "He was certainly not that old—he was . . . Oh." Her brows had risen, as if she had come to some new realization. "I suppose he was."

"So, you had met him—enough to gauge his age?"

"I suppose." She turned her face away again.

Marigold changed tack—for now. "You believe Wilkie Valentine killed Olivia?"

"I can't think of anyone else who might want to do away with her. She was an angel." Imogen Currier dabbed at her eyes. "A feisty, sometimes argumentative, free-thinking angel, but an angel all the same. So passionate. So articulate."

"I am sorry I never got to meet her," Marigold said with sincerity. "She seems just the type of girl I would adore having as a friend."

"Oh, yes," the professor agreed. "You would have liked her—and she you."

Marigold steered the conversation back to less sentimental topics. "What I can't understand is how did this Wilkie Valentine come to meet her at all—he doesn't seem the sort of person who would come to one of her lectures?"

Imogen Currier sighed heavily. "I didn't want to say—we didn't want to say. But it's all my fault."

Marigold resisted the impulse to reassure her. "How so?"

"Because I didn't understand he was a threat," the professor qualified. "I dismissed him—quite literally showed him the door. I didn't think he would go to such lengths. That he would use her to threaten me—us."

"Who is 'us'?"

"My sister and I. Although, I can't think that he understood Olivia was my niece—I never told him so. Although upon reflection, perhaps I should have."

Marigold could not follow what, to her, appeared to be an ungainly leap of logic on the professor's part. "What should you have told him?"

"That Olivia was my niece. It might have made some difference. But he was a Virginian—I suppose they had different ideas in the south."

"What kind of different ideas?"

"About cousins!" Professor Currier closed her eyes again. "But to be honest, I suppose he was bent on revenge any way he could get it."

Marigold felt that skittering of awareness, like an alarm across her skin. "Revenge?"

"For what had happened to him, I suppose." Professor Currier leaned back into her pillow and breathed deeply, as if she were gathering her strength. "We'd kept it a secret for so long—because there was no real reason not to. But I suppose it will all come out now."

Marigold took her own measured, tense breath. "What will come out?"

"Wilkie Valentine thought I was his mother," she said simply.

Marigold did not know when she had been more shocked. Professor Imogen Currier hardly seemed the type of woman to have—done what? Had a secret love affair that had resulted in a child? Like Eliza, Marigold frankly didn't think the professor was the kind of woman who was romantically interested in men.

"His mother?" Marigold finally prompted.

"To be clear, I am not." Professor Currier met Marigold's eye with a weary sort of frankness—but frankness, nonetheless. "And I do not say that because I am ashamed, or any such nonsense, but simply because it is not true. The truth is that he is the natural son of my sister, Lucinda Currier. And she, I was told by the Alms House Hospital in Richmond, passed away at his birth, leaving the orphan child. Puerperal fever," she said as an explanation to Dr. Barker, who had been silent the whole time.

"Sepsis due to streptococcal infection," Dr. Barker elaborated. "Unfortunately, a fairly common occurrence after childbirth in prior days. You have my condolences."

"Thank you," Professor Currier acknowledged. "But it was many years ago—thirty-two to be exact, now that I've stopped to count. My sister had gone away suddenly some months before—left us, much like we thought Olivia had. Perhaps that was what delayed us taking any action to recover Olivia—the stunning feeling of history repeating itself." Her sigh was full of self-blame. "But Lucinda's boy child had already been taken into an orphanage by the time we—my sister Almira and I—were informed of his birth. I sent money for his care—once I knew of both Lucinda's death and of the infant's existence. But by the time I made it down to Richmond—that was where she had gone, though we never learned why—the child had already been adopted by a prominent local family, the Valentines. I thought it best to let be—he was far better off, I thought, with such a family." She closed her eyes and leaned back into the pillows as if exhausted by her story. "Clearly, I was wrong."

"You were not wrong, Imogen," Dr. Barker said. "Not at all."

"I tried to tell him about her—she was such a lovely girl, Lucinda—since he was so insistent and demanding. But he didn't want to listen to what he termed a conveniently made-up story. He had already made up his mind to blame me."

"So, he came to you first?" Marigold had assumed Valentine's entire focus had been on Olivia.

"He did," Professor Currier confirmed, "with his accusations and his anger. When I told him about Lucinda, he didn't believe me. But he went away, at least. Or so I thought. Until he reappeared, courting Olivia. But I didn't realize it was he—Olivia didn't tell us her admirer's name at first, just said there was a fellow romancing her, and that she couldn't seem to discourage him." She shook her head as if she might reorder her thoughts. "I don't know how he found her—I can only assume he saw her with me—and assumed the worst, the way some people do. Like that wretched tabloid."

"Oh, I am sorry. I had hoped you hadn't seen the paper." Marigold exchanged glances with Dr. Barker, wondering if the doctor thought that, with that information, the professor's mistake with her medication was far less easily dismissed as accidental. "Did you read the article?"

"Yes," the professor confirmed. "That was what sent me to my medicine."

Dr. Barker asserted herself into the conversation without any prompting from Marigold. "And you're sure you didn't make a mistake with the medicine, Imogen? You weren't so upset that you perhaps took too much?"

Professor Currier frowned in confusion. "Do you mean that I mistook the dose because I was upset, or that I—" She gasped. "—that I purposefully took the wrong dose?"

"You have been under a grave strain, Imogen," Dr. Barker said quietly. "This latest outrage—"

"Was a fresh insult, yes. And hurtful—entirely so. And I was uncommonly upset—upset enough to want to take the medicine so I might deal with the consequences, so I might speak to Julia and see what might be done to preserve the reputation of the college. I am certainly not the first female professor to be accused of inappropriate or unnatural conduct with a student—"

"Nothing unnatural about it," the doctor said quietly before she continued. "And you won't be the last," she added without much consolation. "It could have been any one of us."

Marigold was struck by a number of thoughts at once.

Firstly, that if Professor Currier had neither taken the extra dose on purpose nor been unmindful of how much she had taken, then another factor—or malefactor—was at play here. And poison was, generally speaking, a woman's weapon.

May Barnacle, with her access to the professor's room and possessions, and her knowledge of the professor's habits, came swiftly back to mind. As did the opinionated members of the Société des Belles Lettres—she had not forgotten them.

And secondly, for her own part, Marigold was taken not only by the quiet conviction in Dr. Barker's voice but by the realization that she had thought about the accusation in the tabloid from the wrong point of view—it affected not only Professor Currier but nearly everyone in the faculty. Female academics were barred by tradition from marrying, which left them open to accusations of being either dried-up old spinsters, full of bitterness and disappointed hopes, or unnatural beings who didn't want the company of a man. They were left vulnerable to derision and calumny no matter what they did.

And this was the future Marigold had wanted for herself—this independent, intellectual life, free from the unequal dictates of marriage. But this independent life had its own costs—accusations that were so commonplace they were shopworn.

But they could still do horrible damage—yesterday's events were evidence of that.

And there was still a part of the sequence of events of the day before that Marigold was curious about.

"So, this feeling of palpitations was not new?" she asked Professor Currier before she turned to Dr. Barker. "She was under your care for this condition well before Valentine showed up in Wellesley?"

"Yes," Dr. Barker confirmed. "I've been treating Imogen for arrhythmia—the disturbance in cardiac rhythm—for quite some time."

"When I escorted you home from your sister's house," Marigold asked the professor, "was that what made you feel unwell?"

"Yes. As I have grown older, my heart's weakness manifests itself in tiredness—weariness," the professor explained.

"Did you take your medicine then, that day, as you had intended?"

"No, actually." The professor seemed to have surprised herself with this admission. "I found myself revived somewhat by our cook's soup. Miss Lucy Dove—although you seemed to already be acquainted with her." Professor Currier's brows rose in question. "She made me the bone broth she mentioned, and I found myself refreshed enough to go up to my room, without feeling the need for the medication. Perhaps it was the broth, perhaps I just needed rest."

"But rest wasn't enough yesterday? What happened then?"

"Mrs. Barnacle brought me the copy of the tabloid," the professor said simply before she closed her eyes momentarily. "Well, you can imagine."

"So, you took your regular dose of the medicine?" Marigold asked Professor Currier. "Two granules of the atropine?"

"Only one, to start. May saw me measure it out—with a glass of water. But instead of regulating my pulse, it became even more erratic. I felt faint and frankly nauseated. Quite distressed."

"So, Mrs. Barnacle was there?"

"Initially. She left me to rest."

How convenient. Certainly, Mrs. Barnacle ought now be treated with some suspicion.

But Marigold had another question that had arisen from the professor's statements yesterday. She took her own leap—of both logic and faith. "Is that when you saw him?"

Dr. Barker looked at Marigold sharply, but Marigold just let the question hang without any explanation or prompting.

"Yes," the professor admitted. "Yes, at least, I thought I did see him. But I heard what Lucy Dove said yesterday—I wasn't entirely insensate—that there was no one there in the room with me. But I could swear he came and stood directly in front of me. I must have imagined it, or worse, hallucinated him. Your Miss Rautencranz said I was confused—she must have been right."

"And exactly who did you see?" Marigold wanted to be completely sure she understood the professor.

"Wilkie Valentine." Imogen Currier all but whispered the name, as if she couldn't even bear to hear it. "I thought he had come back. Of course, it couldn't have been him—he's run off, you said, escaped across the ocean."

Marigold was no longer entirely sure—he could not be in two places at the same time. "What was he wearing, when you saw him in your room?"

"Why . . . I don't know. He gave me such a fright perhaps I fainted." She shook her head, as if in disbelief. "He couldn't possibly have been there, so what does it matter?"

"Indulge me, please," was all Marigold could think to say. "If you close your eyes and imagine him in front of you the way he looked yesterday, what color were his eyes? What was he wearing? A coat? A color?"

"A camel hair coat. And a dark hat."

A spike of dreadful, dawning horror rove through Marigold. Every fiber of her being radiated new alarm. Even as she tried to tell herself that camel hair coats were commonplace and many men wore dark homburg hats, she also knew there were no coincidences.

She made herself speak calmly. "What did Wilkie Valentine wear the first time he came to you with his accusations and anger?"

"The same thing, I suppose," Professor Currier said, before she frowned. "Which is why I am sure I imagined him that way yesterday. He had made an impression on me the first time I saw him—a handsome young man, so well-spoken and polite, so gentlemanly. A wolf in sheep's clothing, if ever there was. A wolf in search of money."

Marigold could say nothing in response, for hadn't she had exactly the same impression? And there were *no* coincidences when it came to murder.

Professor Currier went on. "I told him I had paid all the money for him I was able when he was an infant and that surely he was the responsibility of the Valentines now."

Marigold was distracted back to another question. "Was Olivia Thayer likely to come into any money? If she had married Valentine and they had eloped to Europe as Valentine planned, might she have expected some money from her parents or from you?"

Professor Currier frowned, as if she had not thought of this before. "Certainly—neither her parents nor I would ever have abandoned her, however much we might have disagreed with her actions. She was my heir—in property as well as intellectually—so she might pursue an independent, academic life."

"Did Valentine know that? Did he think he might expect money from the Thayers as well?"

"I don't know, she might have told him, although frankly, there isn't much—we are modest people, of modest means. Our father's estate was modest, as well—mostly spent on our educations. I live very frugally in my boardinghouse, which is comfortable but not lavish by any stretch of the imagination, while my sister lives entirely economically in her husband's family house. I don't believe they light a fire before the first of December, no matter how hard the weather turns. But I didn't tell him about Almira—I didn't want him to darken her door with his threats and innuendo too."

"But he found her—or at least Olivia—anyway? How did he even know where to find you? Richmond is a very long way away."

"I suppose it was because I had signed the papers the Valentines insisted upon, relinquishing any familial rights to the boy. But that seemed eminently practical at the time. The Valentines were far more wealthy than we, my sister and I, despite the war. Or perhaps because of it."

"So, he came to you this fall, accusing you of being his mother and abandoning him?"

"Essentially."

"And he asked you for money?"

"Demanded it," the professor corrected. "Said he would ruin me." Imogen Currier sighed again. "I frankly didn't think it was possible—how could he ruin me? I do almost nothing to draw attention to myself. I have taught at Wellesley for nearly twenty-nine years. I have devoted myself to my students. I have earned the respect of both my fellow faculty members and the administration."

"Naturally," Marigold agreed before asking, "So you told him no?"

"I did. But he swore that he would find a way to make me pay. And he did." Professor Currier took a long regretful breath. "He found Olivia. And the tabloids."

It broke Marigold's heart anew to think that Olivia herself had not mattered—that this vibrant girl with all she had to offer the world, all her passion and intelligence, had been nothing more than a pawn to the man. Just another girl to be disposed of in the water. Tossed away.

The poor girl.

"But I never said a word about her to him, I'm sure!" the professor continued. "Or my sister—nothing about the Thayers at all. I can only assume that Valentine watched me and saw me with Olivia, coming to campus to sit in on classes. And he horned in with his flattery and his anger and his resentment, all hidden behind a veneer of false charm."

"Yes." Marigold could just picture him, flattering and charming his way along the campus paths to the very door of College Hall.

Such arrogance. Such conceit.

Such murderous intent.

Which gave rise to another, conflicting thought. "What would have happened, I wonder, if he *had* convinced Olivia to go with him—if she had succumbed to his blandishments and agreed to elope to Europe?"

Professor Currier shook her head. "It is a blessing perhaps that we will never know. That he didn't have the chance to ruin her and abandon her—for I am quite convinced he never meant to marry her. That he felt nothing for her, really."

"But why didn't he?" Marigold finally asked. "He had bought her a ring—surely that demonstrates some seriousness." Although, the issue of the second Mrs. Valentine—whoever she was—boarding the Cunard liner remained unresolved. "Why would a man who had everything—the Valentines had wealth and privilege, you said. He seems an educated man, who could certainly be able to make his way in the world without resorting to blackmail threats. It seems such a low ambition."

"Low, wicked, and hateful," Professor Currier confirmed. "He said he was out of money—or nearly so. He didn't say why. But he was clearly so deeply resentful. And in the end, revengeful."

Chapter 29

"Life appears to be too short to be spent in nursing animosity or registering wrongs."

Charlotte Brontë

Marigold left the Hospital Wing with a new determination. And new suspicions. Which she would share with Detective Pratt as soon as she could confirm her misgivings.

"Marigold."

"Good morning, Sarah." Marigold stood aside at the door of the Hospital Wing to let Sarah Appleton pass. But to her astonishment—although, to be fair, she hadn't much astonishment left within her—Sarah stopped to talk.

"I was just going in to see Professor Currier. She is a great favorite, you know."

"I do know," Marigold acknowledged. "I am sure she will enjoy your visit with her."

"We . . . I heard about what you did for her yesterday."

"It was all Ethyl, thank goodness, with her scientific expertise. I was only happy I could be of some help." One never wanted to make too much of oneself, especially with a person like Sarah.

"Nevertheless." Sarah nodded awkwardly. "Those of us in the Société very much appreciate what you did for our dear professor."

"Happy to oblige." Marigold might have left it at that, but her suspicions about Sarah lingered, too strong to ignore. But an appeal was better than an accusation. "I was also hoping you might be able to help, Sarah, with this murder of Olivia Thayer." She refused any attempt at ladylike discretion now—even for Sarah. "And this attempted murder of Professor Currier."

Sarah paled. "Attempted murder? Me? How?"

"You said you are this year's president of the Société des Belles Lettres?"

"Yes?"

"And as such, you must have known Miss Olivia Thayer, who was also a member?"

"I did." Sarah looked conscious—the corners of her wide, elegant mouth turned down.

"Why didn't you tell me who she was at the start—at the boathouse, when I found her body?" Sarah had been the first to deny any knowledge of the girl's identity.

"I don't know," she confessed. "She looked so different, so dead," she tried before she finally acknowledged her true motives. "And I admit, I wanted to impede you in any way I could, even if it was to say nothing."

And there was that passivity in Sarah's aggression.

So Marigold said nothing, letting her own silence passively convey her judgment.

"It was not well done of me," Sarah was forced to admit. "I had none of your aplomb and I wished I had. I made . . . a mistake."

"Naturally." It was simple jealousy. From a girl who had every advantage of birth and opportunity. Yet, she was still jealous of others who had far less.

"And the truth is, I didn't particularly care for her or her suffragist views—especially her lording it about the place, joining the Societé before she was a member of the college."

So much jealousy to go around.

"And that man," Sarah added in a low confidential whisper. "That lapdog, always waiting at the door for her." Her eyebrows rose like a triumphal arch. "Girl that age with a grown man."

Marigold was not surprised, but she was very nearly shocked. This was a new characterization of the fellow, who had up to this point been called rough and proprietary, and a ne'er-do-well and a rotter. "Lapdog?"

"He waited around for her, like a dog left outside a shop waiting for its master."

"And she asked this of him?" Marigold recalled Aggie's description of the man who had presumably thought she was Olivia, grabbing her arm in a proprietary manner and speaking to her roughly. "Was he not perhaps more like a guard dog instead? Which begs the question, how are unaccompanied, unattached men allowed to linger"—and lie in wait—"about the college without anyone's say-so? Wouldn't Mr. Duckett or one of the porters drive him away?"

"I suppose." Sarah shrugged. "Somehow they didn't."

Somehow he had charmed them or fobbed them off with some ready excuse, Marigold was sure.

But practical considerations before anything else. "How often does the Society of Belle Lettres meet?"

"Once a month," Sarah answered. "So only two meetings so far. But they've been very productive."

"When are the society's meetings? What time?"

"In the afternoons, between the last afternoon class and the dinner bell. Although often we go in to dinner together," Sarah went on. "Olivia Thayer did ask to stay to dinner at the last meeting. I remember because she asked if Mr. Griffin might be available to drive her home—or at least into town where she lived—on the Barge. But the lapdog—or guard dog, I suppose I see now—was there and insisted on escorting her home."

Marigold felt her alarm begin to pound in her ears. "What day was that?"

"Our meetings are first Fridays, so October fifth."

Two days before he killed her. But that almost made it worse—Olivia had to endure days of Valentine's unwanted, overbearing attention. Poor girl.

"And can you," Marigold heard her own voice waver, "describe this man who lurked in wait for Olivia?"

Sarah's patrician face blanched. "Do you mean that man I saw waiting for Olivia Thayer is most likely the man who—?"

"Who strangled her with his bare hands and threw her into the lake for dead for us to find," Marigold finished. "Yes."

Sarah put her hand to her mouth in horror. "But that man didn't look like a murderer. He looked so gentlemanly. And refined."

That was what Marigold had thought too, hadn't she?

But she had to be sure. "Can you describe him—personally, hair and eyes, not just what he was wearing?"

"Dark hair and dark eyes. A nice noble sort of nose without being a Roman nose, if you see what I mean."

"Naturally," Marigold agreed. "What else can you remember?"

"Tall—seemed taller because he towered over her. Olivia was just a little bit smaller than you, I should judge. But he had a very buttery sort of smile." Sarah shook her head as if she heard the inanity of that description. "You know what I mean—like he poured out the butterboat over her every time he smiled."

"I do know what you mean, Sarah. Because I think that I have seen that smile too."

On James Wilkerson's face.

Wilkerson—not John Wilkes Booth. It was Wilkerson that Wilkie Valentine's name reminded her of. Tall, charming, camel hair coat wearing Wilkerson.

Right in front of her, all this time.

"I have to go." Marigold ran up to her dormitory room, where her typewriting machine sat gathering dust, a tangible symbol of her faltering academic status. She turned a blind eye to its silent rebuke and pulled out her appointment calendar, in which she kept track of classes and assignments—most notably the missed ones—as well as any social engagements she might have, thankful for the habit of meticulously organized note-taking.

She scanned for the last mention of Wilkerson's name—and there it was, Wednesday, October 10th, their conversation in the tearoom, when she had given him her appeal. Which he had never seen printed. Perhaps because he had never intended to.

Perhaps he had only wanted to know what she knew, so he could stay one step ahead of her. And make his escape on the Cunard liner *Ultonia* the next day? Because he had realized that she was slowly drawing closer to identifying Olivia Thayer, and that it was only a matter of time before his connection to the girl was discovered?

It would be in character for such a rotter to turn tail and run.

Except . . .

Her last conversation with Professor Currier echoed in her ears. What if the professor, who was by all accounts and experience a sober-minded, rational, educated woman, really did see someone in her room—perhaps because that someone had actually been there?

But where was he now?

There was only one way to find out.

Her bicycle took her from College Hall through the gate at East Lodge and up Washington Street to the boardinghouse in no time.

She found Lucy in the kitchen with May Barnacle.

"Well, hello, Marigold," Lucy greeted her. "Is the professor better this morning? That was a heck of a to-do yesterday, I don't mind saying. Don't know when I've ever been that frightened."

"I'm sorry for your fright, but I will admit to being very glad you acted as you did, Lucy. Without your quick thinking . . ." Marigold did not want to contemplate what greater harm might have happened—there was altogether more than enough harm as it was. "But in answer to your question, I just spoke to Professor Currier this morning and she is recovering nicely. But she told me again today that she did think she saw someone in her room yesterday. I know you said you looked and the room was empty but did you look through the rest of the house?"

"No," Lucy frowned and shook her head. "How could I do that when I was taking her over to the college to see you?"

"Yes, of course, I see."

Marigold turned to the landlady, May Barnacle, whose conduct—as far as Marigold could see—might not have been entirely blameless. If Wilkerson had charmed Marigold and the porters at the college—and who knew how many others—there was a fair chance he had managed to charm the landlady. "What about you, Mrs. Barnacle? I notice you like to keep a sharp eye on the place from your porch."

"Looking after things." May Barnacle eyed her warily, as if she could not make out Marigold's intent. "I see people come and go from the porch, but it's starting to get too cold to sit out much."

"Were you out yesterday?"

"Well, a little, but I didn't sit out too long. Like I said, too cold."

"Did you hear the professor's cry? Lucy said it sounded as if some furniture turned over? Did you hear that?"

"Well, I was back downstairs by then—come to see if I could get some of Lucy's bone broth that had done so much good for the professor the first time. Because I had taken her the copy of the *Morning Standard* that put her into her taking, you see. I got it from Mr. Henry as I was leaving the butcher shop, and I thought she should see it."

Mrs. Barnacle seemed sincere. "How did she take the news?" Marigold probed.

"Well, how else could she? It sent her straight to her nerve medicine, but that didn't seem to help at all, which is when I came down for the broth."

Marigold looked to Lucy for confirmation.

"That's right," Lucy agreed as she worked. "I was getting out a pan to warm the broth when I heard the crash, and Mrs. Barnacle, she said, 'You go, you're bigger and stronger.' So I went."

So far, so logical. But Marigold remained leery. "And what did you do then, Mrs. Barnacle?"

"I went looking for Homer, in case we needed to send over for the doctor, but the professor asked Lucy to take her over to the college instead."

"Who is Homer?"

"Oh, that's Mrs. Brown the skivvy's boy," Mrs. Barnacle explained. "He comes by now and again in the afternoons—"

"Every day," Lucy interjected beneath her employer's patter.

"—when Mrs. Brown is just finishing up her chores, afore she heads home. Lives down in the Fells." May Barnacle waggled her eyebrows when mentioning the area just beyond the town limits, as if that was all she needed to say.

Lucy was having none of that unspoken opinion. "He's a Black child." She cut into Mrs. Barnacle's litany of unuseful facts. "He most often comes after school—that is, if he goes to school. Sometimes he comes with Althea Brown in the mornings. Doesn't care much for school because he's not often treated right. But that boy is sharp. If he's seen anything, he'll know."

"Did you find Homer when you were looking for him yesterday, Mrs. Barnacle?" Marigold tried to steer the landlady back on track.

"Didn't need to when Lucy told me she was taking the professor over to the college. I turned my mind to what was going to happen to the supper with Lucy gone."

"I had roast chicken I was about to start," Lucy explained. "And that was a near thing with all the coming and going to the college. I had to serve it a little late, the chicken. But sure enough, Mrs. Barnacle had everything ready for me, so that supper was still exactly as it should have been."

"Best cook I ever had," said May Barnacle. "It's like she and that stove are one person. Like manna from heaven, her cooking." She sidled closer to take a whiff from a fragrant pot. "Always got something or another on the hob."

"Thank you, Mrs. Barnacle." Lucy was all gracious acceptance.

Marigold tried to turn their attention back to the murder—and potential attempted murder—at hand. "So, you were either with each other or with Professor Currier?"

"No where else to be," Mrs. Barnacle cackled. "I see to my boarders myself."

"What about the other boarders?" Marigold asked. "Was there anyone else you noticed coming or going?"

May Barnacle scratched her chin. "Once they went away—Lucy and the professor—I straightened up the table that Imogen had turned over—"

Lucy stropped kneading her dough. "I don't remember a table turned over. I thought it was that little side chair—the professor said she'd leaned too hard on the back of it and it went over. I picked that up to help her out of the house."

"Oh, no, her whole side table—the one with the stained-glass lamp—was tipped over. Glass everywhere, but I suspect that was mostly her water pitcher and glass. She had a lovely blue set, that she used to take her medicine."

"And that was broken? And you cleaned it up?"

"Certainly, I did." Mrs. Barnacle was near outraged at the suggestion that her house was less than perfectly kept. "I couldn't have water staining the floor. We keep a clean and tidy house, we do. Everything is top notch. Top notch." She nodded to herself before she nodded at Lucy, as if acknowledging her part in that superior housekeeping.

"Were any of your other boarders involved? Any of them here to lend a hand?"

"I would never ask them to," Mrs. Barnacle protested. "Most of my ladies are professional women—at their places of business or over at the college during the day. Don't recall anyone else about, except Homer and Mrs. Brown. She was airing out my rooms—that's the schedule for a Tuesday. Everything keeps to a schedule, that's how things are kept top notch."

"Thank you, ma'am." Marigold couldn't decide if she was relieved or suspicious that May Barnacle's explanation was so reasonable. And believable. Which meant she had to go on to her next theory and her next witness.

Poison might have been a women's weapon, but there was always the exception that would prove the rule.

CHAPTER 30

"Bullies are cowards at heart and may be credited with a pretty safe instinct in scenting their prey."

Anna Julia Cooper

"Is young Homer about?" Marigold asked. Children were often overlooked by adults—especially men.

"He's usually in the back of the yard. Likes the chickens," May Barnacle offered.

"Likes eating the chickens," Lucy amended. "Likes eating anything he can get his hands on—growing boy."

"Got a hollow leg, that boy does," was Mrs. Barnacle's opinion.

"Might you have something I could take him to ease the hollow feeling?" Marigold asked Lucy. A hungry boy was bound to be more amenable when he was being fed.

Lucy had a plate at the ready. "Leftover buttermilk biscuit'll do him some good. It's stale, from yesterday," she added, probably for the landlady's benefit. "But he'll be glad of it. Just don't use too many big words, Miss College Manners."

Marigold felt her face curve into a smile. After so many days of grim expressions, the feeling was a welcome change. "Thank you, Lucy."

She found Homer Brown playing in the small yard beside the carriage house, throwing rocks to knock over a tin can set on the low stone wall.

"I'm Marigold," she began. "Miss Lucy from the kitchen gave me this plate for you. She told me to come talk to you. She said you're a clever boy with a sharp eye."

"Did she?" Homer's sharp eyes were all for the buttermilk biscuit.

"She did," Marigold confirmed with an encouraging smile as she offered him the plate. "Have at it while it's warm."

The biscuit disappeared before Marigold could formulate her next question. "I was wondering if you noticed anything strange or off about Mrs. Barnacle's house in the last few days? Anyone sneaking around or where they shouldn't be?"

Homer turned his head away and eyed her slantandicular—as Marigold's cousins on Great Misery used to say. "Why you want to know?"

"Because some very bad things have happened to Professor Currier who lives here, and I'm trying to find out who might have done those things."

"I ain't done nothing," the boy declared hotly—hotly enough for Marigold to think he had done something, even if it didn't have anything to do with Professor Currier.

"I'm sure you didn't." Marigold made her voice as bland as a piece of flounder. "But you're clever and you've got sharp eyes, Miss Lucy says. I was wondering if you saw someone—anyone—who shouldn't have been here?"

Homer squirmed a little within his well-worn shirt before he finally admitted. "There was that fellow."

Marigold was alarmed and reassured all at the same time, though her heart started to beat harder within her chest. There were no coincidences. "What sort of a fellow?"

"Nosy sort. Asking questions, mostly."

That "mostly" was laden with dangerous potential. "What questions did he ask you, Homer?"

Homer pulled a long face for such a short child. "Did I know the professor lady?" He tossed up his skinny shoulder in an all-too-casual shrug, as if to ask how such a thing could be of any consequence.

"I asked him which one, cuz there's a passel of 'em living here. But they keep neat and tidy, those professors. That's what my momma says."

"Which professor did he want to know about?"

"The little one, who teaches speechmaking. That Professor Currier—like the picture makers, my momma says."

"Currier and Ives?" Marigold tried the names of the famous, if nostalgic printmakers.

"Got their pictures up in the parlor."

Lucy had the measure of Homer Brown—he was clearly a child of vast curiosity. "What else did you notice?"

"That for a white man, he was pretty hard done by."

"Hard done by?" This was an expression Marigold had not heard. "What do you mean?"

"He dressed real nice, with that fancy hat with the little feathers—I want a hat like that."

If Marigold had not been so horrified by the confirmation of her suspicions, she might have been in sympathy with a hat lover, if not with that particular hat. Although, she did acknowledge, "It is a very dapper hat."

"You know the one—that nice brown one?" Homer's smile was wishful. "But down at the other end, his shoes was all worn down on the heel and sole. He put newspaper inside 'em. I saw the hole when he sat out behind the carriage barn, talking, with his foot over his knee, all casual-like, asking me questions. It was that advert for the soap with the cat doing the washing."

"How very clever of you to notice." Marigold herself had made no notice of the fellow's shoes. She had been too busy making the mistake of trying to flirt her own way into the man's good graces. So much for "seeing things other people don't see." "So, he was low on funds, do you think?"

"Poor as a stray dog, I reckon. My momma said his collar had been turned more than once. He only had a few pennies to pay me. After the first time, I wanted to see the color of his money before I did his bidding."

"And what was his bidding?"

For the first time, Homer lost some of his nonchalance. "I ain't suppose to say."

Marigold took a very pointed, well-honed stab in the dark. "Did he ask you to take anything from the professor's room? Or perhaps break something? Not money or anything valuable, but something that wouldn't do any harm? Or maybe just a prank, like turning over a table, or taking a photograph picture of two ladies, maybe?"

Homer looked uncomfortable. "Promise you won't tell?"

Marigold felt she had to come down on the side of moral right—she did not promise. But under her level stare, he finally confessed. "Said he was going to bring the picture back, so I wouldn't get in trouble. But he didn't bring it back. And my momma whupped me bad."

Marigold's outrage, as well as her terrible sense of guilt, sat together like sour milk in her stomach. Wilkerson had sold the photo to the tabloid—which was then likely used to finance the second set of ocean liner tickets to make his getaway.

"Why didn't your mother tell the professor?"

"Didn't want to lose her job. And if you tell on me and she loses her job, she's gonna whup me something fierce."

"I won't tell if you tell me everything. Was there anything else he wanted you to do?" Marigold asked even though she feared she already knew the answer.

"He wanted me to get that pretty little blue bottle with the cup that fits on top. He wanted me to bring that to him, and I did, and after, he sent me to put it back, so it was all right."

Professor Currier had taken her medication with water from that very blue bottle.

Vindication sat cold in her stomach. "Was that yesterday, Homer?"

"Uh-huh. But he didn't pay me nothing like he promised. He went away at a run, after the professor went into such a taking." Homer pulled a glum face. "Got a whupping then too, just for talking to him. But he said he was going to pay me," he said in his own defense.

Marigold patted his shoulder. "I am sorry his lies cost you a spanking."

"It was a whupping," he said again, in order that she might understand the difference.

"I am very sorry," she said solemnly. "But you know you should not have done something that you knew was wrong—even if he had paid you well for the favor."

"Wouldn't have been enough to take a whupping."

Marigold patted his shoulder in attempted consolation. "No, my dear Homer. Nothing ever is."

She took a deep breath to force herself to think logically, to put herself in James Wilkerson's—or Wilkie Valentine's—worn-down shoes. "Did he ever mention where he was staying? A different rooming house, where they take men?"

Homer shrugged in the way of children who have more important things on their mind, like throwing rocks at trees and avoiding whuppings. "Thought he said he was down the way, maybe, over down Waban Brook. Otises keep a place for menfolk of his sort."

His sort—lying, aiding and abetting scoundrels.

"Is that where he went away at a run yesterday?"

Homer shrugged again. "Nah. He went that way. Like he was going to the train." He hitched his thumb over his shoulder at the unseen station up Washington Street.

"Thank you, Homer." Marigold dug into the pocket of her tweed bloomers for a nickel. "I appreciate your time and your honesty."

"A whole nickel?" He looked up at her with dubious eyes. "Do I hafta tell my momma about it?"

"That is entirely up to you. If you think you can get away without incurring any whuppings—but I'd think twice if I were you."

Homer's sly grin told her there would be no thinking about it, but Marigold had bigger fish—and bigger liars—to catch.

James Wilkerson was Wilkie Valentine. He really was like the villains of Jane Austen's novels—having all the appearance of good and none of the actual goodness.

Marigold set off on her bicycle, following Homer's direction, heading south down Washington Street toward Waban Brook intent upon evidence to not only link Valentine to Olivia's murder but to the attempted murder of Imogen Currier, as well.

He had lingered longer than they had thought, to exact his final revenge against the professor—and to remove the person who could conclusively link him to Olivia Thayer—but was now probably gone for good.

She wheeled up and down a few rutted lanes before she found a hinged sign on a picket fence advertising "Rooms to Let" with a placard next to the door that read "Otis House."

Marigold dismounted, taking a path toward the rear of the house and the kitchen, where there was usually bound to be someone working, if Lucy's example had taught her anything.

"Help you?" Was the cryptic query from the dooryard, where a worn-looking woman very much in the vein of Marigold's first impression of her mother, Sophronia Hatchett—that is to say, a crone—toiled over a washing mangle.

"Yes, ma'am, good afternoon. How do you do." One might adapt one's standards but never let them down. "I was wondering if you had a man by the name of Wilkie Valentine resident here?"

"Who?" The woman turned down her mouth and peered hard at Marigold. "Don't put up with no fraternizing on my property, if that's what you're after."

"No, ma'am," Marigold assured her. "I am only seeking information about Mr. Valentine—I do not seek him personally."

But suspicion was a deep-seated New England trait. "What fer?" The narrow-eyed woman idled closer, as if she wanted a better look at Marigold.

"I am making inquiries on behalf of"—here she gave way to a small lie—"the authorities of the District Police in regard to some suspicious events in the town. Mr. Valentine's name has come up a time or two."

"Has it now?" She wiped her hands on her faded work smock as if she were washing her hands of any knowledge. "Don't have anyone of that name here."

"No?" Marigold could almost taste the disappointment like ash in her mouth. "Perhaps James Wilkerson? Tall, handsome man about thirty years old? Brown hair, brown eyes, nice nose? Perhaps he said he was a journalist with one of the Boston papers? Wears a brown felt homburg hat with quail feathers tucked into the ribbon? Shoes worn down at the heel?"

"Oh, him." The woman harrumphed in disdain. "He was here a week or two—left without paying the rest of his shot. Didn't call himself that—whatever it was you said."

How was it that every time she was proved right she felt worse instead of better?

"What name did he give?"

"Don't recall." The woman narrowed her gaze to mercenary slits. "Paid the first week in advance, in cash." She stuck her hands on her hips. "Cash money is always helpful. Always welcome."

Marigold didn't blink. "If this is an invitation to pay you for your time and information, I am happy to do so."

The woman's smile was pleasantly sly. "You catch on nice and quick."

"Thank you." Marigold searched her pockets to come up with her last coin. "I hope this quarter will suffice to refresh your memory, ma'am, as it is all I have on me."

"That'll do." The old woman pocketed the money in a flash. "Valley, he said his name was. Traveling through, he said. Lovely town, with a lot of young women. Man like him would notice that, wouldn't he?"

"I'll bet he did." Marigold would add Mrs. Otis to the list of people taken in by good looks and charm. "When did he arrive?"

"Four or five weeks ago?" The woman searched her memory. "Maybe more. Paid in cash for the first week. Said as he had some business in town and then in Boston. Said he'd be back and forth. But he hasn't come back."

"When was the last time he was here?"

"Nigh on a week and a half ago. Monday before last. Left at dawn."

The morning after the night he murdered Olivia Thayer.

"If he does come back, would you mind sending a message up to me at the college? To College Hall. There will be money in it, for you, a great deal, if you can get a message to me—without him knowing, you understand. He can't know you're contacting me."

The canny woman narrowed her eyes. "How much?"

Two could play that game. "How much do you reckon a message would be worth?" She would break her own rule and borrow from Isabella if need be.

The crone eyed Marigold up and down, from the top of her boater to the bottom of her cycling bloomers, as if measuring her for a coffin. "A fin."

Marigold narrowed her own eyes. "One dollar," she countered. "A silver dollar if you can get a message to me fast—again, without him knowing."

"Bring it myself for a silver dollar," the crone cackled.

"You do that." Marigold struck out her hand. "Marigold Manners, Wellesley College. Just leave word at the reception room." She would have to begin bribing poor Miss Burke as well, if this crone was added to the parade of persons Marigold was responsible for. "If this Mr. Valley comes back, or you see him at all, anywhere about town, you'll let me know?"

Mrs. Otis's suspicions softened into satisfaction. "Reckon I might could do that."

"Thank you." Marigold didn't want to stand there arguing over the garden gate for a moment longer than necessary—lest the object of her interrogation come waltzing down the lane.

But when she turned to go, she felt an intriguing frisson of recognition at what she finally realized was a kitchen garden laid out irregularly across the yard. It put her in mind of her far more precisely cultivated kitchen garden plot at Hatchet Farm on Great Misery.

But something about the shaggy garden stirred up a breeze in the back of her mind—that cone-shaped flower especially. It reminded Marigold of one her actual mother, Sophronia—although Marigold had no idea she was her mother at the time—who had been deeply conversant in the language of flowers, had added to the kitchen garden for "protection."

"What is that flower, there, along the wall, with the berries?"

The woman's narrow suspicion crept back. "Well, aren't you a clever one. Quick. Nasty too, I'll bet."

"I beg your pardon?" Marigold felt all of the insult and little of the backhanded admiration, but she tamped down her feelings in favor of facts. "I thought I recognized it from my mother's garden, is all, but it's different from what I'm remembering."

"Banewort, I call it. Used in a medicinal tonic I make. Cure putrid throat, along with carbuncles and furuncles. You got any carbuncles need shrinking?"

"No, thank you." Any plant with the word *bane* in it was never benign. And experience—as well as her recent close translation of Antiphon's *Against the Step-mother for Poisoning*—was reminding her that poisons were most often a woman's weapon.

But who was to say who else at Otis House might have noticed and made use of the plant?

There were no coincidences.

"We used to have something similar in my mother's herb garden. She's powerful clever with tonics. But I don't recall anything called banewort. Does it have some other name?"

"Ayuh." The woman's eyes narrowed into cynical slits. "Deadly nightshade."

Chapter 31

"It is my business to know what other people don't know."
Arthur Conan Doyle

Where was unflappable Ethyl with her scientific knowledge of poisons when Marigold needed her?

"Do you use that in your balm for carbuncles?" Marigold asked, as if she hadn't the vaguest idea of balms or banes. "Or the tonic for sore throat?"

The old woman raised her chin. "Depends. Why do you want to know?"

Perhaps the poor woman thought Marigold would set herself up as a rival in ridding Wellesley of carbuncles.

Marigold scratched a vague detail out of her memory and mixed it with a bit of conjecture to allay any lingering mistrust. "My mother makes a watery tincture with the berries, then she distills it down before she adds it to her syrup. Don't know what's in the syrup—she won't even tell me, besides black cherries, though—I know she uses those."

"I don't use no water—just press the berries to get the juice."

"Did your boarder—Mr. Valley, was it? Did he take an interest in your tonics or tonic making?"

Mrs. Otis's eyebrows rose, considering. "Sat with me in my kitchen, a time or two, for company, he said, while I worked. Companionable fellow."

"Did he know you were working with poisons?"

The woman was instantly taken aback. "Not making any poison of any kind, and I'll thank you not to say otherwise. Tonic, I make."

"My apologies. I meant that out of experienced hands, such as yours, the plant might be poisonous—in my hands certainly it would be dangerous."

"I've no doubt," the woman agreed with a caustic laugh.

"I just wondered if your boarder might have understood that—that the plant itself, handled improperly, was dangerous."

"Reckon he was a smart enough fellow. But he didn't make no trouble. Mostly."

There was that "mostly" doing the devil's work again. Marigold would bet that he had made trouble in other ways. "Sounds a charming sort of man."

"That he was. Only wish he'd paid up before he disappeared. Do you think he's not coming back to pay up?"

If he had done what Marigold was sure he had, he would be a fool if he did.

"I think it far more likely that Mr. Valley has absconded to Europe to escape the long arm of Massachusetts law."

"Had enough money for a ticket across the ocean, but not enough to pay me what I was due, did he? No wonder the law's after him."

"You might make a report of his unpaid bill to the town watchmen or to Detective Pratt of the District Police, ma'am." They needed all the evidence they could get. "Mr. Valley, or whatever he was calling himself here, seems to be accumulating quite the record against himself."

"I'll be," the old crone mused. "Seemed such a gentleman, even though he was down on his luck."

"Did he say that?"

"Not directly, though he did say his luck was changing." Mrs. Otis sucked in a resentful breath. "Well, for him maybe, hying off to Europe, but not for me."

"Nor I, ma'am," Marigold said with sympathy. "Mr. Valley seems to have taken advantage of many."

"That why you want to know about the nightshade? Want your revenge on the man?"

"No, ma'am," Marigold answered. "It's because Mr. Valley might have tried to use it to get his own version of revenge."

Mrs. Otis finally looked surprised. "Well, I'll be."

"I need to be getting on." Marigold was anxious to do something meaningful with this new information. "Thank you for your information—and your promise. Good afternoon."

Marigold made as if she was walking her bicycle down the lane to mount it, but as soon as the woman disappeared into the house, she doubled back, wrapped her hand in her handkerchief, snatched up a branch of the plant, blossoms, berries and all, and made directly for Ethyl's bench in the Student Laboratory and Apparatus Room.

She rode one-handed the entire ride, and upon arrival at College Hall, ran all the way up to the fifth floor, appearing far blousier than she cared to be seen.

"Well, as I live and breathe, it's the Inimitable Miss Marigold Manners, looking like—" Ethyl took one look at the specimen in Marigold's hand and promptly snatched it out of her fist and tossed it onto the bench. "Lordy. What are you doing with that? Where'd you get it?"

"From the kitchen garden where Wilkie Valentine—who I'm pretty damn sure is also James Wilkerson but was also going by the name Valley where I found this—was letting a room. It's poisonous, isn't it? The landlady said it was nightshade, which is belladonna, isn't it?"

"No, thank the Lord." Ethyl put on her spectacles to examine it closely. "This is black nightshade—*Solanum nigrum*. It's similar to *Atropa bella-donna*, deadly nightshade, but belongs to a different genus, *Solanaceae*. But what you really need to know is that black nightshade is less poisonous than deadly nightshade."

"You're sure?"

"Sure as I can be," Ethyl swore. "Firstly, the flower isn't tubular and pinkish colored. You can see these are white and star shaped, and they have this mustard-colored anther."

"I wouldn't know an anther from an antler," Marigold sighed, "but I'll take your word for it. You're sure it's not belladonna?"

"Absolutely! But it's the berries that are the absolute giveaway," Ethyl went on. "They're spherical and they have this dull luster. Belladonna berries are much glossier and twice as large."

"So it's less poisonous than deadly nightshade, but it's still poisonous?"

"Lordy, yes. Just not as bad."

"So someone could still make a preparation—say a tonic? Or even just use the straight berry juice to poison something—like a glass of water?"

"I suppose." Ethyl made a face. "I reckon it'd be dang bitter, but I don't know anyone willing to taste test that sort of thing."

"But what if someone was already taking a bitter medicine, like—"

Ethyl's face paled in recognition. "Atropine? Do you mean you think this is how Professor Currier got poisoned even though she said she only took her prescribed dose?"

"That is exactly what I mean. I think Wilkie Valentine was at her boardinghouse yesterday, tampering with the blue water pitcher in her room there—which was turned over and broken, with all the water spilling out, destroying the evidence, after Lucy left to bring the professor here to us. My guess is he simply squeezed the berry juice into the water she used to take her atropine granules."

"Lordy! That sounds just about what probably happened. If it had been from an actual belladonna berry . . ." Ethyl made an exaggerated shiver. "Thank goodness he didn't have the smarts God gave a goose to get it right."

"So, your antidote—even though it was properly for belladonna—it won't have done her any harm?"

"Lordy, no." Ethyl let out a decided sigh of relief. "What we gave her is still an effective antidote, especially as the smaller amount of atropine in black nightshade would be counteracted even more effectively by the physostigmine I isolated from the manchineel."

"Thank you." Marigold felt herself exhale with relief. "But I think we ought to tell Dr. Barker."

Ethyl gave her what could only be described as a grim smile. "It will be the first good news in days. I just pray that it's going to catch on and last."

When they reached the Hospital Wing, Dr. Barker was in concurrence with Ethyl—they had done the very right thing. "And in tracking down this information," the doctor added. "It sets my mind at ease to know exactly what happened."

Marigold's conscience objected. "It's only a very educated guess."

"It's a very logical guess," Ethyl said staunchly. "I don't know how you sleuthed that plant out, but you did it."

"Thank you." One didn't want to make too much of oneself, especially when one had made so many dangerous mistakes. She had suspected the wrong people right from the start, wasting precious time that had nearly run out.

And even now, she might be too late.

She had heard nothing from either Cab or Detective Pratt about either a warrant or the whereabouts of Wilkie Valentine.

"Miss Burke," Marigold approached the reception desk with something that felt bitterly like humility. "Is there any chance that I might impose upon you to use your telephone to consult with Mr. Cox today?"

"I am sorry, Miss Manners." Miss Burke was all concerned solicitude. "The dean is currently speaking on the machine, but if you'd care to wait a few minutes?"

"Certainly, ma'am. I would be most appreciative."

"All right then." Miss Burke turned away before she changed her mind. "I know it's none of my business, but you look like you need a good rest."

"Thank you, Miss Burke. But I'll rest once this murder is solved and the murderer brought to justice."

The older woman looked genuinely concerned. "But my dear girl, that might not be for months."

Not if Marigold had anything to say about it. But time was slipping away just as surely as Valenine had. She sat, though each moment that ticked by was a torture spent in trying to fix the time difference between Boston and Liverpool in her head, wondering if Valentine had even finally got on a ship, and if Detective Pratt's evidence and Cab's connections in legal circles would be able to extend the long arm of the law to cover all of these possibilities.

"Miss Manners? Marigold?" Miss Burke hovered in front of her. "The dean has finished. If you—"

Her query was cut off by the sound of the telephone ringing off the wall, whereupon Miss Burke immediately went in answer. "Wellesley College, Reception, Miss Burke speaking." She listened to the squawk on the other end for only a moment before she turned and waved to Marigold. "I'll expect him directly." Miss Burke rang off. And told Marigold with a smile, "Your Mr. Cox has eliminated the need for your call. That was Mr. Breyer at East Lodge telephoning to say that Mr. Cox had arrived, and that he—Mr. Breyer—was sending Mr. Cox on to College Hall, and he should be here in—"

Marigold did not wait to hear the rest. "Thank you, Miss Burke!" She was out the door and onto the circular drive before she could think better of greeting Cab without taking time to at least make sure her hair wasn't a blousy mess. At least she still had her hat on.

But some things were more important than vanity.

Everything was more important than vanity.

Until the moment when Cab came striding up the drive, his hands pushed deep into the pockets of his tweed jacket and his collar turned up against the rising damp of the afternoon, looking as dapper as if he were walking off a golf course and not helping her to solve a murder.

"Marigold," he called as if there were no one there but the two of them, and her fellow collegians weren't likely hanging out their windows to get a glimpse of him. "I thought I would surprise you, but as usual you're two steps ahead of me."

"You might have safely saved yourself the trouble of the trip—for I think I know, or at least suspect, a great deal of what you are going to tell me." She clasped his hand anyway, reveling in the strange comfort of his physical presence.

"I doubt that." He squeezed her hand. "You look tired."

"La, Mr. Cox, you know just how to flatter." She turned them away from the drive and onto the walk that led toward the west lawn and the golf course. "What news has brought you all this way?"

"I've consulted with the British Consulate in Boston, and they were prepared to detain Wilkie Valentine when he disembarked—"

"But it wasn't him, was it?" Marigold closed her eyes against the feeling of failure.

"Yes!" Cab said. "They cabled Liverpool and were ready to meet the *Ultonia*. But when they went aboard to arrest Wilkie Valentine, it turned out that the man bearing Valentine's ticket—and his wife—had turned themselves in to the captain and shipboard authorities as soon as they had left United States territorial waters."

"They turned themselves in?" Marigold was astonished back into confusion. "For the murder? Had they been working together to defraud Olivia and the Thayers?"

"No." Cab put a hand to her elbow in that way he had of assuring without pawing at her. "For impersonating Wilkie Valentine and his wife. Their real names were Mr. and Mrs. William Wilson of South Boston, who were paid by Valentine to take his place on the ship."

"Impostors. The porter was right about the accent."

"Stand-ins," Cab amended, "but yes."

"Which means Wilkie Valentine is still at large." Marigold only just refrained from groaning in frustration. Their entire focus on the ocean liner tickets had been a time-wasting dead end. "What a complete and utter disaster."

A disaster of her own making. Her vanity, her own sense of being right, while everyone else was in the wrong, had led her to this moment.

The moment when Wilkie Valentine was going to get away with murder.

CHAPTER 32

"So blind is the curiosity by which mortals are possessed, that they often conduct their minds along unexplored routes, having no reason to hope for success, but merely being willing to risk the experiment of finding whether the truth they seek lies there."

René Descartes

"No, not at all," Cab insisted. "After consulting with Detective Pratt and the district attorney's office in Boston, who convened the grand jury to indict Wilkie Valentine, so I could take the warrant to the British Consulate—"

"Which proved entirely unnecessary."

"Perhaps the British Consulate's part, but the rest of the indictment still holds. Wilkie Valentine is now being sought for murder. That information should be in every town within the Commonwealth of Massachusetts, if not the rest of New England, by Monday morning."

"By Monday morning, he could be anywhere." Marigold gave in to her weariness, admitted her defeat. With Cab she would have no misrepresentation or misunderstandings. "But at least now I have a description to go with the evidence, which may be of some small help."

"That is excellent." He reached into his suit pocket to withdraw that neat little notebook she had seen him use with Isabella. "Let me take this down."

"You don't need my word—you can write it yourself." At his frown Marigold confessed. "The journalist, James Wilkerson?"

"Ah, yes. About him. As I told you before, I could find no record of him with the *Evening Standard*—"

"Because he was not really a journalist at all. And that is because I am almost positive that James Wilkerson and Wilkie Valentine, as well as a man named Valley, are all the same person. It was all a ruse to do to me what he had already done to the Thayers—confuse and misdirect."

"Good God."

"Indeed," she admitted. "I've made a shambles of everything. Everything I've done or asked you to do has been completely inadequate to solve this murder and bring him to justice. And I've made a complete and utter fool of myself in the process."

Cab's disagreement was a momentary salve to her feelings. "Surely not, for you have solved the murder, even if he has not yet been brought to justice."

But only a momentary salve. "He could be anywhere by now! Almost from the beginning, I've made wrong turn after wrong turn. Wrong about Professor Currier. Wrong about Sarah Appleton."

"Do you mean to say Sarah Appleton is not a complete pill?

He was being kind. "No, that she is. But she is not a murderous one. At least not yet." Though Marigold had likely given her reason enough. "But I was entirely taken in by Wilkerson, or Valentine, or whatever name he might be using now. I was an idiot to put any faith whatsoever in him."

Cab raised his eyebrows slightly but gave only a mild rejoinder. "I'll grant you that."

"I should have listened to Isabella—she never liked him."

Cab wisely said nothing to that, though Marigold was sure that Cab had suspected the sham journalist too, but was too polite to say so. "I was wrong about Miss Burke. Wrong about May Barnacle. Wrong, wrong, wrong. It's as if I don't know myself."

"Marigold, it isn't wrong to doubt," he said in that quietly steely voice of his. "Doubting that we are right is the thing that makes us better—able to look again and again, and find another way forward. Only fools and maniacs never doubt they are wrong."

It was Marigold's turn to smile. There was that lovely, unparalleled sense of fellow-feeling. "Thank you, Cab. You've reminded me that Descartes's most famous words of wisdom were not 'Cogito ergo sum'—"

"Were they not?" Cab was amusingly dubious. "I'm fairly sure that 'I think therefore I am' was taught in my philosophy and rhetoric classes at Harvard."

"Then Harvard has let you down. No." Of this, if nothing else, she was quite sure. "The full accounting of his wisdom is 'Dubito, ergo cogito, ergo sum.' I doubt, therefore I think, therefore I am. I ought to make them my watchwords," she swore. "So you had the right of it, even if you didn't have your Descartes exactly correct."

"Then I shall continue to doubt away," Cab pledged. "But one thing I never doubt is you, Marigold. Even if you have faltered, you have seen this through. You have identified the man who did this unspeakable thing to this bright, promising young woman. You have seen through the jealousies and lies that tried to hide the truth, because that is what you do."

Marigold felt the hot scald of gratefulness sting her eyes. She had always tried to believe in herself, through thick and through thin, but it had always seemed too much to ask of anyone else. And yet, here Cab was, believing and encouraging her. Again.

"You really are the most extraordinary man."

His smile was warm but somehow guarded. "I've been waiting patiently for you to discover that."

"I've always known that," she told him. "I just don't think I had the confidence to tell you how much I admire you. And appreciate you. And your . . . support."

"Miss Manners." He looked around at their surroundings, gauging their level of privacy. "Is this your rather forward way of asking me to kiss you?"

"Forward? No," she disagreed. "This is forward."

She clasped his extraordinarily well-tailored lapels and held him temporarily captive for a kiss. Because she knew that was all that she was going to get—a kiss, temporarily. Cab was never going to do much more—his misplaced sense of honor wouldn't let him. But still, it was a kiss. A lovely, just exactly what she needed kiss, with his arms stealing around her shoulders to hold her momentarily close.

And she held him, and for that moment, let herself relax into the surety of his presence. Into the ease and confidence she felt when she was with him.

The confidence to be herself, without worry or care. Without striving.

Not that she minded the striving—she liked striving. Yet the constancy of the need to strive was exhausting. Such was their world, where the striving was necessary if one wanted to be something of one's own.

If one wanted to be one's own unapologetic self.

He spoke before she could. "I should be getting back—I've brought papers for Isabella to sign, and she won't thank me—or you—for making her wait for dinner."

"Me? I have nothing to do with it. Didn't even know she was still here, holding court, giving dinners to which she has not invited me."

"Why don't you come with me?" he offered. "Now that the proper authorities are involved, you can rest easy knowing that you have done all you could. You can put this unfortunate murder from your mind and drink Isabella's superior champagne."

Marigold wanted to say yes. She wanted to forget everything, all her past failures and future pressures. But she had classes tomorrow for which she was not yet prepared and expectations she had neglected to meet—for herself if for no one else.

"Thank you." She patted his arm in consolation. "But I really must stay. Antiphon won't translate himself."

"Antiphon?" He seemed surprised. "Far past my humble abilities. You really are a scholar."

"Yes," she said, trying to be truthful while not making too much of oneself. "At least I am trying to be."

"I've no doubt you are succeeding."

He meant to be kind and reassuring. But the truth was that even if she surpassed his abilities by tenfold in any other subject, instead of just Greek translation, she would still never be given half of his opportunities. No one would ever encourage her to go to Harvard Law

School or offer her a position at a revered Boston firm of any kind. Or urge her to run for office or sit on boards or committees or be given even the slightest feel of the reins of power.

To be fair, she had been encouraged to work toward the one position that might be open to her, here at Wellesley. But not at Harvard or Yale or the University of Michigan or anywhere else that would automatically infer that both she and her education were inferior.

It made her furious. And exhausted.

But she wasn't furious at Cab—she was furious at the world. The world that let mediocre men like Wilkie Valentine take their insecurities out on superior young women like Olivia Thayer.

And so, she had to exist in this small part of the world that was made for her. And in doing so, she would do everything in her power to make it safe for young women like Olivia.

"I'll see you . . . soon?" Cab asked.

"Naturally." She gave him a smile that was more confident than she felt. "You will give Detective Pratt this information about Wilkerson being Valentine? And him being behind the attempt on Professor Currier's life? And keep me informed?"

"I will assuredly do so." He stood there, awkwardly she thought, so unlike his usual urbane self.

"Cab? Is there something you're not telling me? I know I'm a bit low at the moment, but I shall rally."

"I know that." He took her hand one last time and held it tight. "I'm just worried is all. This Wilkie Valentine has proved a damn slippery character, who hasn't known when to stop."

"He's a murderer, Cab—do they come in any other stripe?"

"No." He looked at her then, with something like despair in his eyes. "Just promise me—no," he repaired. "Promise yourself that you will be careful. That you will leave this to the authorities and exercise all your considerable intellect in conjunction with your caution, to keep yourself safe."

"Naturally," she conceded. "Why on earth would you think I won't?"

"Marigold." He said her name with a sigh. "Because you never have. And that is why I love you."

Chapter 33

"Re-examine all that you have been told . . . dismiss that which insults your soul."

Walt Whitman

"Miss Manners?"

Marigold looked up from her examination of her coins in their electrolytic solution—which was working perfectly thanks to Ethyl's assiduous assistance—expecting to find Miss Burke ready with one of her seemingly endless summonses.

But it was Eliza Anthony, standing at the top of the stairwell, much as she had the last time she and Marigold had talked. But today she looked entirely different—far less sure of herself.

"Eliza?"

"Do you remember how you asked me to tell you if—"

"Yes." Marigold went to her immediately, for she looked quite green around the gills. "Come sit." She kicked out the chair next to her workbench and guided Eliza into it. "What has happened?"

"I thought . . . I think I might have seen that man . . . from the photograph you . . . The one of the front of the boathouse rotunda?" she clarified.

All the alarm Marigold had managed to push aside came screaming back. Just when she had convinced herself that there was no more that she could do, that she ought to leave the entire matter of evidence and justice to others and concentrate on her studies—

"Where did you see him?" she managed. "When? Today?"

"On the street. In town." Eliza nodded numbly, as if she were still in shock. "At least I think it was him. At the tearoom up on Church Street."

"Yes." Marigold knew it well—it was the one she herself had gone to with James Wilkerson to appeal to him, the day she had enlisted Cab's far superior help.

"Well, he came in. And there was just something about him—about the way he stood there for a moment, with his back to me. His silhouette—the shape he made, you know?" Eliza shook her head, as if to contradict herself. "All of a sudden, I felt entirely all-overish. Just an awful funny, terrible feeling."

"Yes," Marigold completely understood the feeling—she was experiencing it now.

"I was so scared that I had to leave straightaway," Eliza finished. "But I feel so foolish—I might be wrong."

"Not at all," Marigold assured her. "You did the right thing to leave. Did he see you?"

"I don't think so—his back was to me. He was looking in the mirror."

He would be.

Marigold's fright began to abate. The man might be a murderer, but he was only a man—and a vain man at that.

But still, she had to think. And to act. "Did you come straight here? How long ago was this?"

"Yes. I don't know—maybe twenty minutes? I walked—fast, practically at a run, you know? And I don't mind saying it was the worst walk I ever took—I was frightened half to death that I was being followed the whole time."

"Yes." Marigold knew the feeling. "Thank you, Eliza. You've been exceptionally helpful."

"I feel awful foolish now." Eliza began to recover more of her urbane, cynical self. "I suppose I ought to have gotten his name."

"I already know it," Marigold said. "And you did the very right thing, Eliza. It's a good thing you didn't talk to him. That man is a killer."

And Marigold was going to have to stop him before he killed again.

No. She had promised to be cautious. All she needed to do was to get word to Detective Pratt that Valentine was abroad in the town. The officer, with the assistance of the watchmen, would surely deal with the miscreant.

What she needed to do was warn President Irvine and her sister collegians, then telephone Detective Pratt at the town hall, and telephone the Breyers at the East Lodge to be on the lookout.

But the town hall had no telephone exchange.

She would have to go to them then, in person.

Marigold went immediately to her room to change into far sturdier clothing for being abroad than her cotton laboratory smock—her sturdy wool tweed cycling suit with the split skirt firmly buttoned back so she could move freely, tightly laced boots and a well-secured hat to keep the low autumn sun from her eyes.

She was going to need every advantage, physical or mental, that she might have. She needed to be fast and stealthy to avoid being seen by the wrong person.

Which put her in mind of the first time she had visited the Breyers and found comfort in the safety of numbers—she would need all the allies she might manage. Information was power, and every young woman deserved to be armed with as much information as possible.

"Miss Burke?" She paused at the reception room, "I am heading to East Lodge to confer with the Breyers before I go on to the town hall to speak to Detective Pratt. Would you be kind enough to telephone the lodge to expect me?"

"Certainly, but—

"A safety precaution, Miss Burke." And while she was thinking of safety. "Do you think you could consult with President Irvine, and tell her I would strongly advise that the student body be put on alert? Any man—all men—on campus are to be treated with suspicion. All."

Miss Burke, though she drew herself up like a vigilant squirrel, did not blink an eye. "I will do so immediately."

"Thank you." And Marigold was out the door and onto her bicycle and racing down the carriage drive—keeping well away from the remoter foot paths—toward East Lodge.

Mr. Breyer was on the porch waiting for her. "Miss Burke telephoned—"

"Yes, thank you for meeting me. Do you keep a log of all the visitors who come to the gate?"

"Mrs. Breyer keeps it," he answered. "Come in and talk to her where we can be comfortable. Diana, Miss Manners is here, and wants to see the logs."

"I heard." Mrs. Breyer waved her through the door. "Certainly, we keep them same as Miss Burke at the reception room at College Hall," Mrs. Breyer confirmed, turning to retrieve the leatherbound log. "And now you see, we've the telephone." She indicated the matching machine to the one in Miss Burke's office. "We call over to College Hall to expect someone—and Miss Burke does the same—as she just did to tell us to expect you."

"And do you record each person and their name? For instance, when Olivia Thayer came?"

"Now, I don't know if we *always* put down a guest's name if they're with someone we know from the college." Mrs. Breyer frowned. "Not after the first time. Miss Thayer came with her aunt, Professor Currier, the first few times, didn't she?" She looked to her husband for confirmation. "And after that I suppose, she was a sort of regular, so I doubt I made any particular note. Once we get to know students, we don't always write down their names each time."

Mrs. Breyer looked apprehensive, as if she thought Marigold were conducting some sort of audit of her procedures.

"Yes, that makes perfect sense," Marigold assured her. "What I'm trying to get at is, did Olivia Thayer ever have a young man with her when she was walking to campus? Someone who might have been seen to be courting her?"

"No, I don't think so." Mrs. Breyer was frowning again. "She came and went mostly in the afternoons, around three-thirty or so, not during the more popular visiting hours in the evenings. And I often saw her walking home with Professor Currier, who lives just up the street. Young ladies who have young men to socialize with, do so more often in the town, in the tearooms, than at the college."

"We keep an eye out for young men, collegians and the like, all the same," Mr. Breyer asserted. "But I look out for vagrant types too, same as the groundsmen and porters do—sometimes the woods here seem inviting to tramps or whatnot. We run them off, let them know they're not welcome here."

"And has that happened recently?" Marigold thought of Professor Currier's image of Valentine lying in wait. "Have there been any unattached men, either collegians or vagrant types loitering in the woods?"

"Chased a fellow out toward the road from the brook down below the farmhouse a while back. But I think he just wandered in there by mistake—said he was looking for his dog."

That seemed reasonable. But being reasonable was how people went unnoticed. "What sort of a man was he, this fellow?"

"Well, not a vagrant. A gentleman, though he looked like he'd been out some time. Said his dog had got loose and he thought it had come that way. Didn't know he was on college land. Came out easy as you please. Tipped his hat to me and moved on."

Something in Marigold's middle turned to ice. "What sort of a hat?" She heard herself ask, even as she somehow already knew the answer.

"Oh, a nice one—dark sort of felt."

"A homburg with a small quail feather stuck into a brown grosgrain ribbon." Her words were nearly a whisper.

"Why, yes." Mr. Breyer looked baffled. "Say! You don't mean that's the fellow you're looking for? But you said a young man—I thought you meant someone Miss Thayer's age. You know, like a college boy."

"I—" She had unthinkingly repeated Professor Currier's description. "Did the man with—or without—the dog give you a name? Either Valentine or Wilkerson, by chance? Or Valley?"

"That last—Mr. Valley. Lived down in South Natick, he said."

"No." Marigold shook her head. "He was resident in a boardinghouse down off Waban Brook." He probably followed the path of the brook, down under the bridge at Washington Street, where he couldn't be seen, and into the campus unnoticed.

"When exactly did you see Mr. Valley along Waban Brook? Was he coming away from the campus or heading toward it? What day? What time of day? Was he disheveled or neat?"

"Whoa, whoa, now. Let me think. It was some time ago—at least a week back." Mr. Breyer screwed up his face in thought. "And he was coming down the brook, as it flows east out of the lake. Said he was worried his dog might drown."

"Dogs don't drown unless they are tied or weighted down," Marigold said tonelessly. "They naturally swim. Unlike people."

Mr. Breyer looked at her askance. "Well, I didn't think about that. I just told him he had to get out from there—that he wasn't allowed. And he came right out, nice and polite and respectful. Walked off down the road toward South Natick looking all forlorn. He'd been out looking for his dog all night."

"All night? Which night?"

Mrs. Breyer spoke up. "Would you not have put that down in the log, Steven? We're very conscientious about such things, I promise you, Miss Manners. We don't just let things pass. We write things down."

"Did you write Mr. Valley down?"

Steven Breyer went to the log book as if in a trance. Thumbing through the pages, each page a day. Each a day a list of visitors and tradesmen. "Yes," he finally said with great relief. "Yes. '5:15 AM. Found a Mr. Valley searching for his dog, in the dell below the farmhouse. Warned off.' There."

"What date was that, if you please, Mr. Breyer?"

"The morning of Monday, October the eighth. Five fifteen in the morning."

"Which was the morning after the night Olivia Thayer was killed and her body pushed or thrown into Lake Waban. I found her body floating beneath the boathouse that afternoon."

"By jeezum," Mr. Breyer breathed. "Do you think it was him?"

"I do," Marigold said simply. "I am sure that your Mr. Valley's real name is Wilkie Valentine and that he murdered Olivia Thayer.

And I am very glad you have the evidence of the log, so you will be able to say so in a court of law." They didn't just have to have evidence that Valentine was the killer, they needed to bring him to justice. "If he can be caught."

If he had any sense, Wilkie Valentine, or James Wilkerson, or Mr. Valley, or whoever he really was should have been long gone by now, conscious of the noose slowly but surely tightening around his neck.

But he hadn't—he thought he was smarter than all of them. He was certainly more wicked. And more vain.

"We should tell the authorities," Mrs. Breyer suggested.

"I am on my way now to alert Detective Pratt of the District Police along with the watch, and give them as full a description as I might, including all the names he has used." Marigold told him. "But I would ask you to report Mr. Valley to the watch as well, so there is some official record besides your log books—which I thank you for keeping. They will be important evidence in the effort to bring Wilkie Valentine to justice."

"Why don't you let me do that for you," Mr. Breyer suggested. "I can tell them what he looked like, clear as day. You've done more than your share, Miss Manners. You're better off getting back to the college to warn them there."

"Yes," Marigold agreed, reaffirming her promise to Cab. "I'll do just that."

It would be better to know they were not looking for just any man on campus, but this specific man. She would confirm with Professor Currier beyond any shadow of a doubt, that Wilkie Valentine and James Wilkerson and the vagrant Valley were, in fact, the same man.

She ought to telephone Isabella and Cab too—they could identify him. As could Aggie, who had most likely been accosted by Valentine when he was seeking Olivia Thayer.

So many different people, who might give evidence against him, and at least put him in the right place at the right time to make his identification as Olivia's murderer plausible. Because he certainly had not got on that ocean liner. He had been amongst them the whole time, hiding in plain sight. Hiding behind his gentlemanlike plausibility. And his deadly charm.

Oh, the perniciousness of such a thing!

It might have been one thing if the man had strangled Olivia Thayer in a fit of passion and fear, and then regretted the fatal impulse of his actions. But it was wholly another thing for him to have loitered and idled around the town in the aftermath, creating diversions to hamper his victim's identification, stealing photographs and telling lies to the press and anyone who was in any way connected with solving the crime.

Lying to everyone he came in contact with. Lying to her.

He had stolen the photograph—or asked poor young Homer to steal it. He had poisoned Imogen Currier's medicine. Only because Lucy and Ethyl each acted so swiftly was his attempt to kill Professor Currier thwarted.

The depth and breadth of the man's evil was breathtaking.

And frightening.

"Miss Manners?" Mrs. Breyer recalled her to the present. "You go on home now."

"Yes," Marigold agreed. "I will go home."

Marigold started down the path at a run, mounting her bicycle on the fly.

She had never wanted the noisy comfort—as Professor Currier had called it—of her fellow students more that she did at that moment. She needed their company and their humanity to restore her faith in mankind.

Because at the moment, that faith was all but gone.

Chapter 34

"There is no female brain. The brain is not an organ of sex. Might as well speak of a female liver."

Charlotte Perkins Gilman

Marigold headed directly for College Hall. Home, where she might confer with President Irvine on what needed to be done to keep the student body safe until Wilkie Valentine could be apprehended.

For a brief moment, she was tempted to take a different route and different plan. To go north toward the town and Isabella—and with any luck, Cab—at the Wellesley Inn, where she would no doubt also find companionship and comfort and champagne, and feel safe.

But practical considerations came first—and certainly others before self. Non Ministrari sed Ministrare. She could go to her friends at the inn after she had fulfilled her responsibility to President Irvine and the college.

She stood up on her pedals, determined to get there as fast as possible, anxious to crest the rise so she might have the beacon of College Hall in her sights to guide her home.

But suddenly, there he was, in front of her on the path, blocking the way.

The same camel hair coat, now showing some smudge spots, as if perhaps he'd been sleeping rough. The same shoes worn at the heels and soles. But the hat was carefully neat.

Vanity.

She would use it.

For another brief second she thought of trying to ride past him, of keeping on, of defying his pernicious interference. But the path was uphill and narrow, with shaggy shrubs that would tangle her spokes on either side. And she was already out of breath, winded with the fear and panic coursing through her blood like poison.

Perhaps it were better in this instance, to try her own antidote—to use honey instead of her more natural vinegar.

"Mr. Wilkerson," she called casually, dismounting to carefully turn her bicycle as if she were joining him on his walk, and to keep it between them, and to keep moving back toward East Lodge and the Breyers. "I haven't seen you in some time," she said as conversationally as she could. Wanting to appease her way out of any potential trouble. "Where have you been keeping yourself?"

He seemed not to notice her nervousness. "Boston," he said breezily, as if were some foreign place beyond her ken. As if she could have no experience of the world that did not start and end at the rural campus of her college. As if her world was still as small as Olivia Thayer's had been.

"Oh, yes, the *Boston Evening Standard*. Of course." She purposefully mangled the name of the tabloid, but he didn't seem to notice. Or that she was striding faster in her barely manageable fright. "Did you know we identified the girl—the one I found in the lake? It turned out she was very famous."

He scoffed. "I'd never heard of her."

"Hadn't you?" she kept on conversationally, even as her natural vinegar crept back into her tone at his dismissal. "She was to give an important lecture on universal suffrage at the college last Saturday evening. We were all very much looking forward to hearing her."

"You don't believe in all that, certainly," he countered with one of his charming smiles. "You're too pretty."

Whatever appeal Mr. Wilkerson might have once engendered—no, he was Valentine. He was a murderer, not a journalist. She needed to remember that he was trying to manipulate her just as much as she was trying to manipulate him.

Only she needed to be cleverer about it.

But she would not pander. "Naturally, I do believe in universal suffrage as well as equal rights. All the pretty girls do," she assured him blithely. "We're too smart not to believe in our very selves."

That he was equally angered and repulsed by her answer showed only briefly on his face before it was replaced by amused condescension. "Come now. You're just parroting what you heard some ugly, old, dried-up professor say. You don't want to end up like them, surely, all alone with no one for company but their cats?"

"Professor Currier doesn't have a cat. Nor does President—formerly Professor of Classics—Irvine. I myself prefer dogs to cats, though I have no pets at the moment, but I infinitely prefer the natural honesty and companionship of a dog over that of a man any day."

"You can't mean that." He laughed and shook his head as if he were indulging her—for now. "You'll see. When you're older and wiser you'll want to forget all this nonsense."

"Nonsense?" Marigold could not help but give way to her true feelings. "Do you men think that if you just keep repeating an untruth—an untruth you clearly prefer to the actual truth—that it will cease to be a lie?"

He looked at her, really looked at her, as if he was seeing her as she actually existed, not as he wished her to be—or expected her to be to suit his needs. He was clearly baffled.

Marigold decided to give him a dose of his own poisonous medicine—she returned his blithe, supercilious smile and used his same tone. "You'll see when you are older and wiser, you poor dear."

All hint of bafflement vanished to be replaced by darkening anger. "I'm no poor dear, and you're too old to be acting like a spoiled girl who doesn't know better."

"I'm not the one pouting," she pointed out without letting her hopefully infuriating smile slip. "How does it feel to be talked to like that?"

He reacted as if he'd been slapped. "I don't have to stand here and be insulted."

"No, you don't," she agreed brightly gesturing toward the way ahead—the way off college grounds. "Go ahead," her anger goaded her to say. "You're already bound for hell, you might as well get a head start."

For a second, a flash of some dark, fretting emotion passed across his face before he schooled it into contempt. "No, I don't think so." He took her arm in a hard grip. "If I'm going to hell, I'm taking you there with me."

For half a second Marigold was too affronted and shocked—his hand around her upper arm hurt—to take any action swift enough to counteract his grip before he was towing her along, much as she had imagined he had towed Olivia.

She had to think. To come up with a plan that would overpower him with cleverness instead of brute force.

She kept her own hands firm upon her handlebars, not relinquishing the machine, keeping it between them. And she kept quiet, watching him carefully, all but listening to him think. Working out how to keep him mentally, if not physically, off balance.

"I know who you are, you know, Wilkie Valentine." If she had hoped her assertion might stop him, she was mistaken—he kept on at that yard eating pace. "And I know what you did! To both Olivia Thayer and to Professor Currier."

He was unfazed. "Points to you. I'm glad to hear that the old bat's dead too—I wasn't able to stick around to confirm her timely demise."

"If you mean the professor, I am happy to disappoint you. We were able to counteract your clumsy attempt at poison." She could hear the icy heat in her own voice. "We educated women."

His veneer cracked. "You interfering little c—" He jerked her forward, his hand digging painfully into the muscles of her biceps.

"Scholar," she supplied over his curse. "Along with my fellow scholars, who created the antidote. You would have done well to study harder and pay attention in chemistry class."

He let out a curse so raw Marigold felt the tips of her ears turn blue—as she was sure her arm was turning under the viselike pressure of his grip.

But she kept her composure. "If I were you, I would run, now, while you can. You're going to need that head start."

"I can run later too," he gritted out. "I can disappear anytime I like."

"I'm sure you think you can create another name—Wilkie Valentine to Wilkerson to Valley. But that won't change who you really are—a murderer!"

"Perhaps I am," he yanked her to a halt to smile down at her. "But I assure you, I am getting to be a first-class murderer."

She could not help but quake under his glare. Could not help but feel pain under his abuse. But despite the pain, she could not help but be herself—she was logical.

They were nearing the fateful fork in the path where she had found the glove, midway between the Music Hall ahead on the left and Stone Hall up in the trees to the right. Where Olivia Thayer had put up a fight.

Where she too would stand her ground. Somehow.

"Marigold!"

Ahead, on the flat lawn of the Music Hall, Marigold was astonished to see Aggie and Ethyl—one so tall and athletic, the other smaller and so much more academic—waving frantically.

Marigold momentarily let go of her handlebar and waved back.

Ethyl's voice cracked in relief, "Come on up, we've been looking for you!"

"Yes!" Marigold called back, eager to be with her friends. Hopeful that logic and prudence would dictate Valentine's actions now that there were witnesses, and he would let her go. "As you can see—"

Some noise—a cry of distress—came from Aggie. She had put her hand up to shade her eyes from the late afternoon sun but dropped it to cover her mouth.

"Marigold, come away!" Ethyl called, more strongly, waving Marigold up the hill.

But neither girl moved forward. Both seemed stricken, affixed to where they stood.

"I don't think your friends like me." Valentine tightened his hand on her arm, demonstrating the power of his grip.

She would definitely have a bruise.

"Points to them," she said in ironic echo of his words. "I don't think they like most men."

"Typical," he scoffed. "You should stay away from them. It might be catching."

His voice was cold, but he was smiling.

"Marigold!" The pleading in Aggie's voice was something Marigold had never heard before.

She put her own hand up to shade her eyes and saw more clearly the fear on Aggie's face. The fear as she looked at him.

At someone Aggie recognized. Someone she had seen before.

The man who had grabbed her in such a proprietary manner while she was wearing her hat. The hat another girl—another girl he was looking for—had worn. Another girl who was now dead.

And even though she didn't turn to look at him, Marigold felt the realization within him. "Do you know her?" she asked as if she were perplexed.

"Not at all," he lied.

"But she knows you," Marigold allowed. "She's recognized you from that day you accosted her on the golf course because you thought she was Olivia Thayer."

He swore again before he said, "More points to you." But he didn't move. He stood there, the way Eliza Anthony's camera had captured him—tall and dark, with his hat shading his eyes—as if he were trying to make up his mind.

Marigold tried to help him along. "Are you going to kill us all?" she asked.

He turned from the view of the Music Hall to look down at her. "No, just you, I think. You'll give me the most pleasure to kill."

The spike of fear that rove through Marigold stole her breath. And her logic.

But finally she managed, "Did you derive pleasure from killing Olivia? From strangling her." Marigold strove to remember her readings of the Viennese physicians in psychology—another required class at Wellesley. "Did that give you, how shall we say, an erotic charge?"

He jerked her arm in response. "Well, aren't you the hotty totty."

"Because I can discuss both strangulation and erections without confusing the two?"

His grip upon her arm turned viciously painful as he tried to drag her closer, across the steel rods of the bicycle between them. "Why do you girls always think you're smarter than us?"

She could not speak for all girls, but she could speak and think for herself. She was halfway to simply saying, "Because I am," when she saw the look in his eye—the sharp, shocking sight of the menace he had hidden behind the veneer of civilized charm.

But appeasing this man would get her nowhere—except closer to the place where he would try to strangle her too.

She used his own words. "Not smarter than *us*," she said. "Just *you*, I think."

He overpowered her easily, gripping the soft flesh of her upper arm just above the elbow to propel her toward his chosen path—the longer, low footpath away from the better traveled gravel lanes that led past Stone Hall and the Music Hall.

Marigold wrenched back and turned to call for help—but Aggie and Ethyl had disappeared.

And there was no one else who would hear her call for help.

Because she knew in the vast emptiness of the wilderness along the shore of the lake, no one would hear her. Because they were all obeying the college's rules and precepts, and were not going abroad when there were potentially dangerous people about the campus.

Marigold scanned the ground ahead for a weapon—some rock or stick that she might use. Perhaps she might be able to swing the bicycle at him and knock him off his feet.

But he kept too tight a grip on her.

She would have to improvise and fight in other ways. But she hardly knew how.

"Did you kill her because she didn't love you?" she tried. "Because she wouldn't meet you at the White Star docks to board the *Utopia* as you planned? Or because she tried to return your ring?"

"Aren't you clever." His tone was full of scorn. "But not clever or strong enough to stop me." His hand dug hard into her flesh, ensuring her continued cooperation.

"You needn't pinch, Mr. Valentine. I perfectly understand your intent." She was the one who jerked her arms forward this time, doing anything she could to keep him off his stride—either metaphorically or physically. Either would do.

He retaliated by digging in his grip and shaking her a little, so that her hat was in danger of tilting forward over her eyes.

Though she still kept her left hand on the handlebars, her right she reached up as if she needed to steady her hat. And found her resolve.

And readied it.

Ahead, she could see where the path curved along the edge of the small pond that created a natural boundary between the sloping lawns of College Hall and the woods along the banks of the larger lake.

Where the ground was softer and might be less steady underfoot.

"She's really not your mother, you know, Imogen Currier. It really was her younger sister, Lucinda." She presented the facts as reasonably and calmly as she could, given the circumstances. "It's all in the records." She chanced a glance at him as he towed her along—his face was flinty and hard. "For even a pretend journalist, you weren't very good at finding things out."

"I didn't need to," he scoffed. "I've got you to find out everything for me."

"Like the fact that you paid the Wilsons to take your place on the Cunard liner? I'm sure you knew that we would eventually learn about the *Ultonia*—which was why you were clever enough not to get on the ship yourself, given that your coconspirators have already been arrested. Or are they accessories to the crime—you'll have to ask your lawyer. Do you have one yet? Best to be prepared."

"Believe me, I am well prepared."

"To strangle me? One girl gets strangled and the watchmen are in a dither. Two girls get strangled in the same place—you are taking me down to the boathouse, aren't you? I don't know where else you hope to get rid of a body on this campus since they are already actively searching for you."

"No one knows who or where I am."

"My friends, Aggie and Ethyl, do—they know," she countered. "And they'll have gone to fetch the authorities—the Special District Police detective who has been hot on your heels." Her real hope was that the stalwart pair had not done something so ineffective as summon the watch, but were instead arming themselves with Aggie's strong, Scottish metal golf clubs.

"Those two girls?" His scoff became a sneer. "Couldn't fight a fly."

"Perhaps," she lied. She had every confidence in Aggie's ability to crack a wiseacre's skull with a driver. And Ethyl's resolve to help her do so. But instead of saying so, she turned to look past his left and let her eyes widen. "But what about them?"

He fell for the feint.

He turned sharply, yanking her toward his right side, as if he would pull her in front of him to shield himself from the unseen threat.

Marigold felt the pain of his possession all the way up her arm, but she let the impetus of his action propel her toward his chest.

Where she buried the hatpin she had surreptitiously pulled from her hair between his ribs, six inches deep.

Chapter 35

"I no doubt deserved my enemies, but I don't believe I deserved my friends."

Walt Whitman

Marigold's hand stung from the force of the impact. She wrenched herself away. Between them, the shaft of the pin quivered, bristling out of him like a hedgehog's spine.

"You bitch!" he cawed, immediately trying to tear the thing from him.

She had just enough presence of mind to shove the steel cage of her bicycle at him before she ran. As fast as she could.

Up the hill toward the college. Up the hill into the blazing orange late afternoon sun.

Toward freedom.

"Goddamn bitch," he was screaming behind her. He must have thrown the bicycle off somehow. She could hear his hard panting as he came after her, laboring certainly, but still close.

She sprinted up the hill, knowing that he would have at least as difficult a time on the rising ground as she, hoping that her superior knowledge of the terrain would come to her aid. Hoping her stamina would last. Hoping against hope itself.

And then she saw them ahead—a daisy chain of women stretching across her vision, young and old, sweeping down from College Hall, armed with bats and clubs, rackets, javelins, and oars and even, perhaps—if that was tiny Miss Burke—brandishing a ruler.

Every woman in the college, professors and students alike, acting as one, holding hands, or linking arms so as not to be separated from each other. A united front.

An army of women.

She raced toward them, giving it every last bit of speed and stamina she had, reaching out her arms as if they might propel her closer. Close enough to touch. Close enough to be safe.

Their arms closed around her.

"Marigold!" It was Aggie and Ethyl pulling her into their embrace, closing ranks and shoulders to form an impenetrable shield. Marigold hugged them tight, taking strength in their numbers and unity.

It was every woman she had so relentlessly scanned for signs of guilt in the chapel that afternoon that seemed so long ago now. It was President Irvine and tiny, quivering Miss Burke, who looked as if she had not been outside the doors of College Hall in more years than Marigold owned. It was Sarah Appleton and Eliza Anthony. Seniors and freshwomen, friends, acquaintances and strangers still, all forming a shield of sisterhood.

But they were all small, flesh and blood compared to the conscienceless killer who was coming. He was forty yards from them, staggering and swaying as he came, but still coming. Relentlessly.

"Oh, Lordy," Ethyl whispered. "Look at him."

His shirtfront was red with blood, and as she spoke, he toppled, reaching one empty hand forward to save his fall, while the other hand still clutched the wicked shaft of the pin, shiny and glistening in his clenched fist.

It was Cab who reached him first—Cab, who seemed to appear from nowhere, as if she had once again conjured him from her deepest, most private longings. He tackled Valentine to the ground, disappearing beneath a scrum of blue frock-coated officers of the District Police—Detective Pratt massing his men as promised.

At first, they appeared to hold Valentine down—all but sitting on his chest—but then their postures reversed and they were tending to him, holding the man's head up, as if to give him succor.

Don't, she wanted to shout. Don't help him. Don't even touch him.

Valentine was nothing but venom and hurt, violence and poison.

But telling Cab not to do the right thing—not to act like a gentleman, like the best version of himself, full of humanity and pity—was impossible.

Just as impossible as it was for her to stay away. She pushed out of Aggie's restraining arms and went to them where they hovered over Valentine.

"He should have left it in," Dr. Barker said, gesturing to the hatpin still clutched in his bloody grasp. "If he had left it in, it might have kept him from bleeding to death."

"You can't let him die," Marigold swore, suddenly reversing course. "I want him to face punishment for what he did to Olivia Thayer—and what he tried to do to Professor Currier."

"And nearly you," someone put in.

Marigold shook her head, as if that would make the past half hour go away. As if just by deeming it so, she could keep herself from being made into a victim. She refused to be.

She refused to be sweet and kind and magnanimous. She refused to be discreet. "I want him to hang," she shouted. "To pay for the crimes he's done to women. For what men have always done to women! What they have always gotten away with."

"Marigold." The quiet voice at her ear was President Irvine's. "While your passion is perhaps understandable, please think of the example you're setting for all, and perhaps curb your bloodlust."

She would not. She refused.

Discretion had cost them too much.

"It's not bloodlust," Marigold insisted. "It's justice. Justice for Olivia Thayer. And Professor Currier. And Minnie Mallory in Pride's Crossing. And all those other girls in Salem Sound. And in the Connecticut River and every other damn river and lake and pond across this land. The supposed suicides no one has ever cared enough about to make a fuss. To find out what really happened."

Her throat felt raw and tight, and her face grew hot and stinging with the salt tears that were weeping down her face. "You have to understand," she sniffed. "I don't care if it's wicked. It's justice."

"And we hope that justice is tempered with mercy and clear-sighted thinking." President Irvine was just as insistent, only more quietly so. "Not just passion." She put her arm around Marigold's shoulders. "But for now, the passion will suffice very well." She gave Marigold a gentle sort of reassuring shake. "Well done, Marigold. You are, most assuredly, a credit to the college. And to the name of womankind and thinking women everywhere."

"Thank you," Marigold hiccupped. Because somehow, Julia Irvine's approval meant more to her than anything else. And because it had been a very trying, exhausting day, and her arm ached and her hand still throbbed like the very devil, and she was still terribly, terribly frightened, and because Cab was yards away from her and could not see her face, she broke down.

She collapsed upon the grass and finally, finally cried.

But while she had been blubbering on about justice, others had been taking action. Kneeling on the bare yellow grass, Dr. Barker pressed a handkerchief firmly against the hole in Wilkie Valentine's chest.

"Collapsed lung, I should think, along with blood loss," Marigold heard her say. "We need to get him up to the Hospital Wing immediately so we can get a concertina bag pumping air back into his lungs and do what we can to save him."

Detective Pratt and his frock coats swung into action, hefting the man up over their shoulders and carrying him to Mr. Duckett's cart, which now stood at the ready.

It seemed only fitting that the wagon that had conveyed Olivia Thayer from her watery demise should now be hastening Wilkie Valentine slowly toward his, whenever that might be—he would have his day in court, Marigold hoped, and she would be there to ensure justice was served.

But not today. Today, she let the wagon pass by her without following.

"Marigold, darling." Isabella somehow had her much battered hat.

"Oh, Isabella." She reached for her friend's hand. "What on earth are you doing here?"

"You didn't think I was going to let Cab come and save you without support, did you?"

"No, I suppose not. Thank you for saving my hat."

"Of course. It's far too nice to simply leave there—after all, I designed it!"

"Thank you." Marigold accepted the hat with both gratitude and trepidation. And a deep steadying breath because she still felt ridiculously unsteady. "But I will say, I hope I never get that particular hatpin back."

But let that be a lesson to young ladies to secure their fashionable headpieces with sturdy, but potentially lethal hatpins. One never knew when one might save one's life.

And end another's.

"Dr. Barker will keep your hatpin." Cab was suddenly there, in that way he had of lending her an arm without ever seeming to paw at her like a masher. "She said she would see to it that the evidence was properly accounted for."

"Thank you," Marigold said again, for there seemed nothing else she could say. Cab's own wool suit seemed to be stained with Valentine's blood. "Is he—"

"Yes," Cab answered quietly. "I'm afraid Valentine's heart stopped beating some time ago from the wound, but primarily from the blood loss. Your Dr. Barker just didn't want to have him out there in the middle of the lawn. Much better, she thought, to get him out of sight so he could be said to have died in the Hospital Wing."

Always discretion. Always sparing their sensibilities.

Marigold, for one, thought it would be better for all of them to have looked down upon his body and known he was dead, just as he deserved.

But there was another consideration in this contemplation of what he deserved—what she had now earned for herself. "Then I killed him, didn't I?"

"Not in my opinion, and certainly not technically," Cab hedged. "You used your hatpin quite clearly in self-defense, which was witnessed by all—including Detective Pratt, who will no doubt testify to such in his report. And very well and bravely done too." He covered her blood-stained glove with his own warm hand. "But you left the hatpin in—cleverly, or luckily, positioned between the fourth and fifth ribs on the left side, Dr. Barker said. And as she also observed, Valentine was the one who pulled it out, probably tearing a hole in the left ventricle and causing him to bleed out of his heart. No court in the land would convict you of murd—" He stopped himself. "You acted purely in self-defense. Please put your mind to rest."

"I'll try," Marigold said, and took the moment to do just that, taking a deep steadying breath before she rose. "Thank you for coming to my rescue." She forswore the word the moment it came from her mouth. "For helping," she amended. "And . . . everything." She began to feel foolish using such feeble euphemisms. "All you've done. Both of you."

"Naturally, darling," Isabella soothed. "I hope you should expect nothing less from your friends. And you know, I always thought there was something fishy and suspicious and untoward about him, that journalist. I never liked him."

"No, you didn't. And you were right, so I shall after this always heed your instincts."

"As well you should." Isabella brightened. "Which of course means you must marry Cab."

"Isabella." Both Cab and Marigold spoke at the same time.

In Cab's voice, Marigold heard all the disappointment and chagrin of already having asked and been refused. For herself, she knew her own feelings on the matter were bittersweet—especially at the moment, when she was feeling so decidedly vulnerable.

Cab was and, she feared, always would be the finest man she knew. His disinterested assistance in this case was evidence enough of that.

As was that careful way he touched her arm.

"Now that the murderer has been brought to justice—or if he by some miracle can be brought back to life by your resourceful Dr. Barker, he is at least the beginning of the long trail to justice," he amended. "Let us get you out of all this wind and bother. If you're all to rights?" he asked quietly.

Something about his calm consideration took the last of her breath from her. She instantly felt as if her legs were about to give way.

Marigold sat back heavily in the grass.

"Clearly not okay." Cab shucked off his jacket and slung it around her shoulders just as he sat beside her and put his arm around her.

"I'll fetch something bracing," Isabella suggested before she hurried off, leaving Cab and Marigold alone.

"I expect you're feeling a little cold," Cab said solicitously as he rubbed her back. "Shock and fright does that, I'm told."

"You've never been frightened, have you?" Not like that, with someone who so clearly could do whatever they wanted to do to her physically.

Every woman knew that fear. Very few men ever did.

"Do you think me a stone?" was his answer. "I was frightened enough today, trying to find you, hoping, praying I wouldn't be too late—that we hadn't made a fatal mistake in looking for him elsewhere, and in taking so long to realize the truth. I was as frightened as I've ever been," he continued. "More so, because I didn't know if *you* knew."

"Yes," Marigold confirmed. "I came to the realization that Wilkerson and Valentine were the same rotter rather too slowly for my liking."

"But the important thing is that you did come to that realization. Thank God. And you told Miss Burke, who raised the alarm. I think she telephoned every listing on the entire exchange of the town of Wellesley—thankfully including our inn."

"I'd rather thank Miss Burke than God. And Imogen Currier and Aggie Newton and Ethyl Rautencranz," Marigold amended. "They were the ones, who, each in their own way—although Aggie and Ethyl were together on the path—made me realize he was the murderer. Although clearly, Isabella suspected him first. And will never let me forget about that."

"Isabella is fulsome with warnings."

"Is that how she got you up here? Giving you a warning—that I might be falling for Wilkerson?"

"That and her idea to buy a tearoom. And naturally, it worked," he admitted without rancor. "Because she knows I care deeply about you. And want the best for you. And I think the best for you—in case you were wondering—is having you alive and well and carrying on being the Marigold we all know and love."

He loved her.

She knew that—she had always known that, it seemed.

Just as she had always known she loved him too.

Chapter 36

"In order that she may give her hand with dignity, she must be able to stand alone."

Margaret Fuller

But loving someone wasn't the same thing as wanting to get married or set up housekeeping together.

No matter how much Marigold loved him—and judging from the painful lump in her throat, she loved him quite a lot—she did not want to marry him.

Not now, when her dreams seemed closer than ever to becoming a reality.

If she wrote up the story of the Lake Waban murder for *The Argosy*, she might raise all the needed funds for her summer in Kefalonia. And if she returned her focus to her studies and excelled, in the spring she might apply for a scholarship through the American School for Classical Studies in Athens, which might give her enough to excavate in some small style—a second-class ticket on one of the better ocean liners, at the very least, instead of in steerage with her trunks.

It was a heady thought.

Heady and powerful enough to explain to him.

But she didn't have to—Cab had somehow followed her silent train of thought. "I understand you're being considered to be conferred with your master's degree in the spring, as well as your bachelor's at the end of this term? You're to be congratulated. What a coup."

"Yes, thank you," she acknowledged politely. One didn't want to make too much of oneself. "But only if I manage to pull this semester out of the ash can after all this bumbling about instead of studying."

"Somehow I feel you'll be able to put all this 'bumbling about,' as you call it, to good use. *The Argosy* will surely print the next installment of Miss Marigold Manners's adventures."

Marigold could not tell if she was being reprimanded or praised. "Is that how you think of them, these appalling segues we take into murder?"

"Yes," he said firmly. "That is how I think of all the things that you do—adventures. One never knows what is going to happen with you around, Marigold. But one knows that one is never going to be bored."

There was something sadly distancing in his use of "one," as if he no longer wanted to use the very personal "I."

"One lives to entertain."

"That I will dispute—I think you live to *live*." He put paid to her theory of vocabulary. But he looked away from her, out over the shimmering, dimming lake, as if keeping up a close inspection were too hard. "It is one of the things I admire most about you."

"You are very generous." She took the opportunity to look at him—at the chiseled, reliable, dear, dear profile of this singular man. "It is one of the things I admire about you."

"So here we sit." He rubbed her shoulders a little in friendly companionship. "A mutual admiration society of two."

"Here we sit." Marigold realized the jittery sensations had retreated under the warmth of Cab's presence. "Thank you for sitting with me."

"I'll sit with you any time. For as long as you like."

"I like it very much." She let her head rest on his shoulder. Lightly. Just this once.

Marigold let her eyes close in comfort and ease and exhaustion. She gave herself the indulgence of not thinking for a moment. Just a moment. A nice long moment.

The kind of moment a person might think they wanted to make last forever.

But Marigold wasn't a forever kind of person.

Forever would preclude so many other things she wanted and needed to do. Like find Aggie and Ethyl again and thank them, most profoundly. And hug Miss Burke until the little woman's cheeks turned pink with embarrassment. And pledge to President Irvine that she would devote herself to resurrecting her academic reputation. And check on how Professor Currier was recovering. And finish that theme on the influence of Lucretius's Epicurean thought—the natural and rational imperative to maximize pleasure and minimize pain in a person's life—as the foundation and philosophy of America as a country.

And make sure Wilkie Valentine was convicted of murder.

"Marigold? Are you warm enough?"

"Yes," she roused herself to answer.

"You shivered," he observed. "You are still shivering."

"I'm only thinking."

He did not ask what she was thinking about. He just kept his arm around her shoulder and kept up his careful, soothing rubbing of her upper arm.

But she told him anyway. "I was thinking that women very often get killed because they are trying to be likable. I am sure Olivia Thayer said she would go for a walk with Wilkie Valentine because she wanted to be polite and likable, even while she wanted nothing more to do with him. My first instinct was that as well—appeasement rather than anger. It is the paradox of our lives. The moment we do something to make ourselves unlikable—the moment Olivia Thayer rejected Wilkie Valentine's advances, however politely, was the moment she became endangered."

Marigold hugged her knees to her chest in an effort to stop the tremors of horror and frustration from working their way through her body. "I'm sure she kept trying to be polite the whole time he was strong-arming her down to the lake. I'm sure she did. Because what choice did she have? What choice do any of us have in this very real world we live in? Even here in this place that is supposed to be set apart from the cares of the world—set apart specifically so we may learn away from other cares—those cares never go away.

"I've often said that this world is not made for us, for women like me, so we must keep trying to make it over where and when we can, but today I feel as if we can do no such thing. That we must—" She threw up her hands in frustration. "Are we all to go about carrying pistols like gunslingers? Are we to become as violent and despicable as those who would be violent and despicable toward us? Must we embrace wickedness?"

"I don't know," was Cab's answer. "But I for one am very glad you had that hatpin in place of a six-shooter, for it proved itself just as effective."

"My hand still hurts from jabbing it in," she mused before she added, "as well it should, I suppose. One ought to feel *something* when one has stabbed someone in the heart."

"Marigold." Cab gently turned her chin toward him. "He was a very bad man who needed stabbing."

"Yes. Yes, he did," she finally agreed. "Thank you for that, Cab."

"You are quite welcome. It is the least I could do. I can't help feeling I should have done more."

"How?" Marigold laughed her disagreement. "You did everything I asked of you."

"I should have realized that the moment you began investigating the girl and her murder, you would be in danger. That the homicidal impulse, as my readings so presciently taught me, would inevitably turn upon you."

"I should have realized that too," Marigold admitted. "Vanity, I suppose was my undoing. I liked having someone flatter me and take my opinions seriously—or at least appear to take them seriously. Perhaps I should have known that would turn out to be nothing but a ruse?"

"I will always take your opinions seriously, Marigold. Call upon me anytime you have something of import to discuss."

"I'll do that." She took in a deep breath. Their moment was almost over. Just as it should be.

Marigold started to rise and Cab did so too, reaching to pull her up at his side. "Marigold. I hope you know . . . This is an awful time because you've been through such a lot today, but I want you to know that my offer—" He cleared his throat. "My proposal of marriage—in case you might think I might be speaking of something else—still stands. I am utterly mad about you, Marigold, and I always will be."

"Thank you. I love you too." Marigold immediately caught herself being polite and likable—not only because that was what Cab deserved, but because that was what she felt she had to do or appear ungrateful.

She firmed her resolve. "However comforting the idea of being with you—and it is very comforting at this moment—this *is* an awful time, to say the least. I killed a man. And that is not something I will ever take lightly. I imagine I will take it with me always, this token of my failure to see past my own nose."

"I won't let you."

"You can't stop me," she countered. "Even if I did marry you." She hesitated.

"But—" he finished.

"But why does it always have to be marriage? Why can we not just be . . . together for each other? Why must I subject myself to this legal lessening? Why do people expect—expect!—me to love you on your terms, and castigate me for wanting to love you on *my* terms?"

"I . . . I don't know." He reached for her hand. "All I know is that I am glad that you do love me."

"I always have." And the moment she said it, she knew it was true—that all the years she had pretended to ignore him, all the pride that had kept her from enjoying him, were nothing but an excuse she had made to hold that love at bay.

Because she knew, deep down, that as much as she loved him, she loved herself, her ambitions, and her very personhood more. "But—"

"You don't have to explain." Cab shook his head to stop her. "I understand, I do."

He was generosity itself. "Yes, you're prepared to be all noble and fine—and to let me go. Which is not what I want. I want you to be with me on my terms, openly and joyfully and—"

"And outside the law?" he finished.

"Yes." Marigold would not apologize for her want. "What good does the law do me? I don't have any legal rights as a person. Only as a widow, which I do not at all want to be."

"But just to be together . . ." He shook his head. "I can't do that. I am . . ." He struggled to find the right words. ". . . a man of the law. I am expected to live within the framework of the—"

"The society that money and exclusive education and the hidebound opinions of Puritans have built?" Marigold finished, not without some bitterness.

"Such is our world, Marigold," Cab reminded her.

"And don't I know it." She felt like stamping her foot in frustration, so put out was she. But she was not put out with Cab. It was not his fault the world was the way it was. "I am sorry to vent my spleen on you, Cab. I know you don't deserve it."

He chuckled mirthlessly. "What do I deserve?"

"You told me I deserved to be happy," Marigold answered. "Well, so do you. And since I, with my flouting of the conventions you hold so dear, cannot make you happy, I suppose I must let you go to be happy with some other."

"It's impossible, Marigold." He was quietly emphatic. "It's always been you. And I fear it always will be."

There it was, so casually laid between then. So fragile. Like a bomb, the fear.

But as there was nothing she might do to defuse it, she had to let it go. "Come, it is time for me to resume being a college girl and nothing but. Thank you," she said again as she linked her arm with his to walk back to the sheltering hulk of College Hall. "You can help me begin—you've a Harvard degree or two—what do you think of the relationship between Epicurean philosophy and the Jeffersonian ideal of the 'pursuit of happiness'?"

He smiled. "I think Jefferson owned a number of copies of *De Rerum Natura*, both in the original Latin and in translation, so your theory holds a good deal of water."

"So long as that water does not hold dead girls, I think I shall be very happy."

"Good." He smiled down at her. "You do deserve to pursue your own happiness, Marigold. Remember that, always."

Epilogue

"You must be the best judge of your own happiness."
Jane Austen

He always said always.

And for the first time, the word gave Marigold comfort instead of itchy feet.

"You've let him go?" Isabella sat waiting with the sherry in the upholstered reading chair in Marigold's sitting room. Almost as if she anticipated the need for the fortified wine.

"I could hardly bring a young man upstairs to my sitting room after the sun has gone down, Isabella. Even you should understand how that is against the rules."

"I suppose." Isabella conceded gracefully. "I myself don't hold with rules. I'll hold out hope that you asked him to dinner—which I am also hoping you will take with me, at my inn, instead of denigrating my palate with dining hall food." Her face brightened. "Which brings me to another thought I think you'll like—I've come to a wonderful final agreement with your marvelous Lucy Dove. While I could not convince her to become my personal chef—not enough exposure, we decided—she has accepted my proposal to be my partner in a tearoom here in Wellesley." Isabella beamed. "The final documents for the lease were signed today."

Marigold hardly knew what to say. She had too many questions.

So she asked them all. "What do you mean? When did this happen?"

"When? When you had such marvelous things to say about her, and I wrote Daisy to find me some of her recipes that she had submitted to Tad Endicott and Collier's so I could try them out—or rather my chef could. And they were marvelous—and I told Tad that, naturally, because I thought he might like to have an unbiased opinion. And after Lucy contracted with Collier's, I wrote her a note of congratulations, and she wrote me back—exquisite handwriting, and you know I like that. So, when I found she was here in Wellesley, naturally, I arranged to meet her."

"Naturally."

"Naturally," Isabella said emphatically. "One likes to help out where one can, and one likes to have new ventures to think about. It helps spark creativity." She shook her finger at Marigold. "I told you I had a new business venture that Cab was drawing up the papers for."

"You did indeed." After she got over the shock, Marigold found she was delighted. "You have my hearty congratulations. How marvelous for you both. Let us have dinner with her tonight to drink to your success!" She held up her sherry glass in preliminary toast.

Isabella raised her glass in response. "Thank you, darling."

"And thank you." Marigold sat, more weary than she had ever been. "Thank you for your extraordinary friendship. The fact that you are even here"—she gestured to the snug little dormitory suite—"when you could be seated in luxury and comfort at your inn, or in your own home, is testament to what a wonderful friend you are. I'm lucky to have you."

"Darling, the true luxury in this life is having friends worth being with." Isabella held her own glass high. "One of these days, you and Cab are going to realize that."

"Isabella," Marigold began in a tone that would hopefully tell Isabella that she was done with this discussion. "I have plans—good, logical, well-thought-out plans—that of a necessity don't involve Cab."

Isabella sighed in frustration. "I don't see why not."

"Isabella, I have explained about academic institutions requiring women—"

"Your president, Julia Irvine, is *Mrs. Irvine*, I note. If there is an exception for her—"

"She is a widow," Marigold reminded her.

"Ah." Isabella, who was also a widow, nodded in understanding. "And is therefore allowed a different sort of freedom. I see." She took a restorative sip of her sherry. "But it is so unfair," she groused. "You belong with Cab."

Marigold tried one more time, though the words were heavy on her heart. "Isabella, I belong with myself, doing what I have always wanted to do. What I have studied and prepared myself for. Why can you not see that?"

"I do see that, darling." Isabella reached out to take Marigold's hand. "I really do. But I also see something else—that you are most yourself in all your brilliant, proud, determined glory, when you are with Cab, in a way that you are not with anyone else. Not even me. You are the most yourself when you are with him. Except also, dare I say it, a little bit happier and more relaxed."

This was a truth that Marigold was not prepared to admit. Not today. Not after she had so recently spent just such relaxed, happy moments with him.

She rose and went to the window to watch the very last of the afternoon's light leach out of the sky over the lake, casting the water into inky obscurity. "Perhaps," she finally allowed.

Perhaps she was feeling nostalgic for a time in her life when all the things that she wanted had seemed possible. But she understood now that choices and compromises always had to be made. That something or someone was always going to be left out.

"Yes," Isabella murmured behind her. "Perhaps now is just not the right time."

"Yes," Marigold finally agreed with her friend, and found the strange tension in her chest ease, just a bit. "Not the right time."

But who knew if it would ever be the right time.

Although the easing in her chest told her that she still hoped that somehow, someday it would be. But in the meantime—

"I do hope you are going to turn this latest episode into—what did you call them?" Isabella queried. "Spondulicks? *The Argosy* would no doubt like another installment of your murdery tales and should pay you even more handsomely for them. You should call it 'The Wellesley Strangler.'"

"I don't think the college would appreciate the notoriety."

"Then call it 'The College Strangler' and set it somewhere else—Radcliffe or Vassar. They'll be glad of the attention up there in the hinterlands."

"Isabella, you are incorrigible."

"Naturally," Isabella agreed cordially. "Just as I aim to be. And so should you if you're bent on being independent. Incorrigibility is a wonderful characteristic in an independent woman."

And so was persistence.

Marigold took a deep draught of the sherry and let the fortified wine lend her eloquence. "Then what do you think of this for a beginning?"

What was it about hats that always seemed to catch my eye?

THE END

Acknowledgments

Writing might be considered a solitary practice but bringing that writing from concept to publication takes a concerted group effort. My first thanks are always to my brilliant, stalwart Tortoises, Tracy Brogan and Sherry Thomas, whose brainstorming, encouragement, and daily accountability checks kept me on track. Thanks are also due to my wonderful agent, Danielle Egan-Miller of Browne & Miller Literary Associates, for incisive, sanity-saving advice, and for sweating the details, so I don't have to.

But my greatest thanks are to the team at Crooked Lane Books, starting with my first editor there, Holly Ingraham, who shepherded Marigold into existence, and steered me through Book I, Misery Hates Company, and into this Book II. At her departure, Faith Black Ross so kindly took over the editorial duties and brought us into publication along with the rest of her superb team, Rebecca Nelson, Megan Matti, Dulce Botello, Mikaela Bender and Thai Fantauzzi Pérez. It is such a pleasure to know Marigold and I are in such good hands. Thank you, one and all.